Fiona Lowe is a RITA® and RUBY award-winning author who started writing romance when she was on holiday and ran out of books. Now, writing single title contemporary romance for Carina Press and Medical Romances for Mills & Boon, she lives in a seaside town in southern Australia, where she juggles writing, reading, working and raising two gorgeous sons with the support of her own real-life hero! Readers can visit Fiona at her website: fionalowe.com.

Born and raised on the Wirral Peninsula in England, **Charlotte Hawkes** is mum to two intrepid boys who love her to play building block games with them and who object loudly to the amount of time she spends on the computer. When she isn't writing—or building with blocks—she is company director for a small Anglo/French construction company. Charlotte loves to hear from readers, and you can contact her at her website: charlotte-hawkes.com.

Also by Fiona Lowe

Also by Charlotte Hawkes

Hot Army Docs miniseries

Discover more at millsandboon.co.uk.

THE REUNION
OF A LIFETIME

FIONA LOWE

A BRIDE TO
REDEEM HIM

CHARLOTTE HAWKES

MILLS & BOON

First Published in Great Britain 2018
by Mills & Boon, an imprint of HarperCollins*Publishers*
1 London Bridge Street, London, SE1 9GF

The Reunion of a Lifetime © 2018 by Fiona Lowe

A Bride to Redeem Him © 2018 by Charlotte Hawkes

ISBN: 978-0-263-93350-5

MIX
Paper from
responsible sources
FSC® C007454

This book is produced from independently certified FSC™ paper
to ensure responsible forest management.
For more information visit www.harpercollins.co.uk/green.

Printed and bound in Spain
by CPI, Barcelona

THE REUNION
OF A LIFETIME

FIONA LOWE

MILLS & BOON

To Tamara,
for sharing her heartbreaking journey with Finn.

With special thanks to Madeleine and Cate
for the mud story.

CHAPTER ONE

'IT'S RED DAY.'

'Red day?' Dr Lauren Fuller's hand paused in mid-twist on the yellow lid of a jar of Vegemite. She was minding Shaylee—her parents' current foster-daughter—while Sue and Ian were up in Melbourne, celebrating their thirty-third wedding anniversary.

'For reading,' Shaylee explained. 'We wrote a real letter with a stamp and everything. Today we're walking to a big red letterbox. Mrs Kikos says it's really old.'

Lauren knew the postbox. It dated back to 1890, when Horseshoe Bay had been a popular holiday destination and people sent postcards to tease the folks at home. Now everyone just texted. 'That sounds like fun.'

She grabbed the toast as it popped up and swung back towards the table, dodging Cadbury, her parents' aging chocolate Labrador, who had decided he needed to lie right at her feet. After dropping the toast on a plate, she pulled the scrambled eggs off the heat seconds before they boiled. Breakfast at her own house was a much less hectic affair, consisting of fruit and yoghurt, and, if the planets aligned, a quiet online read of the paper.

The eight-year-old girl's gaze suddenly dropped past her new green and white checked school dress—her pride and joy—before resting on her bare feet. Shaylee mumbled something else about red.

Lauren scooped the eggs out of the pan and dumped them over the toast she'd spread with Vegemite. Her mother had been insistent that Shaylee eat a high-protein breakfast before school to help her with her concentration. Lauren knew that wasn't the sole purpose; it was as much about warmth, love and a full stomach as it was about concentration. Shaylee had spent far too many years going hungry when her drug-affected mother's suppressed appetite and muddled brain hadn't considered food a necessity. 'Sit up and eat your brekkie and tell me what you just said.'

Shaylee eyed Lauren carefully as she climbed up onto the breakfast stool. 'Doesn't matter.'

'Of course it matters,' Lauren said with a smile. She'd grown up with a parade of foster-children coming and going in the house and, as hard as that was at times to cope with, if she'd learned one thing, it was that the muttered asides usually contained the most important information.

Shaylee shovelled eggs into her mouth and Lauren waited. The moment the girl swallowed, Lauren said, 'Hit me with it.'

'We have to wear red,' Shaylee said quietly, her head down. 'But it's okay. I love my uniform.'

Lauren's heart rolled over. This little girl had endured so many disappointments in her short life that she automatically prepared for them now. It was odd that Lauren's mother hadn't made a costume for her before she'd left for Melbourne—Sue was huge on things like this. Surely the school had sent home a note about it? But that was something to sort out later. Right now, she had…she glanced at the clock and tried not to groan…half an hour to create a red costume before dropping Shaylee off at school and getting to the clinic on time. 'You eat your eggs and I'll go and see what I can find that's red.'

Her first stop was the bathroom. At the back of the cupboard she found four cans of coloured hair spray, all of dubious age. She picked up the red one and shook it. It sounded hopeful, although she hoped it was fire-engine-red or it wouldn't show up on Shaylee's glossy black hair. Her second stop was the floor-to-ceiling cupboards in the playroom-cum-teenage retreat. Dragging an old hospital linen bag along the polished floorboards, she walked back into the kitchen just as Shaylee finished her last mouthful.

'What's that?' the little girl asked, clearly intrigued.

'Sue's special bag of tricks.' Lauren pulled open the drawstring and started pitching out items—a pink feather boa, a black ushanka fur hat with a red badge, a green fez, an old handbag, a royal-blue waistcoat… As she added more items to the pile, Lauren found herself silently chanting 'Come on, red,' like a roulette player.

Meanwhile, Shaylee was twirling around the kitchen, wearing the Russian hat and a stethoscope. 'Look, I'm a doctor just like you.'

Lauren glanced at the bright red instrument in surprise. It must have been tangled up in some clothing, because she hadn't seen it come out of the bag. If anyone had asked her about that piece of medical equipment, she would have said she'd binned it at the end of her first year of uni after replacing it with a utilitarian black stethoscope. Apparently not. It appeared she had abandoned it here and her mother, ever a magpie when it came to the bag of tricks, must have kept it for dress-ups. Lauren had deliberately not thought about the red stethoscope in years.

Twelve years.

Shut up! How do you even know that?

It was too long ago and far too much had happened in

her life for her subconscious to instantly calculate the number. Especially as the day she'd bought the replacement black stethoscope had been the day she'd moved on from Charlie Ainsworth. At least that was what she always told herself on the infrequent occasions something made her think back to that heady summer a lifetime ago.

'Stethoscopes are like wands,' Charlie had said, slinging a red one around her neck and pulling her towards him before kissing her.

She'd gazed up at him, loving his kind and handsome face. 'They're magic?'

'I wish,' he'd said in a resigned tone, 'but no. They do, however, reflect personality and you, Lauren Fuller, are the antithesis of boring old black. This one is bright and vivacious, just like you. This is the one.'

Lauren felt herself grimace at the now tarnished memory and immediately noticed Shaylee's smile fade. *Damn.* She banished the mothballed memory back where it belonged and forced a smile as she kept rummaging in the bag. 'The stethoscope looks great on you and, ta-dah!' With relief, she shook out a red sequined cape. 'You can be Super Shaylee.'

'Yay!' Shaylee clapped her hands as a look of wonder crossed her face. 'I'm gonna be dressed in red like the other kids.'

Lauren blinked back tears. Why was it always the simple things that undid her? 'You'll be totally red, especially when I've sprayed your hair.'

After dropping a very excited Shaylee off at school, Lauren drove to the café nestled under the Norfolk pines on the sweet curve of Horseshoe Bay. Her usual morning routine was a run along the beach and on Tuesdays and Thursdays she added in a yoga class, but the one constant was coffee. This morning it was just coffee.

'You missed a spectacular sunrise.' Ben, the barista and café manager, greeted her with his trademark grin.

And I missed you. Sun-bleached hair and with a surfer's tan, Ben had moved to the Bay three months ago to run the café. Most mornings as she finished her run, he was walking up the beach with his board tucked under his arm and they always fell into easy conversation. Everything about Ben was easy. This was a new experience for Lauren, because the two men she'd thought she'd loved had turned out to be anything but easy. But that was all in the past and not worth revisiting.

As far as Lauren was concerned, she'd wiped clean her slate of disastrous relationships when she'd returned to Horseshoe Bay two years ago. Determined to learn from her twenties, she was older, wiser and ready to live life on her own terms. The last year had been frantic, most of it spent breathing new life into a busy medical practice that had let the twenty-first century pass it by. Now, with her newly minted decree absolute declaring her officially divorced from Jeremy and with her heart encased in a protective layer of reinforced Perspex—visible but crack-proof—Lauren was finally ready for an easy, straightforward and uncomplicated man.

Truth be told, she was ready for sex. Just recently, she'd been waking up at three a.m. hot, sweaty and aroused, and although she was adept at bringing herself to orgasm, she was ready for someone else to do it. She just didn't want a relationship with its inevitable breakdown and crippling scar tissue as part of the deal. Ben, with his 'live for the moment' and 'no regrets' attitude, might just be the solution she was looking for.

The stumbling block was that at thirty she'd only ever

had sex as part of a committed relationship. Correction; she'd been committed—Charlie and Jeremy not so much—and she was clueless about how to bring up the topic of a no-strings-attached gig. Of course, she could just use a dating app but the two recent cases on the news where women had lost their lives from swiping right warned her she was safer with someone she knew. But in a town the size of Horseshoe Bay, her options were limited.

'I was on mothering duty this morning,' she said, pulling out her purse to pay for her latte.

Ben did a double take. 'I didn't know you had a kid.'

'I don't,' she said, checking the Perspex around her heart and not letting her mind travel to a memory that always brought a troubling combination of sadness and disappointment seasoned with an unsettling soupçon of relief. 'I'm looking after Shaylee while my parents are whooping it up in Melbourne celebrating thirty-three years of wedded bliss.'

'Crikey.' Ben's expression was a priceless combination of respect and horror. 'I can't imagine what that would be like. My brain refuses to go there.'

'I know, right? They got married at twenty-three and are still going strong. It's terrifyingly impressive.' So much about her parents and their achievements was impressive that she was often left feeling daunted by her own choices. How did one even start to live up to their high-set bar?

He placed the metal jug under the steam jet, frothing the milk for her brewing coffee. 'I think I'd find marriage claustrophobic.'

Was this her opening? *Come on, be brave. Be a millennial woman like the ones you read about and take what you want.* 'Sexually or otherwise?'

He shot her a quizzical look as if he was testing the lie of the land. 'A bit of both, really. What about you?'

'Post-divorce, I've had a total rethink.' She swallowed and forced herself to look him straight in his sea-green eyes. 'What's your opinion of friends with benefits?'

'I'm an enthusiastic supporter.' He capped her coffee with a plastic sippy top and gave her a grin. 'And we've been friends for a while now.'

'We have.' For some reason her heart was just beating away normally: lub-dub, lub-dub. Shouldn't it be bounding wildly out of her chest at the fact that the gorgeous Ben was on board with the idea of the two of them tumbling into bed?

He handed her the coffee and swept the coins she laid on the wooden counter into the till. 'Call me whenever, Lauren. I'm looking forward to it.'

'Great!' She heard herself saying, sounding far more enthusiastic than she felt. For some—probably antiquated—reason, she'd assumed Ben would be the one to contact her. Yet this way he was letting her call the shots and after two disastrous relationships, wasn't that what she wanted? Demanded even?

Gah! Perhaps she wasn't as twenty-first-century evolved or as ready for casual, no-strings-attached sex as she'd thought.

Charles Ainsworth—'Boss Doc' to the islanders, Charlie to his friends and on very infrequent occasions to his family—swore as the lights in the operating theatre flickered. 'Bert filled the generator, right?' he asked as he slipped a ligature around a bleeding vessel.

'No worries, boss.' A dark eyed man with a bush of frizzy hair gave him the thumbs-up from the door. 'I fill 'em up. No be in the dark this time.'

'Excellent.' Charlie might be in what travel magazines called 'paradise'—a string of tropical, palm-dotted coral islands floating in an aquamarine sea—but from a medical perspective, he was in a developing country and a disaster zone. During the recent cyclone, he'd had to perform emergency surgery on a boy who had been pierced by a stake that had been hurled into his chest by the terrifying and mighty force of the wind. Mid-surgery, they had predictably lost power, but he hadn't foreseen the generator running dry or him finishing the surgery with Bert and Shirley holding LED torches aloft.

Just another tough day in paradise but at least the kid had survived and only half of the hospital had flooded. If the Red Cross managed to deliver desperately needed medical supplies today, he might be able to breathe more easily. As it was, air was skimming in and out of the tops of his lungs without going deeper and his body was coiled tight, ready to react to the next disaster. He'd been in a constant state of high alert for two weeks.

It's been longer than that.

He shook away the thought. Emergency aid work was, by definition, disaster management, and he had the dubious honour of being an expert. Once the powers that be recognised someone with the skills they needed, they locked onto them and never let them go. Not that he wanted to be let go—he lived for being busy. The alternative didn't bear thinking about.

He stepped back from the antiquated operating table that even on its highest extension was too low for his height, stripped off his gloves and rubbed his aching back. 'Wake him up,' he said to his current anaesthetic nurse, a local islander who had blessedly trained in Melbourne. 'And keep a close eye on the drainage bottle.'

'Sure thing, Charlie,' Shirley said, her teeth a flash of white in her dark and smiling face. 'You get some sleep now, yeah?'

He laughed; the sound as far removed from jolly as possible. 'I'm going down to the wharf.'

'I see your eyes close. You need sleep.' She gave an islander shrug—the one that implied *it will be what it will be.* 'You can't will the boat to come.'

'I can try.' He wasn't about to explain to Shirley that there was no point in trying to sleep, because sleep no longer came. If insomnia had been a visitor in the last few months, it had taken up residence since the cyclone had hit. For the last two weeks he'd only cat-napped. An hour here, a half-hour there, all squeezed in between medical emergencies, general hospital work and helping the islanders clean up the havoc Cyclone Samuel had wrought on them. Although some aid had arrived, it was going to take months for the replacement of vital infrastructure. Not that he'd be around to see it. By then he would have been moved on, dispatched to another place of need and leading another team.

He walked into the basic change room that all the staff shared and stripped off his scrubs. He was shoving his left leg into his shorts when the room shifted and he shifted with it, banging hard into the old metal lockers and jarring his shoulder. What the hell! Was it an earth tremor? He righted himself and listened keenly for rumbling but all he heard was birdsong. He was no rookie at natural disasters and birds didn't sing when there were tremors. Nothing sang then; every animal and insect went deathly silent—the anthem of impending doom.

Trying again, he lifted his right leg, aiming it at the leg hole in his shorts. This time silver spots danced in front of his eyes and then the floor shifted again. He flung out an arm to steady himself and sat down hard on the bench seat. Sucking in some deep breaths, he closed his eyes and waited for the floaters to vanish.

'You okay, boss?' Bert asked, suddenly appearing in front of him. 'You don't look so good. You need a smoke?'

'Don't tempt me, Bert.' Charlie gave him a grim smile. 'I just need to eat.' But just the thought of food made him feel queasy, let alone trying to eat any.

Men's shouts rent the air, sliding in through the open window, and Charlie's empty stomach fell to his feet. He didn't understand a lot of Bislama and his French was tourist-competent, not medical literate, but the last time he'd heard a commotion like this they'd found an islander who'd been trapped under rubble for three days. Despite the joy in finding the man alive, Charlie had been faced with the task of amputating the patient's crushed leg in the hope of saving his life.

'Grab my medical kit.' Charlie lurched to his feet, taking a moment for his head to stop spinning.

'No, boss!' Bert grinned at him. 'This good news. Come on.'

He followed Bert's brightly coloured shirt through the door and down a short corridor until they were both outside and in the glare of a fearless sun. Under the wind-stripped and almost naked palm trees Charlie glimpsed heaven—a group of men and women dressed in fresh and clean Australia Aid uniforms. All of them clutched the distinctive and life-giving red and blue medical packs. At the back of the cluster he recognised the distinctive height of Richard di Stasio—his boss.

Relief carried him towards them, his long strides steady. 'You lot are a sight for sore eyes. That is, if you've brought IV fluids and antibiotics.'

'Would we dare turn up without them?' Richard shook Charlie's hand and his dark eyes did one of those quick head-to-toe assessments that emergency medicos specialised in. 'You're looking a bit rough, Charlie.'

He shrugged as they walked inside. 'It's been tough. You saw what's left of the town on your trip from the wharf? Or what's not left of it, to be more precise. Half the hospital's out of action and we've got limited power. The fuel for the generator's dangerously low, the sat phone's dodgy and I've got three patients battling septic shock.'

'You look a bit shocked yourself.'

'Nah.' He ran his hand through his hair and suddenly realised it was longer than it had been in years. 'No more than usual.'

Richard shook his head. 'You look like you've dropped at least five kilos. Possibly more.'

'The joys of a fish and taro diet. Listen, Richard,' he said, suddenly gripped by urgency. 'I'll happily give you a full report as soon as I've administered those antibiotics to my three sickies.'

'Keith can do that. You're handing over to him and then you're getting on the boat to Port Vila and going home.'

No! Every part of Charlie stilled. 'Don't be ridiculous. There's still mountains of work for me to do here.'

Richard sighed. 'You know the rules, Charlie. First response teams get pulled out after two weeks when second response arrives.'

'Hell, Richard, you know as well as I do that you're the first response team, not me. The only reason I'm on Pipatoa is because I came for a few days of diving after teaching the emergency trauma course in Port Vila. Two days after I arrived, Samuel blew up and I got stuck here.'

'That's irrelevant. The bottom line is you've done the job of first response without the back-up of a trained team. It doesn't take a medical person to see you're completely exhausted. God, man, have you slept at all since the cyclone?'

'I'm fine,' Charlie ground out. 'Besides, you've got me pencilled in for Ghana next week, right?'

'That was before you lived through the most savage cyclone to hit the area in forty years.'

'So?'

Richard's brows rose at the belligerence in Charlie's voice. 'So, HR's been on my case because you haven't taken any leave in eighteen months. Now you've lived through the cyclone, the psych's waded in.'

Charlie's head ached and his gut cramped. 'I don't want to take leave. I want to go to Ghana.'

'Neither of us has a choice in the matter. Even if HR weren't getting antsy about your accumulated leave, you're mandated to take time out of the field and attend three post-disaster counselling sessions.'

'Hell, Richard, I'm not going to get PTSD.'

'You know as well as I do no one's bulletproof. The rules exist to protect Australia Aid workers. As an employee, those rules apply to you.'

'But you're the boss.' Charlie hated the frantic pitch to his voice. 'You can pull strings.'

Richard shook his head. 'Not this time, mate. Besides, it's not the end of the world. There are worse times than summer in Australia to go home.'

It was *never* a good time to go home. Not that he considered Australia home anymore, or anywhere else for that matter. 'How long am I on enforced leave?'

'A minimum of six weeks.'

'What?' His bark of disbelief bounced off the walls and came back to bite him.

'Longer if the psych isn't happy with your progress, but I'm sure you'll be back in action before Easter.' Richard gave him a fatherly clap on the shoulder. 'Look on the bright side. Your family will be happy to see you.'

'Oh, yeah. They'll be thrilled,' he muttered under his breath. 'Any chance the psych will visit me in Bali?'

Richard laughed, completely missing the point that Charlie was deadly serious. 'Send me a postcard from that joint you summered in as a kid. I've always thought it sounded like a place I should take my kids.'

Charlie stared at Richard, stunned that he'd even remembered that conversation—hell, he'd forgotten all about it. He guessed it had taken place about three years ago, on the night of 'the anniversary'. He'd found himself with a bottle of Scotch and, a little while later, Richard for company. He hadn't told his boss the significance of the date—hell, he never told anyone that—but to prevent Richard from asking too many probing questions about why one of his best trauma surgeons was uncharacteristically nursing a bottle of top-shelf liquor, Charlie had entertained him with stories about his childhood summers on the coast.

He'd used words to paint pictures of the old rambling house on top of the cliff, the white sandy beach far below that squeaked when the sand particles rubbed together, the seventy grey weathered wooden steps that led down to the sea and the roar of the surf that filled the air with the zip and tang of salt. He'd waxed lyrical about the exhilaration of catching a wave and riding it all the way in to shore.

Horseshoe Bay. He hadn't thought about the place in years. Despite growing up in the privileged leafy suburbs of Melbourne with every possible advantage, his happiest memories were the holidays at Bide-A-While. He'd spent every long, hot summer there and he and his brother had run wild—swimming, surfing and beachcombing—the sun bleaching their hair white and darkening their skin to honey brown.

When he'd turned sixteen, they added bonfires on the beach and parties to their repertoire. He'd shared his first kiss at Horseshoe Bay. He'd ecstatically given up his virginity in the dunes with—God, what was her name? Other than a flash of white skin illuminated by moonlight, he couldn't form a picture of her, but then again it had been eighteen years ago. His body sagged as the elapsed years unexpectedly clawed at him.

A memory of luminous almond-coloured eyes ringed by jet lashes bloomed in his mind and he smiled. *Lauren.* He may not remember the other girl he'd had his first fumbling sexual encounter with, but it was impossible to forget Lauren. She'd been his saving grace in the worst summer of his life. Old regret ached but he was an expert at ignoring it. It was pointless questioning why life threw curve balls and disrupted the good things. Turning away from the melancholy memories of Lauren, his mind darted to find something to soothe his intense disquiet about returning to Melbourne.

Bide-a-While! While he worked out his appointments and organised a real holiday somewhere far, far away from that southern city—one that fitted in between the obligatory counselling sessions—he'd ensconce himself with Gran down at Horseshoe Bay. With its clear views to the horizon, and a solid two-hour drive from Melbourne, it might just be the wide safety buffer he needed between him and his parents.

CHAPTER TWO

LAUREN TOUCHED THE hands-free green button on the car's console and answered her mobile. 'Hi, Mum. How was The Langham?'

'Just gorgeous! But, darling, I'm so sorry about the red costume.' Sue Fuller's voice boomed around the car. 'Apparently, school notes are going out of fashion and I need to download an app. Anyway, Shaylee refuses to take off her costume and Dad and I want to cook you dinner as a thank-you. Can you make it?'

If anyone ever offered to cook for Lauren, she accepted in a heartbeat, because at the end of long and busy days, rustling up the energy to cook often failed her. 'Dinner sounds fabulous. But fair warning, I missed lunch so I'm starving.' She flicked on her indicator, slowed, turned left and immediately changed down into first gear as the car took on the extremely steep gravel road. 'All things being equal, I should be there by six-thirty. I've only got one house call left.'

'Have you seen Anna Ainsworth?' Sue asked, suddenly sounding more like the district nurse she was than her mother. 'I didn't like the look of her leg on Tuesday.'

'I'm driving to Bide-a-While now.'

'You're doing a home visit? Is she okay? She's one of my naughtier diabetics and in typical Ainsworth style she won't be told anything.' Her mother warmed to one of Horseshoe Bay's favourite themes—the locals' opinions of the well heeled Melbourne-ites who owned holiday mansions in the town. 'You'd think that as the mother of an eminent surgeon, she'd be better behaved. Then again, we all know how Randall Ainsworth likes to throw his weight around and how the rules don't always apply…'

'Mmm,' Lauren hummed noncommittally as her mind drifted back to a summer a long time ago. *Don't go there*, her subconscious commanded. *Do. Not. Go. There.*

When Lauren had taken over the Horseshoe Bay practice, she'd been stunned to learn that Charlie's grandmother had not only left her Toorak home and retired to the house on the cliff but she was now a clinic patient. Not that she'd met Charlie's grandmother twelve years ago, or anyone else in his family for that matter, just like Charlie had never met her parents—some things were best kept secret.

Horseshoe Bay had two populations—the small, permanent one, and the transient tourist population that swelled the seaside village by thirty-five to one each summer. The relationship between the locals and the tourists was a symbiotic one, but that didn't mean it wasn't without its tensions. Stories, some dating as far back as the First World War, cautioned local women about getting involved with tourists. For every positive outcome, there were more than fifty negative ones and most of those revolved around the pocket of big houses high on the hill—the enclave of real wealth.

Growing up, Lauren had absorbed the lesson—have fun with the holidaymakers in the camping ground but don't get involved with anyone on Shore Road unless you want to be used and then abandoned.

As a teenager, she'd mostly avoided the bonfires at the far end of the beach where the rich kids played, although she had been to a couple, reluctantly dragged along by girl-friends who had dreamed wide and big and had inevitably got hurt deep and long.

She hadn't met Charlie at a bonfire or even at the Milk Bottle Café where she'd worked that summer—another favourite haunt of the rich kids. They'd met on a grey and humid afternoon when only the keen or stupid surfers braved the elements, pinning their hope on a fabled storm wave and the ride of their lives.

As the two of them had lain on their boards with their eyes glued to the water, they'd chatted. He'd made her laugh and she'd had the same effect on him, and when the edge of the storm front had hit, it had gifted them five amazing waves. They'd ridden them competitively, try-ing to outdo each other, yet at the same time urging each other on to do their best. Then the rain hit, the wind driv-ing each drop as sharp as the slice of a razor, and caution had kicked in. Once on the shore, Charlie had grabbed her hand and they'd run, taking shelter in a cave.

Sitting at the entrance, they'd watched nature's picture show of lightning jagging its yellow glow across the ho-rizon, complete with the soundtrack of cracking thunder. After two hours together spent laughing and talking about all sorts of things except themselves, he'd leaned in and kissed her.

She'd been kissed before but never like that. His warm and eager mouth had captured hers, making her body melt like chocolate and sizzle with so much heat she'd expected to combust in a shower of sparks. It had been a defining moment. Then and there, she'd chosen to ignore the little details she'd picked up on during the afternoon, like the fact his surfboard and wetsuit had come from the top end of the range. That his accent had been devoid of diph-thongs and that his mention of visiting overseas countries had hinted that travel was such an ordinary part of his life that he didn't even question it.

Instead, she'd told herself he was just 'Charlie' and for the rest of that summer they had spent as much time together as her part-time job had allowed. She'd refused to examine the fact she was keeping him hidden from her family and friends and that he was doing the same to her. Nothing had mattered except the exclusive and private bubble-for-two that they'd inhabited, filled with joy and delight.

And then the bubble had burst.

Twelve years ago. You let it all go, remember? Focus on the here and now.

Unfortunately, the here and now involved treating Anna Ainsworth—a woman she'd never in a million years expected to have as a patient. The families of Shore Road only used the local medical practice if it was an outright emergency and even then the Ibrahims and the Foxworths owned their own helicopters and could fly someone to Melbourne and their own doctor in twenty minutes. But Charlie's grandmother now lived permanently at Bide-a-While and, given her age, required regular medical attention.

Anna Ainsworth wasn't the sort of woman who whipped out photos of her family during a consultation and Lauren had never deviated from the professional doctor-patient relationship and asked about Charlie. Up until seeing the red stethoscope the other day, she hadn't thought about Charlie in a long time and, besides, asking about him would likely only generate questions from Anna about how she knew her grandson. Lauren had kept their relationship a secret this long and there was no reason to admit to it now.

Lauren had never visited Anna at home before but when Lauren matched up the fact the woman hadn't rung to cancel today's appointment with Sue's concerns about her leg, she'd decided a home visit was required. The car crested the hill and there in front of her were the intricate iron gates at the entrance to the Bide-a-While acre. The gates were open and, going by the growth of weeds at the base of the pillars, it would appear this was their normal state these days. 'I have to go, Mum. Talk soon.'

Lauren navigated the car along the agapanthus-lined gravel driveway, the large and heavy white and purple flowers waving in the breeze, and she gave a delighted gasp when the beautiful and immaculately white-painted Victorian house came into view. She parked adjacent to the glorious wraparound veranda that cast long shadows of welcome shade across the treated red gum boards, and the late afternoon sun turned the corrugated-iron roof into a dazzling silver light show.

She automatically imagined women from a hundred years ago wearing white muslin dresses and men in starched collared shirts sitting in the cane chairs, sipping G&Ts after playing tennis on the grass court. Today the veranda was empty except for an aging beagle, who waddled off his bed and ambled to the top of the five steps. He gave her a half-hearted bark as she hoisted her medical bag out of the boot.

'It's too hot for that sort of nonsense, buddy,' she said, leaning down to rub his ears before she pressed the brass door bell. While she waited for the sound of footsteps, she admired the beautiful red and blue painted glass panels around the door.

'Dr Fuller? Lauren. Goodness, this is a surprise.' Anna Ainsworth, still regal at eighty-one, peered at her through her glasses. 'Do come in, dear.'

'Thank you.' Lauren crossed the threshold and found herself standing in a wide hall with deep skirting boards.

'I was concerned when you didn't come to your appointment, especially when Mum…' She smiled and corrected herself. 'The district nurse was worried about you.'

The elderly woman's hand fluttered to the base of her throat. 'I'm so sorry to have worried you. It's just with everything that's happened today, the appointment completely slipped my mind.'

Lauren followed Anna into a spacious living room complete with an open fireplace and a mantelpiece filled with silver framed family photos. 'Is this the best place to examine you?'

'Why not?' Anna's blue eyes, pale with age, sparkled with mischief. 'It's a room with a view that's far more interesting than my leg.'

Lauren laughed and flicked open her bag. 'Oh, I don't know. I get excited when I see healthy skin where an ulcer is healing. I'll start by testing your blood sugar. How's it been?'

Anna grimaced. 'Up and down, like my blood pressure. I had the sniffles last week and at my age it seems to put everything out of whack. I find it utterly frustrating,' she said imperiously, as if the virus was very rude indeed to be causing her problems.

The glucometer beeped. 'Eleven point two. That's high.'

'Oh, that's just because of the tiny glass of champagne I drank.'

'Champagne?' Lauren tried not to sigh and unwrapped the blood-pressure cuff.

Anna leaned forward conspiratorially. 'There are special occasions in life when celebrations are more far important than a spike in blood sugar.'

'Like what?' Lauren asked as she pumped up the sphygmomanometer, deciding it was best to find out exactly what the circumstances were before reading the Riot Act.

'Like my grandson arriving unexpectedly.'

In her stunned surprise, Lauren only just caught the diastolic blood pressure reading as her heart did an odd skip in her chest. She immediately told herself not be ridiculous. Anna Ainsworth probably had many grandsons and even if this one was Charlie, he probably now came with a wife and two point five kids.

'I haven't seen him in over two years,' Anna continued, 'so I'm sure you'll agree that's very worthy of a few sips of champagne.'

'Lauren agrees, but Dr Fuller is a little torn,' she said with a tight smile. 'Now, let's look at this leg.' She slid a bluey under Anna's calf to protect the couch's beautiful Australian wildflower print, before slipping on some gloves and carefully removing the dressing. The skin around the small ulcer was angry and two tiny black dots worried her. She carefully debrided them and reapplied the occlusive dressing. 'That's to stay in place for a week, Mrs Ainsworth, and I need you to promise me two things.'

'Oh, dear,' the woman said, her eyes twinkling again. 'I'm not very good at keeping promises if they're dull and boring.'

'Oh, these are totally exciting, I promise,' Lauren said. 'The first is, when you're sitting down, put your leg up every time. The second is, call me if your blood sugar is higher than eight.'

'Lauren, dear, I think we have definition disparity about what constitutes exciting.'

'Not really. If you don't do those two things, you risk requiring a skin graft and spending a couple of weeks in hospital…' While she'd been talking, she'd gathered up the dressing waste, rolled it up in the bluey and shoved the contents into a bag. Now she tied it with a flourish. 'Now, *that* would be boring.'

'You doctors,' Anna grumbled good-naturedly. 'You do like to win. And I should know, I'm surrounded by them.'

Lauren was about to give in to overwhelming temptation and ask how many Ainsworths were doctors when a tall, gaunt man with a mop of sandy hair and a slightly darker beard appeared in the doorway. Her stomach knotted half in disappointment and half in relief—this grandson wasn't Charlie.

His entire demeanour—from the tilt of his head, past the slight sag of broad shoulders and all the way down to his wide, bare feet—emanated ingrained and longstanding fatigue. His blue eyes—so like Anna's and yet disturbingly less vibrant—were glassy and bloodshot. Lauren couldn't tell if he'd just woken up, was depressed, or if he'd consumed the bulk of the champagne and was, in fact, very drunk.

'Gran, where do you keep the—? Oh, sorry. I didn't realise you had a visitor.'

Lauren tensed as the rumbling voice with a raspy edge raised her skin in goosebumps. *Stop letting your imagination run wild. You know it's not Charlie. You'd recognise him instantly if it was.* Yet she'd swear there was something about his deep voice that held the vestiges of velvet that had stroked her all those years ago.

He was staring intently at her now—probably because she was staring just as intensely at him. His gaze narrowed as if he was closing out all distractions and zeroing in on her and her alone. Suddenly, the sapphire blue of his eyes, which a moment ago had been pale and insipid, lit up like refracted sunshine on water.

It's him. Flashes of fire and ice raced through her—hot, cold, hot, cold—until she tingled all over. She didn't know if she was shivering or sweating, only that her body was alive in a way it hadn't been in twelve long years. That alone scared her rigid. *No, damn it. Just no.* Despite not wanting to, her gaze automatically sought his left hand. No wedding ring. *So what? I really don't care.*

Anna, seemingly immune to the locked and loaded glance crackling with electricity that currently ran between her GP and her grandson, said, 'Charles, darling, this is my doctor, Lauren Fuller. Lauren, I'd like you to meet another doctor who is also my grandson, Charles Ainsworth.'

'Lauren.' His voice rolled over her name, the tone as warm and as addictive as hot caramel sauce. Then his deeply lined face creased in a smile—an older and wearier version of the smile she'd never been able to completely forget. With a quickness that belied his previous lethargy, he pushed off the architrave and strode across the room, his long legs eating up the distance in four fast strides.

Lauren barely had enough time to stick her hand out in greeting, but he ignored the gesture and was instead dipping his head down towards her as if he was about to kiss her. The bolt on the box she'd labelled 'Charlie' and buried deep all those years ago blew wide open. All the hurt and betrayal rose in a spurt of bile, scalding the back of her throat. How dare he think he could just swoop in and kiss her after all this time after what he'd done to her heart?

She instinctively—protectively—took a step back and ducked her head. All the while she kept her hand outstretched as much as a stop sign as in greeting. 'Pleased to meet you, Dr Ainsworth,' she said crisply and professionally, as if she was meeting him for the first time at a conference. She mentally dubbed him Charles as extra insurance.

Her brusque manner was a solid entity and it filled the space between them. He rocked back on his bare feet, his smile fading until his lips settled in a firm, flat line. A deep

V was carved between his dark eyebrows—their ebony so at odds with the rest of his fair colouring—and then the light in his eyes dimmed and vanished completely. The previous stranger with the almost blank affect was back. 'Actually, it's Mr Ainsworth.'

Of course it was. Their time together had been on the cusp of his medical career and Charlie—*Charles*—had mentioned a vague plan of one day working with his father in cardiology. Unexpectedly seething with an anger she'd assumed had faded and aged into acceptance a decade ago, she jerkily zipped up her medical bag. 'It's probably a long time since you've dealt with the less exciting aspects of medicine, Mr Ainsworth.' She hit his title with emphasis. 'But your grandmother's blood glucose readings are currently all over the shop. I'd appreciate it if you didn't offer her any more champagne or cake to celebrate your return.'

'You're planning on killing the fatted calf, aren't you, Gran?' Charles deadpanned. 'It's totally diabetic friendly, Dr Fuller, so we're all good.'

Unbidden laughter bubbled up inside her, just like it always had when she'd been in his company. The memories of how easily he'd made her laugh and smile—how quickly he could talk her out of a bad mood—circled her, tempting her to follow a well-worn path. *It's an overgrown path filled with briars and weeds.*

Lauren cut off the laughter. It morphed into a hard lump sitting uncomfortably in her chest and reminding her how easily he'd broken her heart. Her spine stiffened. She was no longer eighteen—hell, she wasn't even twenty-four— and only a fool failed to learn twice from her mistakes. She was no fool.

'Please ring the surgery in the morning, Mrs Ainsworth, and make an appointment to see me next Thursday.'

'I promise,' Anna said with a little nod to their previous conversation. 'But don't be too hard on Charles, dear. I was the one who suggested the champagne and he's—'

'I'll see you out, Dr Fuller,' Charles said abruptly.

Lauren had already slung her medical bag over her shoulder and moved to the door. 'That's not necessary.' But his hand was on the small of her back and his heat was swirling through her, stealing both her words and her willpower. Without knowing exactly how it happened, she was standing by the front door and he was standing a foot away from her, studying her as if she were a fascinating scientific specimen.

His lips curved slightly—only this time it looked as if the effort to smile was almost too much. 'We've met before, although the last time you saw me I was considerably younger and I didn't look quite so...'

Worn out and faded? What on earth had happened to the energetic twenty-three-year-old she'd once loved? But she didn't want to wonder and she had no intention of asking. Engaging with him would at best achieve nothing and at worst upset her. Desperate to get out of the house and away from the unwanted memories his presence was currently breathing life back into, she reached for the polished brass doorhandle.

'I find it hard to believe you don't remember me, Lauren.'

The mild thread of arrogance that underpinned his bemused words acted like a stiff breeze. The angry coals she had banked years ago flared into life. 'Whereas I find it hard to believe that you do.'

'Of course I remember you,' he said softly.

She could almost see his memories in the words, but she couldn't believe him—didn't trust herself to believe him. Moving decisively, she was quickly out the door and jogging down the steps to her car, determined not to look back. Fortunately, he didn't follow her. If she had anything to do with it, this was the first and last time she'd be in conversation with Mr Charles Ainsworth.

Charlie lacked the energy to run along the beach and was slightly aghast at the fact that Basil, his grandmother's aged beagle, was walking faster than him. It was as if touching down on Australian soil had drained him of all his vitality. His body felt encased in mud and all movement was an effort. He wanted to blame jet-lag for the fact he woke at two each morning, unable to get back to sleep, but who was he kidding? Vanuatu time was only one hour ahead of Australian Eastern Standard Time, so that excuse didn't cut it.

Apart from his first compulsory session with the counsellor and a quick visit to see his brother, he'd spent almost no time in Melbourne. Harry was much the same—thinner perhaps than the last time Charlie had seen him but just as quiet. Charlie had sat and told him about being on enforced leave. Harry had listened, his face impassive apart from a muscle twitch near his eye. He'd not offered an opinion, but that was par for the course. Charlie hadn't expected one.

There was no point lingering in Melbourne so, after leaving Harry, he'd hired a car and driven straight down the coast to Bide-a-While. Now he stared out at the horizon, scanning the calm seas for fins—preferably those of dolphins—and breathed in deeply, willing the salt air to magically invigorate him. With not even the hint of a wave, the bay was empty of its usual cluster of wetsuit-clad surfers and their boards eagerly anticipating the perfect ride.

Charlie vaguely entertained the notion of stand-up paddle boarding, but he couldn't muster the enthusiasm. It seemed like a lot of effort to climb back up the stairs to Bide-a-While, get the key, open the shed, find the board, pour himself into a wetsuit and finally get out onto the water.

Last night, Gran had suggested he walk into town early and buy coffee and the paper. He knew it was a just ploy to get him out of the house and into the fresh air, because she had a state-of-the-art Italian coffeemaker in the kitchen, plus he thought she still had the paper delivered. Still, he had to admit that being out on the beach as the sun rose beat thrashing about in bed, seeking sleep that never came.

Good old Gran. She'd welcomed his unannounced visit with open arms and thankfully with a distinct lack of questions—for now. He'd caught her studying him every now and then, worry clear in her eyes, and he hated that. He'd tried to reassure her—'just following the rules, taking some leave and satisfying the shrink that I came through the cyclone with my head intact'—but even he didn't totally believe his own spin. Cyclone or no cyclone, being back in Australia and without work to keep him busy and his mind full meant the past had a horrible way of sneaking up on him.

It hadn't taken long for the past to insert itself. Last night, the nightmare he'd thought he'd finally banished had visited, laughing at his naiveté. It turned out it had been languishing in the wings, just waiting for him to land on bright red, Aussie soil before making a grand entrance. During its dormancy, it hadn't change in shape or form. It was still him and Harry trapped in caves, wells, mines, barrels—any sort of container, vessel or space. They'd fight their way to the entrance, the surface, freedom, and he'd break through and turn to grab Harry's hand to tug him over the line, only to have his brother pulled away from him at the last moment and vanish in front of his eyes.

The nightmare had released him from its clutches in its age-old way—he'd woken with a start, drenched in sweat, his lungs tight, his chest heaving, and with the sheets tangled around his legs. He hadn't been able to save Harry in real life so why did he expect to be able to do it in a dream?

Although Gran was yet to grill him on work, it was obvious she was on a mission to fatten him up. Since he'd arrived three days ago, every meal had featured at least one of his favourite foods. As yet, none of them had piqued his appetite. It was still MIA along with sleep. So far, the only event to spark his interest had been meeting Lauren Fuller again.

Never in a million years had he expected to find her still in Horseshoe Bay, let alone working as the GP. During that amazing summer twelve years ago, she'd been high on the excitement of starting her medical degree and he remembered her discussing plans to work in indigenous communities. Horseshoe Bay was the antithesis of a desert community or even an indigenous coastal one. Still, all that talk had been a long time ago and plans could change—his certainly had.

Seeing her again had given him a few rare moments of pleasure and it had pierced the numbness and fatigue he was struggling to throw off. He'd felt more alive in those few minutes than he had in weeks. Granted, the feeling had been tempered by her obvious displeasure at seeing him. It was a reaction that still confused him. Despite closely examining his memory in the early hours of the last two mornings, no matter which way he came at it, his recollections of their time together only ever generated a collage of fun, laughter and sex.

Love.

He immediately shied away from the word. Love only brought pain and when he thought of Lauren that emotion was absent. No, he had a deep and abiding affection for her. She'd helped him get through a tough and difficult time and for that he'd never forget her. More than once over the years he'd regretted having to leave her behind. Back then, staying in Australia had been impossible—that hadn't changed.

Despite knowing that, it hadn't been enough to prevent him, in more disconsolate moments over the last ten years, from contemplating what his life might have been like if he'd stayed. *Stayed with Lauren.* But he knew those thoughts were flights of fancy. Even without the disaster that was his family and the fact they'd both been far too young and on the cusp of their adult lives to make a life-long commitment, he was too difficult to love.

But all those details aside, the fact Lauren had intimated he'd forgotten her had thrown him. It hadn't only been excitement at seeing her again that had propelled him across the room to her; it had also been lo—*gratitude.* It had felt like the most natural thing in the world for him to lean in and kiss her on the cheek. After all, that's what old friends did, right?

Apparently not. Her unanticipated frostiness had not only shocked him, it had spiked him, denting his enthusiasm and leaving him feeling foolish. He'd immediately fallen back into old Ainsworth habits. In a moment he still regretted, he'd gone for one-upmanship. He shuddered whenever he thought about his supercilious tone. 'Actually, it's Mr Ainsworth.'

His phone vibrated in his pocket and he pulled it out, half expecting a text from his grandmother asking him to pick up something for her in town.

Nice of you to let us know you're back in the country. I didn't appreciate being made to look a fool when Alison Petty said she'd seen you after visiting your brother and

I told her she must be mistaken. Your mother would appreciate a visit.

His father, he noted wryly, didn't waste text characters on greetings or sign-offs. Then again, it was no real surprise as he didn't use them in telephone calls, emails or face-to-face conversations either. Randall Ainsworth, MBBS, FRCS, PhD had little time for pleasantries—after all, he was a very busy man. As for Charlie's mother appreciating a visit? The jury was still out on that and had been for a long time.

He slid the phone back into his pocket, trying to ignore the unwanted and sticky tug of the complicated web that was his family ties. Visiting either of his parents and pretending that the accusations and angry words had faded into the past was pointless. They still hung in the air as fresh and raw as the day they'd been spoken in the ICU ward by Harry's bed. He was intelligent enough to know that time would not have improved the odds of a visit going well.

Basil barked, the sound thankfully breaking into his unhappy thoughts and diverting him. Charlie watched in surprise as the dog broke into a run. To be accurate, it was more of a brisk waddle but it was faster than the beagle's usual snail pace. He glanced along the beach and noticed a woman running towards them. Dressed in bright fluoro, she was impossible to miss.

Charlie set off after Basil, knowing that not everyone loved dogs, even harmless arthritic ones. He didn't have the energy to deal with an angry resident quoting beach by-laws at him. As he got closer, he noticed the runner's figure—trim but soft and curvy in all the places that made him appreciate a woman's body. He felt something shift inside and for the first time in months his libido sat up and took notice. Basil chose that moment to bark again and Charlie laughed, appreciating the dog's good taste. The noise seemed to penetrate the woman's concentration and, without breaking her stride, she turned her head towards the sound.

Lauren. Even with her face shadowed by the peak of her running cap, he'd recognise those rich brown eyes anywhere. He raised his hand in a wave and caught her momentary prevarication—she didn't want to stop. Well, blow that. He wanted to talk to her and find out why she was being so prickly. 'Morning, Lauren.'

If she wanted to ignore him, she was now stymied by Basil, who was waddling around her feet. She either stopped running or risked tripping over the rotund dog. Charlie decided right there and then that his unexpected wingman was getting a big, fat, juicy steak for dinner tonight. Lauren did an elegant sidestep and then stopped, bent and tousled Basil's velvet ears. She didn't look up.

'Mr. Ainsworth.'

'You used to call me Charlie.'

'We've grown up, Charles.'

She rose gracefully, her full height bringing the top of her head level with his chin. A memory flashed of her curves resting neatly into his dips—the two of them interlocking like puzzle pieces—and how he'd always rested his chin gently on her hair, breathing in her scent. *Apples.* She'd always smelt of apples and he idly wondered if she still did.

A sensation akin to peace rolled through him at the memory. Those six precious weeks with Lauren had been a haven from nine months of hell. A temporary but welcome escape from his family life until he'd made the break permanent with a move overseas. 'Fair enough,' he said, despite the fact he thought her calling him Charles was unfair. 'But don't be surprised if I fail to respond when you call me that. My parents are the only people who use my full name and I rarely respond to them.'

'Your grandmother introduced you as Charles the other night.'

'Ingrained social etiquette. Generally, she calls me Charlie or Stupid, depending on what I've done.'

Lauren's lips wriggled as if she was fighting a smile. 'So, you get called stupid a lot, do you?'

'Just enough to keep me grounded.' He shot her a self-deprecating grin, hoping to be rewarded with a full smile. It didn't happen and it struck him that his disappointment was out of proportion to the situation. Then again, all his reactions seemed to be out of kilter at the moment—they were either way too strong or not strong enough. For weeks he'd been unable to anticipate any of them and not working was making it worse. 'I'm heading for coffee.' He nodded towards the café. 'Any good?'

'As good as you get in Melbourne,' she said, stretching out an arm before standing on her right leg and bending her left up behind her.

The action pulled her top tightly across her breasts and he couldn't help but notice they were slightly fuller than he remembered, not that he was complaining. 'I'm clueless on Melbourne's coffee standards. I don't think I've had a cup there in eighteen months.'

Surprise danced across her high cheekbones and her left foot hit the sand. 'Really? I thought you lived there?'

He saw the curiosity bright in her in her eyes and he seized on it, hoping it was an opening. 'Let me buy you coffee. We can fill each other in on the last twelve years.'

'I don't have all day.'

It was said without an accompanying smile and her resistance crashed into him, wave after wave. If he'd thought he might have imagined hostility when they'd met at Bide-a-While, he was under no illusions now. What confused him was why it existed at all. Although he remembered a lot of arguments that summer, all of them had been with his father and none of them with Lauren. 'What about coffee and the potted version, then?'

She stood still for a second and then her gaze fell to the sports watch on her wrist. He crossed his fingers behind his back. 'Ten minutes,' she said, 'but let's go to another café.'

'I thought you said this one was good, and look...' he pointed to a bloke with sun-bleached hair who was setting up a sandwich board '...it's open.'

'The other one's closer to work.' In an abrupt action that mirrored her words, she broke into a jog.

'Come on, Basil,' Charlie said. 'We're going to have to run to catch up.'

Lauren sipped her latte at the small outside table and blamed running-induced hypoxia for agreeing to chat with Charlie. *Charles, Charles, Charles.* Who was she kidding? He'd always been Charlie and using the formal version of his name wasn't enough to keep old memories—good and bad—at bay. Right now, she was banking on the fact that by agreeing to this ten-minute catch-up of the last twelve years she'd be off the hook. Afterwards, she could cheerfully decline any future invitations without appearing rude. To be honest, she was flummoxed as to why he even wanted to do this when he'd been the one to walk away without looking back.

'So...married? Children?' she asked, determined to control the conversation. It didn't prevent her from steeling herself for the inevitable phone photos of blonde-haired, blue-eyed children in private school uniforms. Or a family shot taken at a resort in an exotic location somewhere. When she'd been younger and daydreaming the vision of her life, she'd never anticipated that she'd be the single, childless woman forced to make polite comments about other people's children. Yet that was exactly what she'd become.

'Let's face it, Lauren. You fail at most things so why are you surprised you can't get pregnant?' Jeremy's words wormed their way back despite her attempt to block them out.

'No to marriage and children,' Charles said in a tone that gave no hint as to how he felt about the situation. 'I was engaged once for a bit, but…' He shrugged. 'It didn't work out.'

Why? She was still processing the fact that he was one of a rare species—a single, good-looking, heterosexual male in his mid-thirties—when he added, 'What about you? Married? Kids? Committed relationship?'

She swallowed as the shame she thought she'd banished came back to bite her. 'Divorced,' she said softly.

'Ah. Sorry.'

'Yeah.' She sipped her coffee, not certain if she wanted his sympathy or not. 'It's not something I ever thought would happen to me but—' *Shut up. He's not your friend. He doesn't need to know.*

'Stuff happens that we can't always control.'

Her head snapped up at his sombre tone. 'That sounds like the voice of experience.'

His eyes suddenly widened into inky black discs. He shot to his feet, tossed the light café table sideways and grabbed her roughly, hauling her out of the chair. She slammed hard into his chest and her breath flew out of her lungs. Fear invaded her, stiffening her body and making her blood thunder through her veins. A scream rose to her throat but before it broke out she was slammed onto the ground and Charlie's body was rolling hers over and over.

CHAPTER THREE

THE TERRIFYING SCREECH of brakes penetrated Lauren's terror, followed by the high-pitched sound of shattering glass. Shards rained down on her. A car horn blared. The acrid smell of rubber burned her nostrils. Her body protectively stilled, every sense on alert, trying to decode the situation—ascertain safety. She opened her eyes and found herself looking straight up into Charlie's cornflower-blue eyes, still dominated by high-alert black. His gaze reflected everything she was feeling—shock, relief and an overwhelming sense of urgency.

'Okay?' he asked, his voice trembling.

'I… Yes. I think so.'

'Thank God.' He pushed himself to his feet and grabbed her hand. She found her footing amongst the glass and vaguely noticed a rip in her pants.

People ran towards them. A man she didn't recognise—his face white with shock—gasped, 'I thought you two were dead for sure.'

'We're fine,' Charlie said, his voice suddenly loud and commanding. 'We're doctors. You call the police and ambulance. We'll check on the others.'

'Go to the doctors' clinic,' Lauren called out, her voice not quite as steady as Charlie's. She pointed down the street in the direction of the surgery. 'Tell Lexie I need the AED and the emergency kits. All of them.'

'Emergency kits. Got it.' The man turned and ran.

Lauren quickly assessed the devastation in front of her. The rear of a small four-door sedan was protruding from the café and the jagged remains of the huge glass frontage hung over it like stalactites. Her thoughts took the obvious path—were the car's occupants alive? Horrifying reality cramped her gut. What about the people inside the café? Had the car hit any of the staff or customers?

Charlie, who was already at the driver's door, looked up as if reading her thoughts. 'Triage inside.'

She nodded and ran. Fortunately, the door to the café hadn't buckled and it opened. Steve, the young barista, and another man stood stunned and rooted to the spot, their horrified gazes fixed on the front of the car. Lauren saw a pair of female legs splayed at a rakish angle and protruding from under the car. As she dropped to her knees, she said firmly, 'Steve. Find me a torch. You…' she pointed to the second man '…do a head count. Tell me who else is hurt.'

Both snapped to attention. 'On it.'

A phone with the torch app activated was thrust into Lauren's hand and she crawled under the car. 'It's Lauren,' she said to the woman, having no idea if she was a local or a tourist. Dead or alive. Conscious or unconscious. 'I'm a doctor.'

The woman didn't move or make a sound. Lauren's hand reached for the patient's neck, her fingers seeking a carotid pulse. It took her a moment but she finally detected a faint and thready beat. Moving forward on her belly, she gained a few centimetres and somehow managed to check the woman's pupils. *Sluggish response to light.*

'Lauren!' Charlie's voice called out to her. 'What have you got?'

'Head injury and probable internal bleeding. Her breathing's shallow but I can't move or see enough to examine her.'

'We need to pull her out.'

'What about spinal injuries? Can't you move the car back?'

'Too risky. The front of the building might collapse. Here.' His hand shoved a neck brace at her and she gave thanks for Lexie's fast arrival with the emergency packs. 'Put this on her.'

'I need light.'

'Got it.' Charlie's face appeared and he directed two phones towards her.

Lying on her side, Lauren's fingers felt thick and clumsy, and while she fitted the brace she agonised over the compromises that always came with triage—save a life but risk exacerbating an injury in the process. 'Brace on.'

'Her name's Celine. Can you support her head while I pull her legs?'

'I'll have to come out and go back in at a different angle.'

'Do it.' Charlie said. 'Fast.'

Feeling like a trainee soldier, she wriggled out on her belly before re-entering so her head and Celine's were next to each other. 'Okay, but slowly.'

'Got it. On my count,' Charlie commanded. 'One, two, three.' The distance Celine needed to be moved wasn't huge but it felt like miles. Lauren concentrated on keeping the patient's spine in alignment. 'And we're clear,' Charlie yelled. 'She's not breathing.'

Lauren rolled out from under the car as sirens blared. Charlie was already doing CPR and she grabbed the automatic emergency defibrillator. Ripping open the woman's blouse, she quickly applied the electrode pads. 'Clear,' she said loudly. Charlie's hands moved off Celine's sternum and he held them up as if a gun were being levelled at him. She pressed the shock button. Celine's body shuddered. Charlie recommenced CPR, counting to thirty before giving the patient two breaths.

'Stop CPR. Analysing,' the electronic voice of the AED instructed.

Charlie lifted his hands 'Look at her trachea. Grab a cannula.'

'Tension pneumothorax?' Lauren handed him a fourteen-gauge needle and swabbed Celine's upper chest. The pressure would be preventing her heart filling with venous blood. With nothing to pump, the heart was a fibrillating mess.

'I'm hoping.' Charlie plunged the needle into the skin between the second rib space in the mid-clavicular line and a faint whoosh of air followed. 'Now we might be able to get her back.'

'Clear!' Lauren said loudly again, before depressing the shock button. Her eyes were glued to the liquid display. Thank, God. 'Sinus rhythm,' she said, catching the relief on Charlie's face. 'Good call.'

He shrugged. 'We're not out of the woods yet. You got this? I'll check on the others.'

'Sure.' She inserted an IV and did another set of observations. Although Celine was breathing and her heart was beating, she was still unconscious. Given the trauma she'd experienced, being out of it could be a good thing but the doctor in Lauren knew her sluggish pupil response was a serious concern.

'Do you need the helicopter, Lauren?'

She looked up at the familiar voice and smiled at her father, who was standing above her in his blue paramedic's uniform. 'Yes. Probable head injury and post cardiac arrest. She needs to go direct to The Edward.'

Ian pulled out his phone and made the call while Lauren helped his partner load Celine into the ambulance for the short trip to the helipad. As the ambulance drove away Lauren returned inside. Charlie was splinting a young girl's leg and Lexie was handing out blankets. Her mother was sticking bright pink sticky notes on people, describing symptoms and seating them in chairs. The young barista was making coffee.

'Who's first?' Lauren asked, ignoring the dull ache all over her body that was probably soft tissue bruising from colliding with concrete.

'Jake Lawrence. He's got a nasty cut to his arm. Do you want to stitch it here or at the surgery?' Sue asked.

'Here might be better.' Lauren saw two police officers talking to an elderly man wrapped in a blanket who she assumed was the driver of the car. 'There's coffee and people need to stay together and talk so they can start to process it all.'

The next ninety minutes passed in a blur. Her father and his partner returned and transported the two patients with fractures to the hospital in Surfside. The police interviewed people who felt up to telling their version of events and while Lauren stitched wounds, she listened to people's outpourings of shock and grief.

'It came out of nowhere. One minute I was paying for coffee and the next... *Crash.* I thought a bomb had gone off.'

But amidst their trauma the locals' concerns were for the tourist who'd taken the brunt of the accident. 'No one expects to be injured when they're drinking coffee on holiday. Will she be okay?'

'I don't know the full extent of her injuries,' Lauren answered truthfully. 'She's got a struggle ahead.'

When there was no one else needing medical attention, Lauren finally came up for air and for the first time fully took in her surroundings. The line of chairs was now empty as people had either been taken to hospital or collected by family and friends. Police tape surrounded the car and blocked the entrance of the café—the blue and white checks declaring it an investigation scene. Steve was sitting with Sue and Lexie, drinking a well-earned coffee.

She felt a hand on her shoulder and glanced up into Charlie's face. Today he was clean shaven and he looked both familiar and alien. She gave an internal sigh. The square jaw and bladed cheekbones she'd loved to run her fingers over all those years ago remained the same, but his skin was older, lined with whatever the last decade plus had thrown at him. The laughter lines that bracketed his mouth were still there but more defined, and on the few occasions he'd grinned, the dimples in his cheeks still showed. That had both reassured and hurt her.

What was new were the deep lines around his eyes. She got the impression that laughter was not responsible for all of them. His golden hair was darker than it had been at the age of twenty-three and, unlike the neat, short cut he'd sported back then, his current style was dishevelled but not in the fashionable 'messy look' way. Strands fell across his high, intelligent forehead, almost poking into his eyes in a jagged and motley manner. Despite that, the hair wasn't long enough to hide the dark shadows under his eyes and the general air of dispiritedness that dogged him.

Her heart did an unwelcome flip of longing tinged with distress, although she was uncertain whether it was for him or herself. She stopped herself from reaching up and cupping his cheek, despite wanting his warmth to fill her palm and to tell her that his essence was still in there somewhere. But she didn't have the right to touch him and, more importantly, she didn't want to touch him.

Reminiscing was like the turn of the tide. On the surface the water looked wonderful and all the good memories enticed her to wade in and throw herself into the experience. But she knew the same jagged rocks that had caused her to flounder once before still lay in wait, ready to plunge deep into her heart. She had no intention of putting her hand up for that all over again.

Trying to shake off unwanted feelings that begged her to only remember the good times, she dropped her gaze and immediately noticed his shirt was ripped and bloodstained. Cuts and grazes criss-crossed his upper arms. 'Did Mum or Lexie look at these? You've probably got glass embedded in your arm.'

'Just like you've probably got glass in your thigh?'

Surprised, she glanced down and realised blood had congealed around the rip in her running pants. She was suddenly aware of a burning sensation. 'How crazy. I didn't feel a thing until now.'

He grimaced. 'Fight and flight response. Adrenaline hides a multitude of ills until it doesn't. Does this hurt?' His fingers ran gently across her lower left arm, lingering on a bump.

She flinched. 'Ouch.'

'Exactly.' He gave her a wry smile. 'Sorry. But I think I inadvertently fractured your ulna when we hit the ground.'

'Don't apologise.' The reality of what had happened was slowly starting to penetrate the protective adrenaline. 'You saw the car heading for us, didn't you?'

'Yeah.' He brushed his hair away from his eyes. 'I grabbed you out of instinct. I probably gave you a hell of a fright.'

'It doesn't matter. You saved my life. Our lives. Thank you.' She moved to squeeze his hand and gasped as sharp pain circled her. Her entire body stiffened and she didn't want to take another breath, knowing it was going to hurt like hell.

'Lauren?' His gaze filled with concern. 'What is it?'

'I think as well as needing an X-ray for my arm I need one for my ribs.'

'Right, you two,' Sue said walking over as if sensing something was up. 'You've both put me off long enough but no more excuses. Lexie and I will look after the clinic and the police are taking the two of you to Surfside to be checked out.'

'That's not necessary,' Charlie said firmly. 'I'm fine. I can drive Lauren to hospital.'

'I don't think so.' Sue folded her arms across her chest. 'According to Theo, who saw it all happen, we're lucky both of you are alive. Let's not push our luck by letting you get behind the wheel of a car just as shock hits and it has you running off the road.'

A look of incredulity crossed Charlie's face that someone would question his plans. 'Ms...um...?'

'Fuller,' Sue said with a smile. 'Sue Fuller. I'm the district nurse and Lauren's mother.'

'I'm Charlie Ainsworth. I'm a trauma surgeon with Australia Aid and I deal with life-and-death situations all the time.'

'I'm sure you do,' Sue said sympathetically, 'but today you're part of the accident too.' She dropped a blanket over the two of them. 'Sorry but this is our last one. You'll have to share. Shane, you can take them now.'

'Sorry,' Lauren muttered, not sure if her light-headedness was from the ever-increasing pain or the fact she was sharing a blanket with Charlie.

His right side flanked her left and his heat poured into her. It skimmed along her veins in a heady mix of lust and yet at the same time it was familiar and almost comforting. Red-hot pain and logical resistance duelled with visceral longing. Her vision blurred at the edges. The room started to spin. She tried to stay upright but her legs lost strength and as her knees gave way, she sagged onto him. His arm circled her and she flinched. 'Ribs.'

'Hell. Sorry.' He dropped his arm lower across her hip but still held her.

Despite his gaunt frame, he felt solid and secure. Without being aware of exactly how it happened, her cheek was resting on his chest and the steady and rhythmic beat of his heart sounded reassuringly in her ear. As his hand gently stroked her hair she heard him say quietly, 'It's okay, Lauren.'

She closed her eyes.

While Charlie waited for the electric kettle to boil, he looked around Lauren's kitchen, opening cupboards and drawers, until he found the mugs and teabags. He had no idea how she took her tea—twelve years ago she hadn't even drunk tea—so he chose a lemon and ginger teabag, figuring that way he didn't have to worry about milk.

They'd only just returned from the hospital. It turned out Lauren's father had been one of the paramedics—yet another thing he'd learned about her today—and Ian had driven them home in the rig. The burly man with salt-and-pepper curls had insisted on taking Lauren to her childhood home but she'd objected. 'Both you and Mum are at work until four so I may as well stay at my place.'

Ian had muttered something under his breath but had driven her to her sandstone cottage. While Lauren had walked down the short path to the front door, Ian had taken

Charlie aside. 'My daughter's stubborn. But you know as well as I do she's groggy after the Endone so she can't be on her own.'

'I'll stay with her,' Charlie had offered immediately, as much for himself as for Lauren.

Something weird and unsettling had happened to him at the hospital when Lauren had been wheeled off to X-Ray. The entire time she'd been gone, he'd been twitchy and jumpy. Flashes of the damn car coming straight at her— at them—had played in a continuous loop in his head, but the moment the porter had wheeled her back to him, the images had stopped. He'd known his thought process of *If I can see her she's safe* had been totally irrational, but if it kept the flashbacks at bay, he'd play along.

'Thank you.' Ian had pumped Charlie's hand generously. 'And thank you so much for your quick thinking and saving her life. You see a lot in this job and...' The experienced man's voice had cracked. 'Well, I'm not telling you anything you don't know.' He cleared his throat. 'Anyway, it's probably a good idea for both of you to be together so you can talk about what happened. Debrief. You know, help with the flashbacks, that sort of thing.'

The kettle pinged and Charlie concentrated on making two mugs of tea. He carried them into the living room where Lauren lay on a couch, propped up on a European pillow and with her eyes closed. He took advantage of the opportunity to study her carefully.

All those years ago it had been her wide smile and enormous eyes that had made him look twice at her, but it had been her laughter that had utterly captivated him. Even before Harry's accident, no one in his family had laughed quite so enthusiastically or seen the humour in obscure things quite like she did. After that tragic day laughter had been silenced, which was why Lauren had breezed into his life like a breath of fresh air. Now he not only longed to hear her laugh, he craved to have her bestow that easy smile on him again. But before either of those things could happen, he had to find a way in, under or around the hectares of reserve she'd thrown up. Apart from the moment she'd slumped against him in the café and her warmth and softness had dived deep inside him, reviving wonderful memories, she'd held herself aloof in a way she'd not done once during their summer together.

'Tea?'

She opened her eyes and turned their slightly glazed and out-of-focus attention onto him. Surprise lit their depths to a seductive caramel hue. It was clear she'd forgotten he was there. He hoped she'd forgotten she was mad at him.

'Thank you.' Her mouth curved up into a sloppy and happy smile.

'My pleasure.' Even though he knew her smile was the result of the narcotic painkiller she'd taken, a lightness washed through him. This was the Lauren he remembered. This was the Lauren he wanted to see more of.

'You look crazy tall standing there,' she said with a giggle, and lifted her legs. 'Sit down.'

He could have sat in a chair but the idea of sitting on the couch with her was far too tempting. As his behind hit the couch cushion, her sock-clad feet slammed across his thighs in the exact way they'd done so many times during that long-ago summer. Back then, he'd loved touching her and he'd taken every chance he'd been offered, along with creating opportunities when chance had let him down. Now, presented with this unexpected happenstance, he wasn't going to let it pass. It was as natural as breathing to slide his hand down her leg and rest it on her ankle, savouring the feel of her smooth skin silky against his palm. She didn't object.

Silently, they sipped their tea. After a few minutes she raised her arm, staring at the ultralight cast with child-like wonder and slightly constricted pupils. 'When I was a teenager, I would have killed for a nightstick fracture. I always envied kids with signed casts.'

'I'll sign it.' He set his tea on the side table and pulled a pen out of his pocket.

'Will you?' Her eyes sparkled and her cheeks danced with joyful expectation. 'What a guy!' Then she laughed; a throaty, husky sound that spun around him like a cocoon, bringing with it memories of hot and sultry summer nights.

Lauren scooted in closer. The action not only brought her arm across his chest for easy access to sign, it also brought her head closer to his. He breathed in deeply, anticipating the scent of apples, but instead he inhaled a complex scent of the tang of the sea, the zip of citrus and a hint of antiseptic. He braced himself for disappointment but it didn't come. The sweet adolescent scent had belonged to the younger Lauren and its innocent notes no longer suited the striking woman next to him.

Like him, she'd changed—life did that to a person. If he was honest, Harry's accident had already changed him before he'd met Lauren all those years ago. He knew he'd used their summer together to take a time-out from the all the pain and heartache of the previous nine months. For a few precious weeks he'd pretended that the accident hadn't happened and his family's lives hadn't been brutally upended. He hadn't expected to fall in love. It had scared the hell out of him.

He was halfway through decoding the change in her scent—what it may or may not signify—when her heat poured into him in like fire water, streaking through his veins and exploding into every cell. The sweet curve of her behind pressed up against the side of his right thigh and the backs of her own thighs now rested on top of his. His heart pounded hard and fast, carrying her heat and scent around him until it pooled in his lap with an odd mix of yearning and urgency.

Stifling a groan, he closed his eyes and silently named the cranial nerves, trying to reverse the effects of his arousal. It didn't help that Lauren was wriggling against him as if she was trying to find a comfortable position.

You're killing me. 'Stop moving.'

She instantly stilled and he realised he'd barked out the command in the same gruff and terse voice he used in the operating theatre when a patient was bleeding out. He cleared his throat. 'Sorry. It's just I'm accused of illegible handwriting at the best of times,' he tried to quip as he struggled to pull himself together. With a trembling hand, he scrawled a message. 'There you go.'

She pulled her arm back and read out loud, '"You'll be surfing again soon. Charlie."' With a sharp intake of breath she moved abruptly back up the couch away from him. When she raised her head, her chestnut brows were drawn down and she was looking straight at him through fully focused eyes. 'I haven't surfed in years.'

Stunned surprise broke over him. In the intervening years, whenever he'd thought of her he'd pictured her on her surfboard, eyes shining and racing him to the shore. 'Why not? You loved it.'

Her nostrils flared and she sucked in her lips as if she was in pain. 'Are your ribs hurting?' he asked. 'Do you need more medication?'

She slowly swung her legs off his, the action stiff and guarded. 'No. Right now I need to be clear-headed.'

'Right now you're better off being pain-free.'

This time her laugh rang out loud and harsh. All the recent softness playing on her face and weaving into her body vanished, replaced by the familiar defensive guard. 'Tell me, Charles. Why did you break your promise to me?'

Bewildered, he stared at her, seeking clues from her tight expression and her return to the use of his full name. He got nothing. He racked his brain, trying to work out what the hell she was talking about but he came up blank. 'My promise?'

Lauren's heart twisted. *He has no idea what I'm talking about.* The pain in her ribs and the throbbing in her arm surged back, morphing from a dull ache to sharp, stabbing pain. As the intensity ratcheted up, her logic and reasoning returned. With it came despair. *Oh, God, what had she just done?* Under the influence of Endone, she'd lost her filter and all her reserve. She'd flirted. She'd snuggled up with Charlie on the couch exactly as she'd done when she'd been eighteen. Only she wasn't a teenager any more—she was a grown woman who knew how much he'd hurt her.

Why had she asked him about the promise? Especially when he'd just saved her life. Not to mention the most important fact, which was that she did not want to revisit a time that had caused her heartache—a time she'd worked so hard to let go. *Hah!* Okay, a time she'd *thought* she'd let go. Obviously, remnants lingered and the speed with which they'd roared back into life when she'd come face to face with Charlie had taken her by surprise. She wished she could hide.

His eyes bored into her. 'What promise?'

He doesn't even remember. Old despair sank its teeth into her. More than anything she wanted to stand up and walk away from him, but she didn't think her legs would hold her. If they gave way again, he'd swoop in and catch her. She didn't trust herself not to give in and let him cradle her close. When his arms had held her in the café, the unexpected sense of being home had been so strong she hadn't wanted to leave. The survivor in her knew that emotions like that were dangerous not only to her peace of mind but to her heart—an organ she'd already shored up and repaired more than once.

The only way to protect herself was to restore the distance she'd so carefully placed between them when they'd met at Bide-a-While—the distance drugs had just jettisoned. 'Ignore me,' she said briskly. 'I'm not making any sense. I need to sleep.'

His gaze was too perceptive, roving over her face, seeking clues. 'I think it's more likely you're making absolute sense for once. You've been prickly ever since we met at Gran's. This promise is connected to that, isn't it?'

She'd forgotten how observant he was and how quick his brain. Perhaps, if she closed her eyes, he might take the hint and leave. Her lids lowered and she shut him out, trying to let sleep claim her.

'Lauren?'

Damn it. He wasn't going away. In fact, she'd bet her bottom dollar he would sit there until she told him. She didn't know which was the worse humiliation; that she'd flirted and snuggled into him or that she'd raised the hurt she'd long associated with him. The answer was simple: it was the latter and now she couldn't back away from it. A long, bone-weary sigh rumbled out of her. 'You told me you were coming back.'

'Coming back?' Bewilderment skittered across his face. 'Where? When?'

The fact he had no clue what she was talking about hurt more than her bruised ribs. 'Do you remember our last night together?'

He was quiet for a moment. 'I have a strong suspicion I don't remember it as well as you do. But before I'm accused of something, I want to say with absolute honesty that our summer together was one of the happiest of my life.'

She flinched as his words poured salt on a wound she knew should have healed a very long time ago. She hated that it hadn't. Hated herself more. 'Your happiest?' she scoffed. 'That's probably because nothing about that summer was real. We immersed ourselves in each other and hid from the world.'

This time he flinched, as if she'd shot an arrow at him and made a direct hit. 'Was that so bad? We had a lot of fun.'

'We did.' She couldn't argue that. 'Then it ended.'

He nodded slowly. 'Just as we both always knew it would. We were young. We'd agreed...'

The arrow returned, piercing her this time, and she couldn't hide the hurt. 'Then why did you move the goal-posts at the last minute and tell me that you were only going to London for a year?' Her voice rose despite her desperate attempts to sound detached. 'I stupidly waited for you to come back.'

A thousand emotions rose and fell in his eyes until all that was left was guilt and pity. 'The intern position I had in London was only for one year,' he said quietly, tugging at his ear. 'Did I actually say to you, "I'll be back?"'

She opened her mouth to say a decisive yes but something on his face and in his voice—not regret but perhaps concern—made her hesitate. She rolled her mind back to a time when she'd sat on the enormous picnic rug at the mouth of the cave. She smelt the hot, sweet fat and the tang of salt from their paper-wrapped fish and chips. She heard the raucous squawks of predatory seagulls brawl-ing for prime position, ever hopeful of scoring food. She tasted the syrupy sweetness of passionfruit soda laced with vodka—her favourite beverage that summer—one she'd not tasted since. It had been their last of many picnics together on the beach.

Two weeks previously, they'd spent a day and a night in Melbourne. They'd had dinner in Lygon Street and he'd told her how, when she was studying at uni, this Italian district would be her local shopping strip. He'd shown her all his favourite haunts in and around the uni, making her bubbly with excitement and keen for the next six weeks to pass quickly so she could start her degree. Then he'd taken her shopping and bought her the red stethoscope.

One small purchase—a gift—had changed everything. The moment he'd swung it around her neck and pulled her into him, she'd fallen in love. What had started out as a summer of fun had morphed into friendship and love. Ignoring all the apocryphal stories about doomed holiday romances, Lauren had foolishly allowed herself to weave a fantasy of the two them continuing to be together long after the summer ended. After all, she'd justified, they'd be living in the same city. The university was across the road from the hospital where Charlie had accepted an intern position. Geography wasn't an issue so why couldn't they build on what they'd started?

'Something exciting happened today,' Charlie said, as she lay with her head in his lap.

She gazed up at him and laughed. 'The fact you actually beat me into shore?'

He grinned. 'That was pretty cool, but it's even better than that.'

Excitement bounced off him, pushing into her and catching her in its web. Had he got the flat he'd applied for? Did it mean he was going to ask her to move in with him? She sat up and caught his hands. 'Tell me!'

'I got an offer from London Central. I'm going to do my residency there.'

Her smile froze. All her daydreams shattered, crashing down around her feet in sharp and jagged shards, digging into her skin. 'London as in London, England?'

'The very same.' He laughed, high on the news.

'Wow.' The one-syllable word was a struggle to form. 'That's...that's so exciting.'

'I know, right?' He pulled her into his lap and kissed her. 'I can hardly believe it.'

She studied his face. It shone with jubilation and anticipation. The fact this news thrilled him to his marrow eviscerated her. She wasn't part of this dream of his. 'I didn't even know you'd applied,' she said, forcing herself to sound upbeat.

'I didn't tell anyone.'

'Not even your parents?' She couldn't imagine keeping anything that huge from her mum and dad. So how come you're keeping Charlie a secret?

'I didn't want to jinx it,' he said, suddenly serious. 'I still can't believe I got accepted. I'm going to have a year in England.'

She wanted to be happy for him, she truly did, but all she could think was that he was travelling seventeen thousand kilometres away from her and she wouldn't see him for twelve long months. Her world, which had been so vibrant and colourful only a few minutes before, was suddenly charcoal grey. 'And after London, then what? You'll come back?'

He smiled and ran his hands through her hair before cupping her cheeks, tilting back her head and kissing her until sensation vanquished all conscious thought.

The memory slapped Lauren and her breath stalled.

No, that wasn't right.

Charlie had smiled at her and then said, 'Yes, I'll be

back.' She conjured up the memory a second time. She saw the smile but the words didn't come.

Oh, God.

Had she interpreted his smile as agreement? Had she been so desperate to hear the words that she'd imagined he'd spoken them?

No!

She tried again but she still couldn't hear them. The idea that she'd replayed this memory over and over in her head until her version of the conversation had become her reality horrified her. Worse still was the thought that her desperation a couple of months later, when darkness had descended over her, had cemented the erroneous belief firmly in place. She knew the only thing that had got her through the heartache and misery after her miscarriage had been her belief that he'd return to her. It had sustained her right up until betrayal had sneaked in and taken its place.

'Lauren.' Charlie's voice was careful and controlled. 'Please understand this has nothing to do with our amazing summer together. The thing is, I would *never* have promised you that I'd come back.'

For so long she'd been so certain, so convinced and yet now… 'How can you be so sure you didn't say it?'

He sighed and the weariness he wore like a coat settled over him. 'Because London was my ticket out of Australia. I never had any intention of returning here to live. I still don't.'

Despite his resigned tone, a hint of harshness lingered in the words. She trawled her dusty and obviously faulty recollections, looking for anything he'd said or done during their summer that had hinted he'd wanted to run from his country of origin. She had plenty of moments to draw on of a laughing and smiling Charlie. Of him daring her to race him both on land and sea, and a thousand clips of his eyes darkening to indigo before he kissed her and tumbled her into bed. Happy, joyous, playful memories with no connection to anything outside their precious bubble. Not one clue that anything was amiss.

The reality was they'd mostly avoided talking about the future because it had meant the end of their time together. 'You did mention a vague plan of working with your father.'

'Was I drunk at the time?' But his lip curled, stealing the joke from the words. He scrubbed his face with his hands before looking back at her. 'Hurting you was the last thing I wanted to do. I had no idea you thought I was coming back. You never said a thing, never dropped any clues, and if you had, I would have said something. I mean, hell, did we even trade more than one or two emails after I left?'

Five. We traded five. But she swallowed the words, not wanting to sound even more pathetic than she'd already exposed herself to be. Only a fool carried a torch for a man who had left her and his country without a backward glance.

But his question had been rhetorical and he didn't pause for a reply. 'I remember you emailing and telling me about your cohort and your lecturers. How you were trying not to sink under the intense workload and asking me for tips.' He gave her wry smile tinged with guilt. 'I was barely keeping my head above water then myself. What's the statute of limitation on apologies?'

'Twelve years and one month.'

'I can just sneak it in under the wire, then.' He picked up her hand. 'I'm sorry I didn't reply to your emails. I apologise for any and all hurt I've caused you.' His eyes flickered with something she couldn't read. 'Seriously, Lauren. I'm truly sorry.'

His sincerity warmed her. 'Thank you. I appreciate

the apology, even though it seems I was the one to get the wrong end of the stick. I'm sorry I didn't give you a warmer welcome the other day.'

'I'm just glad I understand why. I hate the idea you were hurt by this misunderstanding.'

She shrugged and withdrew her hand, not offering the real reason why she'd stopped emailing him or waited out the year. Her surprise pregnancy and subsequent miscarriage was information he *never* needed to know. 'Don't worry,' she said flippantly, changing the subject. 'I didn't pine for long. All the guys in my year were intrigued by my first year of aloofness so I had lots of opportunities to make up for lost time.'

He tensed momentarily before giving her a sideways glance. 'Good to know. So now we've got that all sorted, are we friends again?'

Friends. The feelings his touch had sparked in her today were not the platonic sensations experienced by friends. They told her to run fast and far from the suggestion. But she'd already wrongly accused him of breaking a promise and he had saved her life today. That tilted the scales firmly in his direction. Saying no would be childish and churlish but the idea of being friends with him unsettled her. How could she get around this without appearing ungrateful?

Snatches of conversation played in her head. *'London was my ticket out of Australia' 'I never had any intention of returning.' 'I'm a trauma surgeon with Australia Aid.'*

'I haven't seen my grandson in two years.'

Bingo! Charlie didn't live in Australia. She almost punched the air in relief. If she extrapolated details, it sounded like he only ever spent a few weeks a year in the country so he'd only be in Horseshoe Bay for a few days.

She could easily be friends with him for a few days every second year.

'Of course,' she said, smiling. 'Friends.'

The grin of pleasure that sent his dimples spinning almost made her regret it.

CHAPTER FOUR

THE FOLLOWING DAY, the pain in Lauren's arm was a manageable ache, but who knew bruised ribs bit this much? She'd do something as innocuous as putting a plate in the dishwasher and hot, sharp pain would sear her. It made her wonder at how painful broken ribs must be. From now on she would be far more sympathetic when her patients complained of the same condition.

Moving more slowly than usual, her shower and breakfast had taken longer. Although she had no plans to ever admit this to anyone—especially not to her mother—Lauren had needed to sit and rest for a few minutes after the shower. Lexie had texted, All good here. Will drop around some scripts this afternoon for you to sign.

Sue had telephoned to check in on her, saying, 'Rest. Lexie and I have everything under control. Peter Li in Surfside is happy to see any sickies and we can work around everyone else.'

Lauren had listened to her mother and murmured appropriately so as not to give Sue any clues that she had no intention of staying home. Today was the day Mackenzie Strickland was coming in for her test results and Lauren was determined to be the one to give them to her. The plan for the day was simple—wait until Sue left on her district nurse round and then drive to the clinic, which was why she was now trying not to flinch as she turned the wheel of her car and pulled into her designated parking spot.

Move slowly, she reminded herself as she cautiously got out of the car. She'd driven past the café on her way and had shivered when she'd seen the police tape. Her mind kept going to the question, what if Charlie had been a second slower in reacting? Last night, her sleep had been broken either by the ache of her ribs or by vivid dreams. All had woken her with a start but she wasn't sure which dream had scared her the most—the one where fear had gripped her as she was thrown to the ground or the one where she'd snuggled into Charlie's chest.

This was another reason she was better off at work. Sitting at home gave her too much time to think. She didn't want to think about how close to death she'd come and she didn't want to think about Charlie, full stop. 'Morning.' She stepped into the clinic, using the side entrance.

'What are you doing here?' Lexie's question was terse with surprise. 'You're supposed to be resting.'

'I've rested. I've come to sign the scripts and save you a trip.'

'You didn't have to do that.'

'I wanted to. Also, I know you cancelled everyone but can you please ring Mackenzie and ask her to come in? I don't want her to have to wait any longer than—' Voices drifted up the corridor from the direction of the consulting rooms. 'Who's here?'

Lexie, who rarely smiled, did exactly that. 'Charlie.'

'Charlie? Charlie Ainsworth?' she asked inanely, her brain stalling.

'Of course, Charlie Ainsworth.' Lexie threw her a look that suggested Lauren had lost her mind. 'Do you think I'd let Charlie Petroni or Charlie Rogers into the treatment room without a staff member?'

'But Charlie's not a staff member.'

'He is this week.' Again, Lexie looked at her as if she was a sandwich short of a picnic. 'If you can't remember that then he's right about those strong painkillers messing with your concentration. You shouldn't be seeing patients. Are you sure you should even be driving?'

'I'm fine,' she ground out, suddenly cross. Not that she was exactly sure who she was mad at or in which order. Had her parents overstepped the mark and asked Charlie to work at the clinic? *No.* they wouldn't do that, would they? Had he just taken it on himself to work here uninvited? Would he be that bold?

The voices increased in volume and then Charlie was ushering Mackenzie Strickland across the foyer and out of the clinic, his smile as broad as the patient's. White anger, pure and hot, poured through Lauren. *How dare you! That was my news to give Mackenzie.*

'Who's next, Lex?' Charlie turned towards Reception. 'Lauren?' Surprise widened his eyes and raised his brows, along with a flash of something that vanished as quickly as it had come.

He looked different but she couldn't put her finger on what it was. His ever-present weariness still clung to him, lingering in the lines on his face, but the blue on blue of his eyes positively sparkled. A hypnotic energy whizzed around him in an enticing buzz that drew her in and that's when it hit her. Charlie looked happy.

'May I please speak with you in my office?' she said tightly. Without waiting for him to reply, she stalked down the corridor. The moment he was inside the room and the door closed behind him, she said, 'What are doing here?'

'Talking to you?'

'Don't be a smartarse. Why are you here?'

He sat down in such a casual manner she wanted to

scream. 'I think it's fairly self-explanatory. You're crook and I'm a doctor.'

'You're a trauma surgeon, not a GP.'

'I'm still a doctor.'

'You're on holidays.' She caught the flash of unease in his eyes and it quenched her anger, leaving her feeling rattled. 'You are on holidays, right? A brief visit of a few days?'

'Actually...' His fingers tapped out a tune on his thighs '...it's a bit longer than that.'

Her mouth dried. Her heart rate picked up, pumping threads of anxiety through her. She didn't want or need Charlie in Horseshoe Bay for an extended length of time. She could handle a week. She quickly calculated that as he'd arrived three days ago that meant he only had four left. She could survive four, no problem. Easy-peasy. 'So a week, right?'

'I'm here until Easter.'

Six weeks! No. No. No! She sat down before she fell down.

Charlie watched Lauren's hand grip the edge of her desk before she skated her chair in close. Granted, he'd been accused by women in the past of missing emotional clues but there was nothing subtle about Lauren's anger. She seethed with it—its tentacles lashing and whipping him from the moment he'd spied her across the clinic foyer. That she was angry with him was clear. Why she was angry was another matter entirely.

Yesterday, after they'd cleared up a decade-old misunderstanding and he'd apologised, they'd shared a companionable afternoon watching Bogart and Hepburn on TV slugging it out in *The African Queen*. He couldn't remember the last time he'd sat and watched a movie from start to finish without either being interrupted or interrupting himself. But there was nothing friendly or companionable about Lauren now.

Was it pain-induced anger and distress? He'd been surprised to see her at the clinic, especially as the registrar at Surfside Hospital, her parents, Lexie and himself had all told her she needed to take three days off to give her ribs a chance to ease and start healing. She'd appeared to listen and agree and yet here she was, extremely irritable and unhappy. If they had been fencing and she'd been holding a sabre, he'd have been in danger of being run through.

With a brisk and practised move, Lauren clicked on her mouse and her computer screen flickered to life. 'Please go back to enjoying your holiday.'

Enjoying his holiday? That was an oxymoron. He was more than happy to work. He'd already calculated that if he did two sessions a day at the clinic Monday to Friday— hell, he'd work weekends too—he might just survive the next six weeks of imposed leave. Meanwhile, Lauren's complexion was tinged with the tight whiteness of pain and he wanted to ease that.

'Lauren, why are you pushing yourself? No one expects you to work for the rest of the week.'

'I have patients.'

'Who I'm more than happy to look after.' He'd only done two hours' work so far this morning but already he felt lighter and far more like himself. He loved surgery but he was getting a kick from interacting with patients in a different way. 'It's been a bit like old home week. Mr. Colvin remembered me.'

When he and Harry had been twelve and nine respectively, they'd been given the job of meeting the cray boat on the pier. The instructions from their parents had been simple—buy the biggest two. Harry had always winced at the scream when the cray hit the hot water, whereas Charlie had been fascinated by the chemistry of how applying heat to the shell changed it from a dark blue-brown to bright red. It was probably why he'd become a doctor, whereas Harry— His thoughts veered away from all the unfulfilled potential that had been stolen from his brother. The guilt sneaked in anyway.

'Mr C. brought you a crayfish as a get-well gift. I was going to drop it over to you later but why not take it home with you now?' Charlie gave her an encouraging smile. 'Lexie and I have got this. All you need to do is sleep, rest and recuperate.'

'I'm not asking you to give up your leave.'

'You're not. I'm offering,' he said expansively. 'After all, it's what friends do.'

'No.' She speared him with a mutinous look. 'Friends don't assume.'

Assume? Now she'd lost him. 'I'm not assuming anything. I deal in facts. Your X-rays prove you're injured.'

'Yes, but this is *my* practice. These are *my* patients.'

'Of course they're your patients, but I can help both them and you.' He cast around for an example to prove his point and to shore up his position. 'For instance, Mackenzie Strickland. Her situation wasn't urgent so Surfside wouldn't help her and, yes, technically she could have waited until Monday, but given what she's going through, I was able to ease her anxiety and save you from overdoing things.' He smiled at her, trying to connect and crack her granite expression. 'You know, I got as much of a buzz from telling Mackenzie she's pregnant as I did recently saving a kid's life.'

Two pink spots burned Lauren's otherwise pale cheeks. 'In general practice it's all about the relationship with the patient. For months I've had to give Mackenzie bad news and help her deal with her grief as she experienced yet another miscarriage.' Her voice cracked. 'Another lost dream.'

She sucked in a deep breath as if needing to steady herself. 'The results of her chorionic villi sampling was *my* news to tell, not yours. You don't have the right to swan in here and take over without even consulting me. I don't need your help and I'd like you to leave.'

A thrum of disquiet stirred, underpinned by disappointment laced with worry. He didn't want to leave. He didn't want to walk back through the doors of the clinic and face a long day of beachcombing, reading and going crazy. He wanted to work. Needed to work. 'Surely you can cut a guy some slack for well-intentioned assistance?'

'It's not the sort of assistance I need.'

But I need this. 'I'll be more consultative, I promise.'

'Between Surfside, Lexie, my mother, and me working reduced hours, we're covered.'

Agitation swooped in, pushing out the feel-good emotions of the morning. 'Why risk falling in a heap from working when you don't have to? Hell, I'm here. Why look a gift horse in the mouth?' *Damn and blast.* He'd meant to sound as if he was doing her a favour but all he could hear was the thread of pleading in his voice.

Her beautiful light brown eyes narrowed. 'Why does an Australian Aid trauma surgeon on precious holidays want to waste his time working in general practice in Horseshoe Bay?'

'Hell, Lauren,' he said belligerently, trying to deflect her. 'Do you always give people who are trying to help you the third degree?'

'Only the ones who clearly have something to hide.'

'I don't have anything to hide.'

'Good.' She pressed the intercom. 'Lexie, Charlie Ainsworth is just leaving so as soon as you see him exit the building, send in the next patient.'

'But, Lauren—'

Her finger came off the intercom and Lexie's voice cut off. Lauren skewered him with a look of icy determination. 'Enjoy your day.'

His temper frayed. 'You're being ridiculous.'

'Am I? Picture this. Without asking, I stroll into your operating theatre and do the complicated surgery you've spent days planning and dreaming about.'

'I'd welcome it.'

'Liar. You'd hate it.'

She was right, he'd be ropeable. He sighed. 'Okay, fair call.'

She gave him a long, assessing look and it took everything he had not to squirm in the chair. *Keep it all buried.* He matched her with a direct gaze of his own and threw in a sardonic raised brow. She blinked first. *Good.* Standing slowly, she walked around the desk. As he was still sitting, it was pure power play so he rose and was immediately taller than her.

'Charlie, what's really going on?'

'Nothing.' He shoved his hands deep in his pockets. 'Like I said, I was only trying to help you. I should have curbed my enthusiasm.'

She wriggled her nose. 'I'd understand your help more if we'd had an emergency. What I don't understand is the help with the mundane stuff that can wait, especially on a glorious blue-sky day with great waves. It's almost as if you don't want to be on holidays…'

He gave an 'as if' laugh to move her far, far away from the truth.

Her eyes widened. 'Oh, my, God, that's it, isn't it? It's killing you not to be working.'

Every part of him wanted to deny it but she had him cornered. 'You've got me,' he said with a shrug. 'I'm a workaholic. So, really, you're helping me by letting me work,' he quipped, and added a big grin for good measure.

She didn't laugh. In fact, the expression on her face was more aligned with pity than humour. 'Want to talk about it?'

'No.'

'Okay.'

Okay? What woman ever said that to a refusal to discuss feelings? And yet, twelve years ago, he and Lauren had never talked about their emotions so in a way this 'okay' made sense. 'What do you want me to do next?' he asked, thinking about the patients in the waiting room.

'According to the radio, there's flathead biting off the end of the pier. You might be able to fill your day that way.'

'Very funny.'

She hit him with an uncompromising stare. 'Or you can tell me why you're in Horseshoe Bay when you clearly don't want to be on holidays. Then I'll let you see some patients.'

'I thought doctors were supposed to be caring people,' he grumbled, trying to hide his anxiety.

'We are.' Her hand rested on his arm. 'But we can also be our own worst enemies.'

He gazed down at her, wanting to lose himself in her clear gaze and kiss her until his mind was blank, but she wasn't looking at him with anything other than concern for a friend. *Damn it.* He'd been the one to raise the friend issue. He'd planted that seed. What the hell had he been thinking? Every time he looked at her he wanted to pull her close, hold her tight and breathe in her fresh, sea scent. Who was he kidding? He wanted her naked—under him, over him, with him.

He gave himself a shake and decided the bare bones were all she needed—all he was prepared to give. 'I got caught in a cyclone.'

'Oh, God. That must have been terrifying.'

Not as terrifying as being home. 'Yeah.' He shrugged. 'I'm fine but Australia Aid won't put me in the field again until I've ticked all the trauma recovery boxes. The thing is, I'm better when I work.'

She tilted her head, her beautiful eyes assessing him, and he got the feeling she saw straight through him. 'How long since you last had a holiday?'

'I don't do relaxation.'

'I can see that. You look exhausted.'

Frustration bubbled in his veins. 'Listen, I didn't come to Horseshoe Bay to get the same lecture I'm getting from Australia Aid.'

'That says a lot.'

'Again…' he breathed in deeply and tried to keep a lid on his temper '… I already have a counsellor, so…'

Her brows rose. 'Prickly.'

He wasn't touching that but his temper frayed anyway. 'Can I work or not?'

The cogs of her intelligent mind were reflected in her all-seeing eyes. 'Until I'm back at work, you can do the morning session and finish at one.'

That's not enough. 'It makes more sense for me to do the whole day.'

'Not from where I'm standing. Do you have any idea how drawn you are? How unkempt you look?'

'What the hell does that have to do with anything?'

'It has everything to do with it. A lot of my patients are in better shape than you.' She sighed. 'Look, Charlie, I don't know why you're fighting your R&R but you need it. My offer's a four-hour workday for three days and then we'll review it. Take it or leave it.'

The girl he'd once been able to talk round with flattery and kisses was nowhere to be seen. 'When did you become such a hardball negotiator?'

She didn't laugh or smile and she didn't reply using words—she didn't have to, it was written all over her face. That's when he remembered what she'd told him just before the car had careened at them.

Divorced.

He had an unreasonable urge to punch her ex-husband.

'Watching paint dry is more exciting than this,' Charlie grumbled.

'You have to be patient,' Shaylee said, her elfin face set in a serious and determined expression. 'Ian says the fish know if you're in a bad mood.'

Lauren laughed, loving the way children cut straight through the nonsense. 'There you go, Charlie. Our lack of fish falls firmly at your feet.'

Instead of rolling his eyes, Charlie grinned at her over the top of Shaylee's head—all white teeth and sparkling eyes as blue as the sea that lay at their feet. A bolt of pleasure whizzed through her, zeroing in between her legs with a flash of heat, making her thighs tighten and the rest of her twitch. Being friends with Charlie was killing her.

It was Saturday afternoon and they were on the end of the pier, trying to catch dinner. Lauren's ribs were no longer hurting quite as much and after three days of enforced rest she had a bad case of cabin fever. She'd offered to take Shaylee fishing to free up her parents so they could attend and enjoy an eightieth birthday afternoon tea without worrying about a bored eight-year-old. Lauren wasn't exactly certain how Charlie had ended up joining them on the pier, especially as he appeared to hate fishing, although she suspected he just hated being still. Was that why he was fighting his R&R? Perhaps she should suggest he do an ecotourism high-adrenaline holiday.

I don't do relaxation, he'd said. He wasn't kidding. His line was jiggling up and down in his hand like he had a tremor or a tic. Each day, after his morning session at the clinic, Charlie had called in on her at the cottage and given her a quick handover while he made her lunch. She was positive she hadn't mentioned the fishing plans to him and yet he'd materialised in the car park just in time to help carry the gear. *Why?* For a moment she'd toyed with the idea that he'd taken on board her advice to find ways to chill out but, watching him, she knew the idea to be ludicrous.

'You won't get a bite if you keep jiggling the rod,' she said, deliberately glancing away from his seductive smile.

'I'm creating excitement and anticipation in the fish world by constantly moving the hook.'

She pursed her lips to keep from laughing. 'Interesting strategy. Want to bet on it?' *Seriously? What are you doing?*

His eyes lit up. 'Fifty bucks?'

'I was thinking more along the lines of the person who doesn't hook the first fish fillets the catch.'

'Let's take it one step further. The loser fillets and cooks.'

His dimples twinkled at her, making her feel giddy. 'You're on, Charlie. I'm so going to win this.'

'Lauren!' Shaylee squealed. Her line bobbed up and down wildly.

Charlie shot out his right hand to steady it and Lauren reeled in her own line before scrambling to her feet and kneeling behind Shaylee. 'Okay, honey, we have to do this slowly.'

'It's pulling me,' Shaylee cried with a hint of fear underneath her excitement.

'Crikey.' Charlie tightened his grip. 'You can't do this one-handed, Lauren. Reel in my line and I'll help her.'

She grabbed his rod. 'Slowly, Charlie. Slowly.'

'I reckon you've caught a brick, Shaylee. Put your hands over mine.' Charlie played the line, his hands looking large under the little girl's.

'Bricks don't bite hooks, silly.' But she was gazing up at Charlie as if he was some sort of hero.

Lauren knew that look—a long time ago she'd been guilty of it herself. Now she was wiser. She was never putting a man on a pedestal again. 'Don't break the line,' she instructed—her shame and regret about Jeremy making the words more brusque than necessary.

'Like that's my intention,' Charlie muttered, as he gave the line some slack.

A small crowd of anglers and onlookers gathered around them, many offering suggestions and pondering out loud what Shaylee might have caught.

'Could be a flathead,' a tourist offered.

Spiros Papadopoulos rolled his eyes at the ill-informed holidaymaker. 'Have to be a bloody big one to bow the rod like that. More like salmon or whiting.'

'What if it's a shark?' Shaylee asked, eyes wide.

'Then we'll get our picture in the paper.' Charlie's excitement matched the little girl's.

As Charlie followed Spiros's instructions, Lauren's gaze fell to the play of muscles on his back, easily seen due to the combination of his current lack of weight and the thin and worn T-shirt. Ever since he'd told her about the cyclone, she'd found herself worrying about him. Being caught up in a natural disaster was bad enough but adding in the car accident made him a prime candidate for PTSD. That was, if he didn't already have it.

I have a counsellor. But was he telling the counsellor the real story?

Lauren knew smart people were more than capable of using smoke and mirrors to lead counsellors away from the real issue or issues. She had a gut feeling Charlie was doing exactly that to her, let alone a counsellor. Each day at lunch he'd lean casually against the counter and draw her out. 'Any flashbacks? You sleeping okay? Come on, eat a bit more than that.'

Yesterday, after three days of sitting around doing nothing, she hadn't been hungry, and after eating half her sandwich she'd handed him the plate. 'You have the rest.'

He shook his head. 'Gran's got lunch waiting for me. I'll put some cling wrap over this so you can have it later.'

She wanted to believe he ate a late lunch each day with Anna, except the only problem with that was his grandmother was diabetic. If diabetics indulged in late lunches, they risked collapsing. When she added in the fact that Charlie was underweight for his height and breadth, she was certain he wasn't eating enough. It was the reason that eluded her and brought her full circle back to PTSD.

Or cancer. Or a million other possibilities.

The doctor in her itched to examine him and run a raft of tests. The woman in her wanted to—what? Feed him? Help him? Hug him? Despite trying hard not to want to do anything, she was leaning towards all three.

'Get a net,' Charlie yelled. 'Whatever it is, it's big.' He heaved and his back leaned into her—his warmth and enthusiasm giving her a rush.

She grabbed the net and scurried to his left, ready to scoop the flailing fish the moment it broke the surface.

'Yuk!' Shaylee shrank back into Charlie. 'What's that?'

Charlie laughed. 'It's a cracker of a squid, sweetie. It looks yuk but it will taste amazing.'

Lauren caught the prehistoric-looking cephalopod in the net to the cheers of the crowd and plunged it into the bucket to avoid being inked. Charlie stood up and held Shaylee's arm aloft, as if she was a champion boxer. 'Shaylee, the squid wrangler.'

One of the anglers sighed. 'I've got a state-of-the-art squid jig and you caught it on a hook.'

His friend slapped him on the shoulder. 'You gotta give her the luck, bro.'

'She deserves it,' Lauren said, thinking about Shaylee's mother. 'Hold it up, honey, and I'll take a photo.'

Charlie helped Shaylee hold what looked to be about a two-kilogram squid. As Lauren lined up the yellow square in preparation for the photo, she read unadulterated joy on both their faces. It struck her that it wasn't an emotion either of them wore very often. Tears pricked the backs of her eyes. *Don't be pathetic...again!* 'Smile.'

'Ian! Sue!' Shaylee called after the photo was taken. 'Look!'

Lauren turned and waved to her parents, who were strolling along the pier arm in arm.

'That's a beaut, Shay. Looks like you've been having fun.' Ian winked at Lauren before swinging the little girl around. 'We'll be eating well tonight.'

Lauren's heart rolled. Her father had so much love to give and she was fortunate to be his daughter, even if there'd been times growing up when she'd wished she didn't have to share him with quite so many other children. She loved her parents, but their well-developed sense of social justice sometimes left Lauren feeling unworthy. Although neither Ian nor Sue had ever said anything, she knew they were disappointed they weren't already grand-parents. Lauren was disappointed for them too. For herself. The sad memory of that long-ago miscarriage suddenly rushed her and one lone tear resisted her rapid blinking and spilled over. She was thankful she was wearing sunglasses.

There was a whirlwind of packing up, of Sue and Ian making a fuss of Shaylee and pumping Charlie's hand, thanking him for being there to help, and then her parents and Shaylee were in the car, driving away. Suddenly she was standing alone with Charlie under the Norfolk pines.

'Still think fishing's like watching paint dry?'

He grinned. 'I think it's more like being on call. There's a lot of boring hanging around waiting and thumb-twiddling and then, wham! An adrenaline rush.' He gazed down at her, the shadows cast by the sunlight pouring through the tree branches dancing on his face. 'Of course, the best part of today is that you're cooking.'

'Hah! In your dreams. Shaylee caught it.'

His head dropped closer. 'I reeled it in.'

Her stomach fluttered as his crisp, fresh scent circled her. 'I netted it to stop it from slipping away.'

'I see a problem.' He tucked some strands of her hair behind her ear before his fingers lazily caressed it then slipped along the length of her jaw.

Mini-explosions of delight fizzed in her veins before seizing control of her mind and making all cogent thought difficult. *It's not Charlie making you feel this way,* she quickly reminded herself. *Ben or any other nice guy would generate the same buzz, because it's been such a long time since you've been touched like this.*

Lost in the bliss of his touch, she dug deep to find her voice. 'You…you do?' she said huskily.

But he didn't reply, seeming also to have forgotten what they had been talking about. In an old but familiar way, the blue of his eyes deepened by the second, tugging her towards him as if she were hooked on a line and power-less to resist his pull. A tiny part of her cautioned, *Don't do this,* but it held no sway. Curiosity was a far stronger beast. Would he kiss the same way he had all those years ago? Had he learned anything new? She had. She'd learned a lot—not so much about kissing but about men and about herself.

So, really, if she kissed him, it was all about proving the hypothesis that she was now a world-weary woman with eyes wide open, instead of a naïve eighteen-year-old weaving impossible dreams. This kiss was merely an experiment to prove to herself he was just another man.

She wasn't aware if he lowered his mouth to hers or if she rose on her toes to close the slight gap, but the scratch of his stubble was prickling her cheek as his lips missed the mark. *Not a perfect kisser after all,* she reminded herself. *Yet another faulty memory you've attributed to him.* Then his hands gently cupped her cheeks, tilting her head, and he angled his mouth over hers—warm, soft lips—in a perfect fit.

A sigh rolled through her but she cautioned herself—she'd be a poor scientist if she allowed the first data to overwhelm her.

His touch was light yet firm, generously giving but with a gentle enquiry—*Are you sure you want this?* In the pursuit of her own scientific endeavours, she opened her mouth under his and he slowly and leisurely slipped in. It was in sharp contrast to the younger Charlie, who had kissed her long and hard until she'd run out of breath and seen stars. Regret for the enthusiasm of youth tugged at her.

Did he taste different? While she trawled her mem-ory, her tongue was flicking, savouring and dissecting his flavours. Peppermint, coffee and something delicious. What was it? She stroked his mouth again and he suddenly groaned. His arms wrapped around her hips and he pulled her in close until she was flattened against him. Every part of him pressed her from chest to toe, filling every nook and valley.

Heat exploded, blasting her and igniting her desire until it was a raging fireball that melted her into a puddle of delicious and addictive sensations. Charlie's restrained kiss vanished, replaced by an all-encompassing onslaught that made resistance not only futile but impossible. The squawks of indignant seagulls, the gentle lap of the sea against the sand, the low buzz of traffic and the occasional shouts of children receded. She no longer had the ability to examine, question and deduce.

All that mattered was Charlie's touch, his taste, and the wondrous feel of him. She rested her cast on his chest and gripped his shoulder for support while her other hand roved through his hair. As their mouths duelled hot, hard and with an intensity that demanded their all, her breath came fast and shallow. Silver spots shimmered and spun behind her closed eyes and she didn't know if she wanted to passively allow him to kiss her so she could savour it all or if she wanted to take control and dominate him.

His mouth slipped along her jaw, burning a trail of wonder and promise. Without any conscious thought her head fell back, exposing her neck. She craved his touch like a starving woman craved food and she took everything he offered. As he nuzzled her neck, his lips and tongue marking her skin with his touch, his hair brushed her face. The faint scent of cedar and masculine sweat tangled in her nostrils and she dragged in a deep breath, filling herself with it before kissing his hair. His lips reached the top of her tank top and the swell of her breast. He gave a gentle nip.

Her body jerked. Pleasure whipped her from head to toe, ramping up her need to fever pitch. She was no longer human—she was a mass of spinning and whirling elements driven by a yearning that dominated everything and left her panting. Every cell in her body hungered for him, demanding to be fed and filled. She heard a low, animal-like growl but she couldn't tell if it came from him or her.

Her blood pounded loud in her ears, deafening her, but slowly the insistent buzzing and the shrill and regular ring of a bell penetrated her haze. Gasping, she gripped his head and somehow managed to stutter, 'Ph-phone.'

Charlie drew back, his chest heaving, and he stared at her with unfocused navy eyes lit with a desire that matched her own. The pull was so strong she almost threw her arms around him again but the shriek of a child broke the spell. She took in their surroundings. They were standing just off to the side of a public car park. *Oh, God, who had seen them?*

'You going to answer that?' Charlie asked hoarsely.

Her trembling fingers pulled her phone out of the pocket of her shorts. 'H-hello.'

'Lauren, are you running?' Her mother's voice rattled down the line confused and concerned.

'N-no.'

'Then why are you out of breath?'

Because I've just been kissed senseless. But before she could coordinate her lust-soaked and scattered mind to muster a reply, her mother continued, 'Are your ribs okay? I hope you're not overdoing things.'

'No, Mum. Promise.'

'Good. The reason I'm ringing is that Shaylee says you and Charlie had a bet about the calamari. Something about the person who didn't hook the first catch cooks? Anyway, she got very upset when I started preparing the squid and she's insistent the two of you are coming over to cook it.'

Lauren's stomach fell as she recalled her and Charlie flirting over the top of Shaylee's glossy-haired head. 'The bet was just a joke, Mum,' she said quickly.

Charlie shot her an enquiring look and she shook her head. Just as she turned away she heard his phone ring.

'The thing is, darling,' her mother said firmly, 'Shaylee believes you were serious. You know how often she's been let down and how hard Dad and I have been working to get her to trust us. She's eight, Lauren. She doesn't understand jokes like that. To her it's the truth and I really don't want this to set her back.'

Lauren was spun back in time to her childhood. *You're the lucky one, Lauren. You know we love you. Now, share your toys.* Childhood guilt at being asked again to set aside her own needs tangoed with her adult self and she swallowed a sigh. 'I get it, Mum. I'll come over.'

'Thank you.'

She heard the rumble of her father's voice in the background. 'But you're going to have to teach me how to prepare and cook calamari.'

'You never know, Charlie might be an expert.'

Her mouth dried. 'Mum, I doubt Charlie will come.' *Especially as there's no way in hell I'm asking him to a family dinner.* 'He's in Horseshoe Bay to spend time with his grandmother and we can't steal him away from her.'

'Oh, Charlie's coming, darling, and so is Anna,' her mother said breezily. 'Your father's just spoken to him.'

What? She spun around to see Charlie sliding his phone into his pocket. He gave her a thumbs-up.

Fabulous. Just freakin' fabulous. She slumped against the Norfolk pine, immune to the rough bark sticking into her and the likely chance of resin staining her clothes. So much for a logical, rational and dispassionate kiss proving she was no longer attracted to him. Her experiment had run off the rails in spectacular style. She'd held nothing back and even if Charlie had been a stranger, not an ex, he wouldn't have to connect very many dots to know she'd been on fire for him. Wanted him. Had come close to committing public indecency with him. Even a guy without a surgeon's ego would be strutting like a rooster after such a display.

It took everything she had not to drop her head in her hands and moan. After Jeremy, she was determined never to reveal anything of herself to a man other than superficial and non-important thoughts and feelings. No man was ever going to have power over her again and yet, with one kiss, she'd handed Charlie power on a plate. To add insult to injury, now they had to cook together in the close confines of her parents' kitchen and under the eagle eye of her mother, who saw everything and missed nothing. If Lauren had any chance of surviving this evening with her dignity intact, there needed to be rules—very clear, concise and rigid rules.

Charlie had the sudden urge to whistle and, so help him, he couldn't remember the last time he'd chirped out a tune. His life might be in a tailspin but thankfully some things didn't change—Lauren Fuller could still kiss. His memory hadn't failed him: she was as responsive and as generous with her kisses as she'd been at eighteen. The hot and demanding play of her mouth under his, the flat press of her breasts against his chest and the brush of her thigh between his legs had brought dusty memories roaring back to life in vivid, living colour.

He grinned—it had been a hell of a walk down memory

lane accompanied by the delicious release of a torrent of feel-good memories. Now those memories tempted him with many more—Lauren, naked and with shining eyes, straddling him. Both of them naked, sweaty and moaning as he slid into her—

The hot blast of desire sent his blood south, making him hard in a way he hadn't known in a long while. There was no doubt about it. Lauren was still good for him and, going on that kiss, she still wanted him. He planned to put that knowledge to good use so they both benefited. Closing the small gap between them, he pressed his hands against the bark above her head and gazed down at her.

She slowly raised her head and fixed her luminous eyes on him. He'd been expecting to see the same bright lust that had shimmered so brightly in their depths just five minutes ago. But instead of naked need, they glinted sharp and clear, in focus and with businesslike intent. 'As you know, my parents are expecting us and—'

'Don't stress. I get it.' He tapped his nose. 'No kissing in the kitchen.'

Relief filled her face. 'Exactly. Or anywhere in my parents' house.' She ducked as he lowered his head to steal a kiss. 'And no more kissing in public places either.'

'Spoilsport,' he teased. 'Just for the record, I'm totally on board with kissing in private places.' He waited for her to laugh in agreement, but she swallowed and her tongue flicked out to moisten her lips. It took every gram of restraint that he had not to kiss her.

'Actually, Charlie, I don't think us kissing is a very good idea, full stop.'

If he'd anticipated her reply, it wasn't this. 'Why on earth not? I definitely got the impression you enjoyed it as much as I did.'

She raised her hand as if she was going to brush his

cheek but instead let it drop back to her side. 'Enjoyment has nothing to do with anything.'

'Enjoyment has *everything* to do with it.' For a second he thought he felt her prevaricate, topple even towards the desire that constantly spun around them, drawing them together. But when she spoke, he knew it had been wishful thinking.

'Yesterday we agreed that you're going to continue working one session a day at the clinic. That means, come Monday, we're working together.'

When she had informed him that she was coming back to work part time next week, he'd almost begged her to let him continue working at the clinic. So, they were both working at the surgery, big deal. No matter which way he came at it, he couldn't see a problem. 'But we're not technically working together. We're doing opposite sessions.'

'It still makes us colleagues. Look, I just don't need the locals gossiping and I really don't want my parents misinterpreting anything and…'

'And what?' He needed all the information so he could debunk it and lead her back to what he wanted—Lauren in his arms and in his bed.

She sighed and embarrassment burned two pink spots on her cheeks. 'I don't want them getting their hopes up when we'd only be having fun.'

'R-r-r-right,' he said slowly but thinking fast. First up, Lauren clearly wasn't entertaining a future with him—good.

Really?

Yes!

Second, he knew all about the hopes and dreams parents held for their children. He was also intimate with the vitriol that inevitably followed when hopes shattered and disillusionment and disappointment set in.

He liked Sue and Ian Fuller and he didn't want to set up any unrealistic expectations either, but kissing Lauren had kick-started a need for her that, if he was honest with himself, despite twelve intervening years, had never really left him. 'What if I gave up the sessions at the clinic and we keep us secret?' For a moment she was completely still and then she laughed—a huge, body-rocking belly laugh that shook her, sending her hair bouncing around her face.

Indignation shot through him. 'What's so funny?'

'Oh, come on,' she spluttered. 'Even you must hear how ridiculous that statement sounds. You're a workaholic, Charlie. You're barely coping with afternoons off as it is, let alone filling a whole day.'

It was true. Although he enjoyed Gran's company, he'd sought out Lauren's company every day after work to help pass the long hours. God, he'd even turned up at the pier today to fish when he'd overheard Ian chatting to Lexie about it. Still, right up until now, fishing had paid off in spades.

'And,' she continued, the laughter completely gone, 'I'm not a hobby to help you pass the time.'

'I never intimated that you were.' Her words—so off the mark—stung but he quickly recovered, pushing down his hurt—the intensity of it surprising him. Stepping back, he said purposefully, 'Don't worry. I'll be the perfect guest in your parents' home.'

'Charlie...'

But he didn't want to hear platitudes or excuses—especially ones that wouldn't change a damn thing. He clapped his hands as he did just before surgery when he was focusing his team. 'So, we're cooking calamari. I'll pick up Gran then meet you there. What's your parents' address?'

CHAPTER FIVE

IT WAS UNSEASONABLY humid due to a storm front hammering Horseshoe Bay and bringing a month's rain in a day. Like water pounding over the Triptych falls, it thundered on the roof of the clinic, making it hard to hear, let alone think. The moisture-laden air made Lauren's arm itch like crazy and she was sorely tempted to reach for the plaster saw and break her prickly skin out of its entrapment. Between the rain, the itching of her skin and the needling of her conscience, she was irritable.

'Dennis,' she said sharply in response to her recalcitrant patient's outlandish claims. 'The direct link between smoking and respiratory disorders, lung cancer, bladder cancer and heart disease are not conspiracy theories. There are reams of research backing up hard, cold facts.' She slapped a Quit brochure down in front of him. The king of excuses had chosen the wrong day to trot out this particular argument. 'Either you give up the ciggies or you've got an oxygen tank in your future like Brett Sedara.'

'Jeez, Doc, don't sugar-coat it,' Dennis grumbled. 'What's biting you?'

'This damn cast.' Only it wasn't just the cast. It was Charlie. Over the last four days when they'd crossed paths at the surgery, he'd been excruciatingly polite—Shore Road polite was what the locals called it. The manners of the well-heeled who could wield a social nicety like it was a weapon.

On Saturday night he'd charmed her parents and Shaylee, involving the little girl in the cooking of the calamari. He'd set her up at the bench and as she'd dredged calamari in flour, he'd explained that if she wanted to fish she also needed to learn how to cook her catch. Lauren suspected Shaylee would have been prepared to do almost anything—even deal with the guts of the calamari—if it meant having Charlie's undivided attention.

He and Anna had presented her parents with a bottle of sparkling Chardonnay Pinot Noir, which had not only matched the meal perfectly and tasted like ambrosia but had added a zero to the dollar amount she and her parents usually spent on wine. Sitting around the old oak table with its evidence of decades of family meals scored into the wood, they'd all eaten and drunk their fill while Charlie had entertained them, telling what she guessed were sanitised stories of his off-duty exploits in far-flung countries.

Despite his humour, she couldn't shift the feeling that it was all a façade—a decoy to hide his true feelings, whatever the heck they were. Despite the fact he looked slightly less exhausted than when he'd first arrived in Horseshoe Bay, she was certain that he was suffering. Exactly how or why continued to elude her. She wanted to help him but it was hard to help someone who blocked all serious lines of enquiry.

And then there was the aftermath of their ill-conceived kiss. Given she'd been the one to demand no public displays of affection, or, to be completely accurate, no displays of affection whatsoever, he'd been nothing short of polite with her since. What she hadn't anticipated was the complete absence of banter. She hated that she missed it. Hated discovering that his teasing and flirting had given her a buzz—a lightness of being—that she hadn't even been aware of until it had vanished.

She printed off Dennis's prescription for nicotine patches and after seeing him out, she scanned the unusually empty waiting room. The windows, which had been running with rain for hours, were now splattered with dribbles that slowly formed rivulets. 'Anyone else coming in, Lexie, or are we done for the day?'

'We're done. They either don't want to get wet or they're dealing with minor flooding at home.'

'Do we have any leaks?' Lauren had spent a chunk of her business loan on re-roofing the clinic.

'Looks like it's holding but tomorrow's the test. Sometimes it takes a while for the stains to appear. Seeing as we don't have anyone else booked, do you mind if I take an early mark and check on my house?'

'Good idea. I should check on the cottage too.'

'I'll put the emergency number sign on the door and switch on the answering-machine. I doubt anyone will need us.'

Lauren laughed. 'It always intrigues me how something that is supposedly urgent suddenly isn't if the weather is horrendously wet like this or gloriously sunny.'

Ten minutes later, Lauren was driving home with the air-conditioning blasting. The sun now shone hot and purposeful through a gap in the heavy clouds and steam rose from the road in grey wisps. It felt like tropical Queensland instead of coastal Victoria. The radio announced a flood warning for the Koonya Creek and the SES stressed the importance of not taking any risks by driving through flood waters. School was out and Lauren slowed at the forty-kilometre zone, laughing as she watched lines of children zigging and zagging so they could jump in every puddle.

It wasn't just the primary school students either—the high school teens were getting into the spirit as well.

Turning right at the oval, she was surprised to see Charlie's hire car in the car park with the bonnet up. She pulled in and got out. 'What's the problem?'

He appeared from behind the bonnet wearing a running singlet and athletic shorts. As much as she tried to keep her gaze fixed on his face, she was powerless to prevent it from raking his body top to toe. It had been a long time since she'd seen him in a virtual state of undress and she couldn't blame the humidity for the sweep of sweat that broke over her skin. The only thing that spoiled the view was the fact he no longer smiled at her in quite the same open and welcoming way.

'I got back from running Wild Dog Track and it wouldn't start. Pretty sure it's the battery.'

'I've got jumper leads.'

'Thanks, but I've rung the company. They're sending out another car.'

Their restrained politeness rippled between them, making her ache. She missed the easy camaraderie they'd shared after the accident right up until the kiss. Did he miss it too?

'The creek's flooded so they might have trouble getting through. If we can get it started, you can drive to the garage and I can run you home from there.'

He slapped at his exposed body—at the acres and acres of deliciously bronzed skin that strongly tempted her to touch and taste it. 'Okay,' he said. 'Let's give it a whirl. It sure beats hanging around here in the heat, being eaten alive by mozzies.'

Lauren positioned her car in front of Charlie's rental then attached the leads to her battery. She handed the opposite ends to Charlie. 'Red to red and black to black, as Dad always says.'

'I'm impressed you know how to do this.'

She shrugged. 'Girls need to know car basics.'

'These days blokes with luxury cars are hard pressed to find their batteries, let alone know how to use jumper leads.'

'Lucky this is a basic model, then. Let's start her up.' She turned towards her car and stopped. 'Did you hear something?'

'Just thunder. Looks like more rain's on the way.'

'Just what we don't need.'

'Help!' A strained voice drifted across the oval. 'Please. Help.'

They turned together and a teenager wearing a Horseshoe Bay Secondary College uniform was running towards them. 'I'll get the emergency kit,' Lauren said.

By the time she'd hefted the pack out of the boot, Charlie was a third of the way across the oval and she had to run to catch up. The girl was straining for breath, her chest heaving and her staccato words of 'Madeleine' and 'mud' didn't make a lot of sense. Bent double and panting, she pointed towards the basketball courts.

Charlie was already striding out but Lauren put her hand under the girl's elbow. 'You need to come with us,' she said firmly. 'You need to show us exactly.'

The girl nodded and half ran, half stumbled across the sodden oval, which yesterday had been sun-baked hard like bricks and today was a clay pan. Charlie had stopped and was glancing left and right, turning back to them, his arms outstretched in a question.

'Behind...the...toilets,' the girl panted.

Lauren relayed the instructions in a referee-style call

and picked up the pace. As she rounded the corner of the squat, red-brick building Charlie yelled, 'Stop!'

She teetered on the edge of what looked like a filled-in trench. Some teenage boys stood holding shovels and thirty metres away Charlie was squatting down next to a girl who was chest deep in the mud. Cautiously, Lauren made her way over to them. 'What happened?'

'Apparently, Madeleine was walking and she suddenly went down knee deep into the mud. They've tried digging her out but it's only pushed her in deeper. The rain's turned it into quicksand.'

Lauren took in the average age of the boys—probably fifteen—and said quietly to Charlie, 'Do you think you might have more success pulling her out?'

'Let's hope so. But I'll need something to brace against.'

'Boys,' Lauren called to the muddy crew. 'Go and rip five palings off the nearest fence.'

'Mr Grimes will kill us,' a sandy-haired boy replied.

'I'll take full responsibility. Just go.' She squatted down next to Madeleine. 'I'm Lauren and you've met Charlie. We're doctors. How are you doing?'

'Okay,' she said bravely, 'but the shovels kept hitting my legs. It feels like I'm being squeezed out of my skin.'

'How long have you been stuck?'

'About an hour.'

Lauren exchanged a worried glance with Charlie. Despite the humidity and warmth, Madeleine was wet and encased in mud. Hypothermia was a real risk.

'Can't you just pull me out?' Desperation threaded through the girl's voice. 'Please.'

The boys arrived back with the palings and Lauren passed two to Madeleine. 'Put your arms over them like a noodle in a swimming pool. They'll help support you.'

Using the extra palings, Charlie braced himself before

sliding his arms under Madeleine's armpits. 'Okay, ready? One, two, three.' He hauled—his body taut and his face puce with exertion. Madeleine rose a few precious centi-metres, but the mud held a vice-like grip on her and the moment Charlie took a fortifying breath, he lost the gains he'd made. The mud sucked her back down.

'Stop!' Lauren yelled, horrified the girl was now in deeper than before.

'I can't move my legs,' Madeleine said, her voice quiv-ering. 'It feels like they're stuck under a pipe.'

Lauren squeezed the girl's shoulder. 'Hang in there. We're going to activate plan B.' Whatever the hell plan B was. How on earth were they going to get her out?

Ideas aren't your strong suit, Lauren. Jeremy's scathing voice wormed its unwelcome way into her head. Raindrops the size of twenty-cent coins fell hard and fast, splashing into her eyes. She gazed heavenward.

Are you freaking kidding me?

'Get an umbrella for Madeleine,' she called out to no one in particular. One of the teenagers tore off and she be-came aware of Charlie's blue gaze fixed on her. He was the trauma surgeon who'd worked in field hospitals around the world. She waited for him to direct the play.

'What's your plan B?' he asked, his voice low and ur-gent.

The question stunned her—it certainly wasn't one Jer-emy would have asked. Consultation wasn't something her ex-husband ever bothered with, although she'd been slow to recognise that trait. He would have taken control whether he knew what he was doing or not and forged ahead, shouting instructions left, right and centre.

'Lauren. Tell me.'

As if you have a clue. The echo of Jeremy's derisive tone boomed in her head and she tried to bat it away. She spun around, frantically assessing the scene—nothing in the GP handbook had prepared her for this. Fighting panic, she summoned every problem-solving strategy she could muster and ran through the limited options. 'Pumps.' The word tumbled out of her mouth.

'Pumps?' Understanding broke over his face. 'Of course.'

Really? But she had no time to think about having got it right. 'I'll stay with Madeleine. You ring Dad and tell him we need generators and pumps. He'll notify the police, the CFA and the SES and bring the ambulance.'

Charlie pulled out his phone. 'I'm on it.'

Lauren returned to Madeleine. She could see how much effort the teenager was putting into keeping it all together. 'You're doing really well. Not everyone would be as calm as you are.'

Maddie shivered violently. 'One minute I was walking and then it was like someone just grabbed my foot and pulled. At first, Jessica and I thought it was really funny I was stuck in the mud. When I realised I was slipping in deeper and deeper, I stopped laughing.'

And deeper still. The mud had worryingly reached the girl's neck and Lauren saw grey shadows of exhaustion on her face. Trying to stay warm was not only sinking Madeleine deeper but it was consuming precious energy. Lauren rummaged through her bag and found glucose tablets. 'Eat these for me. They'll help keep your strength up.'

The boys arrived with golf umbrellas and Lauren's ears strained for the wail of sirens and the promise of pumps. *Come on! Come on! Come on!*

'It hurts so bad.' Madeleine's head rested on the wooden paling as if the energy required to hold it up was too much.

'Listen to that glorious sound, Maddie.' Charlie's enthusiastic tone matched his grin and he started singing an old nineteen-seventies pop song. *'Hang on, help is on its way.'*

The stressed and bedraggled teenager smiled back at him with adoration similar to what Shaylee had bestowed upon him. Not for the first time, Lauren wondered why a man who could effortlessly charm women from nine to ninety was still single at thirty-five.

Charlie dropped his head close to Lauren's and asked softly, 'How is she?'

'Exhausted and tachycardic.'

'It's the pressure of the mud. It's like being encased in concrete.'

'I'm petrified she's going to slip under.' Lauren rummaged through her emergency kit, not exactly certain what she was looking for but hoping something would jump out at her. The Guedal airway wasn't going to be any use if Madeleine sank under the mud. Her fingers touched the eye protection goggles and inspiration struck. 'Charlie, I need some plastic pipe. Look round. Have the workmen left any?'

Charlie didn't question her request, he just relayed it to the crowd. People went into action, surging over the area like worker ants.

Lauren was now on her belly, balanced on planks of wood and wondering how she'd somehow avoided treating patients from this position for most of her medical career and yet this was the second time in two weeks that she was lying down on the job. 'Hang in there, Madeleine. Charlie called your mum and she's on her way.'

The girl didn't raise her head from the plank. 'She… gonna…kill…me.'

'No. The moment you're out, she's going to hug you so tightly the mud will seem like a picnic.'

'I'm so-o-o-o tired. I just wanna sleep.'

'Madeleine! Stay awake!' Lauren commanded like a drill sergeant.

The girl startled. 'O-o-kay.'

'Here.' Charlie shoved a length of malleable orange plastic pipe into Lauren's hand just as the mud breached the tip of Madeleine's chin. 'The fireys are here. They're setting up the pump.'

'Tell them to work faster.'

Madeleine's eyes widened and grew frantic. 'I'm scared.'

'It's okay, I've got a plan.' Lauren sounded far more confident than she felt. 'Your job's to keep being brave and calm, okay? It's really important.'

''Kay,' Madeleine said softly—the utter seriousness of the situation now very real.

'These goggles will protect your eyes from the mud.' Lauren fitted them in place. 'And if we need it, you're going to breathe through this tube. It's just like snorkelling, okay? And I'm here. I'm not going anywhere.'

Charlie held coiled rope in his hand that a SES volunteer had given him. 'I'm going to sling this rope under you, Madeleine, to stop you slipping any further.'

The girl could barely nod.

The generator finally fired into life. Usually Lauren hated the monotonous chug-chug-chug sound because it destroyed the tranquillity of bush camping, but right now it not only sounded like music, it was a life-saving promise. Rex Dalton and Charlie inserted hoses into the mud next to Madeleine's legs to draw the water away.

A film of sludge edged up onto Madeleine's bottom lip. The pumps had arrived ten minutes too late.

'Here.' Lauren quickly inserted the tube into the girl's mouth. 'Just watch me and concentrate on breathing, okay?'

As the mud continued to rise, Madeleine's frightened gaze fixed on Lauren's mouth like it was a lifeline. 'Breathe in…' Lauren said, enunciating each word, 'and out. In…and out… In…and out.' *Please don't panic. Please don't inhale mud.*

She wanted to look at Charlie and the fireman, to send her anxiety telepathically, and get some reassurance from them that they were going to win this battle. Save this teenager from a mud coffin. But her job was to keep Madeleine focused on surviving. On breathing. On believing that this group of adults knew what they were doing.

Dear God, please let this work. The crowd fell silent and all Lauren could hear was her own voice against the background chug-chug-chug of the generator and the splash of brown, muddy water as it hit the already drenched ground.

'We're winning!'

The jubilation in Charlie's voice vibrated through her, instilling hope. 'At least I won't have to peg your nose,' Lauren said encouragingly to Madeleine.

The teenager blinked rapidly behind the googles and Lauren knew that if she could talk she'd be shrieking, *No way!*

'Hang in there, Maddie,' Charlie reassured. 'The mud's going down.'

When the sludge had receded from the girl's top lip and back under her chin, Lauren removed the pipe. Madeleine coughed. 'Here, drink this.' She held a water bottle to the girl's lips.

'This hurts worse than before,' Madeleine groaned. 'It feels like bricks on my body.'

'That's because the water's being pumped out,' Charlie explained patiently. 'In a minute, we're going to try and lift one of your legs free. We'll try not to hurt you but I can't promise that it won't. Sorry.'

'Just do it,' Madeleine said stoically.

'You know some women pay a lot of money to have a

mud bath,' Charlie teased, trying to distract Madeleine as he and Rex dug carefully around her legs.

'I'm never going near mud again.'

Charlie and Rex twisted and pulled at Madeleine's legs and Lauren kept up a patter of reassuring banter, trying not to flinch when Madeleine gripped her hands tightly. Her broken arm ached but it was nothing compared to what the girl was experiencing. Time slowed down and expanded. Lauren's rain-soaked clothes stuck to her skin and she felt a shiver race up her spine before settling in her teeth. *Hurry up.*

Charlie was bending over, up to his elbows in mud. 'Okay, Maddie, we're going to try and lift your legs now. If you can help, do it on three. One, two, three.'

Two mud-covered legs finally broke the surface and a cheer went up. Then Rex and Charlie hauled Madeleine onto planks of wood and moved her away from the quicksand trench. 'I'm as filthy as she is so I'll carry her to the ambulance.' Charlie hoisted the teenager in a fireman's lift and as he carried her, he looked like the Creature from the Black Lagoon.

After completing a full examination of her patient, Lauren was satisfied that, apart from dehydration and exhaustion, Madeleine was uninjured. Using half a packet of wipes, she cleaned an area on the girl's arm and inserted an IV. 'Once you've had a shower, something to eat and a sleep, you'll feel as good as new.'

'Thank you both for being there,' Madeleine said gratefully. 'Sorry your cast got all muddy.'

'Don't worry about it.' Charlie said. 'That's easily fixed.'

Lauren glanced at her mud caked arm in surprise. 'It's been itching like crazy so at least I'll get to scratch before the new one goes on.'

Ian ushered Madeleine's mother into the ambulance and Charlie and Lauren clambered out, back into the drizzle. The SES and CFA had packed up and the guys gave a wave as they drove away. 'Thank goodness that's over,' Lauren said, sucking in her first deep breath in over an hour. Instead of fresh, clear air, she got nostrils full of the foulest stench. 'Oh, my God, Charlie. You stink.'

'Speak for yourself. You don't exactly smell like a rose.'

'There's no way either of us are getting into my car like this,' she said as the chill of wet and muddy clothes set in. 'Come on.'

Trying to keep warm, she set off in a gentle jog, testing her ribs. They didn't bite and she picked up the pace. She quickly covered the six hundred metres down the road and around the corner to her cottage. Charlie easily kept up with her, only ducking past in the last fifty metres. As she entered the front garden, a blast of water hit her and she shrieked, shielding her arm. 'Cast!'

Charlie just laughed and sent more water from the garden hose towards her. 'It's water-resistant and it's being replaced. I'm just helping you get cleaned up so you don't track mud into the house.'

'Helping me? You're muddier than me.' She made a play for the nozzle but Charlie was taller and easily held it out of her reach. Normally, she would have gone for a low tackle, gripping him around his knees and bringing him down before seizing control, but she wasn't risking her healing arm. No, she had to be strategic. Distract him then disarm him. *How?* Every time she bantered with him, he shot back a smart reply that came with another blast of water from the hose.

As she ducked another spray, her legs moved slowly, constricted and tangled in wet material. Glancing down, she realised with horror that her summer dress was plastered against her like a second skin, leaving little to the imagination. The now sheer material stretched across her legs and belly, highlighting every bulge and imperfection. Her body had responded to the cold and her bra was doing nothing to hide her round, erect nipples. She was fully dressed yet virtually naked. *Fan-bloody-tastic.*

The spray of water eased and she looked up to find Charlie's hand slack on the nozzle. He was staring at her, his eyes dark with approval and desire. She seized her chance. Scooping up a length of hose, she ran in circles. Water hit her again but it soon petered out.

'Hey!' Charlie said indignantly.

She laughed, holding the clamped hose tightly in her hand until she had the length of it whipped around his knees. She pulled hard and he went down fast, the nozzle falling out of his hand. Grabbing the nozzle, she pressed the lever and sprayed him. Rivulets of mud poured off his body. Momentarily preoccupied by the sight of emerging tanned skin and soaked running gear that outlined him in all his glory, he caught her by surprise.

Suddenly, his hand was gripping her hose hand and he tugged hard. She lost her balance and collapsed onto him.

'Oof,' he groaned as she winded him.

'Ouch. You're too bony,' she said, struggling to move her hip bone off his, but his arms circled her, pinning her against him.

He rolled, taking her with him until she was tucked under him, just like the time he'd kept her safe from the car. Only this time, with his barely dressed body pressing against her, she didn't feel safe at all. This time the enemy wasn't a car but her own body. Rafts of heat and lust rippled along her skin, shimmering in her veins and clenching her muscles in joyful anticipation of sex.

Why not? He wants you and you want him.

You tried that once before and it ended in heartache.

This time I'm all grown up and wiser. This time, just like Charlie, I'm taking what I want.

Shivering with a combination of desire and cold, she looked up into his laughing eyes. 'Having fun? Finally relaxing?'

He grinned down at her. 'I think I am.'

'You play dirty.'

'Well, I am covered in mud. But you've got your own bag of dirty tricks. You totally stole my concentration.' He removed a twig from her hair and whispered in her ear, 'You look totally amazing in a wet dress.'

Silver lights exploded behind her eyes and she was about to kiss him when an arctic blast of cold air tore across her and she couldn't stop her teeth from chattering. She opened her eyes to see Charlie standing above her with an outstretched hand. All signs of playfulness had vanished.

'Come on. You're blue around the lips,' he said, sounding one hundred percent like a doctor and nothing at all like a lover. 'You take the first shower.'

Sadly, she was shivering too much to object.

Later, when Charlie walked into the kitchen wearing Jeremy's plush white bathrobe, Lauren's fingers loosened, almost dropping her mug of hot tea. Before she could say anything, he was fingering the satin piping on the lapel and asking, 'Is it okay to wear this?'

No! Take it off right now! Suppressing a shudder and forcing down her surprise, she somehow managed to say, 'Sure,' in a calm and even voice.

There was something inherently wrong about seeing her ex-lover wearing her ex-husband's clothes. Especially something as intimate as that bloody robe. A bathrobe she hadn't thought existed in her cottage, which had always been a distinctly Jeremy-free zone.

When she'd packed up their apartment in Perth in preparation for her move to Horseshoe Bay, she'd sold or given away all the things Jeremy had left behind when he'd left her. The robe, which should have been on the top of the 'go' pile, must have got tangled up with the towels without her realising. Her mother had unpacked the bathroom boxes and she either hadn't noticed the robe or had erroneously thought Lauren wanted to keep it.

'I thought wearing it would be a lot less dangerous for both of us.' Charlie shot her a wink. 'Just a towel could be risky.'

Her mind froze. Her mouth dried. The image of a bare-chested Charlie standing with a towel slung low on his hips—a towel slipping off those narrow hips—socked her hard. She cleared her throat. 'Your running gear's in the machine, along with your shoes. Although I can't guarantee any of it will ever be the same.'

'Thanks for trying.' As he accepted a mug of tea, he scrutinised her hoodie and tracksuit pants. 'Good. You've lost that tinge of blue. Feeling warmer?'

'Getting there. Tea and chocolate helps.' She carried plates and cake into the lounge room and Charlie followed with the teapot and milk.

She'd just got comfortable on the couch and filled her mouth with a big bite of the moist, rich cake when Charlie said, 'Thank God you were there today. From the pumps to the pipe, you were all over it. Well done.'

The compliment was so unexpected, the cake lodged in her throat. Praise wasn't something she trusted any more—it had an awful way of coming back to bite her. She gulped some tea, taking the time to carefully consider her answer. 'It was a team effort.'

'Sure. But every team needs a leader and today that was you.' He raised his mug to her, the gold monogram on the robe catching the light and glinting.

'Well done, Lauren.' Jeremy, his hair still wet from the shower, raised his coffee cup in a mocking gesture. *'You've stuffed up again. Surely by now you've realised some people lead and some follow. We both know which category you fall into.'*

Her breath sped up. She could see and hear Jeremy as clearly as if he were standing in front of her. She had to be careful. She had to tread carefully.

'It wasn't skill, Lauren. You just got lucky.'

'I was flying by the seat of my pants,' she said, deliberately sounding grateful. 'Like you always say, it was more luck than good management.'

'I don't always say that.' Jeremy sounded uncharacteristically confused. 'I will concede there's often an element of luck involved…'

Startled, Lauren blinked and Jeremy's visage faded. She realised it was Charlie who was sitting at the end of the couch, Charlie who was talking to her.

'Most of today's success,' Charlie continued, 'came down to your clear thinking and good medicine.'

She licked her lips as agitation lingered. Habit made her say, 'I'm sure it pales into insignificance compared with the all things you've done in far-flung places.'

'For heaven's sake, Lauren. I'm trying to give you a compliment.'

He sat forward so fast she automatically shrank back into the couch, pulling the sleeves of her hoodie over her hands. 'Right. Sorry. Thank you.'

Charlie leaned back and set down his mug, but the whole time his gaze never left her, flicking across her face with serious scrutiny. She wished she could vanish in a puff of smoke. 'What's going on, Lauren?'

No way was she doing this. 'Nothing,' she said airily.

'I don't believe you.'

'That's okay.' She reached for more cake. She needed cake to get Jeremy out of her head. She needed the washing machine to finish so Charlie got out of the damn robe. Then she was binning it and all the memories that went with it, and reclaiming the cottage as her safe haven.

'It's not okay, Lauren. If I'd run an emergency like you did today, I'd be basking in the accolades.'

'Some of us are just a bit more humble,' she quipped, desperate for him to drop the topic.

But he didn't laugh. Instead, his face fell and sadness pulled at the corners of his mouth. She had a ridiculous urge to reach out and comfort him.

'Back in the day, during that summer, you were always so full of confidence.' Bewilderment laced his words.

'I wasn't. Your memory's faulty.' She jumped to her feet. 'I need wine. Would you like a glass?' She was halfway across the room before he replied and when he did, it wasn't about wine.

'Who's Jeremy?'

The question stopped her short. How on earth did Charlie know her ex-husband's name? 'No idea.' She had no intention of ever re-entering that dark tunnel.

'Whoever he is, I think you know him pretty well.'

Her heart beat so fast it threatened to lift out of her chest. 'You're wrong.'

'If I'm wrong, why have you gone as pale as a sheet and why is his name on this robe?'

CHAPTER SIX

CHARLIE WATCHED IN stunned surprise as Lauren stomped down the hall before reappearing and holding a pair of bright orange SES coveralls. She promptly threw them at him and he thrust out an arm to catch them but not before a bright orange trouser leg slapped him in the face.

'Get out of that robe.'

'But I'm comf—'

'Get. Out. Of. That. Robe,' she ground out, before disappearing into the kitchen.

As he shoved his legs into the pants and carefully zipped them up over his bare skin, he heard the fridge door squeak, the clunk of glass on the bench and the crack of a seal.

'Are you decent?' she called out.

'Yep.'

'Good.' She reappeared and set down two glasses of wine on the coffee table then scooped up the robe. Jerking open one of the French doors, she hurled the bathrobe into the garden. Lauren closed the door, picked up her glass of wine and took a large gulp.

He hated seeing her like this. He'd unwittingly played a role in the pinched expression that now pulled her lovely features into a grimace. The part of him that hoped to build on their shared fun in the garden and cosy up with Lauren on the couch berated him for asking the damn question about the owner of the robe. But the rest of him wanted to find out what had happened to dent the confidence of this previously self-possessed young woman. She should have been high-fiving him but instead he got the distinct impression she'd been carefully choosing her words and underplaying her achievement. He had a gut feeling that this Jeremy was somehow involved.

'Feeling better?' he asked carefully.

'Not really.' She took another drink and sat down hard. 'But before you think I've completely lost my marbles, Jeremy is my very ex-husband. I thought I'd got rid of everything of his so seeing the robe again was...'

'A surprise?'

'More like a nightmare.'

'I'm sorry.'

'Don't be sorry,' she said tightly, her eyes suddenly flashing. 'I don't want sympathy for my own stupidity.'

He raised his hands in surrender but added, 'You're not stupid.'

She pressed the heels of her hands into her eyes for a moment and when she lowered them she gave him a sideways glance. The fire had gone out of her eyes, leaving behind a gaze as doleful as a chocolate Labrador's. It took all his self-control not to close the space between them and hug her tight. But if he hugged her, he'd want to kiss her. If he kissed her he wouldn't want to stop until they were both naked and sated. And then, high on endorphins, neither of them would want to talk about anything other than nonsense and her story would be lost to him.

Despite the lust that burned hot in his veins, he wanted to know exactly what she'd endured at the hands of a man he'd never met but already hated.

'You want to know about Jeremy? Okay. Here goes.'

A long sigh rolled out of her and she took another sip of her wine. 'I met him when we were both registrars. Work was frantic and I barely had enough time to eat and sleep, let alone find time for a boyfriend, but Jeremy was both charming and persistent.'

'He wore you down?'

'Looking back, it was more like being bulldozed. I'd grown up in a household where I learned to put other people first at all times. Don't get me wrong, I knew I was loved but no one had ever made me the centre of their world like Jeremy did. Sadly, I was like putty in his hands.'

'We're all guilty of loving being the centre of attention.'

'Right up until the attention swings from positive to negative.'

She said the words so matter-of-factly it took a moment for them to sink in. Charlie realised his fists were clenched. 'Is he a short man?' he asked, knowing the type of bloke who often put others down to build themselves up.

She laughed but it held no humour; only the vestiges of anger and regret. 'Metaphorically speaking, I suppose he is, but we were already married before I realised that. Jeremy was desperate to get an ENT fellowship. He'd come to the VRH from Queensland, saying the board at Central couldn't organise themselves out of a brown paper bag. He mentioned he'd been overlooked for a position there because he didn't have the old boys' pedigree. I had no reason not to believe him or even think he had a chip on his shoulder, especially after the scandal broke about all the backroom deals.

'I both admired and envied Jeremy's clear and uncomplicated career goal. I was floundering with my decision and feeling torn in different directions. I lurched between paediatrics and respiratory when, out of the blue, the intensive care consultant asked me to apply for the fellowship.

She was a brilliant doctor and fabulous to work with so I seized the opportunity and threw my hat into the ring. I was up against some stellar people, but to my shock and delight I was offered the job. I was almost paralytic with excitement and by then Jeremy and I were a couple, so he was the first person I rang. If his congratulations seemed muted compared with my parents', I put it down to me catching him during a busy theatre schedule. He made up for it that night with dinner at our favourite restaurant.'

Charlie swallowed a preconceived *humph.*

'Two months later, while I was flying high, working with a fantastic team and learning heaps, the VRH told Jeremy he'd been passed over for the ENT fellowship. He was gutted. It was an awful couple of weeks and then, thankfully, he got a job at The Girton as an unaccredited registrar with a view to being accepted into the training programme within the year. He insisted I move hospitals too. When I refused, saying there was no need because we were both in Melbourne, we had our first big argument. There was a very tense standoff for two days but when he finally came around, instead of make-up sex, he proposed.'

The guy's an idiot. Charlie drank more wine.

'Don't ever play poker, Charlie.' Lauren gave him a wry smile. 'To this day, I hate that I missed the huge neon warning sign. In typical Jeremy style, he applied for a notice of intention to marry and thirty-one days later in a romantic whirlwind of Jeremy's making, we got married at the Treasury building.'

Charlie felt his blood pressure rising. 'You didn't hold out for a big wedding?'

She shrugged. 'We didn't have the money and my parents deserve a retirement. As it turned out, I'm glad we didn't have a big wedding. I would have hated Mum and Dad to have forked out a lot of money when two years later it was over. Romance and grand gestures are not what they're cracked up to be.'

'I'm with you there.'

She shot him a grateful look. 'Anyway, after a year at The Girton, they offered the fellowship to someone else. Jeremy was incandescent with rage. It was everyone's fault from the condescending consultant to the bitchy nurses, the tight hospital administrator, the boys' club of surgeons and me.'

'You? Why you?'

'To quote Jeremy, I'd been given my fellowship on a plate. I hadn't even known which area of medicine to pursue, whereas he had known for years what he wanted. I didn't deserve it—he did.'

Suddenly, her earlier behaviour of pushing all his compliments back onto him fell into place. 'Oh, God, you started to believe him.'

She dropped his gaze. 'Not consciously, but he did have a point. I only had to look at the foster children who passed through our house when I was growing up to know how lucky and privileged my life is.'

'But your luck comes off the back of your hard work, Lauren,' he growled, wanting to hammer the point home. 'It wasn't your fault this guy couldn't nail a fellowship.'

'Logically, all that's true, but emotion clouds everything. I married and I've been taught marriage is a team event. My husband was miserable and I wanted to help. I became his cheerleading squad. I gave him the stats for fellowships, told him hardly anyone gets what they want straight off the bat and I encouraged him to widen his search. I talked to everyone I knew. A job came up in Perth.'

Out of the snippets of information, a picture of control was slowly emerging and Charlie didn't like where it was heading. He didn't want to believe it—didn't want to believe that Lauren would make so many compromises. 'You gave up your fellowship?'

'Not intentionally.' Her old fire was back and he wanted to cheer. 'Jeremy told me there was also a position there for me too. Although I was disappointed to leave the VRH, I rationalised that no one completes their fellowship in one place. Moving would broaden my experience. When we arrived in Perth, the hospital told me they were sorry but the position wasn't available for at least eight months.'

'And your husband knew this when he asked you to quit and move?'

'If you'd asked me then I would have said no. Now I'd give you an unequivocal yes. I was clueless about his jealousy or his plan to completely dismantle my professional life. The thing about the West is, unless you have job, it's very isolating. I made enquiries at all the other hospitals but there was nothing for me except enthusiastic promises. I got some general clinic work and kept up my studies but I was frustrated and miserable. I missed my parents and my friends. Jeremy, on the other hand, was thriving. If I complained, as he'd often done in Melbourne, he was unsympathetic. His standard reply was, "Now you know how I've felt for the last two years."

'Two months after we arrived, he suggested I use the waiting time to have a baby. I jumped at the chance. I never anticipated I'd have any problems getting pregnant because...' She jerkily raised her wine glass and drained the contents, her eyes suddenly wide and frantic. 'Anyway, a year later I still didn't have an intensive care job and I wasn't pregnant either. The tests were inconclusive. There was no apparent reason on either side for our failure to conceive. Jeremy blamed me. Told me if I worried less I'd get pregnant.'

'Useful,' Charlie grunted, unable to stop himself.

Lauren didn't comment. It was as if she needed to block out everything just to get the story told. 'Whenever I voiced my concerns about anything, Jeremy swooped, reinforcing my worst fears. He was working long hours, which became a blessing because almost every conversation we had degenerated into an argument. He'd sit on the end of our bed in that damn robe, twist my words about marriage and commitment, give and take, and dismantle my sense of self. What I hate the most is that I somehow let him.'

'You didn't let him.' Charlie didn't want to think about the guy in that robe or him in bed with Lauren. He wanted to string him up. 'That weasely bastard cut you off from your work, family and friends just so he could feel good about himself. He separated you from everyone and everything that defines you as a person and without anyone to counter his arguments, he went in for the kill. It's an age-old form of torture that's still happening across the world. Thank God you left him.'

An hysterical laugh burst out of her and he flinched. 'I wish,' she said bitterly. 'Don't get me wrong, Charlie,' she said suddenly, patting his knee briefly as if he was the one needing reassurance. 'I'd made the decision to leave but the thing about men like Jeremy is, it's all about control. My exit needed to be carefully planned.'

White-hot rage funnelled through him like a tornado. 'He hit you?'

'No. He wielded words, not fists. But the thing about words is they inflict just as much damage, only the bruises don't show.' She shuddered. 'Status and social standing are important to Jeremy. He was finally working with a consultant who liked him and he wouldn't allow anything to interfere with his plans. Ironically, I'd never warmed to

Jeremy's boss and whenever I met his timid and anxious wife, I wanted to rescue her. Now I know why I didn't like the boss. He was far too much like Jeremy, and his wife was a woman I was fast becoming.'

She grimaced. 'I should write and thank her, because she unwittingly jolted me out of my fog of self-doubt and saved me. Whether my ex-husband sensed a change in me or he feared losing face with his boss if I left him, he took the unprecedented move that goes against all the studies on domestic violence. He left me in a blaze of unsubstantiated malicious gossip that vaporised all my job offers. He wasn't single long and he married again. I tried not to care but I didn't want any other woman going through what I'd endured so I tried to warn his new fiancée. She accused me of being bitter, twisted and jealous, which was, of course, the tale Jeremy spun.'

'You strike me more as battered than bitter,' he said, giving her hand a squeeze. 'So you moved east. Why didn't you pursue ICU?'

'I needed to come home and regroup. I started working here and after a few months, when old Dr Saunders offered me first dibs on the practice, it seemed like a logical step.' She twisted her fingers. 'Charlie—' she said his name with emphasis as if he needed to pay close attention '—my parents think the divorce was a hundred percent due to Jeremy putting his career ahead of me. I'm *never* telling them about the emotional abuse. It would devastate them. They wouldn't understand why I didn't reach out and tell them what was happening. But I couldn't tell them. I couldn't admit that failure when they are so good at marriage. I've never told anyone about it until now.'

He felt her shame wash over him and he ached with it. She didn't deserve to feel any disgrace or embarrassment and he wished he could do something to alleviate her self-loathing. He thought about Harry. 'Sometimes we find ourselves in unexpectedly difficult situations that batter our self-worth.'

She gave him a sideways glance. 'Another lesson you've learned working for Australia Aid?'

'Yep.' *No.* He'd learned that lesson much closer to home and well before he'd met Lauren twelve years ago. But he knew from experience there was nothing to be gained by revisiting the accident and its life-altering fallout. 'Be proud of what you've achieved before and since. Draw on it for strength.'

She scrunched up her face, the action one of pure scepticism. He understood. After what that bastard had done to her, words weren't yet her friends, but he hoped one day they could be again—that one day she'd believe them. Meanwhile, Lauren needed action and he had an idea about how he could help. 'Have you got any accelerant?'

Confusion drew her chestnut brows together. 'Excuse me?'

'You know, metho, kero, fire-starters?'

'Should I be worried that you have pyromaniac tendencies?'

'Nah.' He pulled her to her feet, wanting more than anything to hold her against him and breathe in the lemony scent of her hair. 'But we do need to set fire to that robe. As I was the one to inadvertently bring it and its demons back into your life, I want to be there with you when we watch it disappear.'

She stared at him for a long moment, blinking quickly, and then she cleared her throat. 'I'll get the matches.'

'Thanks for this.' The next morning, Lauren and her new mud-free cast sat in the passenger seat of her car while Charlie drove from Surfside to Horseshoe Bay. He'd insisted on driving her to the orthopaedic surgeon and in the spirit of their new friendship she'd accepted the offer.

'No problem.' Charlie grinned at her.

Her stomach flipped. The distance that had sat hard and jagged between them in the days after their kiss had completely vanished. Who knew all it took was the traumatic baring of her soul? A jet of embarrassment made her look away. Yesterday, in the seconds after she'd completely lost it and shrewishly demanded that Charlie take off the robe, the full ramifications of her meltdown had hit her. In those moments, all she had wanted had been for the earth to open and swallow her—hide her from reality.

Initially, she'd hoped she could pretend nothing out of the ordinary had happened and she'd almost done it—had made a smart comment and ploughed on as if everything had been normal. But one look at Charlie's drawn yet handsome face and the sharp, bright light in his eyes had told her in no uncertain terms that she'd lost every opportunity to keep the mortifying story a secret. She'd fully expected telling him how she'd become mired and lost in her marriage would cripple her with shame. She'd girded herself to read disbelief on his face and hear judgement in his voice, but instead he'd offered her unconditional support.

When he'd insisted she burn the robe, it had been a miracle she hadn't burst into grateful tears on the spot. Charlie had doused the tainted garment with accelerant and then, insisting on a safe distance, had given her the match. As they'd watched the robe burn—thick, black smoke curling up into the heavy, humid air and carrying away putrid memories—he'd held her hand. Afterwards, he'd poured her more wine, raided her fridge and somehow managed to cobble together a fried rice concoction from a limited selection of ingredients.

After he'd left—she'd lent him her car keys so he could

drive home—she'd prepared herself for a rush of difficult memories and the usual play of symptoms—tight chest, shallow breaths and burning pain under her scapula. They always accompanied any thoughts of Jeremy, but they hadn't come. Instead, she'd fallen into a dreamless sleep and woken up this morning refreshed and feeling different. Exactly how was hard to name but she had the oddest sensation of freedom.

'Fancy a coffee?' Charlie asked.

'The last time you suggested coffee, I nearly got hit by a car.'

'Tea, then, if you think it's safer.'

'I'll live dangerously.'

'Coffee it is.'

She'd been too preoccupied with her thoughts to notice exactly where they were but as he brought the car to a halt, the sound of the surf knocked her back into the present with a thud. *Ben's café.* Before she could suggest going elsewhere, Charlie was pulling the key out of the ignition and hopping out of the car.

As they crossed the car park, Charlie said, 'You were right. Ben does make the best coffee in town. But even if he didn't, the view's worth putting up with mediocre Java.' He opened the door for her and ushered her inside before giving the barista a friendly grin and a wave. 'Morning, Ben. My usual and a…' He turned to Lauren, his brows raised in question.

'Too easy,' Ben said, before she replied. 'Lauren will have a skinny latte.' He smiled at her, his dark-lashed sea-green eyes appraising her appreciatively. 'It's good to see you again.'

Shoot me now. The last time she'd seen Ben had been before the accident when she'd virtually propositioned him. Embarrassment flamed her cheeks and everything inside her squirmed. She opened her mouth to utter a vague 'You too,' but Ben was still talking. 'I've missed our early morning chats and phone calls.'

Phone calls? She'd never followed through on telephoning him but he probably thought that was due to the accident rather than buyer's remorse. 'Bruised ribs and strenuous exercise aren't a good match,' she said weakly, tapping her cast.

'Hopefully you'll be match fit soon for *all* activities.' Ben reached for a latte glass.

'The coffees are to go,' Charlie said bluntly, and unexpectedly. He pulled his wallet out of his pocket and slapped a blue bill on the counter.

Ben raised his brows, but his gaze was fixed on Lauren. 'It's a beautiful day with a gorgeous view. Be a shame not to stay and enjoy it.'

Oh, God. Was Ben suggesting he was the view or she was the view? Had he always been such a blatant flirt? Memories of their previous conversations made it impossible not to own that they'd both flirted a lot. Charlie's previously open expression was now closed as tight as a drum. Staying here to have coffee would be excruciatingly uncomfortable, although she wasn't confident that leaving would be any more pleasant.

'Sorry, Ben. We have to keep moving,' she said, lying through her teeth. 'Work calls.'

It didn't. There was never a Friday morning clinic, because that was her nursing-home round. As Charlie could take this afternoon's clinic, she'd switched around her day to fit in with the orthopaedic surgeon. They still had a couple of hours before either of them was required anywhere.

'That's too bad.' Ben clipped a lid on her latte before giving Charlie his change.

'You've undercharged me, mate.' Charlie's use of the moniker wasn't friendly.

'I don't think so, *mate*. Lauren's is on the house.'

As Lauren grabbed her coffee, she swore she heard a growling sound but she didn't hang around to see who'd made it. Instead she gave a breezy 'Thanks, Ben,' and headed for the door.

Half a minute later she felt a hand under her elbow and heard Charlie's rumbling voice low in her ear. 'So, you and the barista have got a thing happening? An arrangement?'

She tried to laugh off his question. 'No-o-o.'

'That's not what he thinks.' He glowered at her.

She schooled her face into what she hoped was a neutral expression, opened the car door and hopped in. 'You're imagining things.'

'I'm not.' He threw the car into reverse, deftly manoeuvred it out of the parking lot and back onto the road. 'I recognise a player when I see one.'

'Takes one to know one?'

His hand hit the indicator and he turned left into Lauren's street. 'I haven't played in a long time.'

Her coffee stalled halfway to her mouth. 'Why not?'

'Work.'

She wasn't buying it. 'What's the real reason?'

The gravel of her driveway crunched under the tyres as he brought the car to a halt. 'That is the real reason.'

They got out of the car and crossed her spongy kikuyu lawn. 'Is that why your engagement didn't work out?'

He shrugged. 'Alysha liked telling people I worked for Australia Aid. She didn't like the reality that I was out of the country more weeks of the year than I was in it.'

With her back to him, Lauren slid her key in the door. 'Why not spend more time in Australia then?'

He followed her inside and tossed her car keys into the

dish she kept by the door. 'Why are we talking about me when the point of the conversation is that the barista was undressing you with his eyes.'

'Why are we talking about me when the point of the conversation is the fact you're using work as an excuse not to have any fun? No wonder you look permanently strung out.'

He was now standing very close to her, his blue eyes shot with navy and his breath stroking her face. 'Are you planning on having sex with that surfer?'

She noted his taut expression and claimed her position. 'I was planning on it, yes. After Jeremy, I don't want a relationship, but I miss sex and Ben's uncomplicated.'

Her gaze narrowed. 'You said *was*. What about now?'

She licked her lips. 'I still miss sex.'

His eyes twinkled. 'Perhaps I could help.'

The tantalising idea hung there between them. She rationalised that she knew him so in that way he was a safer bet than sex with a stranger and this time she didn't want anything more from him than sex. This time she was going in with her eyes wide open, but she needed rules. Boundaries. A known framework that not only kept her feelings in check but protected her from any hidden sinkholes that might unintentionally suck her down to that dark and terrifying place she'd fought so hard to clamber out of last time. 'What about your whole all work, no play thing?'

He grinned down at her, two dimples swirling. 'I'm technically on holidays.'

'Yes, but can you be uncomplicated?'

A flicker of a shadow crossed his face so quickly she thought she might have imagined it. 'Uncomplicated's my middle name.'

Was it, though?

Don't overthink this. Keep it simple. Take it as the gift it is. 'Then, sir, we have a deal.'

She threw her arms around his neck as his hands gripped her hips and he lifted her off her feet, spinning her around. She threw her head back and laughed, savouring the rafts of delight rolling through her.

After setting her back on her feet, he tangled his hands in her hair and kissed her. This time he didn't start slowly or tentatively—this time the kiss was hot, strong and long, filled with the promise of what was to come. It stripped her legs of strength and poured lava-hot need through the rest of her, making her body leap and jump and throb in a way it hadn't done in a very long time. Her blood pounded, her head spun and lights lit up behind her eyes so it took her a moment to realise Charlie was asking her a question.

'Sorry,' she said breathlessly. 'What?'

'Where's your bedroom?'

She grabbed his hand and towed him up to the front of the house. The sight of her unmade bed and the dropped towel from this morning's shower made her stop abruptly in the doorway.

Charlie ran into the back of her. 'Something wrong?'

'Um…it's a bit messy.'

He lifted her hair and pressed a kiss to her neck. 'By the time we're both naked, it will be messier still.'

A shiver of desire shot through her. Spinning around and pressing herself against him, she savoured the long, lean feel of him as she kissed him deeply. Then, without breaking contact, she tugged him towards the bed and fell backwards, taking him down with her.

His hands reached for the buttons on her blouse and she suddenly panicked. 'Charlie, the last time you saw me naked I was eighteen.'

He grinned. 'Yeah. I remember.'

She bit her lip and forced herself to spit out the words. 'I'm not eighteen any more. My body's—'

'Still beautiful.' His voice caressed her with its deep rumble and he tugged the sleeveless silk shirt over her head. 'Well, that's one thing that's changed.'

'What?' *Stretch marks? Five kilos? Less pert breasts?*

He stared appreciatively at her pale pink and black lace bra. 'You can afford more expensive and gorgeous underwear.'

Relief rode in and she laughed. Why had she worried? Nothing had changed. He was looking at her with the same wonder in his eyes that had been there twelve years ago. She brushed her hand across the obvious bulge in his shorts before reaching for the snap but he wrapped his hand gently around her wrist, stopping her.

'Before we get to a point of no return, I don't have any condoms. Do you?'

Her heart sank. 'I don't know. Possibly…or not.'

He groaned. 'Can you look? We were lucky twelve years ago but I don't take those sorts of risks any more.'

Lucky? She blocked further thought. The past and the future didn't belong here—just the here and now. She shot off the bed, ran to the bathroom and rummaged through the back of the cabinet and then in the cupboard under the sink. *Nothing.* What did she expect? Why would there be condoms? She hadn't needed contraception in a very long time.

'We're a poor excuse for singles everywhere,' Charlie called out dolefully. 'Do I need to make an emergency dash to the chemist?'

'Hang on. I've got an idea.' She raced into her study and found a box filled with butcher's paper, coloured markers, handouts, lollies and at the very bottom a blue strip of condoms. She came back waving them like a banner. 'I did an STI talk at the school yonks ago and we practised using condoms.'

Charlie, who was propped up on his elbows, fell back on the bed. 'Thank you, Horseshoe Bay Secondary.'

Lauren crawled up the bed on all fours and straddled him. Charlie laughed, his eyes dancing like sunshine on a calm sea. As his hands reached up and flicked open her bra, releasing her full and tingling breasts, her fingers popped the button on his shorts. She unzipped his fly, releasing him—beautiful, silken and erect. Their eyes locked as they cradled each other for a moment.

'You're amazing.' Their words broke over each other, full of reverence.

'You want to take this fast or slow?' he croaked, as if speaking was difficult.

She stroked him. 'I really don't mind. Either way is good and we've always got the option to reverse the order.'

'I like the way you think.'

He moved with the stealth and speed of a panther and suddenly she was on her back and laughing. Charlie trailed kisses between her breasts and then slowly across her left breast as his hand caressed her right. As his mouth sucked one nipple into its hot depths and lashed it with his tongue, his fingers tweaked the other. Her hips jerked, leaving the bed and pushing against his erection.

He chuckled, the sound wicked and wonderful. 'If you like that, then I think you'll like this.'

He moved slowly and systematically, kissing and licking and stroking her breasts, her belly, all the time murmuring 'God, you're sexy. Beautiful.' She soaked up every compliment and every type of touch he offered, feeling like a woman worshipped. Her body loosened, her legs fell open and then he was kissing the tender insides of her thighs until he flicked his tongue inside her.

'Oh!' She lost herself in the ball of sensation that grew hotter and more deliciously frantic, pulling her higher and higher and tighter and tighter until the pleasure was so intense it was almost unbearable. Yet she wanted more. So much more. Her hands reached for him to pull him up to her but her body took over, wielding total control. Her head thrashed back and forth, her muscles clenched, desperate to close around something, anything. Her hand closed around the edge of the mattress as her legs wrapped around him as if that would somehow help. Be enough. At the point of agonising pleasure, the exquisite ball of sensation exploded, drowning her in bliss.

When she'd floated down from ethereal heights, she opened her eyes. Charlie was smiling at her. 'Going on the sound effects, I gather you liked that?'

'Like would be an understatement.' She laughed. 'Call me Oliver, but I want more.'

'That can be arranged.' But as he moved she grabbed him, accidentally clunking him on his shoulder with her cast. 'Ouch!' He rubbed the spot.

'Sorry. Just lie on your back.'

His eyes glittered. 'Is that a command?'

'If you want it to be.'

Had sex with Charlie been this much fun when she'd been younger? Probably not. Youth may have blessed her with a narrower waist and fewer lines around her eyes but age had added confidence and a few sexual tips to a once limited repertoire. 'Now I've got you where I want you...' Pinching the tip of the condom, she rolled the sticky rubber beast down his length.

'Be careful what you do to me.' His voice was rough. 'It's not that I'm unfamiliar with restraint or the pain of denial, but there's only so much control I can exert on a body that craves to be inside yours.'

Craves. A desperate thrill ran up her spine, vaporising all her plans. Locking her gaze with his, she prayed that after two years of celibacy her body would know what to do and accommodate him. His hands splayed on her thighs as she guided herself over him, lowering herself slowly. She gasped as the tip of him entered her.

'No hurry,' he said, not taking his eyes off her. 'Take your time.'

She could clearly see the effort he was putting into leashing his body and her heart lurched. 'I want this.'

'I know.'

His hands fondled her breasts and something inside her let go. She slid down his length and he filled her. For a moment she sighed at how amazing it felt.

'Good?'

'Way more than good.' She leaned down and kissed him—half with relief, half with desire—and he returned it. Initially the kiss acknowledged her concerns that they still fitted together but then it exploded it into something beyond the realms of anything she'd ever known.

Moving together as one, she savoured every stroke—the combination of silk and power sliding against her—as they created a rhythm that drove each of them upward. She watched sweat slick his body, his muscles bunch and clench, the inky black of his eyes absorbing the vivid blue and then the fast rise and fall of his chest. His eyes closed, his jaw slackened and he bucked and shuddered under her as a look of pure pleasure washed over him, stealing away every vestige of strain and whatever else dogged him.

I did this. The power of it engulfed her already aroused body in a fire of pure ecstasy—ribbons of sensation streamed through her—and she rode them home until she collapsed in a depleted and yet utterly fulfilled mess on his heaving chest.

'Thank you.' His arms enclosed her, holding her against him, and she gradually felt his breathing slow. He kissed her hair. 'Seems like we've still got it.'

Her body was liquid relaxation and it took effort to raise her head and smile. 'Seems so.'

You're home. She tensed as the thought rocked her. *No. No way. It's just familiar territory.*

'You okay?' Concern etched his face.

'Cramp.' She eased herself off him and let him apply counter-pressure to her foot, despite the fact the cramp was in her heart.

CHAPTER SEVEN

'Saw these in Melbourne and thought you might like them.' Charlie handed his grandmother an enormous bunch of hydrangeas. Some were a variegated blue and cream with flat petals twisted into fours, while others contrasted with tightly clustered pale green petals, but all were elegantly wrapped in heavy olive green and rich earth-brown paper and wrapped with a wire-rimmed golden bow.

'Darling boy,' she said smiling at him. 'You remembered my favourite flowers.'

He'd walked past the florist after visiting his brother. 'Harry reminded me.'

Anna gave him what he'd dubbed a 'Harry' smile, sad and resigned. 'Darling boys, the two of you. How is he?'

Charlie shrugged. 'Too thin. The last UTI knocked him about a lot. I left him with a best of Coldplay CD.'

Anna got a far-away look in her eyes as she reached for a vase. 'What was that song he always played on the cello?'

'"Life is for Living".'

She nodded and untied the bow on the flowers. 'Did you catch up with anyone else while you were in town?'

'If you mean did I see Mum and Dad, I think you know the answer to that.' Charlie switched on the coffee machine, suddenly desperate for a shot of caffeine. Desperate to see Lauren. Desperate to bury himself inside her and forget.

'Randall and Patrice are coming down this weekend,' Anna said, studying him carefully. 'Your father asked me not to tell you, but I thought this way you had time to get used to the idea.'

Every nerve ending shot to high alert. 'Lauren and I have plans to go away this weekend.' Well, they would have plans the moment he saw her and told her about them.

'You and Lauren Fuller?'

The surprise in his grandmother's voice made him realise what he'd just said. *Idiot!* A litany of expletives boomed in his head. He and Lauren had a pact to keep things secret to protect Ian, Sue and Shaylee from unrealistic expectations. 'Medical convention,' he said, one beat too slowly.

'Charles Ainsworth, do you think I came down in the last shower?' Anna sighed. 'I have a lot of time for Lauren. Don't hurt her.'

'I don't make a habit of hurting people,' he said defensively. 'I think my work speaks for itself.'

'I'm not saying you do it deliberately, darling.'

Indignation surged. 'What the hell is that supposed to mean, Gran? If this is about Mum and Dad—'

'It isn't. All I'm saying is you dash around the world as if you can't bear to stand still. I wasn't disappointed one little bit when you didn't make it work with Alysha. Nothing about that woman was right for you, but Lauren's different. Perfect almost. Does she know about Har—?'

'I'm seeing a counsellor,' he blurted out, desperate to stop her question rather than a real attempt to open up. 'That's why I went to Melbourne.'

'You're looking and sounding better than the first time

I saw you,' the counsellor said approvingly. 'Nothing like three weeks of rest and sleep to rejuvenate you.'

Nothing like Lauren, Charlie thought, but chose not to mention her. Two weeks of great sex had done him more good than any amount of navel gazing ever would. 'Sea air helps.'

'And family.'

Not for the first time, Charlie thought the counsellor both clueless and useless.

'I'm glad you're seeing a professional,' Anna said, in a tone that said, *finally.* 'And you've talked to them about Randall and Patrice?'

Not if they paid me. 'Gran, don't say anything to anyone about Lauren, okay?'

She tapped her nose. 'I understand. Early days, but, darling, do everything you can to make it work. I'd like to see *one* of my grandsons happy.'

He nodded, not because he wanted to affirm that there was any chance he and Lauren were anything other than friends with benefits but because he couldn't speak. His throat had thickened on the word 'happy' and guilt stole all his words.

'Oh, and, Charlie, I don't ask you for much but…' Anna placed the arranged flowers on the mantelpiece '…I need you here at Bide-A-While this weekend. Lauren will understand.'

And that was when the date hit him. Saturday was the anniversary of Harry's accident.

'You got a haircut.' Lauren ran her hands through Charlie's now neat hair, missing being able to tangle her fingers in its length but happy to see more of his face. 'Trying to impress the counsellor?' she teased.

He didn't laugh but instead rolled her under him and kissed her with surprising ferocity.

She hadn't expected to see Charlie tonight. He'd gone to Melbourne for the day so she'd taken the opportunity of a free evening to go over the practice's financial statements. Fighting a losing battle not to go cross-eyed at the figures, it had been a relief to answer the door and find Charlie standing on her veranda. When he'd lifted her off her feet in a fireman's lift and carried her to bed, her squeals of protest had been token at best.

She gazed up at him, thrilled the dark shadows and drawn skin that had defined him a month ago had vanished over the last couple of weeks, thankfully replaced with healthy colour. It gave her a tingle, knowing she was playing a part in his recovery. Her fingers traced his chest and then she gently pinched his waist. 'You've gained weight.'

He rolled to the side and pulled her in against him. 'It's all that good food you're cooking me.'

'Ha! Ha!' Lauren assembled meals rather than cooking them. She knew she probably let her mother feed her too often but she enjoyed being part of family dinners and hearing about Shaylee's adventures at school. It was as close as she'd ever get to having a family of her own. 'I think it's all the cake Anna's feeding you. She'd better not be nibbling on any herself.'

'I promise you, she's not. She does watch me intently when I eat, though, saying she's enjoying cake vicariously through me.'

'You're such an obliging grandson.'

She waited for him to fire back a cheeky 'That's me,' but instead he sat up abruptly and got out of bed. He fished up his boxers from the floor. 'Hungry?'

For you, always. 'Sure. I bought some prawns off the boat and there's salad.'

'A perfect match for the champagne I bought you in Melbourne. I'll make a start.'

Lauren jumped through the shower, pulled on a pair of comfy shorts and a T-shirt and walked down the hall, anticipating the delicious fizz of expensive champagne. As she got close to the kitchen, she heard Charlie talking to someone. He had his back to her and was staring out the window with his phone pressed to his ear.

'For God's sake, Dad, it's just a CD. I thought Harry might enjoy it.' His hand moved hard and fast against the back of his head as if his fingers wanted to pull at hair that was no longer there. 'Of course I didn't buy it to upset Mum. Hell, I didn't think she even—'

Charlie held the phone away from his ear. Lauren heard an angry male voice but she couldn't make out the words. He slammed the device back against his ear. 'I don't need your permission to give my brother a gift, Dad. This conversation is over. Goodbye.' He swore as he stabbed the screen of the phone with his finger.

Lauren wasn't sure if she'd gasped her surprise out loud but Charlie swung around, his eyes as wild as a choppy wind-blown sea. She saw him rein in his anger from untamed to controlled, but it still simmered in the depths of his gaze. His mouth curved up in jerky increments until it resembled a dimple-less smile. 'All set for dinner? Good. I'll pour that champagne.'

'You have a brother?' Shock shot the question out unfiltered. 'How did I not know this?'

He ripped at the gold foil around the neck of the bottle. 'Because we're all about sex, fun and each other, not boring details.'

Boring details? The words left a slight sting. 'Well, sure, but a brother? Twelve years ago, I told you I was an only child with thirty-six foster siblings. How come you never mentioned your brother then?'

A slight tremor stiffened his hand on the wire cage that held the champagne cork in place. 'Unlike your family, mine's complicated.'

She snorted. 'Thirty-six foster kids, Charlie. *Every* family's complicated.'

'Tell me about it,' he muttered. The amber fluid with a hint of pink frothed in the flutes and he handed her a glass. 'Please don't get all bent out of shape over this. That summer I needed time out from being an Ainsworth. Right now, after that phone call, I need time out from my father, okay?'

A skitter of unease rode over her pragmatism that they were both using each other to feel better. 'Are none of your family close?'

He drained half the glass and set it down on a coaster. 'Gran's the glue. When she's dead, I doubt I'll have anything to do with my parents again.'

An ache wound through her from tip to toe. 'And Harry? That's your brother's name, right?'

His lids hooded his eyes and he sucked in a deep breath. 'I'll always have time for Harry.' For a split second he was perfectly still and then with a flourish he pulled out a chair for her as if he were a maître d'. 'Your prawn and mango salad awaits.'

Before she could ask him anything else about Harry, he'd launched into a funny story about a woman on the tram in Melbourne. When he'd milked that for all it was worth, he talked about the adventures and misadventures of working in Africa. From tales about doing deals with the militia so they could get aid into villages to a misunderstanding where he'd found himself the inadvertent owner of a fifteen-year-old girl and a pig, and how the village chief had only accepted the return of the pig, he didn't draw breath.

Lauren knew his raconteur style would hold fundraising groups enthralled and that these stories would tease out generous donations for Australia Aid, but they left her chilled. Instead of a talented surgeon and captivating storyteller sitting across from her, all she could see was a man holding her very firmly at arm's length. Unlike the evening in her parents' dining room when he'd used a similar story for distraction, this time she'd glimpsed a clue about his distance. His family. Did she dare talk to Anna about it?

'Charlie.'

'Yeah,' he said absently. He was fully occupied in the task of applying *papier-mâché* to the wire outline of a pterosaur for Shaylee's school dinosaur project. It was ridiculous how much fun he was having and he didn't understand why Ian and Lauren had been so relieved when he'd offered to help.

'Thank you so much,' Lauren had said two hours ago at the surgery. Then she'd glanced around and, making sure no one could see them, gifted him with a kiss full of gratitude. 'Mum's in Geelong at a training day and Dad should have been home an hour ago but he's stuck in a traffic jam on the Westgate Freeway.'

'And you've got the family planning clinic. I get it. It's no big deal. I'll pick up Shaylee from school, give her something to eat and we'll get cracking on the project. I happen to know a lot about dinosaurs. Did you know that the—?'

'I'll let you dazzle Shaylee with your brilliance,' Lauren had said quickly, looking at the clock. 'I have to go. I owe you one.'

'And I'm sure I can find the perfect way for you to repay

me.' He'd pulled her close and nuzzled her neck, purely to inhale her scent and carry it with him. Laughing, she'd pushed him away and dashed out to the waiting room to call her next patient.

'Are you a dad?'

Shaylee's question shocked him from daydreaming about extracting delicious payment from Lauren and back to the Fullers' kitchen table. 'I'm not married.'

Shaylee tilted her head, her ebony eyes scrutinising him. 'You don't have to be married to be a dad.'

He remembered Shaylee's fractured family and the fact she didn't know her father. 'That's true. But to answer your question, no, I'm not a dad. Why did you want to know?'

'Cos you're really good at this.' She gave him a beatific smile. 'And you made me an ice-cream smoothie.'

He laughed. 'I learned how to make smoothies because my brother loved them.'

'Did you make them with strawberry ice cream for him too?

'I did.'

Mum, why do I have to make Harry smoothies all the time?

Because you're his big brother and it's your job to look after him.

'Do you still make him smoothies?' Shaylee asked, as she slapped wet and soggy newspaper onto the pterosaur's wing.

Old guilt clawed into him. 'No. He doesn't drink smoothies anymore.'

Shaylee's small hand crept onto his arm. 'It's okay, Charlie. Don't be sad. You can still make smoothies for me.'

Out of the mouths... He mustered a smile against the

numbing ache that circled his heart and patted her hand. 'Thanks, Shaylee. Good to know.'

'Cooee.' Ian walked in, clutching his lunch bag, and immediately dropped a kiss onto Shaylee's head. 'Look at you two. That pterodactyl is coming along in leaps and bounds.'

'Actually, Ian,' Shaylee said in the authoritative tone of a kid who's excited to know something an adult doesn't, 'it's a pterosaur.'

Ian ruffled her hair. 'Is it, now?'

'Yes. Charlie says pterodactyl is a made-up word for the movies.'

Charlie threw Ian an apologetic look but the big man just laughed. 'In that case, we're lucky that Charlie knows his dinosaurs. Can you stay for dinner? It's just me and Shaylee, so we're cheating and having fish and chips.'

'Say, yes, Charlie. Please,' Shaylee begged.

Charlie didn't spend a lot of time with kids but over the last few weeks he'd enjoyed the occasions he'd spent with Shaylee. Even though Lauren said the little girl had her problems, given everything she'd been through, there was something about her indomitable spirit that made him yearn for the time he'd faced each day with enthusiasm. 'Why not? Gran's got her book club tonight so fish and chips sounds great.'

'Did someone say fish and chips?' Lauren walked in, looking tired but smiling.

'Hello, love. You okay? You're a bit pale.' Ian leaned in and gave her a kiss on the cheek.

Charlie half rose, intending to do the same thing, before realising he couldn't kiss her in front of her father and that shaking her hand would just look stupid. He slumped back into the chair. 'Family planning finished early?'

'The last patient cancelled. Apparently, mother nature

resolved her urgency to see me,' she said cryptically to protect Shaylee. 'My order's flake and two potato cakes, please.'

'Yay!' Shaylee clapped. 'Can we play UNO after dinner, Ian? Please?'

'Sure.' Ian winked. 'You beating Charlie and Lauren instead of me will make a nice change.'

'Hey!' Lauren objected. 'When it comes to UNO, I'm star talent.'

Charlie listened to the easygoing banter between father and daughter and the obvious love that flowed between them. His contentment—generated by minding Shaylee and sloshing around in *papier-mâché*—dribbled away, leaving a hollow cave inside him.

Before Harry's accident had changed his family for ever, his relationship with his father had been pretty standard. First came his childhood hero-worship of a man he'd deemed infallible. It had been followed by teenage cynicism, and the need to stretch his wings and break away. After his twenty-first birthday and during his hospital placements, he'd seen his father in a new light—a source of information about medicine and life. He'd been enjoying a more adult relationship with Randall when everything had gone to hell. The chances of that more equal relationship ever happening again were less than zilch.

The late afternoon sun poured through the office window and Lauren's eyelids started to flutter and close as she checked the pathology reports. It was incredibly tempting to put her head down on the desk and grab a power nap but she yawned and stretched instead. Her ribs no longer bothered her, not even the occasional pinch, but perhaps healing bones took more out of a girl then she thought, otherwise she couldn't think of a reason why she was so tired. With Charlie still keen to work, she wasn't yet back to full time and at night she slept like a top so technically she should be jumping out of her skin. She stifled another yawn and jumped to her feet a little too quickly. The room spun and, used to suffering from postural hypotension, she immediately sat down again. Her intercom buzzed.

'Yes, Lexie?'

'Anna Ainsworth's on the phone and she wants to talk to you. She sounds upset.'

It was a worry when any patient called in distressed but the fact that it was Anna, who was of a generation that kept their emotions very much in check, made it more concerning. 'Put her through.'

The line clicked and she heard Lexie say, 'Dr Fuller can talk to you now.'

'Hi, Anna, it's Lauren.'

'Oh, Lauren. Thank goodness. I'm in Melbourne and something's… I need to talk to Charlie urgently. He's not picking up his phone. Do you know what his plans were after he left the clinic?'

She did. The two of them had met for lunch at the cottage, although they'd indulged in each other rather than food. Usually, Charlie fell asleep straight after sex and she was the one wide awake but today he'd been full of energy and she'd been the one wanting to snuggle down and give in to the sweet siren call of sleep.

'I got the better deal today,' he'd said, his blue eyes dancing. 'You have to go to work this afternoon and I've got sunshine and a blue-sky day.'

'What are you going to do?'

'I reckon I'll dust off the surfboard and catch some waves.'

She took in his happy and relaxed demeanour and her heart turned over with joy. Perhaps she'd been catastrophising for all these weeks and worrying about him for no real reason. Had he been right when he'd insisted all he needed was a proper rest?

'Crikey! Don't tell me you're going to recklessly relax and enjoy your holiday?'

'Shocking, isn't it?' He'd grinned down at her and stolen a kiss before jumping out of bed. 'Some days are great days. After work, do you want to bring Shaylee and meet me at the beach? She told me the other day she loves body boarding.'

His enthusiasm had been infectious. 'Sounds like the perfect plan.'

'Anna, he told me he was going surfing, which is why his phone's probably off. Do you want me to go to the beach and find him?'

'Oh, dear, would you? That would be wonderful.'

Lauren could hear the low rumble of voices in the back ground. 'How does he reach you? And what do you want me to tell him?'

'I've got my mobile turned on. Tell him it's Harry. He's got pneumonia and you know what that means. How serious it is.'

Yes and no. Granted, pneumonia was a serious illness, but in a fit young person and with the right antibiotics, recovery was generally swift. Then again, Lauren knew nothing about Harry and, listening to the anguish in Anna's voice, now wasn't the time to ask for details.

'Tell him to come straight away and, Lauren…can I ask you a favour?'

'Of course.' Her mind immediately went to all things diabetic, anticipating Anna might need insulin or something for her pump.

'Come with him to Melbourne. He'll tell you not to, but insist. He's going to need you.'

* * *

Charlie lay on his board just beyond the breakers, taking a breather before trying his luck at some more waves. Surfing might be like riding a bike but it had taken more than a few dumps and the occasional mouthful of water before he'd found his balance. When he finally caught a wave, riding it into shore, the power of the water under him and the board was exhilarating. Almost as energising and amazing as sex with Lauren. He laughed out loud with sheer delight and realised that for the first time in a long time he was happy.

Just like that long-ago summer, Lauren made life sparkle. If he didn't have to go to counselling or endure the upcoming weekend, this enforced break would be perfect. Thinking about the weekend dented his buzz. He hated that Gran insisted he be at dinner on Saturday night. He had no qualms at all in refusing his parents' requests, but he struggled to say no to Gran, especially when she'd welcomed him with open arms and made few demands on him. Although dinner was a big demand. His usual modus operandi on the anniversary of Harry's accident was to drink himself into oblivion. Unless anything had changed, his mother would be happy to join him—she drank to drunkenness most nights, or he assumed she still did. There had been no reason for that to change.

He gave himself a shake. It was only Thursday. Why ruin two perfectly good days obsessing about Saturday, especially when he had waves to catch and the anticipation of a beach picnic with Shaylee and Lauren? He paddled forward in preparation for another crack when a bloke on a board called out, 'Hey! Are you Charlie?'

'Yep.'

'Your old lady's on the beach. She wants you to go in.'

He peered towards the shore and saw Lauren waving.

Perhaps she'd finished early again, although he'd seen her list and it had been full and long. Still, it was sunny and people often forgot their ills. Glancing behind, he saw a wave rising and, determined to show Lauren he still had some skills, he focused on his body, the board and the wave. In a moment of pure providence, his feet were balanced, his rise fluid and he rode the wave, executing a perfect bottom turn before returning to ride the crest again. He was still standing when the wave deposited him gently in the shallows.

Picking up the board, he jogged up to Lauren. Even though his eyes were stinging with salt he noticed she was dressed in her work clothes. 'You're early. Where's your gear?'

She passed him his towel and as he dried his face she said, 'Anna called. She wants you to go to Melbourne as soon as possible.'

His head shot up. Part of his grandmother's ritual in the week before the anniversary was a visit to Melbourne and she'd driven up yesterday morning. 'Why? What's happened?'

'It's your brother. Harry's got pneumonia.'

The rumble and crash of the surf was positively soundless compared with the roar of his blood in his ears. For a long moment he didn't feel anything. Then relief rolled through him but it was immediately kicked hard to the kerb by guilt.

'Charlie?' He saw concern etched clearly on her face along with a parade of questions. 'Do you think Anna's panicking?'

'No.' Resignation cloaked him. 'I have to go.'

'I'm coming with you.'

'No need.' He picked up his board and made a bee-line for Bide-A-While's weathered steps.

'Charlie!' He didn't slow but Lauren, unencumbered by a surfboard, overtook him and blocked him at the bottom of the stairs. 'I'm not sure what's going on but I get the idea your brother's got a condition like cystic fibrosis or severe asthma. Something that makes pneumonia dangerous. I heard Anna's worry and I can see you're upset.' Her hand rested on his arm, warm and caring but firm. 'I'm driving you to Melbourne and that's that.'

He should argue and fight her on this—refuse her offer and drive to Melbourne alone. This was his family, not hers, and no one deserved to have the Ainsworths inflicted on them in the good times, let alone the bad. This was likely to be as bad as it got. Usually, Gran could temper the worst of his bombastic father and acerbic mother but she'd be too upset to manage them.

An idea struck. His parents didn't know Lauren, and that gave her power he could harness. Her presence would be a welcome buffer that would delay the inevitable arguments and accusations laced with disappointment.

'Thank you.'

She stroked his cheek. 'Any time.'

He swallowed the rising self-loathing that he was about to throw her under the Ainsworth bus.

CHAPTER EIGHT

LAUREN STOOD IN a small, sterile room. The only touches of colour came courtesy of a bunch of yellow gerberas, a red CD player and a blue speaker with a white mobile phone charging in the dock. She squeezed Charlie's hand and tried hard to absorb the shocking truth. Of all the scenarios she'd pictured on the two-hour drive, she hadn't come close to this reality.

Charlie had insisted on driving and Lauren had accepted that he needed to divert his anxiety into something tangible, but she'd demanded they take her car. 'Anna will appreciate you driving her back to the Bay in her car,' she'd offered as her reason. If she was honest, since Jeremy, she preferred to be as independent as possible.

The trip had been relatively silent apart from desultory comments on the traffic and Charlie's mutters of 'moron' whenever a car had changed lanes without indicating. Lauren had filled the void with music, setting her MP3 player to shuffle. As they'd crossed the Westgate Bridge, a Coldplay tune had come on and Charlie had flinched before thumping the button on the steering wheel to flick the player onto the next track. It killed her not to press him to tell her what the hell was going on, but he was behind the wheel in heavy traffic—probably another reason he'd insisted on driving. Another way to hold her at bay. And yet Anna had said, 'He needs you.' Did that mean Charlie had told her about them?

When Charlie had pulled the car into the parking lot of a nursing home—the domain of the elderly—a sharp pain had ripped through her. Now she stared at the wraith-thin man on the bed—the ghost of Charlie. Harry, although slightly darker, had his brother's intelligent forehead and widow's peak and a similar shaped nose. Lauren had no idea about the colour of his eyes, because they were closed. A catheter bag was hooked on the side rail of the bed and a parenteral nutrition bag hung high on a stand. A sign inside a Perspex frame on the bedhead declared, 'Nil By Mouth'.

'Hey, bro.' Charlie leaned down and gently brushed his brother's hair from his forehead before kissing him. 'Love you.'

Harry didn't speak, move, flinch, wince or blink. The only movement was the rise and fall of his chest. The only noise was the ominous rattle of each breath and the hiss of the oxygen.

Lauren fought tears. 'Can he hear you?'

Charlie shrugged. 'I like to think so but as he doesn't respond to any painful stimuli it's hard to believe he does. Even so, I still make a recording each week. You know, a private podcast telling him what I've been up to. I try to add a joke and either a funny or interesting story.' He gave her a wry smile. 'I told him about the mud rescue. I send it to his phone and the nurses play it to him a couple of times across the week.'

Her heart quivered. 'How long's he been in a coma?'

Charlie gripped the cot sides on the bed and closed his eyes as a long breath shuddered out of him. 'This week-end it will be thirteen years.'

'But...' Her stomach rolled, making her feel queasy,

and she sat down hard on one of the chairs. 'That means he was comatose when we first met.'

'Yeah. Had been for nine months. That was a bastard of a year but our summer together meant so much to me. It gave me respite from the endless questions and pitying looks. I could just be me. Not poor Harry's brother.'

She wanted to know everything. 'Is he your only brother?'

Charlie nodded and sat down in the armchair next to her. 'He's three years younger than me. Hard to believe, right? He looks decades older than me now.'

She slid her hand into his and his fingers traced the path of the cast across her palm. 'What happened?'

Charlie's eyes glazed over as if telling the story was something he did by rote. 'I was in final year of med school and Harry was at the Conservatorium. He was a hell of a cellist. He inherited the creative gene from my mother's side of the family.'

He grimaced. 'The Ainsworths are far too pragmatic for any of that. Anyway, my parents and Gran were in Europe. Dad was giving a paper at some conference and Harry and I were baching. Of course, we threw a party. Looking back on how many drunk people there were that night, it was a miracle no one drowned in the pool or died from aspirating their own vomit. But the worst thing that happened was a broken coffee table and an indelible stain on my mother's cream carpet.'

He rubbed the back of his neck. 'Like most life-changing events, it happened on a very ordinary day when Harry was doing a very ordinary thing. The Con's opposite the hospital and while Dad was away we had his parking pass. It was a treat not to have to catch the tram, especially for Harry who schlepped everywhere with a cello. I had an early lecture and Harry was dragging his feet. I was at the base of the stairs, yelling for him to bloody well hurry up or I was leaving without him, when he appeared on the landing, shirt half buttoned, feet shoved into shoes, and lugging that bloody moulded cello case. His last words to me were, "Jeez, keep your shirt on."

'I watched it happen but I can't tell you how it happened. One minute he was rolling his eyes at me for being a slave to time and the next he was at my feet. He tumbled head first down the stairs. A lot is a blur. He wasn't breathing. I did CPR and got him back. He was rushed to hospital and they operated, removing part of his skull to allow for the swelling of his brain. The neurosurgeon said it was grim. Mum and Dad were more than twenty-four hours away by plane and I was the one left making the decisions. My funny and irreverent baby brother was just twenty. I said do everything.'

Lauren didn't realise she was crying until Charlie reached into his pocket and handed her a snowy handkerchief. 'You must have been so frightened. Terrified. Overwhelmed.'

'Yeah.' For a second, the shutters on his eyes lifted and amidst the guilt and pain she saw a spark of appreciation. 'He was in ICU for two months without a single sign of any improvement. Every test reinforced this and my father made the decision to remove Harry from life support. We gathered. We said goodbye and we waited. But when everything was withdrawn, Harry continued to breathe on his own. I was euphoric.

'Hope kept me going for months. He had physio and massage to prevent contractures and to help keep some muscle tone. His Con mates came and played and sang. Like Mum, Harry was sensitive and squeamish, so I'd study by his bed, reading out loud to him all the gory stuff in the hope he'd open his eyes and tell me to bugger off.

Gran made sure there were scented fresh flowers from her garden and she did a heap of sensory stimulation stuff.'

It took Lauren a moment to realise that in the list of who'd done what, he hadn't mentioned his parents. 'When did Harry move here?'

Charlie rose and poured himself a glass of water from the pitcher a nurse had brought in. 'The summer I met you. When he was in hospital getting therapy, I could believe he'd wake up one day, but when they bypassed rehab completely and sent him here to God's waiting room with the old, the frail and the demented...' He gulped down the water.

His anguish flailed her. 'That's why you went to England?' *I never had any intention of returning to Australia to live.* But she remembered the overheard phone conversation with his father about buying Harry a CD. She'd just seen him being so gentle with Harry. She'd heard the love in his voice when he'd spoken to him, despite his belief that his brother didn't hear him. The idea that Harry was keeping him away from Australia didn't make sense.

At that moment, a man wearing a beautifully tailored suit strode into the room, his presence commanding every atom of air in the small space. Behind him, an elegantly dressed woman in her sixties hesitated in the doorway, as if crossing the threshold held grave danger. Even without being introduced, Lauren immediately knew they were Charlie's parents. Mrs Ainsworth's hand rose anxiously to touch her pearls but Mr Ainsworth betrayed no such anxiety, although neither did he smile or frown. None of the Ainsworths moved to embrace Charlie.

She shot to her feet and Charlie stiffened next to her. 'Mum. Dad.'

'At least you respond to your grandmother,' his father said curtly.

'And this is…?' Mrs Ainsworth stepped into the room, her accent hinting at old money and elocution classes.

'Lauren Fuller, meet my parents Randall and Patrice Ainsworth. Lauren's Gran's GP in Horseshoe Bay.'

A trickle of ice ran along her veins. *Okay. I get not being introduced as your lover but I would have thought I qualified as a friend.* She tried not to let his descriptor wound her and instead concentrated on extending her hand in greeting. 'Pleased to meet you both. Is Anna all right?'

'Mum's resting,' Randall said crisply. 'I'm sure you can imagine how difficult and wearing this situation is for everyone.'

A wrinkle of tension rolled up her spine at his tone. 'I don't have to imagine it, Mr Ainsworth. I feel devastated for you and your family.'

Patrice made a strangled sound and Randall's commanding aura suddenly sagged under the weight of sadness. He put his arm around his wife. 'No family should have to face this protracted nightmare. Thirteen bloody years.' He cleared his throat and his shoulders squared, clearly pulling himself together. 'If you'll excuse us, Lauren, Charles and I need to speak outside.'

Charlie's hand suddenly gripped her shoulder, his fingers digging in so hard they hit bone. She winced and met his gaze. A tumultuous sea of emotions flickered on his face and then they were swept away, replaced by a remoteness she hadn't seen in weeks. 'You go. I'll wait here.'

He nodded and strode out of the room, leaving Lauren with Patrice and Harry. The noise of his laboured breathing filled the room and Lauren recognised the ominous sounds of the death rattle.

Patrice stood gazing down at her son, stroking his hair. 'I wish you'd met him when he was my darling, talented, impish Harry, instead of—' Her voice cracked. 'I'm sorry.

I'm not like Randall and Charles. I'm not in the medical field and I can't cope with any of this. I never have.'

Lauren considered Randall's pompous manner and the fact Charlie hadn't told her anything about Harry. 'They may not flinch at the hospital setting or be distressed by the sight of a catheter, but I don't think they're coping. Medically trained or not, no one deals well with watching someone they love die.'

'And we've been waiting and watching for so long now.' She looked at Lauren pleadingly, guilt scoring her face. 'I want to remember him how he was, not like this. I don't visit often. Does that make me a bad mother?'

The question made Lauren blink hard. 'No. It makes you human.'

Patrice nodded slowly, but her expression said she didn't believe her. 'Do you have children, Lauren?'

The old ache of loss burned. 'No.'

'Once I had two beautiful boys, two precious sons. Now I have none.'

Surely she meant one? Lauren opened her mouth to ask, *What about Charlie?* but closed it. *My family's complicated.* Sometimes more was learned by silence than by questions.

'Randall and I were overseas when it happened,' Patrice said, almost to herself. 'God, I was in the South of France on a yacht, upset because the wrong champagne had been delivered. We should have been here. Randall rails at the fact he wasn't at the hospital to make the medical decisions. He thinks that if he had been then perhaps things would have been different.'

'I thought your husband's a cardiologist,' Lauren said confused by what Patrice meant.

'He is. I meant he struggled with Charles's instructions that the hospital do everything to keep Harry alive.'

Lauren winced, her heart splitting between a young, bewildered and inexperienced Charlie and his traumatised and grieving parents. 'Hindsight favours an accuracy the here and now never offers. From what Charlie tells me, it was a very confusing time. The doctors involved couldn't have been one hundred percent certain there was no hope. Faced with that crippling type of decision, can you honestly say you would have said, "Let him go."?'

'Randall would have made the decision and perhaps I would have only lost one son, instead of both.' Despite her styled hair and perfect make-up, Patrice suddenly looked haggard as she sucked in a deep breath. 'Things were said in that first year, Lauren. Awful things. Words that fractured our family in ways we'd never contemplated were possible. Nine months after the accident both my sons were alive but unreachable. All thoughts of Charles ultimately working with his father vanished and he's built a career as far away from us as possible. With it went all my daydreams of extended family holidays at Bide-a-While with grandchildren running around the garden.'

Patrice cleared her throat. 'Charles keeps in contact with Harry, though. How ironic is that? He won't talk to us but he talks to his non-responsive brother. If it wasn't for the nurses emailing me Charles's weekly podcast, I'd have no idea where he was in the world or what he was doing.' She tilted her head and her mouth kicked up in a half-smile. 'After listening to the last few and reading between the lines, you're not just Anna's GP, are you?'

He mentioned me? Her heart soared. 'We're friends.'

'I'm glad. He needs a friend.'

Lauren's head and gut spun at the anguish this family had already endured, and was continuing to. Cobbling together what Charlie and Patrice had told her, she realised it was Charlie's guilt and his parents' anguish and self-reproach that kept him out of the country more weeks of the year than not.

Charlie and his father returned to the room, their demeanours equally tense, and Lauren felt the air charge. Patrice rose and, taking Randall's hand, they left the room. 'Are you okay?' Charlie asked her quietly. 'You look pale. Did Mum say something to upset you?'

The weight of the Ainsworths' estrangement pressed in on her. 'I'm...' *tired* '...fine and, no, of course your mother didn't upset me. She's hurting just like you and your father.'

He let out an expletive. 'I just want to be able to say goodbye to Harry without arguing or enduring the arctic freeze that fills the room whenever my parents and I are in it together. Hell, Harry deserves some peace.'

You all deserve some peace. 'I'm sure that's what your parents want as well.' She stroked his arm. 'I'd like to help.'

'Huh! We're long past that.'

And suddenly her need to help him hurt so much she almost cried out. *Stupid! Stupid! Stupid!* Despite everything she'd learned about herself and men over the last decade, despite telling herself that just like him, she was enjoying his friendship and sex while he was in town, she loved him. Not the love of a friend, but a fierce, all-consuming love that cast every other relationship she'd ever had into deep, dark shade. How had she deluded herself that she'd got over him all those years ago when a part of him had once been a part of her and had never completely left her?

'I want to help.' *I can't not.* 'Let me try.'

He rubbed the stubble on his jaw, the action filled with chronic exhaustion—the type that came from years of pain—and she felt his resistance waver. 'What did you have in mind?'

* * *

Charlie didn't know how Lauren pulled it all together, but he would be forever grateful to her that she had. Time was a bastard, bleaching the sharpness of happy memories and leeching them of colour and shape until they were brittle and disintegrated on recall. Over the last decade, Harry had faded from the cheeky and vibrant young man with the off-beat sense of humour they'd all loved and he'd been replaced by a vessel of unrelenting and all-consuming grief.

Few people visited Harry any more, unable to cope with his living death. The idea of waiting and watching Harry take his last breath, when in so many ways he'd taken it thirteen years ago, came with sadness and a guilt-inducing cocktail of relief. If that wasn't enough to send him running from the room, sharing the moment with his parents came damn close. But Lauren had found a way for his parents, Gran, the aunts, uncles and cousins, the nursing staff and even some of Harry's old friends to gather together in the room and give Harry a living funeral.

She'd asked each of them for something that was quintessentially Harry. His cello appeared, as did soundtracks of him playing it, as well as a soft Frisbee, which was thrown around the room. They ate pizza and Vietnamese noodles, the spicy scent of the food replacing the antiseptic tang of the room, and everyone brought photos. They all took their turn holding Harry's hand and telling him and everyone else a 'Harry, do you remember when…?' story. Amidst the numbing grief generated over the long years there was laughter and tears. Charlie was shocked at one point to see Randall cry and equally surprised that during the fraught hours his mother didn't reach for any alcohol, sticking instead to coffee from the machine Lauren had managed to procure.

By six a.m. only the immediate family was left and Lauren slept, snuggled in the depths of the old leather armchair Charlie remembered being in his father's study years ago. He asked a nurse for a blanket and tucked it around her.

'I told you she was special,' Gran said, *sotto voce*.

'I never said she wasn't,' Charlie countered, feeling a familiar tightness in his chest and an urge to protect her. An urge to run.

'I like her.' Patrice glanced at him, her face drawn. 'She's given us something special.'

'Your mother's right,' Randall said gruffly.

First light crept in, its orange rays colouring the white walls, and the rattle of Harry's breathing silenced. Everyone stilled, holding their own breath. The shuddering noise recommenced. They all breathed out.

Patrice sobbed quietly. 'When will it end? I can't take much more of this.'

'It won't be too much longer,' Charlie and Randall said, speaking at the same time.

'Goodness,' Anna said wryly. 'Can we build on this moment of agreement?'

Years of estrangement sat between him and his father like a wide and steep-sided gorge that required the engineering feat of a steel single-span bridge to have any hope of bringing them closer. Did his father even want to try? Did he?

Harry's breathing stalled again. Charlie pressed his fingers to his brother's neck, seeking the gentle press of a pulse against the tips. A surge of tears took him by surprise and he fought them. '*Vale*, bro. Wherever you are, I hope the music's awesome.'

For so long he'd wished his brother's body would recognise it was best just to give up, but now it had finally happened, thirteen years less one day to the date of the accident, the relief he'd expected didn't come. Instead, numbness and cold filled him, along with an abiding sense of pointless futility. He shivered, craving warmth.

'Charlie?' Lauren's arms went around him.

He pulled her in close, burying his face in her hair and jerkily breathing in her salty citrus scent. An edge of the cold thawed and he let his tears fall.

CHAPTER NINE

LAUREN ROLLED OVER and brilliant sunshine bored through her closed eyelids, turning the world vermillion. Squinting, she cracked open one eye and took in the elegant décor and remembered she was in the Ainsworths' guest room. The bedside clock declared it to be one fifty-seven p.m.

Patrice and Randall had insisted she stay at their Brighton home, saying it was too dangerous for her to drive back to Horseshoe Bay on very little sleep, and Anna had agreed. It was only Charlie who'd been unsettled by the idea, suggesting they get a room in a motel. But after last night Lauren knew that had more to do with his tangled feelings about his parents than wanting to hide her from them. She'd accepted his parents' offer, not because she had any unrealistic hearts and flowers notion that Harry's death would offer the family instant reconciliation but because at least it put Charlie in the same physical space as them to nourish any small steps.

Feeling decidedly seedy, she opened her other eye and saw a note on the pillow scrawled in Charlie's almost indecipherable spidery writing.

One p.m. appointment at funeral home.
Text me when you're awake.
Charlie x

When she'd fallen into bed at eight a.m. Charlie had come with her, wrapping her tightly in his arms as if he was scared she might vanish. In this treasured cocoon, her heart had expanded so quickly it had wobbled giddily, tempting her to hope that he loved her too. He did so many small and thoughtful things for her—surely that was love?

The combination of exhaustion and security had drawn her into a delicious slumber, so deep that even when the mattress must have surely moved when Charlie had got up, it hadn't disturbed her. Sitting up quickly, she reached for her phone and suddenly gagged. The taste of stomach acid and the eggs she'd had for breakfast burned her throat. Swallowing hard, she breathed in deeply and slowly, concentrating on keeping the contents of her stomach firmly in place. Back in the frantic days of being an intern, she'd often felt nauseous from fatigue and the same thing always happened to her with jet-lag.

Despite five hours of solid sleep, she supposed that the emotional turmoil of the last twenty-four hours combined with her previous lack of energy couldn't be discounted to have taken their toll.

She texted Charlie: Groggy but awake. Thinking of you. x.

Moving more slowly, she got up and took a shower then sniffed yesterday's clothes. Not too whiffy but then again she didn't have a choice. There was a bottle of perfume on the vanity so she spritzed it into the air and breathed in, checking to see if she liked the scent. Her stomach rebelled at the heavy floral perfume and as she vomited into the white porcelain bowl, she appreciated the small convenience of the toilet in the bathroom. Had she picked up a stomach bug? God, she hoped the Ainsworths didn't get it. That was the last thing they needed.

Her mouth felt like the bottom of a cockie's cage and she

systematically opened the drawers under the sink, looking for a toothbrush and toothpaste. Surely, as this was the guest bathroom, these items would be *de rigueur*. She found neatly folded towels, face cloths, handtowels and a hairdryer in one drawer. The second drawer yielded shampoo, conditioner, razors, shaving cream, aftershave and deodorant for men. She scanned the contents of the third drawer—bath gel, scented deodorant, body lotion, feminine hygiene products and, yay—toothbrushes and a tube of toothpaste. The Ainsworths' guest bathroom was better than a five-star hotel. She tore the packing from the toothbrush, layered on the striped toothpaste that promised to be refreshing, and flicked on the tap.

As she cleaned her teeth, she leaned towards the mirror and examined her face. It was paler than normal with a few beads of sweat above her top lip but she'd just thrown up so that was to be expected. Pulling back her hair to avoid splashing it with toothpaste, she lowered her head to spit and her breasts caught the edge of the raised basin. *Ouch!* She spat, rinsed, rose, and grabbed her towel to wipe her face. As she dropped the toothpaste back into the drawer, a candy-striped tampon tin caught her gaze.

Duh! Tender breasts and tiredness—her period was due.

You just threw up. You've been more tired than usual. The thoughts zoomed in and she batted them away. *I'm tired because my period is due.*

Occasionally, she got a shocker of a period and the clue that it was going to be a bad one was always extremely tender breasts. Given she'd survived being very nearly mown down by a car, stress had probably played havoc with her hormones this month.

You. Just. Threw. Up.

Common sense kicked in. She'd once spent sixteen months not using any contraception, actively trying to get pregnant without any success. She'd only had three weeks of sex with Charlie and they'd used condoms every single time. There was no way she could be pregnant. The odds were virtually non-existent.

But it happened once before.

Her heart lurched and her stomach rolled, propelling her back to hug the toilet bowl. She told herself it was stress, a stomach bug, tiredness, but when she started to rationalise that it was also the phase of the moon, she knew what she had to do. Grabbing her phone, she checked the calendar and sat down on the bed. *Oh, God.* Her period was nine days late. There was only one other time in her life it had been late and that was twelve years ago.

As if on cue, her phone pinged with a text from Charlie.

Hey, sleepyhead. Just finishing up here. Going to take Gran direct to Bide-A-While. Want to drive in convoy and break the journey at Greasy Joe's?

If her stomach hadn't already been empty, the thought of fried food would have propelled her straight back to the bathroom. Charlie knew she loved nothing more than a deep-fried dim sim with a potato cake chaser so he'd want to know why she was refusing a treat. No way was she admitting to feeling sick in front of him or Anna, especially not before she knew the reason, and even then, perhaps not.

Typing, she told him the truth, although it wasn't the whole truth. I have to pick up a birthday present for Shaylee. I'll see you at home. Lauren J

Opening a map app, she typed in 'shopping mall'. An orange bubble lit up ten kilometres away, displaying a large centre. With five hundred stores in the complex, surely she could buy a birthday present and a pregnancy test. But in which order?

* * *

Five hours later, standing in the cottage's bathroom, Lauren re-read the instructions on the pregnancy test, despite knowing them off by heart. They recommended an early morning urine sample for accuracy, but stuff that—the last five hours had been enough of an endurance test and she wasn't waiting another twelve. Charlie had called five minutes ago, suggesting he come over.

'What about Anna?' she'd said, trying to fob him off without appearing to be doing exactly that. 'It's been a huge couple of days for her. Don't you think you should spend tonight at Bide-a-While?'

'I suppose.' The disappointment in his voice rode down the phone, snagging at her heart, and she'd almost relented. But she was far too distracted to see him before she'd taken the test. He'd definitely twig that something was up.

Feeling guilty, she tore open the foil wrapper, telling herself that if the test was negative, she'd go straight to Bide-a-While and watch the sunset with him. She didn't think about the alternative. She couldn't. 'Okay, here goes.'

Counting out loud, she performed the test and then, dry-mouthed and with her heart hammering, she left the bathroom and set a timer. As she paced up and down the hall, glancing at the vanity each time she passed the doorway, part of her insisted that one pink line was the required result—the optimum outcome. The necessary one. But despite a very long list of reasons why being pregnant now would be back to front, she yearned for two pink lines.

The time on her phone beeped. Her sweaty hand gripped the architrave before she propelled herself forward and picked up the stick.

Pregnant.

She stared at the indicator window and felt… She didn't exactly know how to describe it, except it was tangled and complex. Lost yet found. Sheer relief and panic. Awe and dread. All those things. And happy. Illogically happy, because she wasn't fool enough to know that a baby meant Charlie loved her. Biology and lust were so often very separate beasts from love.

How would Charlie take the news?

Her mind rolled back twelve years and once again she was caught on the horns of a dilemma, only this time for very different reasons.

Should she even tell him?

Charlie stood close to the outcrop of rocks that created what the locals called 'far point', watching the hypnotic, graceful swell of the sea rise to a peak before breaking and hurling creamy, salty foam across the jet basalt. Just like the pounding waves, agitation crashed inside Charlie, jagged and spiky, making him restless. Horseshoe Bay no longer offered the sanctuary it once had—his parents were in town. They had been for days and, worse still, they'd befriended Lauren.

Harry's death had changed everything and nothing. He'd spent the work week shuttling back and forth to Melbourne for different events and appointments. His parents had made the decision not to have a funeral for Harry but instead hold a private cremation. He'd been surprised they'd sought his opinion but even more stunned that the three of them were simpatico regarding the decision. The last twelve hours of Harry's life had been the tribute they'd all needed.

On another visit to Melbourne, he'd seen the counsellor and visited the Australia Aid office. On that day, with his mind full, he'd driven back to the Bay and gone directly to Lauren's cottage. His plans had been straightforward—surprise her and tumble her into bed. They had not included his parents sitting around her kitchen table, drinking wine and looking unusually relaxed.

'Lauren's kindly invited us for dinner but as she's working and we're not, we've ordered from Julien's,' his father had said formally. 'Do you wish to join us?'

Charlie didn't know which had rankled more—the fact his father had invited him to dinner at his lover's house or the fact his parents were staying for dinner.

'Are you okay?' Lauren had asked him when they'd been alone in the kitchen, grabbing cutlery and crockery. 'It's just you look a bit pouty. Almost like a teenager who didn't get his own way.'

'I have every right to be pouty. I'm not good at sharing.' He'd wrapped his arms around her then and kissed her. 'I wanted you all to myself this evening.'

He'd expected her to laugh, flash him her sexy, flirty smile and suggest a very fast meal, but instead she'd stilled and studied him carefully. Too carefully—as if she had the ability to see beyond what he chose to show the world. He'd closed his eyes and kissed her, only coming up for air when his father had called, 'The food's here.'

The atmosphere between him and his parents lurched with strain as it had done for years. The only difference that had filtered in since Harry's death was the excessive politeness that barely papered over the scar tissue laid down over the years. The dinner conversation had stayed centred on safe topics. His mother and father had discussed the food, the weather and the cockatoo raid on the lemon tree at Bide-a-While. His father had quizzed Lauren on the challenges of running a country practice and then chatted easily and enthusiastically about the latest advancements in cardiology. Apart from offering an opinion on the satay sauce, Charlie had stayed silent, drinking too much red wine and eventually falling asleep on the couch.

Now cloaked in salt spray mist, Charlie checked his watch. It was time to head back to the Bide-a-While steps. He picked his way carefully along rock ledges, dodging the rock pools and an unwanted encounter with a deadly blue ring octopus, until he reached the white sand. In the distance, he saw a flash of pink—his grandmother's favourite colour—moving down the stairs. He could also make out the shape of his parents and one other person.

Lauren. His heart squeezed in his chest and he rubbed his sternum. Had Gran invited her? His parents? It wasn't that he objected to her presence, it was just he hadn't expected to see her until later. He had the evening all planned—champagne at the cottage, followed by a surprise dinner at Tide.

His agitation did a jig. His parents didn't know anything about his plans but Gran did. Surely she'd stayed quiet and not given the game away? He gulped in a breath, blew it out and tried again, slower this time. He made his way over to the group. Lauren indicated subtly with her finger that his parents had invited her.

'At least it's not windy,' he said, eyeing the timber box containing Harry's ashes in his father's hands.

His mother flinched and his father frowned. Charlie smothered a sigh. It didn't matter what he did or said, it was never going to be the right thing. The saddest part was he'd given up caring.

'It's a glorious day,' Lauren said, throwing him an understanding smile.

He wanted to hug her but that would only highlight the gaping chasm between him and his parents. All public displays of affection between the three of them had ceased long ago and greetings were always fraught with tension that could be sliced, diced and packaged up as ice.

'Remember the Christmas Harry got that stunt kite?'

Anna said, and then turned to Lauren by way of explanation. 'We had a week of calm weather and as each day passed, Harry trudged back from the beach increasingly dejected. New Year's Day dawned grey and miserable with a raging southerly. While everyone sat inside, self-indulgently morose and arguing over a game of Monopoly, Harry tore up and down the beach flying that kite, making it duck and weave and loop the loop.'

'It was freezing, but he didn't care,' Patrice added. 'He was having the time of his life.'

'We all ended up down here,' Randall said, looking at Charlie. 'Do you remember that complicated series of sand dams you and I built?'

Charlie did. He'd been fifteen and if it had been a sunny day, he'd have been off surfing with his mates and his father would have been sailing. Once that day had been a memory he treasured. Now it highlighted everything they'd lost. 'We stayed until the tide came in so we could watch what happened. See whose engineering held the longest.'

'If I recall correctly...' Randall cleared his throat '...we both had losses and wins.'

And didn't that just sum up their relationship, except these days the losses far exceeded the wins.

Shucking their shoes, all of them waded into the shallows and stood in a line—Randall, Patrice, Anna, Charlie and Lauren. Wordlessly, she slid her hand into his—the scratchy feel of her cast on his palm in stark contrast to her soothing support. With the sound of the surf as a backdrop, each Ainsworth said a few quiet words and gently scattered Harry's ashes in a bay that had once given him so much joy.

Lauren watched Charlie link Anna's arm through his as they walked up the stairs back to Bide-A-While. His love for his grandmother was evident in so many caring actions, just as his big-heartedness shone through in his relationships with other people. His generosity towards Shaylee, his easygoing banter with her parents, the way he'd cared for her after the café incident and the thoughtful things he did for her each day—it was just his relationship with his own parents that he struggled with. She was convinced it clouded his soul.

Her heart flip-flopped in her chest. It had been doing that a lot this week—for Charlie and for his parents. For herself. *For the baby.* She blocked that thought. The pregnancy was in its infancy and so much was uncertain. There was, however, nothing uncertain about the Ainsworths. She got a pang of sorrow whenever she thought about them and not just because of the trauma they'd endured but because they didn't seem to know how to take that first step towards reconciliation with Charlie. Her suspicions had been confirmed when Randall had come to see her at the practice that morning.

'We're scattering Harry's ashes this afternoon at Bide-a-While cove. I think it would help Charles if you were there.'

At the difficult dinner two nights ago with Charlie, Patrice and Randall, she'd felt like she was the interconnecting circle in a Venn diagram. She couldn't pinpoint exactly how she felt about that, so she got straight to the point. 'Help Charlie or help you?'

One side of his mouth had lifted wryly. 'Both, I hope. He listens to you.'

Does he? 'I appreciate your faith but—'

'I want to find a way to rebuild my relationship with him.'

Saying sorry to Charlie would be a start. The words had sounded so vicious in her head, they had frightened her. There were always two sides to every story but, despite that, she knew her allegiances lay with the man she loved and, as such, it was impossible to be impartial. She'd put on her professional hat. 'There's a lot of hurt on both sides, but I'm not a trained therapist. Would you consider family therapy?'

The expression on Randall's face—shock and abhorrence—had been Charlie to a T. Lauren had taken it as a very clear no. 'Please come,' Randall had asked again.

It had been the pleading in his voice mixed with soul-sucking sadness that had brought her to the beach. And to Charlie. Always Charlie.

'Don't rush off,' Anna said to her as they reached Bide-a-While's wraparound veranda. Her thin, long-fingered hand closed over Lauren's cast. 'Stay for an aperitif. I have a pitcher of Pimm's.'

Charlie, who was standing behind Anna but facing Lauren, shook his head and tapped his wrist as if to remind her of the time. It confused her, because she'd invited him to the cottage at seven and that was two hours away. 'I'm on call, Anna, so it's a no to the Pimm's, but a tonic water with lemon would be lovely. Can I just wash up first?' Early pregnancy had her running to the bathroom a lot.

'Of course, dear. Straight down the hall to the left.'

A few minutes later, as she exited the bathroom, she noticed a black travel bag in the bedroom opposite. It wasn't a designer bag or even part of a matching luggage set destined for the hands of a porter at an exclusive resort. Fully packed and with a faded fluoro-green combination strap around it, its battered exterior said *well travelled*. A folder sat on top, decorated in the distinctive colours of Australia Aid.

She stared at it as if her gaze had the power to change

the image. It didn't. Her chest tightened and her stomach lurched. Charlie was leaving already?

'There you are.' A smiling Charlie walked towards her. 'I was starting to think you'd got lost.' He leaned in close, sliding his hand along her cheek, and she instinctively pressed against his palm. 'Listen, can we bolt this drink and get out of here? I've got special plans and they only involve you and me, preferably naked.'

Her body betrayed her with a surge of tingling need and she wanted nothing more than to melt against him and kiss him until the world retreated, but that wasn't possible. The real world surrounded them, anchoring them firmly in time and place and making painful demands. She tilted her head towards the partially open bedroom door. 'Your room?'

He grinned. 'As tempting as that offer is, the presence of my family does dampen my desire somewhat.'

She ducked out of his embrace, pushed open the door and walked in. A neatly made bed and no traces of any personal items anywhere to hint that he'd slept here for weeks said it all. Unable to totally school her face to hide her feelings, she turned slowly and faced him.

He swore softly. Stepping into the room, he closed the door behind him and reached for her, his voice entreating. 'Lauren.'

She sidestepped him as memories of the last time he'd left her surfaced. He'd built her a fire at the entrance to the cave and they'd made love on a picnic rug. 'Did you plan on telling me?'

He looked taken aback. 'Of course,' he said emphatically. 'That's what tonight's all about. I've got us reservations at Tide.' His hand ploughed through his hair. 'I'm sorry, Lauren. I didn't mean to spring it on you like this. I wanted to tell you the other night but my parents invaded dinner and the rest of the week's been crazy with getting organised.'

Her mind dissolved into mud-sucking sludge, unable to compute anything, and then panic rose. Fighting it, she asked as calmly as she could, 'Where and when are you going?'

'Java and tomorrow.'

Tomorrow? Sharp pain jabbed her under her ribs. 'How long will you be gone?'

He shrugged. 'For as long as it takes. It's hard to tell.'

The casually spoken words punched her but somehow she managed to silence the agonising gasp that choked her. As she struggled for composure, a prickling feeling raised every hair on her body. 'Hang on. How come you've been assigned to a project before your last counselling session?'

His gaze suddenly moved beyond her shoulder, as if he could see someone at the window. 'After the second visit, she had no concerns so I got the rubber stamp on Wednesday.'

An insidious chill invaded her. 'You didn't tell the counsellor or Australia Aid about Harry, did you?'

His face hardened blanking his cheeks to clean slates. 'For all intents and purposes, Harry died years ago.'

'In some ways, yes, but in so many other ways, no. You and your family have been in limbo for years and no one comes away from that sort of trauma unscathed. Remember the state you were in when you first arrived in Horseshoe Bay?'

His hands flew up in the air as if she was missing the point. 'I'd just come out of a cyclone.'

'I know, but Cyclone Samuel was nothing compared to the emotional cyclone that blew through your family thirteen years ago. For all intents and purposes, you lost your entire family that year.'

'You're exaggerating.'

'I'm not.' A wave of fatigue hit her and she sat on the bed. 'Your mother hinted at what happened between all of you and your father visited me today. They're looking for ways to reconnect with you. I suggested counselling.' Charlie laughed but it wasn't the full bodied, fun-infused laugh that she loved. It was hard and harsh. 'I think I'm starting to understand why you and your father have struggled. You're both too alike.'

'We're nothing alike,' he growled. A sigh followed and he sat down next to her, picking up her hand. 'Can we please not talk about my parents? Let's concentrate on enjoying our last evening together.'

A wave of pain hit her, but before she could say anything he raised her hand to his lips and kissed it. 'I was going say all this at dinner, but somehow now seems appropriate.' He dropped a sweet and tender kiss on her forehead. 'Lauren, you're the most generous person I know. The last few weeks with you have been incredible and I don't even want to think about how I would have got through last Friday without you.'

His sea-blue eyes twinkled at her, affection warm in their depths, and then he reached into his pocket and pulled out a small jewellery box. The knot of worry that had been part of her for almost a week unravelled, spinning joyous relief into every part of her. Charlie loved her. He was committing to her. She loved him. They would both love the baby. Their jobs, his family, the baby—all the complicated stuff—they'd work it all out together.

'I've been racking my brains how to thank you and then I saw this.' He opened the box and nestled inside was an intricate silver sea star necklace with tiny diamonds filling all five arms. 'I thought it would remind you of our rock-pool rambles.'

'But we haven't been rock-pooling,' she said inanely, as her mind fought to comprehend that the necklace wasn't an engagement ring. That he wasn't proposing. That, despite everything, she'd foolishly allowed herself to fall in love with him for a second time. Once again, he was planning to walk away from her without looking back.

She always chose the wrong man. She always got it wrong.

Tell him about the baby.

But for her the equation was simple. If Charlie loved her, then telling him would be a joy. But he didn't love her so telling him risked guilting him into staying, and that would diminish her in ways she wasn't prepared to countenance. After Jeremy, she was never accepting second best again. With devastating clarity she realised that the only thing she and Charlie needed to work out was his role in their child's life.

Embryo. The scientific term centred her. After last time she wasn't naïve enough to expect that the cluster of cells multiplying inside her would develop beyond eight or twelve weeks. She hoped and prayed they would.

If she got to four months, she'd contact Charlie and if she didn't, well, history would repeat itself. The horrifying thought sent red-hot flames of anger through her wrenching despair. What the hell was wrong with this man? Why couldn't he see they belonged together? That they made each other happy? That they deserved so much more than this half-life?

'Of course we've been rock-pooling.' Charlie couldn't believe Lauren didn't remember all the wonderful hours they'd lost gazing into pools. 'Heaps of times. We even got caught by the tide once.'

Her brows drew down and she jerkily shoved the jewellery box back into his hand. 'Why would I want to be reminded of something that happened twelve years ago when you left me and I thought you were coming back, only you didn't?'

Her words slapped him and he tensed. 'I bought it because when I think of Horseshoe Bay I always think of you.'

'You wear it, then.'

Her disregard of the time and energy he'd put into choosing the gift jarred. 'So sue for me doing something nice.'

'Last time it was a stethoscope,' she muttered, rising to her feet. She crossed her arms and faced him.

For a moment, he was distracted by her impressive cleavage. 'What?'

'The last time you walked away from me, you gave me a stethoscope. It's a pattern, Charlie. Use me, buy me a gift and leave me.'

'Hey.' He shot to his feet, indignation simmering. 'I have *never* used you. I regret our misunderstanding last time and I've apologised for it. We're both consenting adults and *this time* we went into this with our eyes open. I've been very clear that I'm only in the Bay for a limited time. I never promised you more. Hell, you laid down the ground rules, not me.'

Her eyes burned hot like glowing embers, scorching him. 'It doesn't change the fact that both times we've got together, you were in the middle of a major emotional trauma. No wonder the sex was electric. You've buried yourself in me to forget.'

The accusation stung. 'The hell I did.'

'Except I turned out to be a patch, as I imagine many other women have been since, and eventually the patch lifts. All of that unresolved pain about Harry and your parents comes rushing back and it gets in the way of every aspect of your life.' Her hands flew to her face, cupping her nose. 'Oh, my God! That's why Australia Aid sent you home.'

The temptation to lift his arms over his head and protect himself from her barrage of words made his muscles tense. 'That is *not* the reason.'

Lauren threw him a pitying look. 'When you arrived in the Bay and discovered I was here, you must have thought all your Christmases had come at once. But you're kidding yourself if you think our fling's helped, because it hasn't. You haven't dealt with any of your demons and I've stupidly allowed another man to use me to make himself feel better—'

'Listen, Lauren.' The room turned a hazy red. 'I am *nothing* like Jeremy. I have never, would never, pull you down to build myself up or degrade you to make myself feel superior or smarter or...' Words failed him that she could even draw a connection between him and that jerk.

'This thing between us...' her voice rang hollow '...it's damaged both of us.'

He rolled his eyes at the drama. 'We're not damaged.'

'I'm honest enough to admit that it's damaged me. A month after you left me last time, I discovered I was pregnant.'

The thought of her eighteen, alone and pregnant reefed him so tightly he had to remember to breathe. 'You never said.'

'No.' A shadow crossed her face. 'As it turned out, I miscarried so neither of us had to make any hard decisions.'

A hundred emotions pulsed hard inside him. He shoved his hands in his pockets and gazed out the window. 'For once luck was on my side.'

'You bastard.' The word exploded over him like shrapnel—stinging, burning and lacerating him with its vitriol. 'This wasn't about you, Charlie. This was about *me*.'

He spun around to see Lauren stabbing herself with her finger. 'There's nothing logical or rational about wanting children,' she said, her voice cracking. 'It didn't matter that the timing sucked. That being a single mother would have changed my life for ever and that studying and qualifying would have been challenging, perhaps impossible. I struggled for months after the miscarriage. I loved and wanted that baby. It was part of you and I love you.'

I love you. A fleeting moment of joy flared before misery and despair doused it. Love only brought pain. If he stayed, the inevitable would happen. He'd hurt her like he hurt everyone he loved and she'd push him away. He'd hurt her and lose her. The thought gutted him. It was better not to try. 'I think you mean you loved me. Past tense.'

'Present tense.' Her eyes softened, filling with sympathy and distress. 'And before you freak out, I don't want to love you. I deserve a man who puts me first. You can't do that because you're a mess but, worse than that, you refuse to do anything about it. I lost myself once trying to fix a man who wouldn't help himself and he took me down with him. I can't do that again. I refuse to. I learned no one can fix another person, that's up to you. The fact you've bamboozled the counsellor so you can flee me, your family and the country tells me that working on your problems isn't happening any time soon. You've used me as a crutch and loving you is only hurting me. I am determined to get over you. I will get over you.'

The words pummelled him hard, raising bruising mental welts. Didn't she understand he loved her too but he was walking away to protect her? And this was the thanks he got for putting her first? A barrage of pain? Animosity stripped him of every skerrick of goodwill and he lashed out. 'At least this time you're not pregnant.'

It was the lift of her chin and the toss of her head that gave her away—that and her recent fatigue and her deep, rounded cleavage. His gut twisted. His heart cramped and his world went into freefall.

A baby. Someone else to let down.

He tore at his hair. 'I don't understand. We used condoms.'

'Believe me, I was as shocked as you. It turns out the ones we used that first night had expired.' She sighed. 'Look, it's too early to even discuss this. If the pregnancy turns out to be viable, I'll tell you, but either way, Charlie, we're over. You're off the hook. I have no expectations and, to be frank, right now you can't offer me anything other than money. I have a life here in Horseshoe Bay with my family, where I'm loved.'

She strode to the door and pulled it open. 'Go save the world because you seem incapable of saving yourself. I hope it makes you happy. Goodbye, Charlie.'

'Lauren!'

But she'd gone. If he chased her then his family would get involved and that was the last thing he needed. He rubbed his face and tried marshalling his chaotic thoughts.

Lauren's pregnant.

The thought paralysed him. He didn't have what it took to be a father. Hell, he hadn't even been able to look after his younger brother. A normal life—a wife and kids and a nine-to-five job—all of it came with too many risks. Life was safer in war zones and natural disaster areas.

You can't offer me anything other than money.

She'd hurled it as an accusation but money was exactly what he could offer. If the pregnancy became a baby, he'd get his solicitor to set up a trust fund. That would give him some peace. He'd email Lauren from the airport and tell her.

He glanced at his old faithful travel bag. Whenever he picked it up, he got a reassuring sense of who he was and where he belonged in the world. He grabbed the handle and lifted. There was a ripping sound, his shoulder wrenched and the bag dangled unevenly, banging hard into his legs. *Damn it.* What the hell else was going to hit him today?

'Going somewhere?' As if on cue, his father stood in the doorway, eyeing the broken bag with obvious disapproval.

'Java.'

'I see.' Randall stepped inside the room.

The room shrank and the air thickened. Charlie turned and looked out the window. Nothing good ever came from his father seeking him out and he refused to be pulled back into Randall's world of pain. *Have you ever left it?* He waited for his father to speak but the silence continued. Eventually, he turned around to check if he was still in the room. 'Spit it out.'

Randall rocked in his boat shoes, looking uncharacteristically uncertain. 'I wish to apologise.'

'For what?' Given the history of their fractured relationship, the last week had been remarkably free of clashes. Nothing came to mind that warranted an apology.

'For what I said to you the day Harry came off life support. And the day he went into the nursing home.'

Charlie's head shot up so fast his neck ricked but he stayed silent mostly out of stunned surprise.

The low sun streaming through the window caught the silver strands in his father's hair. 'I was devastated that my boy's life was cut short in such a random way. You expect your kids to outlive you. None of it made any sense, hell, it still doesn't, but back then I was raging against the world.' He blew out a long breath. 'I now see that the person I was most angry with was myself. I had no right to take out my guilt on you or blame you for not withdrawing treatment earlier. I'm your father and I let both my sons down when you needed me most.'

Randall's voice wavered. 'I've regretted it for a long time. I know Harry's fall was an accident. I know that everything you did for your brother was for all of us. That you did it out of love.'

There was a time Charlie had been consumed with the need to hear his father speak those words, but that was long gone and a low simmer of anger had taken its place. 'Right. Good to know you're no longer disappointed in me.'

'Disappointed in you?' Bewilderment clung to Randall. 'I've never been disappointed in you, Charles. You do amazing work and I'm proud of you.'

I'm proud of you. The surreal moment made his head spin. 'I… I didn't know that.'

'No.' Despondency cloaked Randall. 'What do all the young kids say these days? My bad? I should have told you before but pride is an Ainsworth family failing. After you rightfully told me to butt out of your life, I used that as an excuse to keep my distance. But I've followed your career closely and with great interest. Hell, I've even bragged about you at the club. Can't let Dean Grayson hog all the glory about his son.'

Charlie mustered a smile. 'Leo's research was pretty ground-breaking.'

'And you saved lives under gunfire,' Randall said quietly. 'That takes guts.'

'It was easier than being here.' The words boomed with truth but were devoid of the anger that usually tainted them.

Randall didn't flinch. 'And that's my fault. I drove you away. I'll always regret that and I'm sorry.'

Charlie hardly recognised his father, who to his knowledge had never backed down on any stand he'd ever taken. The impact of the apology sank in, easing some of the long-held hurt. 'Thank you.'

Randall gave a curt nod. 'Are you happy?'

The question hit like a sniper's bullet and he deflected it. 'I'm excited about this new assignment in Java.' *Hah! Keep telling yourself that, mate.*

'I meant outside work.'

Run. 'Not a lot of time for anything else and, talking of work, I have a plane to catch.'

His father joined him at the window and stared doggedly at the horizon. 'I buried myself in work for years and your mother buried herself in the bottom of a bottle. Last year we both had health scares. It forced us re-evaluate and make some changes.'

A fizz of fear made him ask, 'Are you and Mum okay?'

'We are. Better than we've been in years. Getting sick made us realise we'd lost a hell of lot more than just Harry.' He sighed. 'And so have you.'

You haven't dealt with your demons. Sweat broke out on his top lip. 'No need to worry about me.'

Randall's gaze hooked Charlie's. 'But I do. We all do. Your mother and grandmother. We love you. What we want most in the world is for you to be happy and content. Harry's gone. Let's honour him by living our lives the best way we can.'

A whoosh of panic jetted up. 'Look, Dad, I appreciate the apology but it doesn't open the gates to fatherly advice, okay?'

For a moment Randall was silent. 'Fair enough. I'll let you go. I promised your mother a walk before dinner anyway.' He turned then hesitated. 'I will tell you one thing all this loss has taught me. The love of a good woman and children are the greatest gift a man can ever have. It's the source of true happiness.'

This version of his father was bewildering. 'What about the heartache?'

Randall shrugged. 'Life's a bugger. Sometimes you can't have one without the other. Doesn't mean you give up and don't try.'

Right now, you can't offer me anything. Lauren's words buzzed in his head. 'What if you know you'll hurt her anyway?'

Randall squeezed his shoulder. 'Be the best version of yourself, Charlie, and the chances of that are slim.'

CHAPTER TEN

LAUREN SWALLOWED FOLATE tablets and tried not to think about Charlie. He'd be in Indonesia by now, throwing himself into work to keep his festering grief at bay. She blinked rapidly. *Do. Not. Cry.* It wasn't her fault Charlie refused to get the help he needed. But knowing that he preferred to walk away from her, rather than stay for her and deal with his demons, didn't make it any easier.

'I am strong. I will survive,' she said, having adopted it as her mantra after sobbing herself to sleep a week ago. She rubbed her belly. *We will survive.*

Right now, she was clinging to routine to get her through each day. Easter was coming up fast and although she was looking forward to the extra sleep, she wasn't looking forward to four empty days. Her parents were taking Shaylee bush camping. Lauren knew she could invite herself along but as she was barely on top of her morning sickness, camping without facilities was out of the question. So was being in close confines with her parents. She wasn't telling anyone about the pregnancy yet.

Keep busy. Motivated by the idea, she grabbed a pen and, standing at the kitchen bench, she divided a page into four boxes and wrote 'Sleep' in all of them. She chewed the pen. Perhaps she could bake hot-cross buns. The thought made her nausea rise and she reached for the mug of lemon and ginger tea.

Charlie. He'd brought her this tea after the accident at the café.

She steeled herself against the memory of all the many and varied things he'd done for her over the last few weeks. Actions that had screamed love and yet— *Do. Not. Go. There*.

Forcing her thoughts away from Charlie, grief and pain, she returned to the list. A movie at the cinema in Surfside was an option and if it was a nice day she could do a section of the clifftop walk. She opened the weather app on her phone and studied the forecast.

'May I come in?'

The deep, rumbling voice startled and frightened her, making her jump. The phone shot out of her hands, bouncing along the bench. She spun around, her heart pounding in her ears and deafening her as stared disbelievingly at the tall, fair, tanned man in the doorway. A hundred questions exploded in her mind and then adrenaline hit and she lashed out, angry that he'd scared her. 'Most guests ring the bell.'

'Sorry. I didn't mean to surprise you.' He didn't move off the back step.

She didn't invite him in. 'You're supposed to be in Java.'

'Yeah.'

'And?'

'I'm not.' He rubbed the back of his neck. 'Lauren, please may I come in and talk to you?'

Her battered heart limped in her chest and she knew she had to protect it. 'There's nothing to talk about. We said everything that needed to be said the other day.'

'I didn't.'

Don't fall for it. She knew on that horrible evening

she'd done most of the talking to a white-faced Charlie. Obviously, he'd now had time to think. Well, screw that. 'I'm not listening to you justify all the reasons why you can't love me.'

'Good.' He stepped inside, his face contorted and his eyes filled with worry. 'Because I love you.'

Her heart wobbled and her hands closed around the curve of the granite to keep her standing. Had she heard right? God, she couldn't bear it if she'd heard wrong. 'You love me?'

'Yes.'

Her thoughts scattered, unable to make any sense of his declaration. Did he really love her or—? A thought jabbed her so hard it sucked her breath away. 'Is this about the baby? Because if it is, I've already told you I don't—'

'No. I mean…well, yes, in a way but, no… It's complicated.'

She sighed. 'Of course it is. You make everything complicated.'

His mouth whitened around the edges but he didn't deny it. Instead, he opened his palms in supplication. 'I hate that I've hurt you, Lauren. I want to spend the rest of my life making it up to you. Will you let me?'

His sorrow threaded around her heart, tempting her to step into his arms and let him do exactly that, but she couldn't see how anything other than his words had changed. 'Charlie, why aren't you in Java?'

'I pulled myself off the assignment. You were right. I wasn't ready to go back to work. Truth be told, I haven't been functioning properly for a year but you were the only person who called me on it.'

She didn't know what shocked her more—his declaration of love or his acknowledgement that he had a problem. 'So, what are you doing?'

'Dealing with my demons.' He gave her a wry smile. 'I fired the counsellor. I'm seeing one who detects my BS almost as well as you do. He doesn't let me get away with anything. I've spent a lot of time squirming but so has Dad so it's been worth it just for that.'

Her world shifted just a little. 'You and Randall are both having counselling?'

He laughed at her stunned expression. 'Who knew, right? Well, you did. We're having family sessions. Mum too. It hasn't been the worst week of my life but it's right up there. We've unpacked a lot of our guilt about Harry. I thought they blamed me. Hell, I blamed me, but they were too busy blaming themselves. We got mired in that and being together was too hard because it reminded us about what we'd lost. We pushed each other away and I stayed away, because it was easier. Then I got sent home, met you again and nothing's been the same since.

'Everything I've ever told you about both of our summers together is true. I'm more grateful to you than you'll ever know. With you I'm happy in a way I've never been with anyone else. What I didn't realise was that whenever I spent time with you, my self-loathing reduced to a dull roar. I could pretend I was a better person.'

'You're not a bad person, Charlie,' she interjected hotly. 'Harry's death was an accident. You're a good person who has had a bad and life-altering event happen to him.'

'And you're my champion.' He smiled at her, love and affection bright in his eyes. 'I fell in love with you twelve years ago, Lauren, and it scared the hell out of me. I loved Harry and my parents and I'd lost them. I couldn't bear the thought of losing you too so I left first. I've always regretted it. When I saw you in Gran's living room on my first day back, I couldn't believe my luck.'

'If you've always loved me, why couldn't you tell me last week?'

'I was a mess. Things were still a nightmare with Mum and Dad and the baby news threw me for six. I couldn't stand the idea of failing my child like I believed Dad had failed me. I wanted the Ainsworth pain to stop so I ran to protect you and ended up hurting you anyway.'

He swallowed, his Adam's apple bobbing with emotion. 'Every accusation you hurled at me was true. I was avoiding anything that took me close to dealing with my grief and my family. I hate that I haven't been worthy of your love, but I'm here to tell you that I love you. I've always loved you and I'm working on earning your love back. Will you give me time to prove to you that I can be the man you deserve? That with me you'll always come first?'

His entire demeanour showed his remorse and the fact he used words instead of touch sent her resistance tumbling. All summer he'd done little things that had told her he loved her. Now he'd stepped into the emotional fires of hell to prove his love for her and he was taking the extreme and excruciating heat to heal himself and his family.

'Oh, Charlie.' Blinking back tears, she walked around the bench and wrapped her arms around him.

'Thank God,' he murmured into her hair, hugging her hard. 'I don't deserve you.'

She laughed and touched his face. 'Sure you do. You're one of the bravest and most honourable men I know. I love you more than I can say.'

He kissed her then—tender, sweet and long—infusing his love for her down to her marrow. All the way down to their baby.

He sat down and took her with him, cuddling her on his lap. 'I wanted to come sooner. Hell, I almost came back that night, but I thought I'd better arrive having done some of the hard yards so you believed me.'

'Wise man.' Her hands wove through his hair. 'What changed your mind about getting help?'

'It was something Dad said. The old man has his faults but occasionally he hits the nail on the head.'

'Don't keep me in suspense. What did he say?'

'"The love of a good woman and children are the greatest gift a man can ever have. It's the source of true happiness." Then he told me I'd be a fool not to try. But, Lauren, it's not the baby that brought me here, it's you. Of course I'd love a child but that will be the icing on the cake.'

'I hope so.'

He squeezed her hand. 'Whatever happens, we're in this together.'

Her heart wobbled. 'What about your job?'

'That's something we need to discuss. I don't want to be away from you months at a time, but I'm a trauma surgeon and Horseshoe Bay doesn't have a hospital.'

'I'm sure if we put our heads together, we can come up with a plan.'

'I like the sound of that.' He slid her off his knee onto the chair next to them and stood up before squatting next to her. 'You once told me marriage is a team event. Can I join your team and marry you?'

She leaned down and kissed him. 'Consider yourself picked.'

EPILOGUE

It was a blue-sky March day and the Ainsworths and the Fullers had gathered together for family lunch at Bide-a-While.

Randall and Ian stood with a beer in one hand and tongs in the other, each controlling a side of the barbecue with a competitive glint in their eyes.

'Of course, Lauren's got a soft spot for my marinated chicken,' Ian said as his daughter walked past.

'Patrice and I have got a soft spot for Lauren,' Randall said with a smile, raising his drink to her in thanks. 'And she needs red meat, doctor's orders, so my steak will ace that chicken.'

'If you burn it, I'm not eating either,' Lauren said, shaking her head. She never understood why everything with men was a competitive sport.

Charlie had positioned the long teak table on the sea-view side of the veranda and Patrice and Sue had decorated it beautifully with blue and white hydrangeas and sea star scatters. Lauren had contributed a salad but, really, she'd only assembled it after Charlie had done all the dicing and slicing. Marriage hadn't made her a cook but between them, and helped along by casseroles and dinners cooked by Anna and Sue, they ate well.

Charlie was dividing his time as a surgeon between

Surfside and Werribee hospitals. Although there were some late nights, he managed to be home five nights out of seven. Initially, Lauren had worried that, despite all his insistence to the contrary, the politics and lack of a need to 'fly by the seat of his pants' in a well-stocked hospital would frustrate him. None of those concerns had come to fruition. 'I want to be where you are,' he'd say whenever she asked. But he had signed both of them up to staff an Australia Aid clinic in Pipatoa at the end of the year. 'Bit of a working holiday but, I promise you, there will be plenty of time to relax.'

As long as Lauren didn't have to cook, she really didn't mind.

'Five minutes,' Randall called. It was the cue for everyone to assemble at the table.

Lauren was filling champagne glasses when Shaylee appeared on the veranda, her face pink with excitement. She was holding a large white platter heaped with creamy calamari. 'Charlie says it's our best yet.'

Lauren smiled. Cooking calamari had become a bit of a Charlie and Shaylee tradition. 'Does that mean he's been sampling pieces as he cooked?'

'Damn straight.' Charlie walked up behind her, wrapped an arm around her waist and dropped a casual kiss on her mouth.

She rose on her toes and increased the pressure, flicking her tongue tantalisingly along his lips. His hand tightened and as he pulled away, his eyes glittered. 'I'll be holding you to that promise,' he whispered.

'Yes, please.'

As Sue and Patrice whipped fly nets off the salads, Anna walked onto the veranda, holding a squawking and indignant baby. 'Someone's woken up hungry.'

'Timing, George,' Charlie said fondly, scooping his son

out of his grandmother's arms and kissing the top of his sweaty head. 'I'll change him.'

'Already done,' Anna said. 'Come and sit. Lunch is ready.'

Lauren sat down and Charlie placed their downy-haired baby boy, with his Ainsworth vivid blue eyes and his distinctive Fuller nose, into her arms. He latched onto her breast with gusty enthusiasm, his eyes fixed solemnly on hers. Her heart lurched. Four months ago he'd slithered into Charlie's arms and stolen all their hearts. George had solidified all the hard work Charlie, Randall and Patrice had put into rebuilding their relationship and his presence had fully healed what had become a clean wound. The Ainsworths were a family again and Lauren was thrilled to be part of it.

Chatter ran around the table as platters of food and bowls of salad were passed to everyone. Charlie filled a plate with food for her, teasing that, as a father, he'd expected to cut up George's food, not hers, and then he handed it to her with a fork. As George had a sixth sense about being hungry at almost the same time her meals were served, she'd become an expert at eating one-handed.

When everyone had a full plate in front of them, Randall tapped his glass and the conversation faded until the only sound was cello music playing softly in the back ground. He rose to his feet and placed a hand gently on Patrice's shoulder. 'On a day that represents our deepest sorrow, we are blessed to be surrounded by family. To Harry. With all our love.'

'To Harry,' everyone murmured, raising their glasses.

George chose that moment to pull off the breast, look around and burp loudly.

Charlie tipped back his head and laughed. 'That's got to be Harry saying G'day.'

'Remember how he used to bate me by burping loudly at the dinner table whenever I served rice?' Patrice smiled. '"Chinese custom, Mum," he'd say with a perfectly straight face.'

A few more Harry stories followed before general conversation took over and then Shaylee was clearing plates, ever hopeful it would speed up the serving of dessert. 'Can I have a cuddle?' Sue scooped a now contented George out of Lauren's arms and went and sat next to Patrice.

Lauren stood and spied Charlie standing on the lawn, gazing out to sea. She jogged down the steps and slid her arm through his, giving her daily thanks that she had the privilege of being loved by this generous and caring man. 'Penny for them?'

'I was just thinking… It's been a hell of a year.'

'Good, though.'

His blue eyes sparkled. 'The best.'

'The amazing thing is I'm confident there's a lot more to come.'

'I love you.' He pulled her in close, tucked her head under his chin and sighed contentedly. 'Thank you for loving me.'

'Right back at you.' She pressed a soft kiss to the base of his throat as his warmth circled her and the rhythmic beat of his heart tapped reassuringly against her chest.

She was home.

* * * * *

A BRIDE
TO REDEEM HIM

CHARLOTTE HAWKES

MILLS & BOON

To Derek,
thanks for reading my books.
Also, for telling people that you do so! x

CHAPTER ONE

SHE WAS STILL SHAKING.

Whether it was through humiliation, anger, or simply an utter sense of failure, Alexandra Vardy—Alex to only her closest friends, Dr Vardy to most of her patients—couldn't be sure.

Whichever it was, it wasn't now helped by the advancing form of infamous surgeon Louis Delaroche, whose smouldering, rebellious, bad-boy self had been plastered over the media for a decade. Between the tabloids, the internet and various entertainment news channels in all manner of graphic shots, the man was the hot topic of conversation at water coolers across the world on practically a weekly basis. And still nothing could have prepared her for the assault on her senses at being alone and this close to him.

Alex gripped the stone balustrade of the ornate external balcony, sucked down lungfuls of the cold night air that penetrated her one and only ballgown, and reminded herself to keep breathing.

In and out. In and out.

'Why were you discussing Rainbow House with my father?' His low voice carried in the darkness.

'Discussing?' She squeezed her eyes closed at the un-

pleasant memory of the run-in with Jean-Baptiste Delaroche. 'Is that what you call that verbal mauling?'

'Do you want to tell me what happened?'

It wasn't so much a question as a quiet command. Typical Louis. But not sinful playboy Louis; this was all pioneering surgeon Louis. The one gift he gave the world to stop it from burying him completely. She'd seen him in action and his skill was simply breathtaking.

Still, that didn't mean she was about to trust him now. Especially when her thoughts were such a jumbled mess.

'Why would I want to tell you what happened? Aren't *you* supposed to be the mercurial one of the Delaroche Duo, not your father? Isn't he the good one? The one the media hails as one of the true philanthropists of a generation?'

She had truly believed in that image of Jean-Baptiste, had really thought that he would help her once he knew what was planned for Rainbow House. It had never crossed her mind that he might have actually been party to the plans.

To her horror, Alex choked back an unexpected sob. Not with Jean-Baptiste, and not now with Louis. Part of her wanted to flee this balcony, this party, this night. But she couldn't. Not while the fate of Rainbow House still hung in the balance. The centre was the last common ground she and her father shared. If she lost that then she lost him. And they'd both lost so much already.

She might not trust Louis, but she couldn't bring herself not to listen to him.

'That's my father,' Louis concurred tightly. 'Such a good man.'

'You don't agree? Of course you don't.' She threw up her hands in desperation. 'The whole world knows there is bad blood between the two of you. Are you as jealous of your father's good name as they say you are?'

Rather than replying, he lifted his shoulders casually and turned her question back on her. The cool, unflappable, playboy Louis the media loved to hate.

'You still think he deserves his good name? After he just tried to have you thrown out of here?'

Of all the ways he might have spoken to her, Alex wasn't prepared for the hint of warmth, of kindness.

Almost as if he actually cared.

Her head swam and suddenly it all felt too much.

'I… I don't know.'

Before she could catch herself, she slumped back against the stone balustrade, trying to order the thoughts racing around her head. A fraction of a second later, Louis was shrugging off his tuxedo jacket and settling it gently over her shoulders before resuming his position between her and the doors back inside the estate house. Whether he was protecting her from any security detail should they come looking or blocking her escape, Alex couldn't quite be certain.

The only reason she'd even attended the annual Delaroche Foundation Charity Gala Ball had been in the hope that she would find a quiet moment alone to speak discreetly to the eminent surgeon Jean-Baptiste and ask him if he might possibly reconsider the foundation's unexpected decision to take over and shut down the desperately needed Rainbow House.

She could never have predicted that the media's beloved 'knight in shining scrubs' would turn on her so instantly and with such venom, even going so far as to instruct his security detail to parade her through the ballroom before throwing her out. *To make an example out of her.* Jean-

Baptiste's snarl still echoed in her head, causing fresh waves of nausea to swell up inside her.

It turned out that Jean-Baptiste might be a world-class surgeon but, contrary to newspaper talk he wasn't a particularly nice man when he chose. Briefly, she imagined telling the world what the man behind the mask was really like. But no one would ever believe her. Jean-Baptiste was an institution. If she dared to openly criticise him they'd be more likely to turn on *her*.

It was a cruel twist that now, before she'd even had time to lick her wounds, Louis Delaroche—the one man now left who had it in his power to help her, but who never would—should have taken it on himself to deal with her. Crueller still that she couldn't silence the little voice inside her that kept reminding her of that glimpse of a caring, driven Louis to which she'd so recently been privy.

But surely it was a false hope to think she could turn to Louis? Just because she'd recently seen just how deeply he cared for his patients didn't mean he would care about Rainbow House. Or that he would care about anything the Delaroche Foundation did. At the end of the day, he was still a playboy.

Work hard, play harder, that was Louis's motto. His were never mere parties but Saturnalias; he never merely drank, he caroused.

Why, face to face with him now, did it seem so difficult to remember that side of his character?

Even now, as she tilted her head to take him in, his famously solid figure now framed by the light spilling onto the balcony from the French doors behind him, she wasn't sure what to make of him.

Louis was the man who the media simply revelled in loathing. Not least because his weekly exploits—both sexual and otherwise—sold copies by their millions the world over. Since his mid-teens, Louis had been building a reputation for being larger than life with a penchant for the kind of wild parties the average person couldn't even imagine. The scandalous occasion he and his rich friends had stolen one of their parents' super-yachts for a raucous party, only to subsequently sink it, was probably one of the tamer of Louis's outings.

And he got away with it all because he was one of the most gifted young surgeons of his generation. Women wanted him and men wanted to be him. Was it any wonder his ego was as gargantuan as the rather crudely reputed size of a rather specific part of his anatomy?

Well, she wasn't going to be yet another addition to the lusting harem that had trailed around after him all evening. Neither did she have the energy for an unwanted fight with another Delaroche male this evening.

Shock still resonated through her, but something else followed it. Something stronger. An inner core strength that had got her through losing her mother and her brother. Had got her through a lifetime of disappointing her father since birth. Got her to med school, to pass top of her year, and to the placements she'd wanted most.

She would *not* cry in front of Louis. She'd already been the object of one unwarranted Delaroche temper this evening, and she'd be damned if she'd let another Delaroche take his pound of flesh, too. Steeling herself, she raised her chin to look up into the dark shadow of a face she didn't need to see to have imprinted in her mind.

'Thank you for rescuing me from the humiliation of being thrown out in front of the press waiting outside, but you have…people to get back to. And if you don't mind, I'll find a back way out of here and get safely home before your father realises I didn't get *made an example of.*'

'I don't think so.' His voice was lethally quiet. 'You still haven't told me why you were discussing Rainbow House.'

Frustration lent her courage and she let out a humourless laugh.

'The fact that you don't even know says it all.'

He took a sudden step towards her and made a sound somewhere between a growl and...*something*, his lips curving upwards into a shape so razor sharp it could hardly be called a smile.

Awareness shot through her, her heart thundering almost painfully in her chest. Her senses all immediately went on high alert, the stunning crispness of the cool night fading into nothing compared to the man in front of her. A reminder of why Louis was one of the world's most powerful eligible bachelors.

She gripped the rough stone surface of the ornate balcony tighter and it was all she could do not to back away further. To hold her ground rather than tumble over the edge. He was too distracting. A six-foot-three package of corded muscles, so lean and powerful and strong, its beauty was almost too much. No amount of scandalous headlines or scurrilous articles could have prepared her for the effect of being this close to Louis in person. And alone with him.

Not even the proximity the previous week when her mentor had granted her coveted entry into one of Louis's surgeries.

The moment when she'd seen Louis's incredible surgical skill for herself. The moment she'd seen a different side to the heinous media image when he'd shown such care and kindness to his patient and their family. And evidently the moment she'd begun to lose her grip on reality, for pity's sake.

Some small sense of self-preservation pounded inside her and she let out a disdainful, if somewhat nervous huff.

'Remind me, what *is* the collective noun for a group of immaculately coiffured, designer-ballgown-dressed, primly preening women who spend all evening zealously clamouring around a less-than-selfless playboy?'

'I believe they're called high-society contacts.' He flashed a wolfish smile that was more bared teeth and another shard of awareness sliced straight through her. Mercifully, Louis appeared oblivious. 'This is a charity ball, after all. I'm sure even you must understand that the aim is to raise as much money as possible.'

'I hardly think it's the charities they're here for,' Alex scoffed, recalling the covetous expressions on a sea of female faces when Louis had abandoned them in the ballroom in favour of her.

Only *he* could have made several hundred women look on with more envy than interest as he'd snatched her from his father's security detail, only to frogmarch her away, back through the vast estate house and finally here outside in the relative privacy of one of the many ornate stone balconies.

No doubt he thought she should be grateful to him for that much, Alex grumbled to herself as she rubbed her elbow and told herself that it was only tingly from the pain of Louis's grip. Certainly not the thrill of his touch.

That would be lunacy.

'I don't care who or what brought them here.' Louis shrugged. 'As long as they support the Delaroche Foundation. The sooner they part with their surplus money, the sooner I can say I've done my filial duty and get out of here. Which brings me right back to why you were discussing Rainbow House with my father.'

He advanced on her again, her feeling of suffocation nothing to do with the lacy choker at her throat. Because even without the name or the heritage there would never have been any denying Louis Delaroche. He carried himself in the kind of autocratic and exacting way that many men tried to emulate but few could ever master. For Louis, it seemed effortless, an intrinsic part of who he was. He only had to murmur 'Jump' and those around him would frantically turn themselves inside out to become metaphorical pole-vaulters.

Alex sniffed indelicately. Well, his ubiquitous charm wasn't going to work on her. She was determined about *that*. How ironic it would be if, after a life of trying to do the right thing, striving to be somebody worthy of living in this world, someone who could maybe one day make a difference, she should be toppled by something as prosaic as falling for the proverbial *bad boy*.

Even now Alex could imagine the sadness on her father's face. The knowledge that he'd been right about her all along. That she was worthless. That it was laughable she should have gone into medicine, a profession in which she was supposed to *save* lives when she only ever destroyed lives. *Their lives.* Her mother's and her brother's.

Mum and Jack. Or *them,* as she'd come to think of them. Grief slid over her, as a familiar as a set of scrubs yet in many ways equally as impersonal.

Not that her father ever blamed her aloud. Never made such an accusation. Never once even breathed it. Rather, it was the fact that he'd always been careful *never*, ever to mention it—never, ever mention *them*—that screamed louder than anything he could have said.

He was always so careful, her father, to keep subject matter defined. Work was fine, personal life was a no-go. Rainbow House was the only thing the two of them shared that had any connection to Mum and Jack at all.

And so her father must feel it, deep down. That kernel of loathing that she felt for herself. Rainbow House was the one good thing they shared. She *had* to save it. Whatever the cost.

That last thought helped her to steel her spine again. Lifting her head, she met Louis's stare head on, refusing to be distracted, however tempting the packaging had turned out to be.

'Rainbow House is a place for children with life-changing illnesses and their parents,' she informed him. 'A place that helps as many children as possible to find a cure, and offers respite for those who can't get the solution they need, whether it's a transplant or an operation. It sends families on that one precious memory-making holiday together, and helps fulfil as many bucket-list wishes as possible. Just the kind of place the Delaroche Foundation is famous for supporting.'

'I know what it is,' Louis remarked wryly, but the edge to his voice cautioned her.

Was she missing something? What?

'I asked why you were discussing it with Jean...my father,' he interrupted her musing, his voice sharp.

'I'd have thought you should be one of the first people to know what was going on at Rainbow House,' she snapped. 'But since you don't, here it is. Your precious Delaroche Foundation is trying to shut it down.'

'It is not my precious foundation. And even if it was, Rainbow House is part of the Lefebvre Group.'

'Which was bequeathed to you,' she announced triumphantly, ignoring the part where he'd known about the group. She wasn't sure what to make of it. Louis was hardly renowned for being interested in anything other than surgeries and sex. Although, for all his vices, he kept his great obsessions clear and distinct from one another.

She had to give him that much.

'It was bequeathed to me as a kid. But the group has

been doing a fine job of governing itself without me stepping in and wasting my time. I operate, or I party. I don't have time for charity as well.'

She couldn't fathom the expression that pulled tight across his face. As though his words didn't match his feelings on the matter. All of a sudden she remembered the Louis she'd seen in the operating room barely a month earlier.

She'd heard the stories about Louis's skill as a surgeon ever since she'd been a medical student. Only a couple of years older than her, he was already years ahead of his peers, apparently having observed his father's surgeries ever since he'd been old enough to stand on a box long enough in the OR. It was said that schoolboy Louis had been able to answer questions even second-year house officers had struggled with.

But last week had been the first—the only—time she had actually witnessed Louis in action for herself. It had been an incredible experience.

Louis didn't simply measure up to the stories, he surpassed them. A surgeon of such skill and focus that he eclipsed any other surgeon she'd seen. And when she'd mentioned it to her mentor—the anaesthetist who must have promised Louis the earth in order to get him to allow her in to observe in one of Louis's infamously closed-door surgeries—Gordon had merely rewarded her with one of his conspicuously rare smiles.

She'd finally seen what Gordon had known for years, that Louis was a pretty unique surgeon. The more she'd run back over the surgery all week, the more she'd realised that it hadn't been luck that the entire procedure had gone so smoothly, so without complication. Louis had made so many tiny, almost imperceptible adjustments so instinctively throughout the operation that he'd headed off any little bumps before they'd even had a chance to develop.

Some surgeons reacted well to incidents in the OR, others were a couple of moves ahead. Louis, though she hadn't realised it immediately, was akin to a chess grandmaster who could foresee multiple patterns ahead and then made the best single move, even if it wasn't the most obvious one.

She might even go so far as to say Louis was gifted. And after years of feeling proud—perhaps maybe even a little superior—that she was immune to some of the best-looking but arrogant doctors she'd worked with throughout her career, it was galling to realise that, of all people, playboy Louis Delaroche should be the man to breach her defences.

Not that she was about to let him know it. She rolled her eyes at him and pressed on.

'You're wrong. The board isn't doing a *fine* job at all. As I understand it, the Lefebvre Group is now almost wholly comprised of the Delaroche Foundation, ever since the death of the old chairman a few months ago. Your father's foundation has been voting to transfer various assets from the Lefebvre Group to the Delaroche Foundation, at very advantageous prices.'

'They can't do that.'

'Tell that to the board,' she spat back. 'Some of these assets they intend to keep and some they want to shut down or sell off. Rainbow House is located in the centre of town, it's prime real estate. Shut it down and any developer would pay millions for the site.'

'No.' Louis folded his arms over his body, the move only highlighting the powerful muscles there. 'That won't be why he wants to shut Rainbow House down.'

'You're telling me he has no choice?' She dragged

her gaze back to his shadowed face. 'Because I can't believe that.'

'I didn't say that he didn't have a choice. I said he isn't
driven by the money.'

Disappointment bubbled up inside her. She couldn't
explain why she'd imagined she'd sensed a possible ally
in Louis, but watching it slip from her grasp was almost
like watching her own father slip away from her. They
amounted to the same thing.

'Seriously? You, of all people, are now claiming he's
philanthropic after all?'

'I'm not claiming anything. I'm simply telling you that
selling the site for millions won't be the reason he's closing it down.'

'It's a much-needed centre. It benefits hundreds and
hundreds of children and their families. We work hard to
raise our own funds and we don't ask much more of the
Delaroche Foundation than lending their name to it.'

In that instant it was as though everything around them
had frozen, leaving only the two of them locked together
in some kind of void.

'You work there?'

'Yes.'

'Why?' The question came out of nowhere. Not a
challenge but a soft demand. Unexpectedly astute. Un-
avoidable. As though he knew she had to have a personal
connection.

She couldn't explain it, she only knew—somehow—
that it wouldn't pay to lie to him.

'I volunteer there,' Alex began hesitantly. 'With my
father. My brother was… Years ago…we used Rainbow
House.'

'Your brother?' Louis demanded sharply.

She flicked out a tongue over her lips, managing a stiff nod of confirmation.

'Yes. Jack.'

'And now?' His voice softened a fraction, he sounded almost empathetic. A flashback to the Louis who only usually emerged for his patients.

If anything, that just made it harder for her to keep her emotions in check. Alex fought to keep her voice even, the air winding its way around her.

'He died. Twenty-one years ago. He was eleven. I was eight.'

'I'm sorry.'

Simple. Sincere. And all the more touching for it.

'Thank you.'

Instantly the air finished winding its way around her and instead began slowly constricting her. Like a python immobilising its prey. And she felt she was sinking into the depths of those rich-coloured eyes.

She fought to control her heart as it hammered so loudly within her ribcage that he must surely be able to hear it. And then abruptly, rather than suffocating her, the silence seemed to cloak them, drawing them a little closer together and almost suggesting an intimacy that hadn't been there before. She realised she was holding her breath, not wanting to break the spell.

Funny, because she was usually so quick to move conversations on from talking about her brother.

'So that's why Rainbow House means so much to you.'

'Right,' she agreed, shutting off the little voice that urged her to tell him about her father.

Where did that come from? That was no one else's business but her and her father's. Certainly not Louis's. She lifted her head, determined to throw it back onto him.

'I suppose that's why I don't understand why Rainbow

House doesn't mean as much to you. Given what it meant to your mother.'

The icy change was instantaneous. She might as well have struck him physically. He reacted as though she had. Reeling backwards before he could stop himself, even as he recovered his composure.

'I don't know what that means. So when is this closure supposed to be taking place?'

It all happened so fast that anyone else might have missed it. They probably would have. But she wasn't anyone. It was her skill for observing the little things, picking up on the faintest of shifts, whether in patient symptoms, monitor readings or merely attitude, which made her particularly good at her job. A skill in which she had always taken such pride.

Right now, it was an unexpected glimpse of the less-than-perfect image of Louis that he carefully hid from eager media eyes. She couldn't help pressing him.

'It means I know your mother was Celine Lefebvre, and I know it was your maternal family who founded Rainbow House over fifty years ago when your aunt, your mother's younger sister, was diagnosed with childhood leukaemia.'

'How quaint that you know a little of my family history.'

His voice was as fascinating yet deadly as the ninja stars that her brother had always dreamed of one day being able to master. A dangerous cocktail of sadness, frustration and desperate hope flooded through her.

'I also know that your mother fought hard to keep Rainbow House open over twenty-five years ago when original Lefebvre Group members who had been appointed were running it into the ground. That was around the time she convinced your father to set up the Delaroche Foundation and oversee the group until you were of an age to take control. I'm guessing that she expected to train you to run it but…she never got the opportunity.'

'Which means it's nothing to do with me now.'

She wished more than anything she could decipher that expression behind his concrete-coloured eyes. But the longer she stared into them, the more unreachable he seemed to be. Her voice rose in desperation.

'She left control of Lefebvre Group to you. You could stop the foundation from doing this. Surely, for the sake of her memory, it shouldn't be so far beneath your concern?'

'Careful.'

It was one word of caution and it shouldn't have sounded so menacing. So full of control. But it had, and Alex shivered, feeling the sharp edges of the stonework cutting into her fingers.

'Rainbow House meant everything to your mother. The stories people have about her are limitless. She's a legend with everyone I know there.'

He turned his face a fraction, inadvertently allowing the light from inside to illuminate him. But she wasn't prepared for the expression of pain that pulled his features tight. It sliced at something raw deep inside her, something that she'd spent decades trying to bury. She slammed it away before it could get to her.

'I have no intention of getting involved,' Louis bit out.

'Is that why you rescued me from your father, then?'

She could hear the quiver in her challenge, knew Louis could hear it, too. Still, she refused to back down.

'I didn't want to see you humiliated in front of the press. It wouldn't have made the Delaroche Foundation look good, especially on such an important gala night.'

'Rubbish.'

She had no idea where her courage was suddenly stemming from, but she wasn't about to question it.

'You wanted to know why we were talking about Rainbow House. You can tell me you don't want to get involved all you like, but clearly you do want to. Clearly a part of you *needs* to.'

'How interesting that you appear to know me so well.' He flashed his teeth at her in another intimidating non-smile. 'Let me guess, you know that Jean-Baptiste and I don't get on so you think I'd be prepared to go up against him with the board because of some sentimentality over a place my mother once patronised.'

'It's more than that, and you know it.'

She valiantly ignored the way her heart somersaulted within her chest. The way his mannerisms spoke to something undefinable within her. A blasé attitude that masked a vulnerability he didn't want anyone to see.

No doubt anyone else would have believed him. He sold smouldering disinterest all too well and even she herself couldn't help but be drawn in. Louis was stunning, and edgy, and utterly mesmerising. But she was sure she could see past the front. That particular emotional Achilles' heel was something she recognised only too easily.

'It's true that vastly exaggerated stories concerning some feud between Jean-Baptiste and me—his prodigal son—have been gleefully published by the press for almost a decade—'

'You mean two brilliant surgeons, bonded by blood, united by mutual contempt?' Alex cut across him. 'Yes, I might have heard something about that. It's a media favourite.'

'Indeed. But that doesn't mean I care enough to take on Rainbow House merely to thwart him. It would cut into my playboy lifestyle too much—surely you've read about that, too?'

'I think it's an act,' she heard herself state boldly. 'I

think you and your father have been in competition for as long as you can remember. He's one of the most image-conscious men I've seen, and I think your infamous play-boy routine was your way of sullying the Delaroche name.'

'Nice theory. And if it was true, I'd say it's a resounding success, wouldn't you?' He quirked an eyebrow as though she amused him.

But Alex wasn't finished yet.

'Ah, but it hasn't worked as well as you'd hoped, has it? Because as much as the media love to hate you, they also hate to love you. If they ever realised quite how much you care for your patients, I think they'd be having bank holi-days in your honour. No wonder you keep such a close-knit team around you—can't have people realising you're actually a good guy underneath that bad-boy exterior.'

Something skittered over Louis's face.

'And that fantastical notion is what you're basing your hopes on? You're relying on some non-existent version of me to save Rainbow House?'

'Why not?' She shot him an over-bright smile. If he was her last chance then she might as well go down fighting. 'Besides, it's not such a fantastical notion if I'm not the only one who thinks you could save the place.'

She had him. She could see it. And it gave her a thrill to realise she had hooked him so easily. But reeling him in, that was going to be the impossible part.

'Go on then,' he conceded, and she had to give him credit for not trying to disguise his intrigue.

'Half of your board.'

'Allow me to let you onto a little secret. Even if I wanted to save the place, I couldn't.'

'You could. All you have to do is take over control from the Delaroche Foundation, the way your mother always intended you to do.'

'Are you always this argumentative?' His lips twitched and Alex wrinkled her nose.

'I'm not arguing, I'm only pointing out—'

'So it's just me, then? I suppose I should take it as a compliment that I get under your skin.'

'You do *not* get under my skin,' Alex huffed, before realising that her fists were clenched into balls, hidden as they were by Louis's jacket. 'Well, if you do then it's only because I find it frustrating that you could help us—that you spend your professional life saving people, even if your personal life is in the gutter—and yet you stand on the sidelines and refuse to get involved.'

'You've got it all wrong,' Louis bit out. 'You're looking at me like some kind of white knight, but there's a reason Jean-Baptiste has that reputation and I don't. Besides, as I was saying before, I couldn't help you even if I wanted to. My mother might have left control of Rainbow House— or, more to the point, the Lefebvre Group—to me in her will, but not before my father had her insert a clause making one further stipulation.'

'Stipulation?'

'I have to be married.'

'Married? You?'

He simply shrugged. 'Quite. So you see there's no point looking to me to rescue you. Unless you care to marry me then I'm the last person who can help you.'

CHAPTER TWO

'YOU MUST BE DRUNK.' The disdainful wrinkle of her nose cut him far more than it should. 'As usual.'

'Most probably,' he lied smoothly, knowing he couldn't blame her low opinion of him entirely on the media.

But the truth was that he hadn't had a drink in months, maybe even the best part of a year. And even then it had been a rare brandy with a close friend. Ironic how easily water could be mistaken for vodka, if that was what aligned better with people's assumptions.

Strange thing was that he hadn't missed the alcohol or the wild parties. The latter had never made him feel any less alone, whilst the former had never even made a dent in the block of ice that had encased his heart for as long as he could remember. Or at least ever since his mother's... *death*. But, then, he'd never wanted it to.

Until recently.

If he'd been able to foresee how his first few dates with the it-girls of the moment would have resulted in a sex story that would define his playboy reputation for the next decade and a half, he might have thought twice about something that had been meant to be *harmless, private fun*.

Now it proved impossible to change. People didn't want to see him grow up.

Worse, he couldn't be bothered to prove it to them.

'Nonetheless, a marriage clause remains,' he proclaimed. 'And clearly I don't intend to satisfy that particular parameter.'

'Oh, but that's ridiculous!' the woman exclaimed, *sotto voce*, wrenching him mercifully back from the precipice of memory. 'I know the Delaroche family can trace its ancestry back to thirteenth-century aristocracy, with a palace for a family home, but this is the twenty-first century. Why would they have put such a clause in?'

'Perhaps for the very reason of thwarting you now.' Louis grinned, enjoying the way she flailed her arms around in frustration.

'Very amusing.' She glowered at him.

'Thank you.' He tried for modesty, but not very hard. 'And it's twelfth century.'

'Pardon?'

'Twelfth-century aristocracy, not thirteenth. And it isn't a palace but a chateau which, quite frankly, is mostly cold and draughty despite the modern improvements. We do, however, have a moat and a drawbridge.'

'As so many of us do.' She affected a deep sigh but her eyes twinkled and sparkled, and made him feel so much more *alive* than he had felt in…a long time.

He shifted to the side slightly to allow the light from inside to fall on her face. Pretty, wholesome, yet with a mouth that he wondered if she realised was as sinful as it was. He watched in absorbed fascination as emotions danced across her features like any one of the ballets he'd accompanied his mother to on the promise of an afternoon of ice cream and activity of his choice. But it had never been a chore, for either of them.

She'd been fun like that, his mother. And they'd been close. Or at least he thought they had been. He still found it hard to accept that she'd taken her own life. Had chosen to leave him. Even now, when he thought back over his life, those first seven years with her were still in vibrant Technicolor. He could even still hear her laughter, so unrestrained, so frequent. And then she'd…gone, and everything since had just been different hues of black and grey. Only his surgeries gave him that same feeling of invincibility.

And now this woman, whose name he didn't even know, had streaked into his life with a burst of colour and he couldn't explain it.

'You know, you could get married if you wanted to,' she said, a note of desperation in her tone.

'I beg your pardon?'

'Don't look at me like I'm mad.' She scrunched up her face. 'But you could. Any one of those women down there would leap at the chance to marry you.'

'Are you suggesting I get married just to inherit control of a place I don't even care about?'

'You do care,' she pointed out. 'You wouldn't have rescued me from your father or indeed still be here, talking to me about it, if a part of you didn't care.'

'You're mistaken.' Louis frowned. 'And as for the idea of marriage, you really think it would be morally just to inflict *playboy me* on any woman?'

She actually snorted at him. No one had ever done that in his life. She was either very brave or very foolish.

He found he was intrigued to discover which it was.

'If you put the idea out there, I can see a whole host of volunteers ready to play the part just to be married to Louis Delaroche.'

'Is that so?'

'That's so.' She nodded firmly and he tried not to let his eyes slide to the way it made her breasts jiggle in that sexy sheath of a dress.

Man, what was wrong with him? *Jiggle?* Really?

'It's honestly that simple,' she insisted, dragging him back to the present. 'You get married and the Lefebvre Group passes to you.'

'I'm sorry,' he couldn't help but tease her, 'you're putting *marriage* and *me* into the same sentence and you're calling it simple?'

She wrinkled her nose again and the guileless, girlish mannerism shot straight to his sex. So different from the manipulative females he'd been dating for too long. Who he was better off dating, because they were as jaded as he was.

Alex wasn't jaded.

Alex was vibrant, and direct, and he felt as though she was breathing new life into him.

He should leave now. Before he sucked all the life *out* of her.

'And how about you?' He dropped his voice to a whiskey-gruff tone.

Unable to quash the urge to seduce her.

It worked, as he'd known it would. If she glowed any brighter, one of the helicopters bringing guests in to the ball might have mistaken her for a helipad beacon.

'Sorry?'

'How about you? Would you be prepared to play the part, just for me to save Rainbow House?'

He told himself he'd meant it as a joke, to see how far he could push her. He suspected that wasn't the real reason.

'Not if you were the last hope for mankind.'

She tipped her chin up with defiance, meeting his gaze as though she was completely immune to the obvious attraction that sparked and cracked between them. But he knew how to read people, how to read women, and the staining on her cheeks revealed that she wasn't as unaffected as she pretended to be.

'It seems you have me at a disadvantage.' He held his hands palms up in placation. 'Since you know who I am, while, regrettably, I don't know who you are, shall we start over, this time with introductions?'

She narrowed her eyes, apparently searching for a catch. Her breath was still coming out a little raggedly. He took care not to focus on it. Or the way her pulse flickered at the base of her throat in a way that seemed to scrape inside him.

'Alexandra Vardy,' she acknowledged at length, although her tone was clearly still defensive. 'Alex.'

'Alex, then,' he replied. Then frowned. 'Alex Vardy? I know that name.'

She appeared pleasantly surprised despite herself, even if she subsequently shook her head, as though it didn't make any difference.

'I was in your surgery last week.'

'I don't think so,' he challenged her. 'My surgeries are strictly closed-door procedures. I attract too much press interest. The last thing my patients need are journalists sneaking in because they can watch one of my surgeries without being challenged.'

'The cervical cerclage on the woman with the twenty-week-old foetus,' Alex answered softly.

He raised his eyebrows, scrutinising the woman again.

'Indeed. Well, since you were in my surgery, for the record, her name was Gigi Reed. And she'd already named her unborn baby Ruby, just in case.'

'You remember their names?'

'It was a difficult case.'

'Not for you.' She eyed him anew. As though reassessing him.

Louis gave himself a metaphorical kick. He shouldn't have let her know he knew his patients' names. Gifted but arrogant, that was his reputation and he was fine with that. He didn't need anyone outside his trusted team to realise that he could probably name every patient he'd ever operated on, as well as linking them to their procedure.

What was it about this woman that fired him up the way she did?

People mattered to him. His patients mattered. They always had.

'The additional complications in this case and the fact that the woman turned out to be such a high-profile businessman's daughter have made it a high-interest story.' He went for one of his famous shrugs. 'Hard to forget her name.'

'Except that Ruby's name has never been mentioned.'

She didn't let up, this woman. He shouldn't find her tenacity so appealing.

'Fine, you've got me. I remember my patients' names. They matter to me. Their procedures matter to me. And Gigi's was a good operation. She'd suffered three miscarriages in the past, probably what had weakened her cervix. Stitching it closed might help prevent premature labour.'

He didn't add that the procedure carried significant risks, or that every minute, hour, day was crucial. He didn't need to. Alex clearly understood that or she wouldn't have been in his OR. The question was, who had let her in, and did some heads need to roll?

'It's a hail-Mary procedure that very few surgeons could have even attempted. Fewer still could have actually pulled it off.'

She bit her tongue before she could add whatever else it was she had been about to say. He found himself strangely curious. About what this woman...what Alex thought of him? He eyed her thoughtfully. Finally breaking free of her spell, falling back on what he knew best.

He advanced on her, watching with grim satisfaction as she braced herself, her eyes darkening with the mutual attraction she clearly didn't want to acknowledge.

'So you're Gordon's protégé.'

Another humble blush.

'I wouldn't put it quite that way.'

'I would.' His eyes never left her. He took another step towards her, watching her every reaction. 'He speaks exceptionally highly of you. He really fought your case for you to be in that surgery. I don't just let anyone in, you know.'

Was he still talking about his surgeries, he wondered, or had the conversation suddenly split off into a second, less overt direction? When had he let that happen? He deliberately advanced again.

'You should.' She almost covered the slight quake in her voice and he flashed another wolfish grin. 'You're an exceptional surgeon—any doctor would be inspired by watching you.'

The unexpected compliment caught him off guard. Why did it mean more when it came from this stranger's lips?

'Should I be offended that you sound so surprised?' he drawled in an effort to conceal his rare unsettled state. 'I understood my reputation as far as my career went was exemplary.'

The hollow, unimpressed laugh unbalanced him even further and Louis didn't know what to think. He was always in control, always so assured that he found this current state of flux anathema.

'True, but with your hand-picked teams and closed surgeries, which most of us mere mortals have never actually witnessed in person, you'll forgive us for considering that your shining reputation could have been coloured by the simple fact that you're a Delaroche.'

'Is that so?'

'It is.' She affected a shrug. 'There's only one thing I don't understand.'

'Oh, and what's that?'

'The Delaroche Foundation has been given credit for the entire Gigi Reed procedure in the press. His name might not have been mentioned outright but the leaked article in the paper certainly made it appear that Jean-Baptiste was the surgeon, not you. Yet neither you nor any of your close-knit team has bothered to set the record straight.'

Why was it suddenly so hard to shrug it off as he would have had no trouble doing had anyone else been asking him?

'It's good for the Delaroche brand.'

The line his father had fed him since he'd performed his first exciting surgery. Jean-Baptiste's successes were his own. Louis's successes were those of the foundation.

And he didn't care. Because, really, what else could his father take from him that he hadn't already taken? Plus more accolades meant more expectation, which in turn meant more responsibility. And up until recently he'd been content with just his surgeries and his hedonistic lifestyle, as the media seemed so fond of calling it.

'I've heard you say that before.' She glanced at him astutely. 'To the press. How many times have you passed up taking credit for something that would have improved your godawful reputation with the media?'

'What if I don't want to improve my reputation? What if my playboy label gets me more…*benefits* than getting the credit for weird surgeries ever would? Besides, despite everything, I already have a good reputation with the media as a surgeon, so why worry about more?'

'Given how well documented your sexual exploits have been in the media over the past decade, it's a miracle you even know what day it is half of the time. Shame. I heard from Gordon that you were a decent enough lad in your late teens. A bit arrogant, conceding that you were in med school while other kids your age were still doing their A Levels. Then suddenly you turned into the player of the century.'

He arched one eyebrow in quasi-amusement and watched her swallow once, twice. The sexual tension between them was unrelenting.

'And you wonder why my father reacted as he did. Are you always this combative?'

'I wasn't at all combative with your father,' Alex retorted hotly. 'I'm not a confrontational person.'

'I find that hard to believe.' Although, as it happened, he didn't find it hard to believe at all.

The mutual attraction was messing with his head almost as much.

He folded his arms across his chest, as if entertained. A move that he knew from experience only enhanced the strong muscles in his chest, his biceps, even his forearms. Muscles he had acquired through serious hours pounding the streets or in his home gym in a futile effort to exhaust himself into sleep pretty much whenever he had time on his hands and no stupid party to distract his racing thoughts.

Despite her obvious inner fight, Louis watched as Alex tracked his every movement with her eyes, lingering longer than he knew she wanted to.

'So you're Apple Pie Alex.'

'I've never liked that nickname,' she bit out.

He ignored her, knowing his amusement only riled her up even more and wondering why he felt so compelled to keep pushing her as he was.

'Why do you suppose your colleagues call you that? Because you're wholesome and sweet, or because you're boring?'

For some reason, it cut right through her even though she tried not to let him see it. Instead, she rolled her eyes with a hefty dose of melodrama to distract him.

'Because apparently I'm comforting. Just like my grandmother's recipe for apple pie, which I foolishly brought in one day.'

'Comforting?' His chuckle rumbled out of nowhere. When was the last time he'd wanted to tease in this way? 'What? In the same way that a tankful of piranhas is comforting?'

'I'm very even tempered,' she snapped.

'I can see that. And for your next trick...?'

It was intended as a gentle ribbing, but by the expression on Alex's face she was genuinely struggling with her supposedly out-of-character attitude. He felt chastened, and yet he got a thrill out of this verbal sparring with her.

'I was polite and respectful with your father,' Alex said firmly.

'So, like I pointed out earlier, it's just me.'

'Yes.' She nodded, making him grin again, much to her chagrin. 'No. Oh, you're impossible. I just meant that I'm more on edge now, after...your father.'

'You're even cuter when your temper flares.'

'And you're condescending.'

'So I've been told,' he replied, unfazed. 'Many, many times before.'

'We're just going around in circles here, aren't we?' she said through gritted teeth. Then abruptly pushed off the balcony and sashayed past him, apparently tired of the conversation.

He wasn't sure that anyone had ever tired of a conversation with him before. Certainly they'd never walked away from him. He felt something like admiration surge inside him. As well as something more recognisable. Like lust.

'Come, now,' he admonished. 'You can't really be leaving. You haven't even heard how I plan to help.'

She didn't even turn around, merely slowed her walk and cast her head over one delectably bare shoulder.

'So you finally *do* plan to help? That's a start, I suppose. All you need now is to return to your harem and decide which one of them you'd prefer to join you in no doubt unholy matrimony.'

'Oh, I've already decided that.'

'Really?' She spun around in surprise. 'You really are going to do this, then?'

It was just that Alex was a challenge, Louis told himself. And normally he would relish the challenge. All too often he would have beautiful women falling over each other to throw themselves at him. He wasn't proud of the fact that he indulged, frequently and indiscriminately, but it had suited his bad-boy reputation and he'd often told himself that he was just a red-blooded male like any other. But sometimes a challenge was fun. Especially if it came in the kind of package standing in front of him and pretending she wasn't fighting the chemistry sizzling between them.

But right now wasn't normal.

It all came back to the name he hadn't heard in years. Decades even.

Rainbow House.

He'd thought about it more tonight than he had in all the last years combined, banishing it from his head to the pitch-black depths of nothing, with all the other painful memories of the happy life before his mother had gone from it. But what had pretending it didn't exist accomplished? His mother was still gone and Rainbow House had been one of her legacies. Even decades on it shouldn't amaze him that his old man was still trying to erase every last one of them.

For the first time Louis had a compulsion to stop him. To save at least one good thing his mother had achieved. He told himself it had nothing to do with the captivating woman currently gliding away from him. He couldn't explain why Alex talking about the place should reinvigorate it with such colour, such life. He only knew he wasn't ready to relinquish it—relinquish *her*—just yet.

'I've made my choice, but I might need your help,' he announced gravely, watching her take a single step back to him almost against her will.

'My help?'

'Sure.' He strode towards her, supressing a grin at the way she flicked a tongue out so deliciously over her lips. 'You don't think it's going to be easy for me to get any potential father-in-law to agree to giving me their daughter's hand in marriage?'

The closer he got, the more she leaned the top half of her body away from him. But her feet remained planted in place, almost as if her head was telling her to back away but her body was telling her something quite different.

He knew the feeling.

'Oh, come on.' She gave a bark of laughter. 'You can't really expect me to believe you'd do something so chivalrous?'

'Why not?'

'Because…well, because…you're you.'

'Nice that you noticed.' He really shouldn't be enjoying himself this much. 'But as it happens, I do like the odd tradition now and then. My family is, as you say, traceable back to the twelfth century.'

'You don't say?' She widened her eyes in mock surprise. 'Then surely any potential father-in-law would be falling over themselves to literally throw their daughters into your arms. Particularly the classy women you date.'

'I'm shocked that you would cast such aspersions, Dr Vardy. Nonetheless, I have the distinct suspicion that it was matter of charming half of their daughters into bed out of wedlock that must have turned them against me in the first instance.'

'Only half?' she quipped tartly. Too tartly.

'No, well, one can't be too greedy.' He shrugged dismissively, neatly changing the subject. 'Of course, you appreciate that the more you lean back from me the more you angle your hips towards me? One might even say *invitingly.*'

Her eyes widened, her scowl deepening, and she faltered backwards just as he'd known she would, giving him the perfect opportunity to reach forward and halt her fall, hauling her body closer to his as he did so.

'You did that deliberately,' she said irritably, though he noticed that for all her objection she remained in the light circle of his arm, though she could have pushed him away if she'd really wanted to.

It only served to fuel Louis's desire. He could tell himself that this was all part of his plan and that he was still in control, but he knew that somewhere along the line, that had ceased to be entirely true. He could no more explain this attraction as he could fight it. He'd been attracted to women—plenty of women, though nowhere near in the disgusting numbers that the papers so deliriously hypothesised—but never like this. Never on a level that he knew wasn't merely about the physical.

'I can't seem to help myself,' he drawled, his tone intended to conceal just how unexpectedly close to the truth that statement was.

Even now, as his eyes took in the rapid pulse at her neck, the stain of lust spreading over her skin, the sudden huskiness in her voice, doing something as simple as drawing a breath suddenly became an arduous hindrance.

He leaned forward and she stepped back. Right up against the stone balustrade, allowing him to place an arm on each side and effectively cage her.

'What are you doing?' she whispered. Hardly a protestation of his position. Still, he needed to be sure.

'Making sure you don't run away.'

'I'm not running away.' He recognised that hoarse desire in her voice. He'd heard it plenty of times before. But never with anyone who made him as hard as she did.

Like he was some hormone-charged teenager.

'You know my reputation,' he ground out. 'You should be running.'

'I know your reputation,' she concurred. 'But right now I don't know anyone else who can help me stop your father.'

It was hardly the rebuttal he realised a part of him had been hoping for. As if he hoped she might see past the bad-boy exterior to the honourable man he knew had probably died a long time ago.

Pathetic really.

Louis had never wanted, never sought anyone else's approval. He would leave that to his father. Though how he was the only person to see through his old man's veneer to see that he'd only set up the Delaroche Foundation as a way to earn himself a knighthood, he would never understand. Let Jean-Baptiste revel in his unearned glories as much as the vainglorious old man wanted.

His mother would surely laugh out loud to know that Rainbow House was still a thorn in her husband's side. Even now.

It was only when he caught Alex watching him curiously, his arms still trapping her in place, that he remembered himself, and banished the unwelcome thoughts from his head.

He pushed backwards, releasing her with a theatrical flourish, exultant when she didn't go anywhere.

'So, Dr Alexandra Vardy, how about it?' He flashed her a wolfish smile, playing the habitually drunk playboy role for all he was worth. After all, why else would a bad boy like him make such a ridiculous suggestion? 'Want to marry me and stop my father from committing any more of his dastardly deeds?'

CHAPTER THREE

'SOMEONE PAGED ME?' Louis burst through the doors of the pre-op room, taking in the unfolding events in one careful sweep.

'I did. I suspect an anaphylactic reaction in your patient,' Alex answered quickly but calmly, her attention going straight back to the patient in front of her even as she addressed the anaesthetic technician. 'Freddie, let's set up an IV. Start with eight milligrams of dexamethasone and point one milligrams of adrenalin.'

'What happened?' Louis stepped over quickly without, she just had time to notice, getting in the way of her staff.

Surprisingly he didn't wade in, but waited silently for her to finish issuing her brief, perfunctory instructions to her team.

It could be no coincidence that she had suddenly been assigned as part of Louis's on-call team tonight. She'd been avoiding him for two days since she'd walked—though she still had no idea how her legs had kept her upright after his audacious marriage suggestion—away from away him.

Clearly, this was his way of flexing his authoritative muscle. An irrefutable demonstration of the power he wielded in this hospital. She'd spent the last few hours enacting scenarios in her head in which she had confronted him about it. But right now it definitely wasn't the time.

'The patient was clearly hypovolaemic when she was brought in,' Alex informed him. 'She was clammy in appearance and tachycardic.'

'She presented in the emergency department a couple of hours ago following a salpingo-oophorectomy three days ago,' confirmed Louis. 'All signs led the resus team to suspect intra-abdominal bleeding, which was when they referred her to us.'

Cool, professional, approachable. No hint that he even remembered what had happened between them on that balcony. How she had been within a hair's breadth of kissing him, of letting him kiss her. If he'd pushed it that tiny bit further, she knew she would have.

Every spare moment since, she'd wondered why he hadn't.

Was it insane that every time she'd thought of him, a gurgle of laughter had rumbled within her?

The thing about arrogant men was that they had altogether too high an opinion of themselves to be likeable.

Yet Louis was wholly unaffected by his stark male beauty, and he didn't take himself too seriously. He made her laugh.

It didn't fit.

Still, she couldn't afford to dwell on it. Forget her illicit fantasies about him, he was standing right in front of her, right now, and he was all professional. The way she always prided herself on being.

She pulled her head back in the game, relieved to realise that she hadn't missed a beat.

'Yes, I completed the handover twenty minutes ago. She appeared calm despite the circumstances. Blood pressure was one-twenty over seventy and heart rate was eighty-four beats per minute. Intravenous access was difficult, probably as a result of the hypovolaemia and the suspected internal bleeding, but she did have a cannula in situ, which we used.'

'You used it for general anaesthetic induction?'

'Right, then we intubated.' Alex nodded. 'There was an initial delay of results for the carbon dioxide output but the tubes were in correctly, there was misting and the chest was rising symmetrically. I began manual ventilation, which I thought felt restricted, and when I listened to her chest I heard wheezing. I had already started to suspect anaesthesia-related anaphylaxis, which was when I told them to alert you to the situation.'

There had been no need for Louis to come in. As the anaesthetist, this was within her remit rather than his, but she could understand why he wanted to see for himself. In many respects she was still an unknown quantity to his team. Typically Louis.

'You're using her foot—?'

'To gain additional venous access? Yes,' Alex cut in, straightening up with a satisfied nod and taking the bag of colloid fluid from her team. 'Good. Right, let's start infusing and get her blood pressure back up and her cardiovascular volume. Freddie, start drawing up another point one milligrams of adrenalin.'

But before she could get much further the patient went into cardiac arrest.

'I'll start compressions.' Louis moved instinctively to the table, allowing her to continue administering the adrenalin.

They both knew that while in ordinary circumstances the surgical procedure would be called to a halt, due to the acute nature of the internal bleeding, it wasn't an option in this situation. She had no choice but to get it under control.

Good thing she'd never been one to crumble under pressure.

Still, it was a relief when Louis confirmed cardiac output had been regained and Alex was able to insert both a central and femoral line, even as she issued further instructions to her team to treat the anaphylaxis before continuing their pre-op procedures.

'You're re-administering anaesthesia?' He frowned, still watching her closely.

Her pride kicked in. She couldn't help it.

'I thought I might.' The tongue-in-cheek tone was clear but now the patient was stable, and after the tension the team had been under a little dark humour always worked to buoy morale. It was just the way hospitals seemed to work, in her opinion.

It wouldn't make the team work any better to keep stress levels high. Still, she kept her eyes on the monitoring equipment as she spoke.

'If it's internal bleeding then I can't imagine you could afford to postpone the operation, and with all the excitement the last thing the patient needs is to come out of the anaesthetic in mid-operation, wouldn't you agree?'

'Never preferable,' he agreed, as she concluded her tasks and gave him a slight nod. 'We're ready?'

'Ready,' she confirmed, knowing that, even if the surgery was carried out quickly and without incident, the postoperative management was going to be crucial.

It was going to be a long night. And yet, when the patient came out of it treated and cared for, it made it feel like the best job in the world.

If only she didn't have Louis to deal with at the end of it.

* * *

'Good call on the anaphylaxis case.'

Alex visibly stiffened as he called to her from across the atrium. It was a deliberate ploy on his part so she couldn't continue to duck out, having pretended not to see him, as she had been doing for the last nine hours.

And the atrium was the perfect trap. During the day it was a bustling hub of staff, visitors and mobile patients. Right now, it was relatively deserted, save for the trio around Alex's small table. It was one of the reasons he'd chosen this moment to corner her, when the fewest people were gawking. But she didn't need to know that.

Let her think he hadn't considered her at all.

He couldn't disappoint that way.

He sipped his coffee and sauntered deliberately over to where they sat, pulling out a chair and sliding down easily into it. Alex barely glanced up as the over-eager pair began falling over each other to introduce themselves to him, and he politely acknowledged them then affected insouciance, all the while taking in every possible detail.

By the expressions and body language of the group he'd lay a bet that the two women had barely socialised with Alex before yesterday's papers had come out, and more specifically the grainy, pixelated image of him escorting her out of the kitchen entrance of the gala event the other night—clearly taken by one of the kitchen staff on their mobile phone, he was already dealing with them—and suddenly Alex had become everyone's new best friend.

Another thing he was guilty of.

Louis managed to smooth out the grim expression before it could settle on his lips. He refused to apologise or feel remorse. It had been him or being publicly ejected through the main doors by the security team. Though she'd probably have been the first woman to choose the security team after his outlandish proposal to her.

There was no reason for him to still be grinning about it.

'Ladies, it's a pleasure to meet you but I wonder if Alex and I could have moment?'

She sucked in her breath audibly and he knew what was coming the moment the women left the room. Sure enough, as soon as the doors slammed Alex practically exploded.

'Oh, why don't you just drive a tanker of fuel into the damned fire?' she seethed. 'They'll be gossiping all over the hospital as we speak.'

'Isn't that the idea?' He grinned. 'Generate publicity and all that.'

Her eyes narrowed.

'The papers are already speculating, thanks to that photo,' she hissed. 'Grubby little rumours about how I'm the latest notch on your bedpost.'

'Ah, well, the quicker you agree to marry me, the less *grubby* they can make it. The story will go international and you'll be the woman who tamed me.'

'No woman will ever tame you,' she snorted. From anyone else he would have taken it to be a compliment, but for some reason her contempt needled at him.

He pointedly ramped up his grin.

'Of course not. But the story is bigger if they think you have. And the more publicity the more chance we can help Rainbow House before my father gets his way.'

She frowned.

'I thought that if you got married, you got control of the Lefebvre Group and then Rainbow House and others like it would be safe anyway.'

'You might think that,' he agreed, carefully concealing his amusement that she'd just revealed she had actually been considering it, despite her rather vocal rejection

of the idea last night. 'But I've been looking into the specific clauses ever since the gala. It seems that unless we
get married before the official vote on any transfers then
any such decisions will still carry through.'

'For pity's sake.' A torn expression contorted her face.

So this was what it felt like to be such a heel, putting
more pressure on her than she already had. But, then, she
was the one asking for *his* help. She just needed to set her
prejudice against him aside for long enough to agree this
was the only way given the short timeframe she'd given
him.

Not that he really blamed her for her vacillation. He'd
hardly set himself up to be keen to help.

The sound of her fingers drumming on the plastic table
echoed in the vaulted space.

'Why?' she demanded abruptly.

'Why what?' It was a feeble attempt to stall but her
question had caught him off guard.

'Why do you want to help Rainbow House at all?' She
eyed him shrewdly. 'You didn't when I first asked you. And
then said you did but really it was all a joke to you. Yet
suddenly you're getting me onto your surgical team and
trying to collar me in public places. So, what's going on?'

Louis arched one brow.

'You know what they say. It's a surgeon's prerogative
to change his mind.'

'No one says that, Louis.'

'I do.'

'Yeah, well, as far as I'm concerned, you don't count.'

He feigned a hurt expression.

'You cut me to the quick.'

'I highly doubt it. But if I did, I suspect that with the
number of women literally falling over themselves to bag
you, I'm sure you'll get over it remarkably quickly.' She

crossed her arms over her chest and he resisted the impulse to tell her that the action only thrust those pert breasts of hers to the fore.

He could save winding her up with that one for another day. Right now he was enjoying the show too much. Namely the *Feisty Alex* routine; so far removed from the wholesome *Apple Pie Alex* but which, now he'd done a little digging, he'd discovered was a closely guarded fact amongst a select handful of her closest friends, Gordon being one of them.

What did it say about him that he actually *wished* to be part of Alex's select circle?

'So, should I take that as your answer then?'

He snapped back to the present.

'Say again?'

'I asked why you really wanted to help me suddenly. You chose to deflect in your usual manner.'

'You don't pull any punches, do you?' His grin widened.

'With you? No. I don't think I can afford to.'

'I like that,' he mused, taking another long swig of his coffee. She might want something from him but she wasn't about to pander to him. He was all too accustomed to people pandering to his wishes. Not least in the bedroom. 'That why I think you'd be the perfect marriage choice.'

'I'm flattered,' she drawled. 'So why not tell me why you're so fixated on your marriage idea all of a sudden.'

'It wasn't my plan,' he reminded her smoothly. 'It was *your* plan. You're the one who asked me to help. And you're the one who suggested I get married simply to satisfy the clause in my mother's will.'

'Well…yes,' Alex faltered. 'But…but not to *me*.'

'You really want me to inflict this charade on some other woman?'

Why was he enjoying this quite so much?

'I doubt they'd feel remotely *inflicted on*,' she sniffed. 'While for my part, my picture is in the paper as your latest lover. One of hundreds if the papers are to be believed. My reputation is, for want of a better word, tarnished.'

'All the more reason for you to agree to marry me.' He shrugged.

'I don't know.' She toyed with the paper cup, long fingers playing with the corner of card, unpeeling it carefully, meticulously. 'You're right, I wanted your help but I was desperate. I suppose a part of me never thought you'd agree to it. And now you have… I can't help but wonder why.'

'Does it matter?' he wondered aloud.

'Yes. Are you motivated by getting one up on your father in this ridiculous game the two of you seem to be permanently playing?'

'Does *that* matter?'

'Yes, Louis, it does. Because you're infamous for being a loose cannon and if I have any hope of controlling you then I need to know what sets you off.'

'Now I can definitely tell you *that*,' he countered suggestively.

'Louis…' Alex sighed, a soft sound as though he actually *exasperated* her.

And suddenly he didn't want to play the charade with her any longer. He was exhausted with playing up to perceptions of how he should be. All he wanted to do was kick back and let the mask slip.

'Louis,' she bit out abruptly. 'Is this about getting your own back on your father?'

He should lie. Come up with another typical quip. Instead, he heard himself respond.

'Maybe. A little. You know, before last night I hadn't thought about Rainbow House in years. Did you know I usually travelled with her? Backwards and forwards between Chateau Rochepont and the UK? Did you also know that Rainbow House is where my mother died?'

Died; suicide. Pot-ay-to; pot-ah-to.

He tried to stuff back the pain he'd thought long since buried. Play it down as he had in the past. But, for once, it didn't seem to fit back in its dark, wretched cage. Instead, he plastered a smile on his mouth and pretended he didn't hear the way Alex had sucked in a breath and shot him a look of pure horror.

'I didn't know that.' Somehow that made him feel better. 'Is that why you haven't taken on her legacy all these years?'

'Partly.'

He hadn't been able to bear it. Taking on the legacy of a woman who could have achieved so much more. Who had chosen to take her own life when she could have followed her passion for the Lefebvre Trust; who had chosen to leave her desperate, seven-year-old son behind.

His only consolation was the fact that only he and his father, and whoever had discovered her that day, knew the truth. It wasn't in anyone's best interests to disclose such facts. The last thing Rainbow House would have wanted was negative media attention. Covering up his mother's suicide had been the one decent thing his father had ever done. And even that hadn't been for altruistic purposes.

'Her name was Celine, but you already know that.' He had no idea why he was still speaking. Why he was telling her things he'd never uttered to another soul. But it was like a faulty tap and now he'd opened the faucet he couldn't shut it off again.

'She didn't have the greatest life. She was pretty but rather naïve when she met Jean-Baptiste. By the time she found herself pregnant with me, she was nineteen. My grandfather on my father's side was only too keen to unite two aristocratic families while my grandfather on my mother's side believed that Jean-Baptiste was doing the honourable thing in marrying Celine.'

'And that was a bad thing?' Alex was cautious.

'With hindsight my mother was too young, too innocent to handle a man like my father. She would have been better off without him, but an unmarried pregnant woman was still a scandalous thing, especially in this area, back then. My grandfather just wanted to be sure that Celine and her son and rightful heir to the Delaroche estate— me—would be acknowledged.'

'Were you close?'

'Very.' And suddenly he was fighting off a slew of unwelcome emotions. It was enough to evoke so many memories, but he would *not* remember her soft voice, her contagious laugh or the fresh scent of her hair when she'd hugged him. He would not remember how they'd spent every single day together, out on walks along the section of Canal du Midi where the chateau was, or collecting pine cones in the surrounding woods. And he would not remember how she'd taught him about the birds and their songs, only for *him* to have to teach *her* all over again when he was six and had discovered she'd got it all wrong.

He *could* not remember it. He'd long since found that detonating those flashbacks in the deepest, darkest caverns of his soul had been the most effective way to eradicate them.

'Jean-Baptiste was as vile a husband as he was a father.' Louis flipped the subject quickly. 'What you saw that night is only a glimpse of it. He's a bully and a coercer. Gradually, systematically, he beat my mother down until she felt she was worthless.'

'She couldn't leave him?'

'We talked about it. We agreed how different life would

be without Jean-Baptiste's money or connections, and we concluded how much easier it would be to breathe without his restrictions. That last trip to Rainbow House was to be her final one. When she flew back we were going to leave. Then she…died.'

He understood why she'd had to be free of his father, but he could never forgive her for choosing such a way out. For not simply packing a bag for them both and fleeing in the dead of night. For leaving him behind.

'I'm sorry for your loss, Louis.'

Her words wrenched him out of whatever black pit he'd been sliding into. He fell silent, old grief washing over him. And then, for the first time, a hint of something resembling a soothing calm.

He stared at Alex.

Was that because of her? He couldn't be sure.

She was watching him warily. Opening her mouth, then hesitating and closing it again.

'What is it, Alex?'

She bit her lip.

'For what it's worth, your father isn't as loved by the Delaroche board as you, or the media, seem to think.'

He didn't know what flooded through him then.

'What do you mean?'

'It means there are some members of the Delaroche board who would like nothing more than to see your father ousted.'

'That's absurd.'

She shook her head.

'No, it isn't. I told you, I've been working at Rainbow House for over a decade. People talk. People talk to me. There are quite a few people who had seen that other side of your father, the one the press seem oblivious to. I hadn't believed it until I saw for myself the other night. But if you came back, Louis…if you took control of the Lefe-bvre Group, I think there may be quite a few members who would support your nomination within the Delaroche board as well.'

'But you don't know for sure.'

Why did he even care? He had his surgeries, and when he wasn't at the hospital he had his hedonistic lifestyle. He didn't want anything to do with either the Lefebvre Group or the Delaroche Foundation. He didn't belong in that world. He should stick to what he did best.

Except something niggled at him.

He thrust it away.

Alex had asked for his assistance and, though he couldn't explain why, he wanted to help her. Wanted to make sure she and her father kept the fragile connection between them, the link to her brother. The kind he had never had with his own father, and had lost with the death of Celine.

'If you want to save Rainbow House then you're still going to have to marry me.'

'There has to be another way. Your position in full control of the group can't really be wholly dependent on whether you're married or not.'

'Only it is. And, yes, I could probably fight the clause if I wanted to. Get a top legal team and find some way around it, but it would take time. And I don't think Rainbow House has that time. Not if the vote to transfer is imminent.'

'Which means you have to get married imminently,' she said.

'Right. So, Alexandra Vardy, how much does Rainbow House really mean to you?'

It was a bit of a loaded question, he recognised that as soon as he asked it. But rather than another of her wise-cracks, she shot him a sideways look.

'It means more than I could tell you. I just don't know if we can pull this off.'

'You doubt me?'

She heaved a deep sigh.

'No, as it happens. I've seen how driven and focussed you can be. What you can achieve when you want to. I just don't know if you want Rainbow House enough.'

'Well, you're going to have to make a decision.' He felt unbalanced. Intoxicated. Her decision had been like an intimate caress to the hardest part of his masculinity. Nothing like the fawning, gushing compliments that so often peppered his day yet meant absolutely nothing to him.

'You can trust me and maybe we can save Rainbow House, or you can fail to trust me and we save nothing.'

The last thing he expected was her sudden wry grin.

'Hobson's choice, then.'

Whether she'd intended it or not, it had the effect of chasing away the uncharacteristic melancholy that had threatened to sweep through him. He suspected she understood that, which was why she'd chosen to back away.

It should bother him more that she'd been able to read him so easily when he prided himself on the fact that no one else ever could.

'It is. Although regrettably I don't have an extensive stable of horses.'

She laughed, and the sound cascaded through him like a pleasant waterfall.

'You can't really expect me to believe that. Only the other night you told me that your family home is a castle. You truly don't have huge stables?'

'The stables are long gone. Or at least the horses are gone and the stables have seen better days. They're not really a priority for my father. Does that count?'

'And what about the media? Do you think you'll need to get them onside?'

'Possibly. Which I think is where you would come in. I think you'd be the perfect person to charm them.'

'Wow, thanks, I'll look forward to it.' She pulled a face. 'So you think they'll believe you're no longer the fickle, play-hard womaniser Louis who has never dated a woman longer than about a week in his life, just by taking a girl-friend...sorry, I mean a fiancée?'

'Why not?' he murmured. 'Eligible playboy bachelor tamed by sweet girl next door, it's an age-old story and people love it.'

It should be a cliché. But if it was then he was staring right at half of it.

'I'm not the girl next door,' she snapped, before soft-ening her words with a smile. But it was more brittle than those that had gone before. And the sudden change snagged his attention.

He wanted to know more about Alex, and she'd just given him the ideal opening.

As though sensing a chink in her armour, Louis suddenly leaned closer and abruptly the huge, vaulted space felt as claustrophobic as a three-by-three tent. The seductive Louis was back, edging closer, and even sitting down his body was definitely one built for sin. Heat swept through her afresh but she ordered herself not to be such a fool, not to fall for it. It was simply an act he knew how to play to perfection.

'Then who are you, Alexandra?'

The too-sharp edge to his gaze unnerved her, the at-traction still zipping between them. Inconvenient and un-deniable. One misstep and she got the impression he could convince her to lay her soul bare. She wanted to get back to the banter they'd had before but she had to tread carefully.

'So, Louis…' She forced a smile, buying herself a little more time. 'If I did agree to marry you, how do I know you'll honour your promise to me about Rainbow House?'

'You have my word.' He shrugged, making her splutter. Her eyebrows shot up to her hair.

'That's it? The word of a renowned playboy.'

'I might have a reputation as a playboy, but shouldn't that make me honest rather than a liar? I never promise women something I can't give them.'

'Is there anything you can't give women?' she said, regretting it the moment it came out of her mouth. It would only inflate his already giant ego.

'I appreciate the vote of confidence.' His crooked smile *did* things to her. 'And you're right. There's only one thing.'

'And what's that.'

'Marriage,' he deadpanned. 'Commitment.'

'Idiot.' She actually swatted him. She waited for him to react but he just ramped up the killer grin.

'I deliver in all other areas.'

'So I've heard. You have quite the reputation for delivering.'

'Indeed I do. Care to put it to the test?'

Her whole body reacted, thrumming at the soft teasing of his tone. Grey eyes pierced into her like the short, sharp scratch of a needle into a vein. The air between them appeared to crackle. His eyes locked onto hers and she couldn't make herself break contact.

'I'm harder to dislike than you thought, aren't I?' he teased.

'You keep telling yourself that,' she bit back, but it lacked any edge.

And here they were, full circle. He *was* harder to dislike than she'd believed from his media reputation, she'd been learning that over the last few days. In fact, the more time she spent in his company, the harder it was to see the two sides of him as the same man. She sniffed delicately.

'So if we want to get married then first we have to get the media invested in your apparent redemption.'

If Louis flinched at the term, he recovered quickly.

'That's the plan,' he agreed. 'Although, full disclosure, there's nothing remotely redeemable about him left any more. Too many years of playing the wild, arrogant playboy have meant my soul has long since been sold.'

For a moment she wondered if he truly believed that. There was such an odd tilt to his expression. And then it was gone.

Still, she felt compelled to answer.

'If Jean-Baptiste can convince the press and public alike that he's some kind of benevolent force, then I'm sure you, too, can learn to play the part.'

'Don't tell me that was a compliment.'

Before she realised it, he leaned forward, his fingers sweeping over her forearm. The fleeting contact was electrifying.

'Take it,' she suggested, wishing her voice didn't sound quite so husky. 'It's the best you're getting.'

'Oh, no, trust me. You'll be doing way better than that before the ink is dry on this so-called marriage. Many of them comparing me to a deity, just as you're reaching orgasm.'

Why was it that every time she thought she'd struck a nerve with Louis, he came back more scurrilous than ever? Was it his way of concealing some vulnerability, or was she just imagining something that wasn't there?

Either way, she had to stop reacting to him, stop taking the bait.

'I haven't even agreed to it yet.'

'But you want to.' Hard, male triumph. 'Finally we're getting there. Tell me, what exactly do you have to lose?'

She stared at him for a moment, wishing she could read his thoughts and then wondering why she cared so much.

It didn't make sense.

'My soul, perhaps?' she offered.

And maybe something else she didn't care to admit.

He laughed, and then suddenly he leaned in. And she found herself wondering what she would do if he closed the gap and kissed her. He was so close, so big, so… *Louis.* Even his teasing had made her body hum with desire.

If he kissed her then she had a feeling she would kiss him back.

And then she would hate herself for it.

For that reason alone, she pulled away and forced herself to stand up.

'You will come to me, Alex,' he murmured, so quietly that at first she wasn't sure if it was just the thoughts in her head, taunting her. Knowing what she was trying to tell her body it didn't want.

'I won't.'

'Oh, you will. And when you do, you'll come willingly. Eagerly. And I'll be waiting.'

'This has to be a business arrangement, Louis. Not for pleasure. We have to set out the ground rules now.'

'Why not for both?' he asked, low and sensual. 'We'll discuss it tonight. Over dinner. Where the press can see us and we can start the clock ticking. The car will collect you at eight. Be ready, Alex. Don't keep me waiting.'

CHAPTER FOUR

THE NIGHT WAS not going as planned.

True, the press were outside, tipped off by an *anonymous source,* as arranged. And he had pre-ordered the soufflé to suggest that he had given this date care and forethought. But the so-called date itself hadn't gone as intended.

He was too distracted, too fascinated by the woman who was sitting opposite him.

He should have spent the last hour discussing with her the next steps in their plan. Instead, he'd spent it watching her, studying her, trying to learn about her. She was a breed apart from any other women he'd previously…entertained. Not just because she was a doctor, and the kind of skilled anaesthetist he should have known Gordon would want to mentor, but because of *her.* Because there was something about the woman that he found utterly compelling.

She was driven and she was focussed, both qualities he'd never looked for in a lover before. Qualities, if he was honest, that he'd gone out of his way to avoid. Sex was simple, but cerebral attraction was a complication he could do without. And there was no doubt he found Alex Vardy utterly desirable; physically and otherwise.

As if sensing his scrutiny, she lifted her eyes, a scowl knitting her forehead. When she pursed her mouth he was helpless from imagining dragging his thumb over that plump lower lip, dipping his head to taste the sweet heat of her mouth, pulling her body close against his. It was nonsensical. And pathetic. And it made him feel like the kind of hormone-ravaged teenager lusting over the hottest girl in school he'd never been.

Yet here he was. Imagining.

'Do you have to look at me in quite that way?' she grumbled suddenly.

'Sorry?' He flashed her the slow, easy smile that women never failed to respond to.

Alex, however, appeared less than impressed.

'*That* way.' She waved her hand abstractedly in the air towards him. 'As though I'm some kind of puzzle box and you're trying to work me out.'

Another little nugget of information about her that he found himself seizing upon.

'You enjoy puzzle boxes?' He swirled the wine around his glass. Experience told him the act in itself was enough to convince the casual observer he was drinking it.

'As it happens, yes,' she fired back. 'Though I've no doubt they would be considered too geeky for someone who prefers the kind of X-rated pursuits that you do.'

'I wouldn't write me off so quickly. You clearly have no idea how attractive geeky can be.'

'Right.' Had she really rolled her eyes at him? 'Because you're well known for your attraction to geeky women.'

The laugh rumbled low in his stomach. He loved these flashes of her feistier side, made him hungry to learn more. And that fact alone should bother him more than it did.

'I think the fact that you like puzzle boxes makes you all the more—what shall we say?—*interesting*.' His scrutiny deepened. 'Do you have a collection or something?'

She smoothed out the frown before it could crease her face, careful to keep her tone level.

'By the way, are you actually planning on drinking any wine? Or do you think by swirling it around the glass every now and then that I'm going to believe I'm not drinking alone?'

The corners of his mouth twitched involuntarily.

'I'm impressed. Most people wouldn't have noticed that fact.'

'I'm not most people.'

'No. You aren't.' He dipped his head to the side, relishing the stain that spread across her cheeks.

'Is that supposed to be a compliment?'

She was going for nonchalance but was clearly unpractised. Without her scrappy side, her innocence was even more endearing. Louis grinned.

'You know it is.'

A silence descended over their table and, while he was content just to watch her and assess, after a few moments Alex shifted awkwardly, glancing around the room. All about them couples were talking in low voices, laughing together, even cuddling in their booth-style seats. If the whole idea was that the press saw them together and began to wonder, surely the only question on their lips would be if they were even there together in the first instance?

'Shouldn't we be…doing something? Generating interest?'

Another wicked grin cracked his face. Why was it that she was so deliciously easy to bait?

'Nice to see you're suddenly so keen. What do you suggest, then? Rampant sex underneath the table? The tabloids would go frantic for the chance to squeal to the world that I indulge my insatiable sexual needs in restaurants the length and breadth of the country.'

She pulled a face.

'Just the country? Surely you're ambitious enough to take on the world?'

Was it perverse that he got such a kick out of the fact she never seemed to let him get away with a thing? He dropped his voice to something approaching intimate, and leaned forward across the table to take her hand.

'Right, now, who says I'm not just interested in you?'

Far from delighting her, it earned him a withering glare from his companion.

'I bet you say that to all the girls.'

'True.' The accusation scratched its way under his skin despite his attempt to let it roll off him. Usually, it was a line delivered with considerably more aplomb. A truth in the face of irrefutable physical evidence.

'I also know that as much as you're pretending to want to pull your hand away, the flare in your eyes and the way your breath has quickened tell me that what bothers you most isn't that you don't want me touching you, but that a part of you is enjoying it far more than you think you should.'

Alex really defined the idea that beauty was more than just skin deep. He admired her passion. He admired her drive. He admired the lift of her head as she met his gaze proudly, the cool smile on her lips enough to fool the casual observer.

'You're mistaken, but then with an ego as big as yours that shouldn't surprise me. But I'm not pulling away because I know that if we go ahead with this charade then I can't afford to look like I'm not interested in you.'

'You keep telling yourself that. We can both feel the attraction here.'

His smile sharpened, tugging low in his stomach like a primal challenge.

'You're a pitiable Lothario.'

'I freely confess to the latter; however, I'm fairly sure no one's called me pitiable before.' He chuckled. 'At least, not to my face.'

'I'm equally sure you haven't been called plenty of things to your face,' Alex bantered quickly, 'but that doesn't mean you haven't been called them.'

Unperturbed, he lifted his wine glass to his lips and prepared to take a sip, the hint of a smirk deliberately moulding his mouth.

'Oh, no doubt.'

There was no reason on earth for him to get such a kick out of bringing out a side of her that other people didn't seem to see.

'You really don't care at all, do you?'

There was also no reason for her disdain to needle him the way that it did. For him to go from amused to regretful. For it to suddenly be so hard for his practised smirk to stay in place.

Since he was seven years old he'd spent his life ensuring he *never* cared about what people thought. Because the only person whose opinion had ever mattered hadn't cared enough about him to stick around. People could say and think whatever they liked, it had never bothered him. If anything, it had been mildly entertaining.

There was no reason on earth why he should experience even a trickle of regret when he wondered how Alex might judge him.

'I didn't say that.'

'You didn't have to.' She was trying to sound scornful but it lacked the necessary bite. 'It's etched into every apathetic bone in your body.'

'I'm glad you've been paying so much attention.'

'You play up to those cameras, don't you? Give them the volatile Louis show they all love to see? Play the buffoon? And know you get away with it because half the female population seems to be in lust with you.'

It should antagonise him more. People simply didn't defy him. Instead, he found himself relishing her tenacity. Her refusal to be intimidated.

'You exaggerate your court-jester routine, your insouciance, and your sexual prowess.'

'Trust me, there's nothing remotely exaggerated about my sexual prowess.'

He savoured the way she flushed, the increased rise and fall of her chest, the darkening of her pupils, the faint flare of her nostrils. He told himself that he only cared because it would make it easier to deceive the paparazzi if there was at least a degree of genuine chemistry between the two of them.

He knew it was a lie.

'So,' she continued after a moment, 'this afternoon I told you why Rainbow House mattered to me when I told you about my brother Jack. Now you're going to tell me why Rainbow House is so important to you.'

It was his chance to redefine the parameters. To remind her, and himself, that this was a business deal, nothing more; that she didn't have the right to demand anything of him. Louis opened his mouth to tell her, one of his well-honed put-downs ready on his lips.

His gaze swept over Alex's face. Sincere, open, ingenuous. Like no one he'd ever known before.

And for the second time in as many days he found himself opening up and letting the dark ghosts of his past emerge into the light for the very first time.

* * *

She hadn't expected him to answer. She'd thought he might brush it off, the way he always did when any of his work colleagues politely made personal enquiries. Or else make a scathing remark, as he did when the media prodded him considerably less politely.

Perhaps what startled her most was the way Louis shifted to face her square on in his seat, or maybe how he lowered his voice so that she had to edge in closer to hear, as though their conversation wasn't for the rest of the world to know. It might even have been the way he toyed with the pepper shaker in the middle of the table as though he was feeling suddenly, uncharacteristically, unsure of himself.

It was several long moments before she realised she'd stopped breathing.

'My mother didn't die in an accident at Rainbow House, the way everyone seems to think. She committed suicide.'

'That's ludicrous. My brother was in and out of the place around the time your mother died. He would have been around six, which means I was probably three. My father would have known.'

Her breath came out in a single whoosh. He ignored it, continuing with even less emotion than he had shown when choosing their expensive bottle of wine this evening.

'Have you ever thought about why, if she was such a hero in rescuing a place like Rainbow House from the brink, she isn't more celebrated by the centre? Why her connection to the charity has been all but erased? Why you only knew about her because your brother was a resident all those years ago, and because you still care enough to volunteer there now?'

'Well…yes. But…'

'No one talks about her. Certainly no one who was

around at the time. I'd lay a bet your father never mentions her.'

That was true. In fact, when she'd mentioned Celine and the Delaroche connection to her father, he'd ignored her. It was only when she'd mentioned her idea of attending the gala to speak to Jean-Baptiste that he'd snapped at her and told her not to be foolish. He, who wanted to save Rainbow House as much as she did.

'Nevertheless...'

'It happened, Alex.'

'How do you know?'

'My father told me at the time. Told me he'd managed to cover up the details surrounding her death and that as far as the press were concerned, there had been an accident.'

She heard the scornful snort; realised it was her.

'Your father?'

'I didn't want to believe it. I spent the best part of a decade telling myself it was a lie, and that one day I'd uncover the truth. I was seventeen by the time I was in a position to do that. I discovered that there had been no official police investigation, although an internal investigation had taken place with as few personnel as possible. A couple of them had since died, but no one left was talking. At least, they only confirmed the story that the press knew, none of which matched my father's all-too-vivid account.'

'Louis...' she began. She wanted to ask so many questions, wanted to comfort him. It was impossible to tell whether he would have accepted her sympathy or shut down again. She couldn't risk the latter. Gripping the table, she hardly even dared to blink.

'Most of the evidence had long since been destroyed. I barely managed to get hold of a few photos, which was all that remained. There was one of a ripped-up bedsheet, and my mother's favourite handbag, and the broken pearls from her necklace on the floor next to the beam they had cut to get her down. It all matched the story my father had told me. He hadn't been lying.'

'I can hardly believe it,' Alex offered tentatively. 'The woman I've always heard about from my father was so happy, so generous, so full of love.'

'She was. And, I suppose, for all his flaws I have to be grateful to my father for at least preserving her good reputation. Hushing up the details and ensuring the press reported nothing more than a tragic accident was the kindest thing he could ever have done for my mother.'

'So…is that…' She paused, thinking of all the best memories of her brother she'd clung to over the years. 'Do you still remember the good times with her? How close you were?'

He shrugged and she couldn't explain it, couldn't justify it, but somehow she sensed that—far from the negligent attitude Louis had used to fool the press for so long—a maelstrom of feelings actually raged beneath the surface. Undetected by others, stuffed down by Louis.

'I remember her leaving the chateau the previous night. She'd promised to take me with her because I loved the plane so much, but I was sick that day and she had to leave me behind. She told me she loved me, and that she would fly home as soon as she could. I waved to her out of the window as her car went down the drive. She even got out just before the moat and waved back. I never saw her again. Twenty-four hours later she'd taken her own life.'

'Louis, I…'

Before she could finish, almost out of nowhere, the atmosphere changed and the razor-sharp, dominant veneer for which Louis was so famous slipped back into place.

'Ah, your chocolate soufflé. Savour it, I'm assured it's the best in Europe.'

The conversation was over and Louis was sampling his dessert and throwing compliments to the chef as if every mouthful wasn't sticking in his throat the way she knew it would have done for her.

But she wasn't fooled. He wasn't unmindful or unaffected. He simply didn't trust her. Alex wondered if he had ever trusted anyone.

How long had he isolated himself in this way?

As long as she had?

It shouldn't matter and it certainly shouldn't make a difference. But it did. She understood him better now, and what she'd learned had thrown her somewhat. He wasn't at all what she'd imagined, even with the twist of the surgeon she'd seen in action the previous month. Every time she saw him, spoke to him, it felt as though she was discovering a man no one else even knew existed. And even though she knew she should know better, she craved to learn more.

It was thrilling, and nerve-racking, and utterly bewildering. How was she supposed to react to everything he'd told her? She could barely even digest it all. She needed time, in particular to ensure that she wasn't at risk of losing all perspective and actually doing something as foolhardy and foolish as falling for the man.

But her biggest fear was that time wasn't a luxury she had right now.

The decadent dessert felt like wet concrete in his mouth. Worse, Alex was looking at him as though she could see straight through every bluff he cared to conjure. The way she had almost from that first encounter.

Still, he shouldn't have told her that. He shouldn't have told her any of it. If he could have shovelled back his words and rammed them all back inside then he would have.

Except that he wasn't sure that was even true.

No one had ever been able to read him the way she seemed to, a fact that ought to concern him far more than it did.

They finished their so-called date in strained silence. The only consolation was that, from all the covert glances and barely concealed smirks they were receiving, people were only too happy to draw their own, rather different conclusions.

For all her mental reservations about the two of them, Alex's body language right now betrayed the fact that on a purely physical level she was far less hesitant. Without the benefit of hearing their conversation, any casual observer would no doubt mistake her awkward fidgeting for eagerness to conclude the meal and get back to more private surroundings so they could continue the date on more intimate terms. Whether Alex liked it or not, she wasn't schooled enough in the art of seduction to mute the sexual attraction that crackled between them, blazing as brightly as a beacon warning of impending invasion.

The irony wasn't lost on Louis.

Neither was the fact that fooling the press into thinking they couldn't get enough of each other was only the first part of the plan. But the idea of *sex* and *Louis* was practically a given. What they really had to convince people of was that there was more to it than simply *sex*. They had to make the world believe the two of them shared a connection, an area of common ground. A foundation on which they were about to build a real relationship.

It should ring more alarm bells that he knew just how to snag Alex's focus.

'Did you enjoy your morning with our team? In the end?'

A man could quickly grow to love that wide, uninhibited smile. The one that told him she'd already forgotten herself. And their surroundings.

'I loved it,' she breathed. 'You get some incredible cases. Well, of course you do. But, I mean, you're one of most fascinating surgeons to observe. Your entire team is so well knit.'

'It's taken years to build the perfect unit, people with not only the skills I need but also the attitude I like. And the ability to leave all egos at the door.'

'Yes, I saw that.' Alex nodded, then blushed. 'Even you. I hadn't really expected that.'

'I'll take it as a compliment,' he commented wryly. 'I was impressed at just how easily you slotted into the team.'

'I did?' She looked inordinately pleased and something tugged inside him.

It felt good to compliment her. Especially as it was so well deserved.

'You were everything that Gordon said you were, and more.'

'I wondered if…?'

She leaned in eagerly, but whatever she was about to say died on her lips as several camera flashes went off.

Louis barely remembered standing up, much less moving around the table. But one minute he was in his seat and the next he was pulling Alex to her feet, holding her close and ignoring the way she stiffened against him, while the staff ushered the photographers outside. It would only be later, on the drive home, that he would wonder at his instinctive reaction to protect her, shield her, when the entire point of the so-called date had been to flaunt their relationship to the world.

But for now, all that consumed him was the way Alex felt in his arms, her initial reticence already melting away as her body softened, curving into his, moulding herself to him. As if they had been designed to fit together.

'Let's go,' he muttered, waving the apologetic maître d' out of their way and tapping his watch and making a call to ensure his driver would be out front in a matter of minutes. Telling himself his body wasn't celebrating the way she pressed herself tightly against him.

'I can walk by myself,' she muttered, though she made no move to push away from him.

'But it would look better if you didn't want to,' countered Louis, refusing to acknowledge the voice suggesting he was motivated by more than just the way it looked to others. 'Better if you preferred to be in my arms.'

'But not like your typical Louis Delaroche date.' She shook her head, toying with the fabric of his shirt, as though she was willing her hands to brace against him and push him away.

'Isn't that the point? That you're meant to be unlike anyone I've been with before?'

'Still, like you said, I don't think wholesome, boring, grandmother's *Apple Pie Alex* is going to convince the press. Do you?' She barely gave him time to reply. 'If we want to convince people that you're a changed man, we need to give them a reason they'll believe. A spicy apple pie. The Apple Pie Martini.'

'Sorry, the what?'

But she didn't stop to answer.

Flattening her palms against his chest, Alex propelled herself back and pulled herself up to her full height, more like the confident, feisty woman he'd seen that first night. The smile she cast him shot straight through him and to his sex and then she spun around and glided out the doors and into a sea of camera flashes, appearing for all the world like she was born to a life in the spotlight. Part girl next door but part fierce Amazonian. It filled him with a sense of pride, of…almost *possessiveness*.

He couldn't explain it, all he did understand was that it meant the papers, once they found out who she really was, would be eating out of her hand in days. And that was before they saw the sheer drive and determination that governed her world.

How much more was there to Alexandra Vardy? What might he discover if he had the chance to peel back one skin after another? Why was he so damned intrigued by this one woman?

The questions jostled around his head with such eagerness that for a moment he almost forgot to follow her.

He, who never followed anyone.

Bursting through the doors, he covered the ground to her in a few long strides. Sliding his hand to the small of her back and guiding her the last feet to the kerb as their car headed towards them.

'Quite a show,' he murmured, leaning in to whisper in her ear, and exalting in the fact that only he could see her quickened, nervous breathing.

'I think it got the message across.'

'Perhaps. But a kiss would seal it.'

'I don't want to kiss you.'

'Liar,' he whispered, angling his head even closer to her ear so that her lips couldn't be seen by the cameras, but there was no mistaking the way her body trembled. It sent waves of desire through him. 'Love and lust are easily mistaken for each other. And there's no denying you and I have the latter. We both feel it.'

'I don't feel anything,' she refuted, but her voice lacked any conviction.

'Is that so?' he growled.

She was going to stall. Louis refused to give her the opportunity. He yanked her in, his mouth claiming hers and silencing any further objections.

Hot and glorious, and full of sinful promise. It wasn't like any other kiss he'd ever known. His mouth moved over hers, the whisper of her tongue against his fanning the flames that raged inside him. This was the kiss he'd been imagining all night.

Maybe even the kiss he'd been imagining his whole life.

As though she was the drink he'd never been able to find anywhere else, and the only one that could ever quench the thirst that had plagued him for what seemed like for ever. It wasn't just the way her tongue now scraped over his in sweet response. It wasn't just the way she tensed, relaxed, and then pressed against him, her breasts splayed against his body, generating a heat that burned right through clothing he desperately wished he could just rip off. It wasn't the way she tasted of need and longing and ultimately of promise.

It wasn't any of that. Yet it was all of it.

His head was spinning and, as hard as he tried, there was only one thought he could seem to hold onto.

He couldn't let her go. Not after this. He couldn't risk her backing away again. He liked this spiced version of Alex. Maybe a little bit too much.

When the car came, it was as much an interruption as a relief to break apart and bundle her inside.

The sudden silence was a jolt after the fracas out there.

'Where do you live?' Louis asked after a moment.

'Sorry?'

'What's your address?' He barely recognised the raw voice but it was hardly surprising when she was still trembling in his arms. And this time, he knew, it had nothing to do with the press.

'Why?'

'Because we're heading there now. You'll have half an hour, forty minutes at the most to pack everything you need and you'll move in with me.'

'I will not,' she squeaked.

He sighed. The sort of gently impatient sigh one might have bestowed on a small child who refused to hear what was being said to them. Alex would never know what it had cost him to rein himself in as he had.

She opened her mouth to speak but he cut in smoothly.

'You have no choice. Surely that's obvious to you?'

'Why should it be?' she challenged uncertainly.

'Because now the press have linked us, they're going to hound you until they get more. Camp out on your doorstep, harass your friends and relatives. You need to move somewhere it isn't as easy for them to gain access to you. Not only for your sake but also for the sake of your family.'

'I don't have a family.' The words were out before she could bite them back, as she clearly wished she could. She tried to pull out of his arms but he refused to let her. 'Just my father.'

'And your mother?'

She flinched, pressing her lips into a thin line, but at least she wasn't trying to pull away from him any longer. For the first time it occurred to Louis that he'd been so busy telling her things he'd never told anyone before that he hadn't thought to have her investigated as he usually would have. He vowed to remedy it as soon as he could.

'Either way, I'm sure you don't want him to see your every movement in the papers when they climb trees, or break into your back garden for the photos that capture a day in your life.'

He hated the way she recoiled from him.

'Oh, God, my father. He'll see photos of that kiss in the papers tomorrow.'

'And in the news tonight,' Louis pointed out gently.

She covered her face with her hands.

'It's what we wanted,' he reminded her. 'What we *needed* them to believe.'

It had just happened faster than he'd intended. And he couldn't pretend he'd been entirely in control. She had a way of making him act like a desperate kid. Either way, they'd set out their proverbial stall. Now they had to sell their wares, starting with ensuring she now moved in with him.

The car was pushing through the crowd and somehow he knew he needed to get her to agree now. Before the moment between them was broken.

'Put it this way, I have to go to France for a month or so. There are some cases that I've been waiting to complete out there. You'll be safer in my penthouse than on your own, but you won't have to worry about me seeing you with bed-hair.'

He took the snort to be a mirthless laugh. He didn't know why he was so suddenly desperate for her to agree. It wasn't just about making sure she was safe, he knew that. He suspected it was something far more primal. And that was dangerous.

'Alex?'

'Okay.' She dipped her head fractionally, clouds skittering across her eyes.

He could read the sense of foreboding that she desperately wanted to shake. Her feeling that she was somehow capitulating and that he had won. But it didn't feel like a win. He didn't know *what* this feeling was.

He only knew that the very ground was shifting precariously beneath his feet and it was all to do with this one woman.

Worse, Louis had no idea how to keep himself from plummeting into the void head first.

CHAPTER FIVE

'IT'S THE STUFF of spy movies, isn't it?' Alex was still struggling to regain her composure after the kiss as the plush lift whisked them silently from the underground garage to Louis's private penthouse.

'Sorry?'

She waved a negligent hand in the air, wondering if he could see the way it trembled, even now, at the memory of his mouth against hers.

'I mean, the exclusive key card to access the security pad just so you can enter in some private code. And that's before the lift had even closed its doors.'

Alex fought valiantly to appear light-hearted, but how could Louis fail to hear her heart drumming out its wild tattoo on her ribcage?

'That's what money buys,' he said with a shrug, that hint of darkness she was beginning to recognise meaning he'd have given it all up in a heartbeat just for one question to be answered. *Why his mother had chosen to do... what she had.*

It was a sense of helplessness that she understood only too well. It was getting easier and easier for her to read the man who had confounded the press for so many years. They had him pegged as this complex genius playboy.

They didn't understand him at all. And the two of them had a lot more in common than Louis realised.

She wasn't sure whether she'd realised it on the drive from the restaurant to her home, or from her home to here. But she'd realised it. She wasn't foolish enough to think that she'd worked out the entire puzzle box that was Louis Delaroche, but she'd at least figured out the first stage of him. He was as lost and hurt as she was, if for different reasons. And for each of them, that unbearable void couldn't be filled by another person and so they'd each been driven by their work.

That was why she felt such a connection with him. And in turn it explained why she'd acted so out of character outside the restaurant back there. Why she'd allowed herself to be kissed so thoroughly in front of a sea of flashing cameras. Why she'd come alive in his arms in a way she'd never before believed possible.

If only it was that simple.

If only she could pretend it really was just a mental connection rather than a physical one. How easy and convenient that would be. But there was more to it. It was less cerebral, more visceral. Louis fired up a need in her that she hadn't even known existed until he had come along. As if he had crept under her skin and infected her with some kind of thrilling fever.

And she liked it.

It didn't matter how many times she tried to tell herself that Louis had only kissed her to distract the press from her obvious gaucheness, she still craved more. Physically she felt drained and yet energised. She *ached* for him.

Lifting her fingers, Alex traced them lightly over her lips. She could still taste him on her mouth, feel his solid chest against her tender breasts, recall his strong hands tracing patterns up and down her spine.

In her whole life she'd always prided herself on her fight over flight attitude, but in this instance she knew if it hadn't been for Rainbow House she would have turned and run. She couldn't say how she knew it, but Louis Delaroche had the power to devastate her just as he'd devastated so many women before her. It turned out she wasn't as immune to that kind of man as she'd always assumed.

But, then, Louis wasn't *that kind* of anything. There were no others like him, he didn't so much break moulds as stick them on a mine and blow them to a grey mist.

So, here she was, in the lift to Louis's penthouse. And on top of all her roiling emotions it was difficult not to feel at least a little intimidated by Louis's obvious wealth and luxurious lifestyle. Especially when she thought of her own little flat and what he must have thought, pulling his flashy supercar into the communal car park packed with small older cars, scooters and a plethora of battered bicycles chained up together. A world away from the exclusive garage below, adorned with flashy cars recumbent in their generously proportioned, allocated parking spaces.

'Are you coming in?' The low voice broke through her reverie. 'Or do you intend to ride the lift all night?'

With a strangled sound Alex lurched forward, as if her legs didn't quite belong to her, and out of the lift to where Louis stood at the door to his penthouse. The edge in his voice accompanied by the hard, distant expression—as though he could read her thoughts on their kiss and scorned her for them—only made her fears swell.

And then she stepped past him into the room and everything rushed from her mind.

'That view is incredible,' she gasped.

One minute she was too close to Louis and the next she found herself across the room, palms flattened on a bank of glass looking out at the twinkling city as if she was somehow on top of the world. Or, at least, the closest she had ever come. The lights spread out for miles under a blanket of night and even some of the tallest buildings, which had always appeared enormous to her even from the fourth floor of the hospital, were now dwarfed by the breathtaking views from Louis's penthouse.

No wonder Louis walked, talked, acted as though the world was his for the taking. To him, it was.

'Is this how you seduce all your dates?' she asked, thinking that it really was a breath-taking view. 'All your *real* dates, that is?'

The pause stretched out for longer than was normal but when she turned, she wasn't prepared for the curve of his lips that developed into a full-blown smile of... *warmth?*

It blasted her, as though opening an incinerator door.

'I can't say any of my previous so-called dates have ever been interested in the view. Not the one out there, anyway.'

She shot him an exasperated look, and felt a little better.

If she had to work alongside Louis while such inappropriate longings poured through her then she needed to rediscover the light banter, the teasing back and forth they'd touched on earlier.

It was better than the alternative. Than the...kiss.

'Are you ever more impressed with anything other than your own brilliance?'

'Aren't you impressed by my... *brilliance*?' He quirked an eyebrow.

Something rolled and flipped low in her belly.

'I'm more astounded by your indefatigable arrogance.' She tried for loftiness but her own lips refused to do anything but curl upwards in amusement. His devilish grin of response wrecked her insides.

'Thank you.'

'It wasn't a compliment.'

'Oh, I would strongly disagree.' His rich, amused voice reverberated around her.

Abruptly, he moved to stand beside her, his head turned to the same view she saw, as if trying to see it through her eyes. She suspected he had long become immune to its beauty. She wasn't prepared for him to grow so quiet and serious.

'But, to answer your original question, lots of things impress me. Even astound me. Especially the strength of some people's human spirit inside and outside my OR. What you told me about your life back at the restaurant.'

His unexpected compliment made her yearn for more. Alex clenched her fists against the glass, silently cursing such weakness.

'There was nothing impressive or astounding about my life. People have it far worse.'

'And many don't. Either way, few of them use it to drive them on to becoming the star pupil of one of the most sought-after anaesthetists in the country, let alone the hospital.'

She could barely think straight, let alone talk.

'That was just work. And a bit of luck.'

'That was *you*,' he corrected softly. 'You asked if anything impressed me and you're right that few things do. But I'm telling you that you're one of them.'

She hated herself for the way her heart suddenly soared. If she wasn't careful, the press and the Delaroche Foundation board weren't going to be the only fools to fall for this charade.

She really was like a breath of fresh air.

He'd spent the entire drive fighting the urge to kiss her over and over again. To taste that delicious mouth from every angle. It had been like some kind of torture being so close to her and not allowing himself to indulge. And as for that interminably long ride in the lift…she could never know how close he'd come to hitting the emergency stop.

Yet now here he was, standing side by side with her and staring at the view as though seeing it properly for the first time in a long time—perhaps the first time ever—because of Alex. Because she was so genuine.

None of the women he'd ever brought up here had cared about the view. They weren't the kind of women who would ever have been interested in such simple beauty. But Alex wasn't similar to those women. She wasn't swayed by the superficial, she cared about the things that mattered, about people who mattered. She made *him* start to care again. Not about his patients—that was a given—but about something other than medicine. About Rainbow House.

He'd never thought anyone could make him do that.

He'd been fighting an attraction to her ever since that first night on the balcony. Even now, he couldn't stop himself from thinking how Alex could make a room light up just by walking into it, just as his mother had once done. Alex could make *him* light up. And he didn't want her to stop.

The realisation slammed into him with such force he felt as though every last bit of air had been sucked from his body. As though his lungs were crumpling in his chest. He wanted Alex. Not just to finally wrest his inheritance back from the Delaroche Foundation, as had once been his mother's intent, and not just to save Rainbow House from his father.

He wanted Alex because she made him feel. Something. Anything.

Not for ever, of course, because that would be nonsensical. He didn't *do* long-term relationships. He never had. But for as long as this charade lasted, he wanted it to

be more than simply a charade. He wanted it to be more…
real. He wanted her.

Worse than that. He wanted to *know* her.

'What is it?' Alex touched his arm and he realised she
must have repeated the question at least once.

He shouldn't answer. He should shrug it off. He certainly shouldn't indulge this fantasy of his of getting to
know her as if they were in the kind of real relationship
he'd always studiously avoided in the past.

'What is it about the view that so enraptures you?'

'I don't know.' She frowned, taking a step away from
him. 'What is it usually about such a magnificent sight?'

Defensive. Just the way he'd surmised.

'When I was a kid my mother used to say that views
like these made her feel as though the world was spread
at my feet for the taking. That, standing in front of it like
this, she believed I could do anything.'

'You're a Delaroche, the world *is* yours for the taking,'
Alex countered, but her words lacked any real heat.

'I couldn't control everything, though,' he said quietly.
'Any more than you could with your brother. Jack, did
you call him?'

A momentary pang of guilt made its way through Louis
as he watched her turn stiffly back to the window, her
fingers braced against the glass as she stared out mutely.

'Do you volunteer at Rainbow House because you want
to, or because you feel you somehow owe it to your father?'

'Because I want to, of course,' she snapped automatically.

He didn't bite, but neither was he about to let her off
that easily.

'Is that really all there is to it?'

Her knuckles paled as she pressed her fingers down

harder. As though some internal battle was going on in her head. Louis could imagine what it was only too easily.

'Perhaps a bit of both.' The admission came through gritted teeth.

'You feel responsible for your father's happiness? Responsible for Jack's death?'

'It's complicated.'

'It often is.' He couldn't explain why his heart twisted for her. 'But it doesn't always have to be.'

Her head was fixed away from him, her gaze trained on the vista below. But he would lay a bet she wasn't seeing any of it. Not a single building, or road, or tree. The haunted expression hovering over her beautiful profile betrayed her otherwise calm exterior.

'You don't understand.'

'So enlighten me.' He knew he was pushing. He couldn't seem to help himself. 'I can refute as many clichés as you can come up with, Alex.'

And then she smiled. A soft half-smile that looked more sad than anything else. But she turned her head and she finally looked at him.

'Jack was my older brother. He was diagnosed with diamond blackfan anaemia aged two. They tried other treatments that didn't work. I was conceived shortly afterwards in the hope that my stem cells would save him.'

'You were a saviour sibling,' Louis realised abruptly.

'Back before the time when embryos could be checked for compatibility. It was a leap of faith for my parents.'

'Alex, I had no idea.'

'It didn't pay off,' Alex continued, as though she hadn't heard him. 'Once I was born they carried out the tests and found I wasn't a match. Jack died seven years later.'

'I'm sorry,' he said simply.

The hush in the penthouse swirled softly around them.

'Your parents didn't try again?'

'My mother died when I was…a baby. They didn't get a chance.'

Her expression pulled tight and Louis couldn't shake the thought that he was missing something. Before he could say anything she was already speaking.

'I don't know what they would have done otherwise. Jack and my father had always been very close.'

He wanted to reach out and pull her into his arms. Comfort her. But he could read her well enough to know that she didn't want that. She might at least be looking at him, but her body was still steadfastly facing the world outside.

Strong. Resolute. Determined.

Apple Pie Alex indeed. Anyone who called her that didn't understand her at all. They completely missed that steel core that ran right through her from that blonde head to the soles of her feet.

The matching pair to the one which he'd always prided himself ran through him.

'So you volunteer at Rainbow House because your father does? Because you still feel responsible for not saving your brother?'

Quietness settled around them afresh before Alex finally answered.

'I suppose that's part of why I started. But I find it fulfilling.'

'And it's just you and your father?'

He wondered if her father had blamed her for not being able to save Jack. If the man had taken his grief out on his little daughter.

She narrowed her eyes at Louis. Too shrewd, he realised.

'Yes. It's just been the two of us ever since I was seven. And my childhood was fine, since I know that's what you're asking. My father loved me, in his own way, he supported me through university and with my career. We might not be as close as some families but he did lose his wife and son after all. It's hardly unusual that he might be a little closed off.'

'And you lost your mother and brother.'

He knew the words hit their mark. He could see her flinch. And he didn't know if he hated himself or her father more. Whether her old man had intended to hurt her not, he'd clearly withdrawn, taking demonstrative love with him.

She didn't need to say the words, he could read them all over her lovely face. Her father had fallen apart. Two people he'd loved most had gone. And instead of pouring that love into the one child he had left, he'd pulled away from her.

Her father might not have overtly said or done anything to hurt her, but clearly his absence of words had been almost as damaging. Certainly, Alex still felt she had something to prove to him. She was still the one fighting to keep their only area of communication alive. Fighting for Rainbow House.

At least he himself had experienced the unconditional love of his mother for the first seven years of his life. If Alex had lost her mother, and her father had known her brother's death had been inevitable once Alex wasn't a match, then had she ever experienced even that fraction of joy he'd had?

He doubted she'd thank him for pointing that out.

'Is that what got you started in medicine?'

'You mean, did the fact that I felt guilty about not being able to save Jack drive me on to try to save as many other people as I could?'

'That isn't what I was asking, no.'

They both knew her reaction had revealed far more than she had intended. Her lips quirked up into a rueful smile.

'Then clearly that's a bit of a hot button for me.'

Her quiet honesty tugged at something inside him. Louis lifted his shoulders, suddenly fighting to stay in control.

'We all have them.'

'Right.' She turned around finally, her back leaning on the glass.

Fearless. Proud.

A fracture splintered through his chest.

He told himself it was just part of the game. The better they knew each other, the closer they could appear to be for the cameras. But then her smile suddenly widened, the faintest hint of a gleam in her eye as she spoke.

'I could let you into a little secret.'

And he knew that telling himself such lies was tantamount to slapping a sticking plaster over a gaping wound and hoping it would do the job.

'What's that?'

'I wasn't always as driven or wholesome as everyone seems to think.'

It was impossible not to be swept along with her. How was it possible she could lift the mood with a single smile, a single look?

'Let me guess, you got a B in one of your medical courses,' he teased.

She actually rolled her eyes at him.

'You see? No one really gets me.'

There was no reason that should rankle as much as it did. No reason for him to take it as a challenge. To want to be the first—the only—person who she couldn't say that to.

'Go on, then.' He arched his eyebrows. 'Shock me.'

She pushed off the glass abruptly, strolling across the room to the view on the other side.

'I almost got expelled when I was fifteen. I nearly didn't even get my GCSEs, let alone my A levels.'

'You did?' He snorted. 'Sorry, no chance.'

'It's true.' He could almost believe she was enjoying this. Shocking him. 'I suddenly realised I was this teenage girl who had lost her mum and I fell into all the typical traps. I couldn't see the point of school, or learning. The doctors hadn't been able to save either her or Jack, so what was the point? I fell in with a different crowd and started ditching school, playing truant.'

'What, to go and drink cider and sit around the local park?' He was incredulous, but that only served to make her laugh all the more.

'Actually, we went to the local pool hall and spent all day in there. The brother of one of the group worked there, so if anyone ever came looking he'd let us out the emergency exit. Wow, I used to love that game.'

'And you did that for weeks? A month?'

Why did this only add to the admiration he had for her? The fact that whatever demons she'd had in the past, the intelligent, quick-thinking, professional doctor she was today only proved she'd beaten them all.

'Almost a year. My father eventually took me in hand. Told me some home truths, like what my mother would think of me if she saw me.' She raised her chin and for the first time Louis realised how fine the line was that she was treading, between laughing and crying. 'It was the first time he'd ever really talked about her to me. Before that, everything I knew, all the photos I had of her had come from my grandparents.'

'Yet you turned your life around again,' he breathed. 'Look at you now.'

'Yes, I turned it around.' She tilted her head from one side to the other in a devilish little dance. 'But not before I'd been put back an academic year. It was mortifying, but some of the others from that crowd hadn't even been given that opportunity so I knew I had to swallow it. I worked. God, I worked. I worked so hard that by the time I came to sit my GCSEs I'd already been put back into my old year group. After that I never looked back.'

'Never?' he challenged softly, her slow smile burning hotly through him as she shook her head.

'Never.'

'Then how about we do a little fun, nostalgic looking back now?'

He had no idea why he did it, but Louis held out his hand, waiting as she saw it, tried to resist it.

'What do you mean?'

'Trust me,' he prompted quietly.

'Why?' Suspicion warred with curiosity.

'Do you trust me?'

The question was so much more important than he'd intended. And her answer suddenly carried that much more weight.

Instead, Alex chose not to say a word. She lifted her eyes to his, scanning his face and searching for answers to questions she couldn't bring herself to ask. And then, just as he was about to wonder at the sense of what he'd done, she crossed the floor almost as if against her own will, and fitted her hand into his as he led her to the helical staircase in the centre of the room.

Wordlessly she kicked off her heels and jogged lightly up the stairs behind him, her fingers still laced through his and her trust in him implicit.

Something barrelled through Louis. He needed to call a halt to everything now. It suddenly felt all too intimate.

She felt too intimate.

Sex was one thing, but being emotionally close to someone? That was something he didn't want to risk.

Instead, he pulled her next to him, his arm slipping around her waist, not sure whether he was talking about the view or what was happening between them.

'Open your eyes,' he ground out brusquely.

CHAPTER SIX

ALEX STARED AT the full-size snooker table, a gurgle rumbling up from somewhere deep inside her.

'It isn't quite the quality of table I learned on.' She grinned. 'But I appreciate the nostalgia.'

Louis laughed. 'It isn't quite the quality I learned on either. I was taught by Arnaud, our estate hand—though he's now the estate manager. They had a beat-up pool table in one of the old stable blocks. My grandfather used to sneak in there a few times and he and I would have a game. When he died, Arnaud was the closest thing to a father figure I had left.'

'Is the table still there?'

'I doubt it. But the stable blocks are mine, maybe I'll renovate them one of these days. There's a covenant to say I can use them for any activity, providing it's legal and doesn't damage the estate.'

'You want a game?' she asked quickly.

'Why not? Snooker, billiards or pool?'

'You choose.'

It was daft and fun and none of the ways she would ever have imagined her evening with Louis ending up. No doubt he would say the same thing.

It was amazing how the time disappeared after that. Lost in a haze of happier childhood memories—at least, comparatively—and the unexpected discoveries that they loved many of the same books and bands, shared some similar interests and wanted to travel to similar destinations. Even politics wasn't off limits and they marvelled at their similar opinions and indulged in a couple of lively debates where they did differ. They laughed, drank wine and talked, even finding an old action film they both remembered, which spawned yet more nostalgic memories.

Her only real moment of envy came when he told her he'd visited Machu Picchu on a trek with his grandfather, while she knew she would probably never get that opportunity. When she remembered how their lives had differed. Still differed now.

It was the kind of first date she could only have dreamed of in the real world. The fact that it had happened so organically, so unexpectedly, with Louis—on a first date that hadn't even been real—made it both inspiring and aggravating at the same time.

'You're a revelation,' he told her abruptly, stopping as they passed one another around the table, allowing his hand to cup her cheek.

And all she could do was stand still and let him, afraid to move lest she break the spell. Her insides turned molten, not least when he dragged his thumb across her lower lip.

'Why don't you act like this in public, Louis?' The question slipped out before she could stop it. 'Why always the playboy act?'

'Who says it's an act?'

She might have thought regret shadowed his eyes, but that couldn't be right.

'I do. I don't think you enjoy it any more, if you ever really did. But I can't help but wonder if it's how you protect yourself from forming relationships. Because you're afraid you'll lose someone else the way you did your mother.'

* * *

Louis hadn't banked on the way she seemed to creep into his head without him even noticing her advance. The way that when she looked at him, the expression in her ice-blue eyes was hot enough to melt entire glaciers, speaking to his very sex.

He should shut her down, but he couldn't quite manage it. Time to turn the tables instead.

'I can think of a lot more interesting pastimes than a sixty-second pop psychology session,' he countered suggestively.

'You do see that you use sex as a distraction when the conversation heads off into waters you don't like?' she demanded.

Her voice was a little too husky. Still, it hadn't escaped him that she had a point.

'You credit me with too much guile.' He summoned a practised grin and stepped closer to her. 'Maybe I just enjoy sex. Pure, unadulterated, animal sex.'

She held her ground but he didn't miss the way her pulse jumped at her throat. Did that pretty flush currently sweeping over her pretty face also extend to that indecently sexy body of hers? How he'd love to find out.

'Stop it.'

A half-hearted mutter at best. He let his hand skim over her jawline and her breathing grew shallower, the swell of her soft breasts visible with each inhalation. His palms actually ached to touch her, to discover whether her nipples were as taut, as perfect as they'd felt against his chest a few hours before.

'Why? You can't deny there's an attraction between us. We both felt it even at the gala, and if there was any doubt then that kiss back at the restaurant dispelled it.'

He took another step, his hands restrained in his pockets, letting her be the one to reach out and make contact, palms flat against his chest but by no means pushing him away.

'Fine.' A gurgle of triumph rumbled in his body at the vaguely strangled sound. 'There's an attraction there, I can't deny it. But, apparently unlike you, I can control myself without having to pursue every desire that takes hold of me.'

'Do you pursue any?' he demanded, and she gave a quiet gasp.

'Are you calling me frigid?'

'I wasn't.' His tone was even, unconcerned. 'But I find it interesting that *you* should choose the term. Is it something you've been accused of in the past?'

She lifted her head defiantly.

'No. It is not.'

'Ah.' Louis nodded gently. 'Then it's merely your own hang-up.'

'You…don't know what you're talking about.'

The moment of hesitation said it all. A heavy silence swirled around them for a moment until Louis chose to take pity on her.

Or himself.

There was no room for the sentimental side of Louis Delaroche. It wasn't what people wanted to see. It wasn't what he wanted to see. And he didn't appreciate the way Alex kept excavating little memories that he'd long-since buried.

He'd rather go back to the arrogant playboy Louis than be the man who still wondered at what might have been.

As if sensing him closing off to her, Alex tugged herself free and backed away. This time he didn't try to stop her. She seemed to get under his skin both mentally and physically.

His lips still burned with the memory of their kiss. The

ghost of it still lingered, haunting him with its feigned promise. *Rattling* him, when nothing ever got to him. Making him feel out of control, vulnerable.

The thought pulled him up sharply. He wouldn't allow himself to be vulnerable. Emotions were for those too weak to control themselves. Surgery gave him the only buzz, the only kick, the only sense of triumph and pride that he needed. Especially when he carried out intricate, hail-Mary procedures that lesser surgeons shied away from even when they had nothing left to lose.

He might need to tame his wild, arrogant playboy reputation in order to finally start to wrest the Delaroche Foundation from the hands of the self-serving Jean-Baptiste, but that didn't mean he had to change who he was under the surface.

Since when had he allowed himself to become confused over just how fake his relationship with Alex really was?

How had she slipped under his skin?

What he felt when he was around her was lust, pure and simple. Surely he should know that better than most?

It was merely the circumstances of their meeting, Alex's fierce drive to save Rainbow House coupled with the fact they were both struggling with the loss of a parent who had loved them, only to be left with a parent who had never wanted them, was confusing the issue. The bond they seemed to share was an illusion, nothing more. That was all there was to it. The sooner he recovered his infamous, flirtatious side, the better.

'I think maybe we should go to bed,' she cut into his thoughts, offering him the perfect recovery.

Alex realised too late the suggestive nature of her comment.

'Is that so?'

His lazy drawl might have been the most sensual sound she'd ever heard in her life. It certainly shot through her to her very core.

'Alone, I mean. Not to the same bed.' She sounded ridiculously flustered. 'That is… Oh, it sounded far less suggestive in my head.'

But instead of teasing her a little more, as she'd expected, Louis simply placed a hand on her arm, apparently oblivious to the jolt of electricity that zipped from her shoulder to her fingertips.

'Relax, Alexandra, I know what you meant. Come on, I'll show you to your suite.'

'My…suite?'

'You would prefer to sleep in my suite?'

She shook her head even though, leading the way back down the incredible staircase, he couldn't see her.

'Of course not. I just assumed…well, I thought…the couch.'

She was sounding more and more like a stumbling, naïve fool as the moments wore on, she realised in dismay.

'I suppose you could sleep on the couch if you prefer, but I can assure you that the bedroom is decidedly more comfortable.'

'You know that isn't what I meant.'

He didn't acknowledge that. But, then again, he didn't refute it either. Alex wrinkled her nose as she hastily snatched up her discarded footwear, which to her eye painted an intimate, if inaccurate, scene, and followed him back into the rather grand hallway, where he was collecting her small case, and through a double archway she hadn't spotted upon her arrival.

'Your suite is this way.' Louis headed up the corridor, stopping, in a rather gentlemanly way, at the double doors and putting her bag down, as if whatever lay beyond was to be, at least for the time being, her private sanctum in which she could feel secure. 'Through there you have a bedroom, bathroom and sitting area. Should you want me for anything, I'll be in the master suite down that way.'

Alex turned obligingly as he indicated the opposite end of a corridor, which was probably the same length as her entire back garden. Possibly longer. It was difficult not to feel intimidated and only reminded her that, if this hadn't been a charade, such a coupling could never have worked.

'See you in the morning.'

The words seemed to pulse in the air. As Louis turned and walked away, a thousand different responses flew around Alex's head until, in the end, she plumped for one.

'Yes. See you in the morning.'

But he had already turned back into the main living area and out of sight. And even when she closed the door to her suite, she stayed against the door for a long time, remembering his touch and his taste and craving more.

CHAPTER SEVEN

A LOW, UNFAMILIAR sound jarred Alex out of slumber the following morning. Not that she had any idea how she'd managed to fall asleep, plagued as she had been by visions of Louis, and by erotic memories of his mouth claiming hers over and over again.

Even now her body burned with all the things she'd wanted him to do. Although the ridiculous winceyette nightgown she'd chosen to wear—the one she'd been sent as a Christmas gift years ago and had never once even considered wearing—wasn't helping. She almost hadn't packed it, hadn't lifted it out of the dusty package from the top corner of her wardrobe when she'd been racing around her home the previous night. But then she'd thought of Louis, and how weak her resolve seemed around him, and she'd decided to make a point to herself by bringing it along.

Was she really being foolish, denying herself the night with Louis that she so obviously wanted, simply because of fear? Or was her refusal to indulge such a base urge a logical, well-considered matter of self-preservation?

Alex couldn't be sure. All she knew was that she'd wrestled with the dilemma until the small hours, and now she was exhausted with her brain apparently unable to process what had woken her. She squeezed her eyes shut, her ears straining that little bit harder.

Wait? A vacuum cleaner?

She swivelled her head, which felt as though someone had exchanged it for a wrecking ball, and peered at the clock. What confused her most? The early hour or the notion of Louis vacuuming?

Common sense finally made an appearance. Scurrying out of bed and through her suite, she opened the door the tiniest crack and peered out. Of course it wouldn't be him out there.

Louis was the kind of man to employ a cleaner. And someone to do his dry-cleaning. And someone to take his dry-cleaning away in the first instance. Basically, Louis had *people*. But *people* could not catch her sleeping in the guest suite at least fifteen metres down the hall from Louis's suite. Alex squinted, praying for someone to step into view yet dreading the idea that they would. The sound appeared to be coming from the hallway off the corridor, but she couldn't see anything. She leaned back on the wall, her mind racing as she tried to figure out what to do next.

Why wasn't Louis out there, stopping them? Funny, but she wouldn't have taken him for a heavy sleeper.

Reaching into the closet, her hand only hovering for a moment, Alex slipped the previously unused dressing gown off the hanger she'd placed it on the previous night, slipped her phone into her pocket, and prised the door open again.

There was still no sign of movement, but she would have to pass the archway to get from her suite to Louis's master suite. It was, as they said, now or never.

Scuttling down the hallway as quietly as she could—it only occurred to Alex that the sound of the vacuum would have masked her footsteps by the time she reached the archway—she paused to peek around the corner. The unmistakeable figure of a woman clad in a tunic, black trousers and sensible shoes vigorously working a machine confirmed Alex's fears and sent her heart bouncing violently up into the region of her oesophagus.

With a final dash across the door opening, Alex hurried to the end of corridor, and after her first tentative knock went unanswered, she let herself in before the cleaner rounded the corner and spotted her. With relief, she noted the suite was a mirror image of hers, although the décor was a little more masculine, the sofas more Louis-style, the elegant, darker wood of the furniture giving the impression that the room was naturally Louis's, rather than having been carefully selected by some designer with a brief. Her eyes were drawn involuntarily to a broad antique-looking desk. Beautiful, unmistakable workmanship, a piece of furniture that she might have even chosen for herself.

Her stomach twisted and flopped. It was getting harder and harder to reconcile the fast lifestyle, typical bad-boy Louis with the sophisticated, complex man she was getting to know. But she shouldn't be here, it was very much Louis's personal space. And she was invading it.

In two minds, Alex hovered where she was. Then she edged back to the door that led back into the hallway and nervously wrapped her fingers around the door handle, wondering if she should leave. She inched the door open, only for the sound of the vacuum to assail her again.

No, leaving was definitely not an option.

Alex scrambled back across the room and pressed her hands to the set of doors on the other side, which could only lead through to the bedroom, and rapped softly, her voice little more than a whisper.

'Louis?'

Silence.

She rapped again, sharper this time, but there was still no response.

Her pulse beat wildly at her wrists, making her arms almost tingle with anticipation. As if she'd run a marathon when all she'd done was manage a brief hallway sprint. But it wasn't about the distance, it was about her proximity to Louis's bedroom right this moment; the fact that entering the room where he slept, where his bed was, seemed so utterly personal.

For the first time in years, Alex dithered. Then the sound of the vacuum grew suddenly louder and she knew the cleaner must have rounded the corner into the corridor. Time was running out.

Pulling her lips into a grim line, Alex sucked in a deep breath, placed her palm on the door handle and pushed. The door offered no resistance at all, swinging easily despite its obvious solid weight, and silently inviting her into the room beyond. It took her everything she had to step through.

Light danced playfully off every surface, startling and disorientating her, but there was no mistaking the source. A bank of glass lined one side of the bedroom, but rather than giving out to the city view, as in the other rooms of the apartment, inviting blue waters lay on the other side of this windowed wall. For a moment she thought she was peering into an aquarium with no sea life in sight, although something had to have been in there recently as it was these agitated waters that were catching the light and bouncing the reflections back into the bedroom.

Louis's bedroom.

For a moment she'd almost forgotten. Yet now she looked around it was hard to believe she'd missed the oversized bed on the other side of the room, which looked as though it had been hewn from the oldest, strongest, most striking of English oaks.

It was also *unmade*.

Alex swallowed. Hard.

Crisp, white sheets had been thrown off and there was a single dent on a plump Oxford-pillowcased pillow. Her mind accelerated away from her, dragging her along as though she were tied to them with ropes. Louis, naked, in those sheets. Had his mind tossed and turned last night with images of her, the way hers had of him?

Probably not. That shame was no doubt hers alone. At least he wasn't here to witness her bursting in on him. *But where* was *he*?

Abruptly a movement at around ceiling level snagged her attention and she whirled round to catch a figure diving into the water that she now realised was a swimming pool. Louis was cutting through the water, fast and skilful, his front crawl one of which even a world-class athlete would be proud.

Did the man have to excel at everything?

He was spellbinding. Hard, unyielding lines, breathtakingly masculine.

A low ache made itself felt between her legs. The same low ache she'd been pretending she didn't feel all night. The same way she'd pretended she didn't recall exactly how his hypnotising physique felt against her body.

But she'd only been fooling herself. She remembered it all. How he'd felt. How he'd tasted. How he hadn't simply kissed her but had claimed her. Somehow branded her. Here, now, in his bedroom and looking at him through the glass wall, she couldn't fool herself any longer. It was time to abandon the notion that she could somehow control the spark that darted and sizzled between them. Somehow master it. She could no more command the attraction they shared than she could save a terminally ill patient, although her analogy felt just as deadly.

It was as if the more she tried to deny her attraction to Louis, the greater his hold over her became. He demonstrated a determination, a drive, a competitive edge in every facet of his life, even right here in the privacy of his own pool. Characteristics Alex had always found to be utterly compelling, but never more so than in the utterly focussed Louis.

And more and more she was moving away from the idea this mad scheme with Louis was a hail Mary to save Rainbow House for now, and towards the consideration that Louis might be her best chance ever for securing the future of the place for a very long time in the future.

Somewhere along the line she'd gone from suspecting his motives to trusting more than she'd trusted anyone in a very, very long while.

When had that happened?

As if sensing her thoughts, Louis turned his head, his gaze slamming without warning into hers, and she felt pinned to the spot with the intensity of it. Her whole body came alive when he stared at her that way. As though he saw nothing else but her.

She had no idea how long they stayed that way. It could have been seconds, or even a minute—she had no doubts that Louis was some kind of Poseidon, able to hold his breath for just as long as he desired under that water. She watched, riveted, as he kicked out, propelling himself up to the surface and to the edge, where he pulled himself out of the water with apparent ease.

And then he was gone and still she stood there, staring into the roughly churning water and wondering why she suddenly felt so lost. She started towards the glass wall, her nose almost pressed to it as she looked up to the water's surface.

'Something wrong?'

Alex spun around, her tongue apparently glued to the roof of her mouth.

'Alex, is everything all right?' Louis demanded, descending a set of stairs in the bedroom that had been concealed like an illusion against the panelled wall behind it. Just as the layout of the room had concealed the fact that there was a mezzanine level at all.

But it wasn't the clever architecture that had humiliatingly stolen her voice. Bare chested and glistening with beaded water, a towel now wrapped around his waist, Louis's presence filled the space, making it feel too small to contain him, pressing in on her and leaving her unable to even draw a breath.

She opened her mouth to speak but nothing came out. Louis's mouth curled up in almost grim triumph.

'Or perhaps you were just missing me after all?'

The wryness in his tone licked through her like flames racing over a wood-dust floor, and in its potency it created a smoke fog in her head, smothering all but the most inappropriate, indecent thoughts. She tried to snag her eyes from the tiniest of rivers making their way down the contours of the muscular V of his body but found that she couldn't. Her fingers itched to follow the path of the water, to trace their route, to smooth their flow, to actually *lick* them away.

Ludicrous.

And still she couldn't shake the image. Couldn't seem to regain control of her senses. She went first hot, then cold, and then impossibly hot again. And all the while Louis kept on approaching her, closing the space between them tantalisingly slowly. She needed to move, back away, turn to the side, do *anything* to halt his advance. It took her all her time to swallow. Hard.

'Though if it were the latter I'd have expected something a little...*less* than whatever it is you're wearing right now.'

That damned winceyette nightie. His grin was as wicked as if he could read her mind. It shouldn't have been possible to make the situation any worse and yet as Alex flushed and her hands clutched at her chest to pull the material together—unnecessary since it already might as well have been a tent over her entire body—she realised she couldn't have done a better job of broadcasting her lust if she'd hired a big screen in the car park of the hospital itself.

'Where did you get it from?' he continued, his rakish grin scraping through her, raw and exhilarating. 'Your ninety-year-old grandmother's wardrobe?'

'Very funny.'

To her chagrin she could hear the huskiness in her voice. Louis's eyes glinted but, try as she may, she couldn't seem to loosen her grip. If anything, she found herself gripping the fabric even tighter. Still he didn't slow his advance and Alex was forced to crane her neck up to watch him.

They both knew it was a deliberate ploy on his part.

'Is this your idea of seductive nightwear?'

'This is my idea of never becoming another notch on Louis Delaroche's bedpost nightwear,' she muttered, wishing her traitorous body had also bought into such a notion.

'Ah, I see.' Reaching her, he stepped right into her personal space and placed his hands on her shoulders, as if testing her.

Pull away, her head screamed. Her body—with the mental equivalent of sticking its fingers in its ears—refused to move a millimetre.

'Is it working?' he enquired over-politely, as if he was unaware of the current flowing between them, his touch like an flash on her skin.

Alex wavered. There was something she had to tell him. A reason she was here. For a brief second it was there, on the periphery of her mind, and she mentally lunged for it, but then Louis let one hand slide off her shoulder, his fingers brushing over the cotton, his touch scorching her flesh underneath, and for the life of her she couldn't remember anything any more.

'Is this really what you slept in?'

Her cheeks flushed, she could feel the heat. As if he knew she'd hated every second of the unfamiliar, rough material when she could have been wearing a lot less and revelling in the high thread count of Louis's luxurious sheets.

'Where did you get it from?' he pressed, his amusement refusing to abate.

Much like her embarrassment.

'My great-aunt sent it to me when I bought my first home. She thought I might get…cold.'

'She didn't think that, as a doctor, you could probably afford a place that had its own heating?' He arched an eyebrow.

It was a battle just to unstick her tongue from the roof of her mouth. It felt as though she'd just swallowed a spoonful of peanut butter.

'She remembered her first home. She had coal fires but no central heating. She's quite old, ninety-six. But still going strong. Anyway, I guess you weren't too far off the mark with your first observation about it looking as though it was something I'd got from my ninety-year-old grandmother's wardrobe.'

She was babbling. It was as much a giveaway as anything.

'Is that so?' True to form, Louis was tracing his fingertips across the material over her collarbone and she couldn't help but shiver. The corners of his mouth turned up ever so slightly. 'It's in remarkably pristine condition. One might almost believe you'd never worn it before.'

'Well, I have,' she lied, shame rippling through her at just how easily he seemed to see through her.

'When?' The challenge was stamped on every quirk of his too-perfect face.

Alex gritted her teeth.

'Lots of times.'

'Is that so? Because it looks almost as if you wore it just for me,' he continued softly, taking another step closer so that the breath caught in her throat, her body completely forgetting how to breathe. 'Tell me, Alex, who were you trying to remind to keep their distance? Me? Or you?'

She couldn't answer. She didn't dare. Whatever she said, she'd surely give herself away. His eyes bored into hers and for the longest time she couldn't drag her gaze away, couldn't deflect him. His fingers still traced a pattern on her skin, making her whole body tighten. She craved him in a way she'd never known possible.

'Does it matter who I wore it for?' she managed. 'The fact is that I'm trying to make a point.'

'That's what I thought,' Louis muttered gruffly, his hand moving quickly to cradle the back of her head as he tugged her to him. 'You realise you wouldn't have to make a point if you weren't fighting your instinct, of course?'

It was a rhetorical question, which was good since she couldn't seem to make her voice work. Her blood thundered through her and, so help her, she angled her head in tacit invitation.

'I thought it would…put you off.'

'I hate to tell you,' he continued in a voice that sounded anything other than displeased, 'but it isn't working. If anything, my imagination is filling in the blanks with re-markable enthusiasm.'

'Is that supposed to be a compliment?' Her voice shook. Something still pressed in on her mind but she couldn't locate it, couldn't remember what was so urgent other than Louis, right here, right now.

'More a statement of fact.'

The low purr was reminiscent of the promising hum of a highly powered supercar moments before it roared into action and burned everything else into nothing in its wake. She shivered in anticipation. Turned inside out by Louis, even though he hadn't done anything. Yet.

But she wanted him to. Oh, how she wanted him.

He dragged his thumb across her lower lip and heat bloomed in her anew.

'Kiss me.'

Deadly soft, but nonetheless an unequivocal demand.

She could have done so many things—refused him, decried him, walked away from him. Instead, she did the worst thing possible. She obeyed him.

Tipping her head back, she arched against him, rising just slightly onto her toes, and closed the gap between them, a thousand fireworks exploding in her head, her chest, and lower, as she finally pressed her lips to his.

CHAPTER EIGHT

IT WAS NOTHING Louis had ever known before.

The moment her hot, slick mouth fitted to his, an urgent need clawed within him. Even more raw and desperate than it had been back out there, in front of the restaurant.

Because this time there was no audience. This time they couldn't pretend it was all about the game. This time there was nothing to stop them.

He deepened the kiss and the fact that Alex was lost, barely able to keep her grip on him in an effort to keep herself upright, only intensified the moment. From the delicious drugging draw of her fingernails over his muscled shoulder blades to the feel of her hair slipping through his hands like the finest silk.

His tongue slid deliciously over hers and she let out a sound that made everything tighten, coil in his lower abdomen. He cradled her cheek as though she was as precious as the irreplaceable, valuable sculptures dotted around his penthouse. And she cast every one of them into the shade.

It was bliss to kiss her. He paid homage to her lips, the corners of her mouth and then her jawline, blazing a trail of hot kisses down the neck and exulting in the way her whole body quivered in response.

When she moved against him again, moulding herself to his chest and pressing her breasts against him, he wanted her with a ferocity he hadn't known before. Up against the panelled wall, in his bed, anywhere. Everywhere.

Every way.

He wanted to feel her without the barrier of the stupid winceyette nightgown, but he could use it to his advantage. He could make her wish she'd never brought the damned thing. Spanning her ribcage with his hands, he moved his palms to circle her and flicked his thumbs over nipples straining even beneath the heavy material. She swayed instinctively against him again, a muted cry slipping from her mouth—and a curse—and triumph stabbed through him.

'Regretting your choice of night attire yet?' he murmured against her throat, feeling her pulse fluttering wildly beneath his lips.

'Shut up and take it off,' she moaned hoarsely, and he smirked all the wider.

'Soon. There's no rush, we can take our time.'

Her eyes flew open. One minute heavy-lidded and dark, the next squinting at him and taking in his grin. A low gasp escaped her.

'You're enjoying this. Teasing me.'

'Of course. Like I said, there's no rush.'

'You say it as though you're perfectly in control,' she muttered. 'Only I know you're not.'

Carefully, deliberately she moved her hips, rocking against him until she felt the unmistakeable ridge of his arousal. Solid, insistent, almost painfully hard. He hadn't such an ache, such a desperate throb in a long time. Suddenly her hands moved to the twist of his towel, which still hung low on his hips, tugging the knot and releasing it before he could react. And then she was touching him, her fingers gliding up and down his length and sending him wild with desire.

Louis groaned. Things were moving fast. Too fast. This wasn't the way he did things. He was never so…desperate. He had to slow it down, get back in control of this runaway train of need. He grasped her wrist, encircling it with his finger and thumb, and moved it from him. She protested even more when he moved her entire body from his, ignoring the way the loss of contact made him feel abruptly lost. Bereft.

Then he lifted the ugly, tent-like nightgown over her head in one easy movement, balled it up and tossed it across the room. And finally she was standing before him in nothing but the tiniest, sexiest scrap of lace he thought he'd ever seen.

'Exquisite,' he commented thickly, his hand sweeping over her shoulder, down over her chest, one perfect breast, and skimming over her abdomen before running a finger over the thin velvet band of her underwear. He traced patterns over her lower stomach and dipped low enough to brush against her hot, feminine heat, revelling in her gasp, then back up over her torso, leaving her aching for so much more.

'It's peacock-blue,' she blurted out abruptly. Rattled.

That she was so responsive to him, so brimming with need only made him all the harder. She poured through all his senses. A strange kind of insanity ran through his blood. He was consumed by her.

'I wasn't talking about the underwear,' he managed gruffly, 'so much as the woman wearing it.'

'Oh.'

So demure, so modest, so unaware of her own sexuality. *So his.*

His lips curled upwards slightly. Such a possessive sensation should have alarmed him. It didn't. Instead, he simply lowered his head and kissed her again, and she drank him in as if she thought this was her one and only chance.

It was like the most delectable adventure, kissing and nibbling and licking his way from her eager mouth, along that pretty jawline and down the long line of her elegant neck. He dawdled and dipped into the sensitive hollow that made her tremble so sublimely in his arms. When he rolled one glorious nipple in his fingers before bending his head to suck on it, his tongue swirling a pattern of its own, she called out as her fingers bit into his shoulders, her back curving as though she offered herself up to him all the more.

'I can't get enough of you,' he mumbled as he moved to lavish the same attention on her other breast.

She choked something out, but it was almost incoherent to him, and he couldn't bring himself to stop long enough to ask her to repeat it.

His hands glided over her body, acquainting himself with every contour, every feature. Imprinting them into his head. Maybe into his very soul.

Every now and then he allowed his fingers to dip lower, but never for long. And never where she wanted him most, if her soft moans and body rolls were anything to go by. But Louis suddenly found he had his own battle to win. He wanted to make this first time last, to make it perfect for her, but his own body—up until now always well within his expert command—was threatening to spin out of his control. Every time she arched her body into him, brushing against his sex in a silent plea, he had to fight the carnal urge to pick her up, throw her on the bed and bury himself inside her until she was crying out his name and neither of them knew where each of them ended and the other began.

Almost feverish with lust, Louis dipped his head again,

his teeth grazing the hollow of her neck with just enough pressure to make her gasp. To make her hips rock against him in another silent plea.

'Tell me you want me,' he commanded, the faintly salty taste of her skin teasing the end of his tongue. But he forced himself to stop, to put a gossamer-fine layer of air between them.

She could barely answer.

'What are you doing?'

She twisted to get back into his arms. He held her away.

'Say the words,' he rasped, pausing but not lifting his head.

He was reckless, and abraded, and pounding.

'I want you,' she managed to choke out. Then, as if she felt bolder, the assertion came again. More confident this time. 'I *want* you.'

'Where?'

A crimson stain spread over her lovely cheeks.

'You know where.'

'Tell me,' he ordered.

He needed there to be no doubt, no ambiguity. He knew what she thought of his morals to date. He had to hear her say what she wanted. For her to know she'd said it.

Shakily, she took hold of his wrist; moved his hand to the heat at the top of her legs, her whisper so quiet he had to strain to hear it.

'Here.'

'Here?' he enquired casually, as though it wasn't killing him to restrain himself.

She bit her lip, a jerk of a nod.

'There.'

'Better.' He didn't even try to disguise the naked need in his voice.

But it didn't matter. He had what he needed.

He nudged her over to sit on the edge of the bed. Dropping to his knees in front of her, his hand lifting one of her legs over his shoulder, Louis hooked the flimsy scrap of lace aside and pressed his mouth to the centre of her hot, honeyed need, drinking her in at last.

Alex heard herself cry out. A low, husky sound, and then nothing. She couldn't. She could barely even catch her breath.

Every single nerve in her body reacted as he licked into her core where she'd felt heavy, *so heavy*; yearning for him with a need that was almost crippling.

He muttered in French, but Alex didn't need to understand the words to know it was fierce, thick with desire. For the first time she felt desirable and wanton. Just as provocative, as sexual as the women he usually dated. Except that she wasn't, and she wasn't sure if there was something she should be doing for him. If there was something important she was forgetting.

'Louis…' She lifted herself slightly onto one elbow and tried to shift away from him for a moment.

Louis lifted his head a fraction until his smouldering gaze met hers.

'Relax,' he murmured, his breath the most sensual whisper against the softest heights of her thigh, making her all the more molten inside. 'I want to taste you. Claim you.'

He slid his hand under one leg, lifting it slightly as he shouldered his way under it, granting himself better access, and he lowered his head again, the way his eyes still locked with hers only making it all the more erotic. And then he licked into her again and it was like an explosion of fireworks across Alex's eyes.

Louis toyed with her, kissed her, sucked on her, his dexterous fingers and devious mouth working in harmony to render her completely incapable of any action. Any thought. Blood roared in her ears and she could feel his hair through the fingers she couldn't recall lacing against his head. She gave herself up to sensations she had never felt in her life before. Surely never would again.

She could feel fire inside her growing as he stoked it. Higher and higher. His long fingers slipped in and out of her even as her hips bucked involuntarily against his sinful mouth. Wild need coursed through her, dizzying, searing, clearing her mind of that last, insistent thought. He was moving faster now, making her clasp at the luxurious bedsheets in a hopeless attempt to gain traction, her gasps and pants fast and shallow.

And then he twisted his wrist and Alex stiffened and shuddered and then simply fractured. She splintered into a thousand perfect shards. She cried out his name again and again. Still he didn't stop. Kissing her, holding her, playing with her, until she finally, *finally* stilled.

For several perfect moments Alex could almost imagine it was the start of something new. Then, abruptly, the outside doors to the suite banged, the sound of the vacuum invading her ears, and as Louis's grip loosened for a single instant, Alex rolled back on the bed, exhaling in dismay. But not for what she'd let Louis do, instead simply for the fact that they'd been interrupted.

That was what she'd forgotten.

'Your cleaning lady,' she breathed heavily. 'That's what woke me up this morning. That's why I'm here.'

His low curse reverberated between them and he crossed the room in two long strides. They were lucky the woman was still in the sitting area on the other side of the bedroom doors.

'Wait here,' he barked out. 'She can't see you like this.'

'That was what I thought…' Alex blurted after him.

But he was already gone, leaving her alone in the middle of his bedroom. And the shivers that accompanied her were nothing whatsoever to do with the temperature.

What had she been thinking? Losing herself with Louis to the extent that she'd even forgotten someone could walk in on them at any moment. That wasn't who she was. It wasn't who she'd ever been.

But it was who playboy Louis was.

It was one thing to agree to this charade of a relationship, the engagement to come and ultimately the marriage. To pretend she could be bought as a wife. It was quite another to actually *act* as though she was some booty call mistress.

The worst thing about it was that a part of her didn't want to listen. A part of her wanted to wait for Louis to come back through those doors and pick back up with her exactly where he'd left off.

Hot shame flooded through her.

Scampering off the bed, she searched the room for the nightgown that he'd balled up and tossed. It wasn't hard to spot, lying on the floor on the other side of the bed like some huge, cheap rug.

Mocking her.

She hurried over and snatched it up, tussling with the long, ruffled sleeves, which had been pulled inside out in the moment, pretending she didn't see the buttons that he'd torn off in his haste.

Righting it, she tugged it back over her head, telling herself she was glad it was as frumpy and unflattering as it was, and moved to the doors to listen.

She could hear the tone of the conversation, as one-way as it was, even if the words themselves were too muffled to get the detail. Still, she could tell that Louis was brief, firm, yet nonetheless polite; was forced to admit that it was a world away from the arrogant, entitled man who the press loved to hate.

Then he was closing the door as he stepped back into the room. Just the two of them, again. Him in his towel, her in her nightgown, just as they'd been at the start of this thing. Still, this time he kept his distance, staying across the floor from her.

She didn't know whether to feel relieved or hurt. She only knew that the air felt thick around them. Oppressive. And she didn't know what that meant.

'She's leaving,' Louis stated flatly, but somehow she didn't get the impression that he just meant the bedroom corridor.

Alex shook her head. Why did everything feel so muggy?

'Who's leaving?'

Louis offered a clipped nod.

'Janelle, my cleaning lady. For the day. Just give her a few minutes.'

'You can't be expecting to just pick up where you left off,' she accused, guilt lending her voice a harsher quality.

'You want to pretend you don't want that?' He raised an eyebrow, faintly mocking her.

'I'm not pretending anything.'

'So you admit you want me.'

She swallowed.

'I don't want you.'

'Is this the game we're back to playing?' he asked quietly, dangerously, enough to make her skin prickle in warning. 'Because I can tell you now, Alex, that I'm bored with it.'

'We agreed this was a business arrangement. A marriage in name only. We agreed there would be no sex.'

If only her body wasn't protesting every word she was saying.

'We didn't agree anything of the sort,' Louis stated calmly. 'It was never discussed.'

'Because it went without saying.'

'No, because I always assumed somewhere down the line you'd give up your ridiculous notion of pretending this intense attraction between us didn't exist.'

'So you always planned to seduce me.' She crossed her arms disdainfully.

'I was always expecting this moment to arise. I was always waiting for you to tell me you wanted me. And exactly *where* you wanted me,' he countered, the deliberate emphasis causing another blush to colour her cheeks.

'That's why you made me say it.'

'I just wanted to hear it,' he said softly. 'And I intend to hear it again and again in the weeks and months to come.'

'You won't,' she bit out. 'Because this will never happen again. Nothing like this can ever happen between us again.'

'That's where you're wrong, *amour*.' His calm tone was almost worse than if he'd been angry. 'Because now that I know just how much you want me, now that I have irrefutable proof of how incredible we would be together, I have no intention of this marriage being merely a charade.'

'You can't make me…'

'Of course not,' he scorned. 'Neither would I ever dream of it. But I would never have to. You will come to me.'

'No, I most certainly won't.' Was her thudding heart because of her conviction, or because she was terribly afraid that he was right?

'You will,' he assured her, his wicked smile going right to her core, where she was still soft, still wet from his masterful play. 'Just like you did this morning.'

She couldn't seem to stop her teeth from worrying at her lip. As long as they were in such close proximity there was a good chance she would once again give in to the baser needs that Louis seemed to have unearthed in her.

She tipped her head back, barely stopping herself from rising up onto her toes.

'Then it's lucky you're working away in France for the next month or so.'

As victories went, it didn't feel like much of one. Rather, she felt empty at the prospect.

'Luckier still that you're coming with me.'

She told herself that her heart didn't leap. His unwavering gaze didn't help matters.

'I can't. I have work.'

'You can and you have to. I'll deal with the hospital. If we're to convince the press we're together, that this engagement is a true whirlwind romance and not a sham, then you have no choice. That's if you want me to claim control of the Lefebvre Group and save Rainbow House, of course. What is more important to you? This false sense of pride or Rainbow House?'

He had her. They both knew it. She still quashed the part of her that rejoiced at the knowledge.

'Then this nonsensical exchange is over?'

She opened her mouth to object but knew she couldn't. His wry smile still turned her on.

'Good. So, we shall be staying at Chateau Rochepont—'

'Your family estate?' she cut in. 'The press will have a field day. You've never taken any woman back there.'

Her body felt compressed, tight, too small for her skin. It was only intensified by his inscrutable expression.

Had this always been part of the plan? Or had it developed in the last few minutes?

'All the more reason to make a point of it now, don't you think?'

'I can't—'

'It's non-negotiable.'

He was back to his Louis voice. Imperious, inflexible. Part of her didn't even care. He wanted her with him. Nevertheless, she shook her head.

'Louis, I can't… I need more time… I…'

'The point of you moving in here was to be with me so that I could help you avoid the media after last night at the restaurant. If I'm not around, who will protect you?'

'I can look after myself,' she argued. 'Besides, surely the very fact that you have all this security to get up here makes it safer than my little house. I still have to go to the hospital, carry out my work.'

'They can replace you.'

'I owe it to Gordon to give him time to choose a replacement.' She knew that would halt him. Louis respected her mentor as much as she did. She pressed her advantage. 'A *temporary* replacement.'

'Fine. I'll give you three days. But don't say I didn't warn you that the press would hound you. I'll trust you not to let them rattle you.'

'Louis—'

'Three days, Alex, and then you *will* join me out there,' he said, shutting her down. 'It will be the perfect setting for a public proposal to cement our plan.'

Her throat was suddenly painfully dry.

'The plan.' She wasn't sure how she managed to nod, let alone speak. 'Right.'

'And, Alex…' His voice rasped, pushing down the feeble defences she was frantically trying to reinstate. 'We will be revisiting what happened here this morning. I can promise you that much.'

She told herself that the gurgling sensation was her stomach roiling at Louis's highhandedness, and not a bubbling excitement at being alone with him for the next month or so.

She almost believed it, too.

CHAPTER NINE

'RIGHT, I NOW have your bloodwork results, your MRI and EMG. And I can say that I believe that facial decompression surgery is a good treatment option in your case, since there isn't any damage to the facial nerve itself.'

He smiled gently as his patient and her partner promptly dissolved into tears of joy. The paralysis that had left one half of her face severely drooped had affected her confidence and quality of life considerably and other less invasive treatments of the paralysis had been unsuccessful.

It was good to be delivering positive news, but ultimately Louis couldn't help but feel happy today for anything which would keep his mind off the fact that Alex would be arriving in less than a couple of hours. In fact, she would probably be getting ready to board the plane right about now.

It still needled him that he'd had to fight her about taking his own private jet instead of some commercial airline. That she hadn't just obeyed him. Accepted that the private plane would make her life—and flight—far more pleasant. No doubt she'd been making a point to him. But he didn't care. She had acquiesced in the end and she was coming, and the latter was what really mattered. The chemistry had been there all along but the fact that, for the first time in his life, he was resisting it had to be the reason Alexandra Vardy got under his skin in a way that no other woman ever had.

While she'd pretended to him, and to herself, that she didn't want sex, he'd kept his distance as best he could. But hearing her acknowledge that she wanted him had been pivotal. It had been the moment he'd realised that if he wanted to conquer this apparent *longing* he'd inconveniently developed for the woman, he was going to have to take every opportunity to slake this effervescing thirst for each other.

He'd told her to call it a break away, and he hadn't been entirely joking. Getting Alex away from work, from the UK, from the press, would no doubt help her to relax. Make her see that denying the attraction that thundered between them was only feeding it all the more. Once they'd slaked their physical desire they could get on with the task in hand without such unwanted complications.

He carefully ignored the voice that echoed in his head that he was being naïve, and pulled his concentration back to his patient before it could wander too far. Another thing that had never, not once, happened to him in his professional life with any other woman before.

'At this stage my plan would be to carry out a mastoidectomy, which is where I would remove part of the mastoid bone behind your ear in order that your inflamed facial nerve might have enough room to expand, thereby relieving some of the pressure that is no doubt causing some of the symptoms of your facial paralysis.'

'That's wonderful,' the woman choked out. 'I can't believe it.'

'I'm sure you already know this,' he encouraged, 'but the facial nerve, also known as the cranial nerve VII, serves many vital functions, not just the motor function that allows you to smile and frown. Although we always prefer the smiling.'

His gentle joking elicited a smile, as he'd hoped it would, keeping them positive and engaged so that he could get across as much important information as he could.

'The anticipation would be that, as well as some facial control, you should experience some degree of return of gland function in your eyes, nose and mouth, making it easier to close your eye and even to blink, so there would be less need for the eyedrops all the time; and improvements to both your senses of smell and taste.'

'And if the drooping is reduced then she'll be less prone to accidentally biting her inner cheek, right, Doc?' the patient's partner asked, and Louis couldn't help noticing the way the couple squeezed hands in a silent, supportive conversation of their own.

Though there was no logical explanation, it made him think of Alex all over again.

'It should,' he agreed. 'So fewer ulcerations and infections. But, as I said, it won't wholly reverse the paralysis. And I do need to warn you that it might take up to a year for optimal results, and there will still be a significant degree of asymmetry.'

'That's okay,' she managed, her barely contained emotion making her sound slightly more indistinct than usual. 'It's better than what I have now.'

'And how is work?' Louis asked as carefully as he could. 'Are your colleagues understanding about your condition?'

'Actually, I'm a teaching assistant specialising in children with severe learning difficulties. Some of them just asked outright, a few of them were a little unsettled in the beginning, and some of them struggle anyway with emotions and empathy. However, I'm lucky that for the most part, as long as I act the same towards them, give them the same love and care, it doesn't really matter to them how I look.'

'That's good.' He forced an understanding smile onto his face.

Even as he walked the couple to the door, his mouth still talking to them, his mind was on Alex.

Why was it that everything seemed to pull him straight back around to her? The way that, unlike his patient, it hadn't mattered what she'd done, she was never going to win her father's love. Never going to make him forgive her for not being a match for her brother. For not being the saviour sibling. Something that had never been within her control.

And yet, despite all that, she still fought so damned fiercely for Rainbow House.

How many other kids were like Alex?

Like him?

It struck him that there had to be more he could do to help. Not just Rainbow House, but places like it. For Alex. For his mother. For himself.

He might be pretending to the world that he was changing, he might even convince them all. But that was all about perceptions. Up until now he hadn't really believed he *would* change. Not deep down.

Maybe he could.

Alex seemed to believe it.

Closing the door behind the couple, Louis picked up his ringing phone, knowing exactly who it was going to be, and part of him wished he could just ignore it and will his father away.

And yet he should be celebrating. Rejoicing in the fact that if Jean-Baptiste was calling him, it was because he was beginning to panic. Because his father was being forced to recognise that support for Louis was beginning to gain momentum.

It should fill him with jubilation. Instead, it was shadowed by Louis's delight in knowing that in a matter of hours Alex would be back in his life. Tonight, he was determined, she would be back in his arms.

His father was little more than an unwelcome interruption.

'Oui?' Louis demanded curtly, clicking it onto speakerphone and sliding the phone across his desk as he busied his hands with sorting a few files.

His father's fast, angry tone barked at him in Franglais, a sure sign that he was mad.

'You're seeing *la putain* who tried to corner me at the gala *soirée*?'

Louis sucked in a deep breath. Then another.

He would not allow himself to be baited.

'I'm seeing Alexandra Vardy, a respected doctor at Silveroaks Hospital. She's Gordon's protégé,' he added with painstaking breeziness. 'I know you'd be impressed if you saw how skilled an anaesthetist she is. Oh, and I should also inform you that Alex is coming out to the estate.'

'No, she most certainly is not.'

'Too late, I'm afraid,' Louis injected with deliberate calmness. 'She's already around thirty-six thousand feet.'

The silence suggested his father was uncharacteristically apoplectic in his characteristic rage. Louis almost smiled into the silent phone, though it was a hard, brittle excuse for a smile.

'I forbid it,' Jean-Baptiste spluttered eventually.

And there again was the easily enraged man Louis knew all too well. It was gratifying to know that not everyone had been fooled by the knight-in-shining-scrubs reputation that the media had painted all these years.

'I'm not asking permission,' Louis stated in a tone so cold he could bet it would rival the Norwegian ice hotel where his father had taken his latest squeeze. 'The estate is my home, too. I'm merely taking this opportunity to inform you. Call it courtesy. This way, you don't have to engage in another disagreeable phone call to verify what will no doubt be in tomorrow's papers.'

'I know you lied to my security team to save her from the humiliation of being ejected from the ball like the unwelcome stray dog that she was. I know you play to your reputation as a playboy, Louis, but even you could have done better than scraps like that.'

Jean-Baptiste was goading him. Louis knew it. And still he clenched his fists at the barely disguised snide tone. He couldn't let the older man think he was winning. Not where Alex was concerned. Still, he had no idea how he managed it.

'Alex did mention you and she had had a little…misunderstanding that night.'

'Un malentendu?' the older man exploded, as much at Louis's calmness as at his words, but it still felt like a hollow victory. 'It was no misunderstanding. She threatened to go to the press with how the Lefebvre Group and the Delaroche Foundation are composed of one and the same board. The vitriolic little *putain* tried to claim she knew that I was transferring assets simply to sell them off and line my own pockets.'

'We both know that isn't true although, to be fair, her assumption was based on her knowledge at the time.' Louis forced himself to stay civil. He would not lose his cool. He *could* not. 'But don't worry, I've since set her straight.'

'Meaning?' The snarl rolled down the line.

'Meaning that I assured her you weren't using the Delaroche Foundation to shut down Rainbow House simply for financial gain.'

Deliberate, aimed, striking true. The silence was almost lethal.

'You told her about your mother's accident.'

'More or less.' Louis shrugged. 'They weren't my exact words.'

The gutter-level curses his father was uttering were another long-overdue, satisfying strike. Louis had a few choice names of his own he would like to throw back. But he didn't. He restrained himself, knowing Alex wouldn't approve, and it was amazing how her good opinion was suddenly driving his actions.

The cursing stopped abruptly and silence cracked instead. Air practically whistled down the phone. Icy and foreboding.

'Be very careful which side you choose to be on, Louis. Or you may find yourself dealing with questions about your mother concerning things I'm certain you would far prefer the press didn't know.'

The threat insinuated itself through the ether, filling up Louis's office until he was reaching for a window, as if the toxicity was as real as the air he was breathing.

He reached a hand up to tug at the shirt collar that suddenly seemed to have closed around his neck. He had no idea how he kept his voice as calm, as level, as he did.

'Are you threatening to tell them she committed suicide?'

'What do they say, the truth will always out?'

Emotions coursed through Louis so fast and so violent that he wasn't sure how he remained upright.

'Then perhaps it's time it did,' he managed. 'Perhaps they might ask the questions I was always too afraid of you to ask. Such as why such a strong, loyal, connected woman should be so beaten down by her husband that she felt she had no alternative than to do what she did.'

With that, Louis terminated the call. Before any of his father's poison could get to him. Before he could wonder at how, since Alex had come into his life, he suddenly had the strength to turn the tables on his father.

And that was just the start, he thought triumphantly. With her by his side, he could save Rainbow House for Alex, even if that meant temporarily claiming the birthright he'd refused to pursue all these years. The responsibility that he still didn't care to take on.

Not that it mattered. Once things had settled down he would appoint a good chairman and leave the ship in some other captain's eminently more capable control. As long as he had his surgeries. And Alex.

He couldn't stay in the room any longer. Not after that call. Snatching up his coat, Louis hurried out of the door, barely locking it behind him, and then down the stairs rather than wait for the lift.

In less than an hour Alex would be here. And he found he could scarcely wait.

Take it slowly. Don't make her bolt.

He could work the rest out from there.

Alex gazed out of the small aircraft window, trying to quell the muffled *rat-a-tat* of her heart against her chest and feeling more confused than ever.

When she'd embarked in England not ninety minutes ago, she'd been feeling a horrible combination of irritability and fragility, resenting every moment of what was to come even as the plane had climbed into the grey skies and plunged into the thick cloud cover. She'd tried to lose herself in a book, and when that hadn't worked, the latest medical journal. She'd refused the first two glasses of champagne that a silent but efficient attendant had brought to her. But at some point, right after the cloud cover had broken and warm sunshine had poured through the tiny window, she'd accepted the third attempt, stopped mumbling her speech and allowed herself to breathe for the first time in days.

Now she gazed down on the deep blue waters of the Mediterranean, glinting like jewels in the brilliant sunlight, and felt that little bit more carefree, that little less drowned in responsibility. Her champagne flute stood freshly refilled, her paperback abandoned on her lap, and her head filled with indecent images of Louis from that morning in his penthouse.

Even the memory of him made her feel alive. The anticipation of seeing him again was creating a low hum in her body that only seemed to grow louder the lower the plane descended through the French skies.

But she'd meant what she'd said when she'd told him it could never happen again.

Now, more than ever, she had to stick to her word. The last few days had been hell. Louis had warned her that the press would be unstoppable but she hadn't believed him. Instead, they'd been worse.

She turned her head to the tabloid that sat rolled up in the bag by her feet. As if *Apple Pie Alex* from her colleagues hadn't been bad enough, in the last couple of days, ever since the Louis kiss in that restaurant, the press had chosen to dub her *Vanilla Vardy*.

Vanilla Vardy too virginal for Lascivious Louis!

It might have been a compliment to her. It wasn't. It was as though even her kissing technique was plain and uninspiring and the tone all too closely matched a similar tabloid article from the other day that had breathlessly proclaimed:

Vanilla Vardy wins Luscious Louis Sympathy Vote!

As if they knew how he'd touched her that morning. She may not be a virgin per se, but it had been like she'd never been touched before, and certainly not with such an effect.

As if they knew that her response to him had been so visceral, so carnal that she'd barely even recognised herself.

She wondered if he was laughing at her the way the public would be if they'd seen the way she'd come apart so quickly in his arms. Congratulating himself on ruining her for any other man. Because he surely had.

And yet it took a real effort to bring herself to feel even a degree of remorse. To tell herself that she wasn't frustrated that they had been interrupted, or that the moment had been shattered, and that she hadn't had the courage to finish what Louis had started.

Because she'd wanted to. Oh, how she'd *ached* to. In that moment she'd known that she might never get another opportunity like that in her life, since no other man in her past had even come close to making her lose control the way she had in his bedroom. She couldn't imagine any other man in her future ever would either.

No one else would ever be able to match Louis, the way he'd made her feel, the way he'd made her writhe, the way he'd made her shatter.

There was only one Louis Delaroche.

Which was why that had to be her one and only slide into temptation. She couldn't afford to lose herself again. Couldn't afford to let him get under her skin the way he seemed to be so skilled at doing. Couldn't afford to indulge in all the fantasies she'd had over the last few nights, in which, instead of simply lying back and letting him pleasure her so thoroughly, she'd met him halfway. Doing things to him she knew she would never have the courage to try.

And that was why she had to keep her head on her shoulders from now on.

Only it wasn't that simple. Because for her, at least, there had been more than just the sex. Louis had awakened a side to her character that morning that had lain dormant for so many years that even she herself had thought it long gone. That daring, mischievous side to herself that she'd thought had died a long time ago. And she'd accepted that it was gone, almost welcomed its demise.

Who would ever have thought that Louis would be the person to resurrect it?

It didn't help that she'd received a concerned call from her father that morning to tell her that Rainbow House had been visited by a new team of hotshot lawyers who claimed they were working on behalf of the Lefebvre Group. He'd said that they'd managed to get through a temporary injunction to stop the transfer of assets to the Delaroche Foundation. And then her father had asked, in his gruff way, if their new advocates had anything to do with Louis Delaroche and the fact that photos of her and Louis kissing had been plastered all over the papers. He'd gently warned her against doing anything that wasn't *right*. That even Rainbow House wasn't worth certain sacrifices.

And she'd lied and assured him that the two things weren't related, even as she'd swelled with happiness and something she didn't care to identify that Louis had begun to fulfil his part of the deal. That he hadn't grown bored with the venture now that he'd claimed her as his.

But that still didn't mean he was finally ready to do

the right thing and take up the mantle of the Lefebvre Group, as his mother had always wanted him to do. Until he accepted that, surely it was yet another reason why she needed to separate the two, the business agreement from the sexual attraction.

It was only as the plane bumped down that Alex realised they'd landed, and the Morse code tapping of her heart became more urgent. More panicked.

Relax. He won't even be here.

Why would the great Louis come to meet her in person when he had people to send for that?

So was it any wonder that her stomach flipped and twisted when she descended the steps to see him waiting on the runway for her? Perched as he was on the bonnet of a sleek, black car, his impossibly long, muscular legs stretched out in front of him, a crisp suit shirt, sleeves rolled up and open at the neck.

'What are you doing here?'

He grinned, and her stomach knotted some more.

'I trust you had a pleasant flight? Didn't find my private plane too much of an ordeal after all?'

'It was wonderful,' she conceded.

'Bon.'

Before she had time to think, he thrust to his feet, pulling her into his arms and snagging her mouth with his.

It was happening too fast. She wasn't ready.

Her body was on fire with fresh need.

Startled, she pulled away, but his iron grip on her only tightened, his head bending so that only she could hear the mild reprimand. It should have felt threatening, instead it felt thrilling.

'I might remind you that the aim is to show the world that we have fallen madly, desperately in love. We've caught the public interest and we are being observed. All the time.'

'There's no one around,' she choked out, trying to look around.

Louis caught her hair, anchoring her head in place but looking for all the world like a passionate lover.

'Do not look, there is always someone around. The trick is to pretend you don't know they're there.'

'I *don't* know they're there,' she reasoned, wishing her heart would drop back into her chest instead of lodging itself somewhere around her throat.

'There's at least one guy with a long-lens camera on the outer perimeter, on the other side of the runway. The give-away is the odd glint of sunlight reflected by the glass,' he informed her. 'So kiss me, please. As if you really mean it.'

It may as well have been the excuse her body had been looking for to override any last shred of common sense. Leaning slowly backwards, her eyes meeting Louis's and never leaving them, she dropped her shoulder bag with exaggerated care and then looped her hands around his neck.

'As if I really mean it, you say?' she challenged, proud of the way her voice didn't shake, even once.

His gaze darkened.

'For the camera.'

'Oh, of course.' She quirked her lips, delighting in the flare of desire in his face.

Either he wanted her just like he had the other night, or he was a really, really good actor.

And then she kissed him. Met him. Matched him. Their mouths moved against each other, their tongues dancing a slow, sensual rhumba. This time it was she who eventually broke the contact, seeking out that impossibly square jaw-line until she reached his ear, grazing the lobe with semi-gentle teeth as she moved to the sensitive spot behind it.

His reaction was instant. And evident. Heat pooled between her legs at the unmistakeable feel of him. What *she* had managed to elicit. As though she had some kind of power over him. It was a heady sensation. She lost track of where they were, what was around them and she rocked against him, her body splayed against his.

'*Dieu*,' he growled in her ear, barely catching her hand from sliding down his chest to his trousers. 'Is this where you choose to come to me? Out here, on the tarmac?'

She blinked, crashing back to earth. Remembering where they were.

'I… The photographer,' she whispered hoarsely.

'Has more than enough, believe me.' His voice was harsh, tight. 'Now, get into the car.'

It took everything she had to stay calm and not scramble to get inside, wondering if she'd ever felt so mortified. When Louis joined her on the butter-soft leather she couldn't help her yelp of discomfort. Though she noticed he did nothing to close the gap between them.

'Quite a show,' he accused her.

She had no idea how she managed to raise one eyebrow at him, her voice shockingly level.

'I thought that was the whole point.'

'I asked for a kiss, not an open invitation to take you right there on the runway. *That* part of it is something I'd rather do with you in private.'

'Really? This, from the king of sex spectacles?'

'With other women, Alex,' he bellowed. 'Not with you.'

It sliced her deeper than she'd thought possible. An unambiguous slap in the face of just how gauche, how sexually unsophisticated she was.

So much for keeping her head around him. One minute in his company and she was losing her mind and her morals. It was more confusing than ever. Like being a human pendulum, swinging wildly from one extreme to the other.

Now, like a wounded animal, she retreated to her corner of the car to lick her wounds. Louis, on the other hand, stewed silently in his.

CHAPTER TEN

IT WAS LIKE some kind of illogical torture. Sitting here, at the restaurant, both equally frustrated yet having to flirt, to play the loving couple, just to conceal their row from the other curious diners so that they could forge ahead with the main goal of tonight. To stage their very public engagement.

The timing couldn't have been worse. After this afternoon he was still smarting. *Smarting.* As though their contretemps had actually got to him.

And yet it had. Even now, when he thought back over what had happened on the runway, he couldn't work out where it had all sprung from.

A row.

As if they were a proper couple.

It was almost enough to make him laugh. And somehow the thought chipped the first sharp corner off the block of granite that seemed to have taken up residency in his chest.

'I apologise,' he murmured. 'For what I said to you this afternoon.'

She looked up at him in surprise, then belatedly smiled. To him, it was too brittle to be a real smile, but he knew that, even to fool the hawk-eyed photographers, it would appear to be the sweetest, shyest smile.

'You mean for reminding me how I don't match up to any of the other women you've…*dated?*'

The smile didn't even waver. If anything, he felt it become that much sharper, like a scalpel blade pressed against his chest. But it was her words that had him taken aback. He fought to keep a frown from his face.

'That certainly isn't what I said.'

'Yes, it is.' She nodded vigorously before remembering herself. She leaned forward across the table so no one could possibly overhear them, although they both knew it would simply look as though she was captivated by him.

Incredible how much he suddenly wished that was true.

'You'll have to refresh my memory.'

Her pretty blush would certainly make it into tonight's papers. As would the way she steeled herself, like a woman boosted by love. Like a woman *in* love.

He should be pleased she could play the part so well.

'Fine. You told me you were more than happy to have sex with other women. Just not me.'

He laughed then. To his ears the sound was hollow and full of disbelief, yet the restaurant diners seemed oblivious to the undercurrent at his table. The not-so-covert stares only became all the more indulgent. As if they truly believed they were watching a couple happy to be together.

But what are *they watching?*

He hastily muffled the voice in his head. But it was too late.

'Is that why you were angry? Upset?' He caught her chin in his hands, not too roughly but enough to force her to look at him, to read the truth in his gaze. 'I said I didn't care if the world saw me with any of those other women, or read those ridiculous kiss and tells. But I never wanted the media to gossip about you in that way. You deserve better. However, I did *not* say I didn't want to have sex with you. We both know nothing could be further from the truth.'

She didn't want to believe him so easily. He could read

her like the latest medical journal. But she was wavering, and that could only be a good sign. Abruptly, he was filled with the urge to convince her, to reassure her. As though what was between them was real and not just a charade.

'I want you, Alex. Fervently. I want you any way you can imagine, and probably a fair few you can't. You have no idea how close I was to losing myself right out there on that runway. I don't lose myself, Alex. I never lose myself. *That's* why I was so mad.'

'I lost myself, too,' she whispered after a moment, a hot flush blooming on her cheeks.

It was adorable. *She* was adorable.

Before he could stop himself, he leaned across the table and kissed her. Her response was as perfect as it was instantaneous. She made him feel like a king.

'I promised myself I wouldn't go there again.' She smiled ruefully, her eyes sliding to the flashbulbs that were going crazy outside the windows. 'Especially in front of them out there.

It was a jolt to realise that he'd almost forgotten about the press, too caught up in Alex herself. He should take a step, regroup. Only he couldn't, he was enjoying this far too much. He couldn't help it. He toyed with the stem of his glass.

'So what happened?'

'You happened.' She managed to make it sound exciting and irritating at the same time. 'I was all set, I had my speech all prepared...'

He frowned. 'Your speech?'

'About how that morning could only be a one-night stand.'

This time his laugh was genuine, if a little regretful.

'I'd hardly call it that. We got interrupted.'

'Which was a good thing,' she assured him, but the way

she refused to meet his eyes told him she didn't even believe her own words.

'Liar.' He slid his hand across the table and took hers. It could have been part of the act, but it wasn't. You wanted that morning as much as I did.'

Her teeth worried at her lip before she offered a sheepish smile.

'Perhaps.'

Sweet. Perfect. Alex.

Before he knew what he was doing, Louis slid out of his seat, his hand drawing the ring box from his inside suit pocket. As though his body knew what he was doing even before his brain did. As though he was acting on instinct and desire, rather than their carefully laid plans.

As though he was only partly playing the part.

And he knew Alex felt it too. The expression on her face certainly wasn't as composed or cool as it would have been if she hadn't been as caught up as he was.

He told himself that it was a good thing that it made their charade all the more convincing.

But that wasn't even the half of it.

'Alexandra Vardy…' The words certainly weren't any he had composed in his head beforehand. They would be relayed from the diners, to the press and around the world within minutes. He told himself that was the point of saying them, but he knew that wasn't entirely true.

'You make me want to be a better man. A better human being.' His voice dipped then, huskier than he might have intended. 'Marry me.'

Her fingers had shot to her mouth, her wide-eyed expression relaxing into one of tentative hope. An unexpected fierceness shot through him; the sense that such open innocence should be cherished. Protected. She gave a halting nod and then she dropped her hands to cup his face. Something shot through him that he couldn't put a name to.

Didn't want to.

And still he couldn't break the moment.

'Say the words, Alex.'

She knitted her eyebrows at him, but he found he couldn't let her off with it; couldn't explain why he needed to hear her say the words.

'Say it,' he murmured.

She opened her mouth, closed it again, and then took a deep breath.

'Yes. Yes, Louis, I'll marry you.'

The fire that burst within him made no sense. Still, he stood up, gathering her into his arms and kissing her as though they were the only two people in the room. In the universe.

A blazing, hot, white light in the middle of darkness.

He might have known it couldn't last.

They were still caught up in his thoughts when the maître d' hurried over, his usual elegant, practised glide all but abandoned, not even attempting to speak in English for Alex, even though he'd been doing so all night.

'I apologise for the interruption but there is an urgent call for you, Monsieur Delaroche. A serious Motocross accident involving young Florien. They think he might die.'

Everything receded from Louis's head. Florien, the grandson of Arnaud. This was what he, Louis, excelled at—surgery, helping people medically. If there was an accident, Louis intended to be there.

Alex watched Louis, wondering what was going on. His grim expression was one she didn't recognise and his gabbled French was too fast for her to even attempt to understand.

She knew there had been an accident…someone's leg…a fracture maybe. Or a break.

The call he made was brief, factual. Louis was already standing and pulling a wad of notes out of his wallet, his apology curt.

'There's been an accident?' she prompted as he snatched up his jacket.

'I'm sorry, yes. A Motocross accident,' For the first time Louis looked at her. 'Florien, Arnaud's grandson.'

'A crash?'

'He was making a jump when he realised he wasn't going to make it and so he threw himself off the bike. But he didn't throw himself far enough.'

That suggested impact. And if it was the top of his leg, Alex knew it didn't sound good.

'Femur fracture?'

'Could be.' Louis shrugged as they exchanged a grim look. 'It's too dark for them to see if there's any shortening of the leg but I know Florien, he's quite a tough kid. Still, it sounds like he's in incredible pain.'

They both knew that with a femoral break the surrounding muscles would spasm, pulling one end of the broken bone past the other. It *would* be painful but more significantly it could cause bleeding as well as muscle and nerve damage.

The stress of the afternoon, and the euphoria of the proposal, fell away in an instant. Because of the femur's proximity to the femoral artery, it was possible that a patient could haemorrhage to death from an isolated femur fracture. Until they got to Florien they wouldn't have any idea how serious it was.

And Alex had a feeling Louis was about to tell her to

stay at the restaurant while the maître d' had someone send a car from the chateau to collect her.

'Forget it,' she told Louis, standing up before he could open his mouth. 'I'm going with you. If it's as serious at you fear then I might be able to help.'

It was almost gratifying that he didn't argue. He simply squeezed her hand, had a quick word with the sombrely nodding maître d' and headed out the door.

She rushed to keep up with him, both of them silent as they jumped into the car. Louis revved the engine into life and they roared away, eventually turning off the road and onto a dirt track barely fit for a dirt bike, let alone a car.

'Hold on,' he advised.

Alex braced herself as the car hurtled over bumps and divots, the bottom of the car grinding worryingly as it hit the ground. Even with Louis's skilled driving it was going to be wrecked. But, then, anyone with less skill than Louis could never have got it over this terrain in the first instance.

She saw kids desperately waving their arms fractions after Louis did. The car pulled up sharply by the boy, barely at a standstill before Louis was out and racing across, the cries of pain letting them know how close Florien was.

The terrain was, frankly, not designed for high-heeled shoes.

Alex gathered up her dress and made her ungainly way behind Louis, who turned abruptly.

'I keep a gym bag in the boot with a change of clothes,' he called out, and then he was gone.

Alex gratefully made her way to the back of the car, throwing it open and grabbing the bag. A pair of shorts, a T-shirt and a tracksuit greeted her, as well as a welcome pair of socks. Within minutes she was changed and hurrying the short distance across the ground. Even so, she was still a fair way behind Louis and by the time she reached them he was on his phone and barking out instructions in French.

Beyond him, lamps had been placed in a circle, shining light on a young boy lying flat on the ground. But even from that distance there was no doubt it was a femoral break, with one leg significantly shorter than the other and clearly at an unnatural angle. She made her way down the dirt mound.

'Mid-shaft, closed fracture,' Louis informed her as soon as he'd finished on the phone. 'I've updated the emergency services and made sure an air ambulance is on its way. But they're going to need to package him up before they transport him.'

She nodded. 'Straighten the leg and slip the femur back in place, or at least as close as,' she said, her voice quiet.

'We can speed that up for them so they can get him to hospital quicker.'

'You have a traction splint back at the chateau?' she guessed.

'No, we'll make one in the field.'

Her stomach dipped with uncertainty.

'I don't know how.'

'I'll teach you,' he said simply, matter-of-fact.

Despite her reservations, she instantly felt more confident.

'What about pain relief? We can't try to move the leg without anything.'

'In this instance there's no compromise,' he stated. 'I need you to find the materials.'

Quashing any reservations, she nodded her head.

'Okay.'

'Good.' His brief smile filled her with warmth. 'First I need a couple of branches. One should be about a metre and half long to run from his armpit to his foot, the other should be about just under a metre to run from his groin to his foot. Forked, if at all possible.'

'What diameter do you want them, or does it matter?' she hedged.

'They're going to support the leg so I'd say make sure they're sturdy and thick. At least four centimetres.'

'Okay.' She was beginning to get the idea, and Louis's characteristic strength was infectious.

Whatever had happened in town this afternoon, maybe they could put it aside after all.

'You're also going to need to find a stick to go on the underside of his foot and several lengths of something to lash them together. Rip up material if you have to.'

'What about belts? I bet his friends would give us theirs.'

'Good,' Louis said approvingly. 'If we pad the area, that could work. We need to pad the area where the sticks will go so get as much clothing together as you can.'

Galvanised, Alex cast around and grabbed a few of Florien's friends. Telling one of them to start collecting spare coats, jumpers, any clothing he could, and thrusting a lamp into the hands of another so that they'd be able to see what they were looking for, Alex managed to get the others to follow her as she headed to the wooded area a short way away. Once she got there, she could use the branches around her to get across to them what they were looking for. As far as she was concerned, the more eyes there were, the better.

It was easier than she'd expected to find a selection of branches, especially with the help of Florien's desperate friends. Discarding those she knew wouldn't be suitable, they gathered the rest up and headed back to where Louis was to select whichever he thought would work best.

She'd planned to sort out the rest of the clothing once she got there, but was hardly surprised to see Louis already had it in hand, as well as consistently checking on his patient and looking for a pulse. He looked up as soon as she approached.

'Everything okay?'

'Not bad.' She tried not to let her heart kick. 'What about Florien?'

He kept his expression deliberately neutral for those around them, but the look he exchanged with her was one of mutual understanding.

And something else. The former bonds of connection were returning.

'I'll be happier when I get the traction done and there's a good pedal pulse.'

'The branches are there.' She indicated them, understanding his concern. 'Hopefully there'll be some useful lengths in there.'

'Great.'

Reaching over, he ran an expert eye over the selection and then chose two longer pieces, offering each up to the outer side of Florien. Quickly he discarded one and then, after a quick word to the group, which promptly produced an army-style knife, he began to dig out a notch in one end of the other branch.

Alex watched fascinated as he did the same with a shorter branch, offering them up to the boy on either side of the leg requiring traction. Then he began to secure the longer branch to Florien by sliding padding and a belt around the boy's waist.

'Can you reach?'

Hastily, Alex slipped her hand under to find the other end of the belt that Louis was passing under their patient's back, and as she caught on to what he was doing, he left her to it as he moved on to tie another, securing it around the top of the boy's leg, this time including the shorter branch. When she was done at Florian's waist, Alex moved lower, making sure not to tie anything on his knee but keeping well above and below, still padding as she went.

It felt easy and natural to be working together, Alex realised. They instinctively knew each other, could anticipate the other, taking it in turns to soothe Florien and try to reassure him, despite the pain he had to be in. A little of the earlier trust was back. Working together just as they had in Theatre was reminding them both of the connection they'd shared.

At least, Alex hoped it was.

And then they were at the ankle, and Louis produced a long length of bandage.

'First-aid kit in the car.' He half smiled as she glanced at it in surprise. 'I need it for this bit more than anywhere else.'

'You're going to tie the ankle,' she guessed.

'Yes, but watch.'

Curious, Alex observed as Louis tied it around Florien's ankle, then twisted each end around the final small branch, which he fitted under the boy's foot. Then he slid in a winching stick.

'Now.' He leaned in to Alex's ear. 'You twist, I'll deal with Florien. Whatever you hear, keep twisting until his legs are the same length and you know the bone is re-aligned. The quicker you can do it, the sooner the worst of the pain is over for him, understand?'

Louis was trusting her, depending on her, and that felt

good. Not to mention the fact that she wanted to help this poor kid as much as she could. Lifting her eyes briefly to Louis's, she gave a sharp dip of her head.

'Ready,' she murmured.

And then she twisted. Over and over and over, blocking out the sounds of Florien's screams as Louis talked to him and reassured him. She only knew that the smoother and faster she could perform her role, the better in the long run. And then she had done it. His leg was straighter, the femur realigned as close as they were going to get it, given the crude equipment they had, and Florien's legs were the same length.

'Okay.' She raised her voice loud enough for Louis to hear, shaking away the stray hairs that clung to the sweat on her face.

'Nice. Now secure the winching stick so it doesn't reverse and loosen what you've just done, then slip each end of the cross-branch into the notches I made in each of the splint branches.'

'Like this?'

'Exactly,' Louis confirmed, turning back to Florien to confirm to him that it was over. Then he checked the pulse in the boy's toes and foot.

'Good pedal pulse, no swelling, toes are nice and pink. Good result, Alex, well done.'

His praise felt inordinately good, but more than that they'd been working well together and somehow that had eased her discomfort since her arrival better than any gourmet meal could have done.

'Take my car back to the chateau and speak to Brigitte. Florien's mother has already been contacted and is on the way to the hospital but Brigitte will know the best people to call to look after the younger siblings over the next day or so.'

'Okay.'

'And, Alex,' he called softly. 'I'll see you back at home.'

CHAPTER ELEVEN

IT WAS LATER than she'd thought it would be by the time Alex trudged up the stone steps and through the silent chateau. She didn't need to search for Brigitte as the older woman came hurrying from the kitchens as soon as Alex entered. Hugging her and nodding, taking a moment to talk about other things, which left Alex's head spinning, the older woman bustled away. Her parting words were to tell a dazed Alex that a fire had been lit and food set out if she was hungry.

It was a welcome suggestion, especially when the first waves from the blazing fire began to thaw Alex's frozen toes. The engagement ring glinted in the firelight, and a different kind of warmth blew gently through her chest. Despite the long night and the exhaustion beginning to set in, the thought of going to her room without Louis was one she didn't care to entertain.

Louis. The man who would soon be her husband. Her stomach flip-flopped. Their charade aside, if she wasn't marrying playboy Louis, but instead marrying the version of the man she'd seen out there tonight, the man who hadn't thought twice about helping the son of one of his employees, treating him with no less care or respect than he would his top bill-paying patients, then she could actually be the luckiest unconventional bride around.

She quashed the nerves that betrayed her. The flutter-ing sensation that maybe, just maybe their marriage could be so much more than just a charade. If only she could convince him to stop punishing himself for something he couldn't possibly have had any control over.

Alex froze.

Wasn't that exactly the mistake she'd spent her own life making? *No, it couldn't possibly be the same thing? Could it?* Lost in thought, she collapsed back into the wing-backed chair and stared into the fire.

She didn't know how long she waited, or that she'd even dozed off, but when she awoke Louis was in the room, throwing a couple of logs on the dying fire, the first rays of morning light peeking from around a kink in the heavy curtains.

'What time is it?' She stretched, her neck moving awk-wardly.

'Around dawn. You should have gone to bed.'

'I was waiting for you.'

'I accompanied Florien to the hospital.'

Why didn't that surprise her?

'How is he?'

'He'll recover.' Louis nodded grimly.

'But no more Motocross.' She hazarded a smile, unpre-pared for the shockwaves that coursed through her body as Louis smiled wryly in return.

'Not for a good while. But, knowing Florien, he won't be able to give it up for good.'

'Obstinate, then, just like all young men?'

'We Lefebvre men are the same.'

The room fell silent, only the logs spitting in the fire-place disturbing the air. And Louis's gaze was on her, reaching out to her, although she didn't think he even re-alised it. The fact that he had just identified himself as

Lefevbre rather than Delaroche offered her a glimmer of hope that he was finally beginning to accept he wasn't like his cruel father after all; that he had more of his mother's kindness about him than he realised.

Something skittered through Alex and she unconsciously fingered the ring on her finger. Once Louis accepted that he didn't need to punish himself any more, he would truly be unstoppable. He could change anything he wanted to—*if* he wanted to—and maybe they could really begin to trust each other.

'You know that's who you are,' she began tentatively. 'Alex…'

She couldn't let him interrupt her. Couldn't let him run away this time—although he would never, in a hundred centuries, believe that was what he was doing.

'You don't have to be either your mother or your father. You can be yourself, and who you are is pretty special, Louis. Or at least could be. You're the best parts of the Lefebvre and Delaroche lineages. You could take up your mother's legacy and create something even more prestigious than the Delaroche Foundation. But, unlike your father, you'd be doing it for all the right reasons.'

His lips pulled into a cold, hard line. But he was still standing there, still listening to her. That had to stand for something.

'This again? Why do you keep pushing this? Just because I helped Florien tonight doesn't make me who you want me to be.'

He was right, she couldn't seem to let it go. But suddenly it felt vitally important. She could tell herself it was her last chance to secure Rainbow House, to make her father realise just how much she would sacrifice to make up for what they had lost, but she suspected it had become more than just that.

She suspected it had become more about Louis, and the way he resisted the good part of himself because he didn't feel he deserved it. He was punishing himself for his mother's death and, for some reason, that hurt *her*. As though layers were being peeled away, from the inside out.

Very much as though *Louis* mattered to her. More than she had ever thought possible.

But that couldn't be right.

This was about her father, and Rainbow House. Nothing more, nothing less, and that was what she had to stick to.

'It isn't who *I* want you to be,' she pressed. 'It's simply who you *are*. You must see that. You're a good man. Everyone who works with you knows that. Brigitte was telling me that only tonight. Every single one of your surgical team, eager to please you every chance they get, knows it. Even the press know you're a good surgeon. They laud you every time you operate.'

'Brigitte said it?'

'Brigitte told me she'd worried when you'd first told them you were bringing someone to the chateau, but that since she's seen us together she hopes our marriage will be a very happy one.'

'Our marriage is a sham.' Louis frowned.

It hurt far more than it should. Alex struggled to answer him.

'Of course I know that. But the point remains, people want the best for you. Did you know she also told me that she knew we were trying to regain control of the Lefebvre Group?'

'There's no such thing as secrets in a place like this.' Louis shrugged, his shuttered expression only heightening her frustration.

'According to Brigitte, your mother once intended for the stable blocks here at the chateau to be turned into

a respite centre. Holidays for families from places like
Rainbow House and the other charities sponsored by the
Lefebvre Group.'

'Is that so?'

Louis gritted his teeth. It was a warning she should
heed, but she couldn't. Or she didn't want to.

'It is. Brigitte said your mother even got planning permission, and that your father signed documents to that
effect.'

'My father would have long since got rid of any such
papers.'

'Not if your mother lodged them at her own solicitors.
In trust.'

It was a dangerous game, but she couldn't seem to stop.
Aside from their silly argument, things had seemed so positive between them before they'd got the message about
Florien. And even then, they'd worked together harmoni-
ously, just as they always did. She felt as close to Louis as
she was likely to get.

So why did that knowledge deflate her so?

'Let me guess, Brigitte thinks that, too.'

'Right.' Alex nodded, shoving her misgivings aside.
'You could reinstate your mother's plans and make it one
of the first successes of the Lefebvre Group.'

'And call it Rainbow House the Second? Maybe Rainbow Court?' His anger was apparent. 'Alex, how many
times can I tell you that I don't want to take over the Lefebvre Group? Or the Delaroche Foundation. The Lefebvre
Group was my mother's drive, her passion, because it was
something away from my father. But to me, it holds too
many bad memories. The Delaroche Foundation has only
ever been a vehicle for my father to gain a knighthood. It
has never been about helping people, for him.'

'So you can be different.' She stood up, took a step

forward and then stopped, her arms dropping to her sides helplessly as Louis folded his own arms across his chest as though warding her off.

'No. I am who I am. I'm a brilliant surgeon...' he shrugged as though it was a fact he acknowledged but wasn't boasting about '...but I'm not a good man. I tried to make sure I was nothing like my father, yet everything I've done has made me more like him with every day.'

'You mean the playboy nonsense,' she sniffed. 'Why do you insist on punishing yourself with that? It's only a part of who you were, not even who you are now. You're a surgeon above all else. You have determination, persistence, passion.'

'For surgeries, Alex. I have that passion for surgeries. I could carry out procedures day and night and I would never tire of them because they inspire me and every surgery is different. But the Lefebvre Group was my mother's passion and her footsteps don't lead somewhere I want to follow. I don't even like the man I become when I think of that place and everything it took from us.'

'So if you don't like that man you become, change him. Turn it into something positive. If anyone can achieve that, it's you, Louis.'

'It wouldn't be enough,' he said abruptly. 'Do you think this is the first time I've regretted some of my choices? Those first kiss-and-tell encounters that gave me the reputation as a playboy? I'd been trying to hurt my father, damage the Delaroche name, make people look twice and realise that Jean-Baptiste wasn't their knight-in-shining-scrubs, but a brilliant surgeon with a grubby personal life of his own.'

'You were eighteen. We all make stupid choices when we're younger—sometimes when we're older too—but

most of us don't do it in the public eye where it follows us
around for years to come.'

'That's hardly the point,' he ground out angrily, but it
was the pain behind it that clawed at Alex, deep inside.
'I'm not *most* people. I'm Louis Delaroche. My grandfather was a Lefebvre. I should have known better.'

'You lost your mother,' she exclaimed, 'your guide, over
ten years earlier! By your own admission your father was
hardly the greatest role model.'

'I don't want to enough.' He shook his head. 'I'm selfish,
just like him. I know the Lefebvre Group needs a chairman, and I know that was meant to be my role. It was what
my mother always wanted me to do. But I don't want any
part of it because I can't get past my own hurt. I'm angry
with my father for his affairs, which drove my mother to
the edge, and I'm angry with her for choosing the way
out that she did. Most of all, I'm angry with myself that I
wasn't good enough to give her something to hold onto.'

It was the most honest he'd been with her and something sang inside her at the knowledge. She was desperate to go to him, to hold him, but she didn't dare move for
fear of breaking the moment. A minute ago they'd been
standing across the room from each other, only a few metres but it might as well have been a yawning chasm, and
now suddenly it felt like he'd thrown the first rope across
the divide. The first step to building a bridge.

The logs spattered and a clock chimed in the entrance
hall, the sound echoing along the silent chateau corridors.

It was only when Louis exhaled, moving as though he
was about to turn and leave, that Alex finally spoke.

'I do understand your guilt, Louis. You blame yourself for your mother's death. I know what it's like to carry
around a burden of responsibility that isn't your own.'

'Your brother.' He blinked, as though remembering it for the first time.

She swallowed, her heart accelerating uncontrollably.

'Not just my brother. My mother, too.'

Louis stilled, his jaw locked, the pulse ticking away the only tell-tale sign that he wasn't as calm as he would have her believe.

'You don't. Not like this. I know you mean well, but these are my demons.'

Shutting her out like he always shut out everyone. Leaving her no choice but to go to the one place she'd swore she would never go. Even now, she knew it would cost her.

She hoped Louis was worth the risk.

'I never told you how my mother died, did I?' she heard herself say.

And suddenly there it was, the pain that was always there—like a dull ache that never, ever went away—but now it was rearing up, sharper and more biting than it had felt in years.

She stuffed it back down and forced herself to meet Louis's gaze, her momentary pause losing her what little advantage she might have had. He raked a hand through his hair.

'Alex, I don't want to get into a "my pain is worse than your pain" contest. I'm just explaining to you why I don't want to take on the Lefebvre Group.'

'And I'm just telling you how my mother died,' she managed quietly, her fingers gripping her book so he couldn't see how she was shaking.

The air thrummed with tension, breath bated to see who would fold first.

Eventually, Louis dipped his head in perceived acquiescence, moving around the chair and flopping down to lounge in his deliberately insouciant fashion.

She drew in a slow, discreet breath and counted to ten before uttering the words she hadn't said for decades.

'My mother died in childbirth. After she'd been in labour with me. The child who had been conceived as a potential saviour sibling for their son, but who would turn out not to be a match, was also the direct cause of her mother's death. So, you see, I do understand a thing or two about guilt and responsibility.'

She hated that look he shot her then. The look of pity. The one she'd grown to resent so much as a kid that she'd started telling people her mother had died in a car accident.

'Don't look at me like that, Louis.'

She braced herself for the platitudes.

'How? How did she die?'

As though he could read her. She cast him a ghost of a grateful smile.

'Placenta percreta. The placenta had grown through the uterine wall and invaded her bladder. They couldn't do anything. Everything ruptured and she bled out.'

'I'm sorry. I can't imagine…'

'I content myself with the knowledge that she got to hold me, at least for a few moments. And she told my father to love me and made him promise to tell me every time I needed him to that she was grateful for the chance to meet me.'

'Did he?'

'No. He never told me. He tried to, in his own way, but he couldn't bear talking about her. In the end it was my grandparents who used to tell me but it wasn't the same. I always felt he blamed me, deep down. And so I blamed myself. When my brother died, my father retreated even more and so I took on that responsibility, too.'

He shook his head, his fist balled as though he was angry on her behalf. As if he wanted to protect her.

As if he *cared*.

'I didn't tell you this because I wanted your sympathy.' She made her voice crisp, unemotional, telling herself that she'd dealt with that pain even though she could still feel it, rattling the heavy chains on its prison door, even now.

'I told you because I wanted to show you that I let that experience drive me to become a doctor. To become someone she would have been proud of. I know you play the bad boy because you think it's somehow your punishment, but honestly I think that's nonsense.'

She knew he was about to stop her but she held her hand up to silence him. If she didn't tell him now, she'd never get the chance to say it.

'You were seven, a child. You can't hold yourself responsible for someone else's happiness. You could be doing so much more. Even if you can't do it for her, you owe it to yourself to be the kind of man you have the potential to be. If only you'd forgive yourself.'

He'd only felt helpless once before in his life. The night his mother had turned her back on him.

Louis was determined tonight wasn't going to be the second time.

But seeing Alex so distressed, and knowing how worthless her father had made her feel—not by hurling the kind of vicious jibes that his own father had but by staying silent and withholding his love—made Louis furious, powerless and mournful all at once.

And yet he couldn't let her off so easily.

'You talk about me forgiving myself. But have you?'

He could tell by the rush of panic in her eyes that he was right.

'Of course. That's why I can volunteer at Rainbow House. I've confronted my ghosts.'

'I don't buy that, Alex. I know you volunteer to main-

tain that last connection with your father. But if you for-
gave yourself then you wouldn't need to hang onto him.
You'd tell yourself that it was time he met you halfway.'

'Who said I didn't enjoy volunteering there for myself?' she blustered.

'You. You've never once given that as a reason. You've
always linked it to your father.'

She stilled. He thought she'd even stopped breathing.
Then she blinked rapidly, as if tears were stinging her soul-
ful eyes, and guilt poured through him.

'I'm sorry, I shouldn't have said that.'

'But you were right,' she whispered. 'I'm just as tethered
to my past as you are. I wanted to help you see that you
weren't helping anyone by punishing yourself. I thought I
could help you move on.'

He didn't remember standing up or crossing the room
to scoop her into his arms. But suddenly they were there
together and all he could do was to hold her body close to
his, try to make her feel safe and secure. And cared for.

So what did that mean?

He let the question wash over him as her blinks gave
way to the first silent tears. He carried her out of the door,
up the grand, sweeping staircase and to her room. And he
let her hold onto him as if she would never let go as he settled her on the bed, nodded wordlessly when she begged
him not to leave her, lay down beside her and cradled her
as sobs racked her, crying for probably the first time in
decades. Finally allowing herself to grieve for the things
she'd lost as well as the things she'd never had. Finally
letting go after years of trying to build bridges with her
father and holding her feelings inside.

And when the tears at last began to ebb and the hiccups
subside, when, exhausted and depleted, her eyes tired and
swollen, sleep crept over her, he continued to hold her.

Long after the house fell silent and the fire died in the hearth. Long into the night until the tendrils of slumber wisped around him. Right into the first hints of light and the sounds of the dawn chorus.

As his eyes began to open again, Louis tipped his head from one side to the other to ease the crick in his neck. After last night he ought to feel drained. Wary, even. Instead, he just felt as though a weight had finally been lifted from him. Hearing Alex share her story with him and knowing she hadn't told anyone else had changed things for him somehow.

Suddenly, he no longer felt the isolation he'd never realised he'd been experiencing. His brain was fired up with renewed drive. An energy effervescing in blood that coursed eagerly through his veins. If he could only work out what to do with it.

He'd spent years playing genius, playboy Louis, convinced there was a reason that he was renowned for his surgical skills on the one hand and his sexual prowess on the other. But the truth was that he'd been little different from any other nineteen-year-old kid with money and women throwing themselves at him. The only thing that set him apart was the name he'd been forging for himself in the surgical field.

The press had only jumped on the playboy story because it had sold more papers for them. And he'd let them because it had seemed easier. Because it had been convenient. But Alex made him want something different. Something…*more*.

Maybe, and he wasn't saying definitely, taking on the role of Chairman of the Lefebvre Group was something he should consider. Maybe he and Alex could make their sham marriage work for them, and pull together to really achieve something good. Maybe their marriage could be more than just... *No, that was going too far.*

But still they could make a good business team. No one else could ever have dared to talk to her the way he had last night. He, in turn, could never have trusted anyone else with the truths he'd told her this past week.

Easing his hand from under her neck, Louis slid off the bed, covering her with a blanket and taking his time so as not to disturb her. The hot, powerful jets of the shower sluiced over his body and, with it, any residual anhedonia of the previous night, of the previous decade.

He barely brushed the towel over his body before pulling on jeans and a tee, clothes that he hadn't worn in years but which welcomed him from the back of his burr-walnut wardrobe. Louis snatched up his phone, his fingers scrolling efficiently through old contact numbers. With a final glance at Alex's sleeping form, he slipped out of the room.

It was well into the morning before Alex appeared, having tracked him down to where he was meeting someone in the east wing drawing room. She looked as deliciously fresh and bewitching as ever. He forced himself not to stare at her.

'I'm sorry.' She backed up immediately. 'I didn't realise you were in a meeting.'

'Don't leave.' He waved his hand immediately to beckon her over. 'Étienne is just leaving, we were finishing up anyway.'

She only hesitated for a moment before advancing with a sweet smile, her hand outstretched in greeting as the man dropped a light kiss on her hand, making his introductions and apologies as he excused himself to run to another meeting.

'Étienne Morel is a lawyer. His father was my mother's personal lawyer, who never had much time for Jean-Baptiste.'

'You're looking into what Brigitte said last night,' she breathed, the expectation dancing in her eyes almost too much for him to stand.

'I'm making tentative enquiries, shall we say,' he cautioned. 'I cannot promise anything. I will not promise. Don't get ahead of yourself, Alex. I am simply…weighing the options.'

He could see by her body language that his words were falling on deaf ears but her delight got under his skin in a way that wasn't prudent and, if only for a short while, he gave in to the temptation of indulging her.

'Étienne's also looking into finding the Lefevbre Group tie-in with the Delaroche Foundation—maybe fresh eyes can see a loophole. In the meantime, he found the plans Brigitte mentioned easily enough. The idea was to convert the old stables into small holiday apartments for disabled people and carers. They already had made provisions for wheelchair access and additional security features.'

He waited with a strange tenseness as she perused the drawings, her finger tracing every last inch of space, her soft voice reading the French aloud, translating.

'Right. Accessibility but with more practicalities. This could be safety gates, well-fenced gardens, and ensuring doors and windows can be locked to prevent any little Houdinis.'

'Perhaps building a couple of swimming pools but ensuring they were both secured.'

'Perfect.' The look she sent him pulled straight down to his sex. He thrust it away. 'For some families it might be more about assuring them that they're coming somewhere safe and secure, and assuring them they can relax in the knowledge that no one is going to be judging them.'

'I also considered respite holidays,' he said, searching her expression.

'Proper respite holidays?' Alex asked slowly. 'Where the carers also get a proper holiday, not just a bit of break?'

'Why not?' he challenged. 'We could offer twenty-four-hour nursing care, attracting qualified, highly experienced nursing and care staff if we refurbished the west wing of the house and turned it into high-spec accommodation. Furthermore, this estate has always provided plenty of work for the surrounding communities, and the decline since my father took over has hit people around here hard. We could also run annual courses to train suitable locals or anyone else willing to come here.'

'You could offer quality hospitality,' she mused. 'A relaxed atmosphere with plenty of excursions and lively entertainment?'

'Right.'

'Is there a lot to do around here?'

The grin curved his lips and her eyes darkened, intensified as she watched him. It was dangerous ground. He needed to back away.

He couldn't.

'I think you should take a tour of *our* little town and its environs.'

CHAPTER TWELVE

'So this is the Canal du Midi?'

'This is the Canal du Midi in style,' Louis corrected, pouring her another wine as their sleek boat cruised leisurely along.

This day was driving him slowly mad.

Or, more to the point, Alex was.

Despite all his words of caution to himself, his constant reminders that their engagement was one of convenience and not choice, he found himself sucked into the charade that the press were lapping up everywhere they went. And showing Alex around his town, the place in which he had grown up, and seeing her obvious pleasure at some of the sights that had so captivated him as a child wasn't making the task any easier. Her freely given smiles, the way she charmed everyone he introduced to her, her uninhibited laughter.

He'd watched her. And he'd wanted her.

The small canal boat ride had been her idea. He'd loved it as a kid but his tastes had run to more refined, elegant super-yachts in the last few decades. Sitting here with Alex, he couldn't help but wonder why.

They'd moored to take a stroll to a canal-side patisserie for an impromptu lunch of baguette and some local produce. Right now she was taking long gulps from a bottle of ice-cold water, the long line of her neck making him think of anything other than the history lesson about seventeenth-century canals that he was meant to be giving her.

Worse, Alex was apparently oblivious as she screwed the top back on her water and set it down to look around them.

'Why are there so many felled trees around this area?'

'They're diseased, they needed to be felled,' he said ruefully.

She looked aghast and it felt better than it should. Seeing her care about some of things that he cared about, as though they were in perfect sync.

But they weren't. It was all pretence. So why was that so hard to remember?

'All of them? Why?'

'They were plane trees, planted back in the early nineteenth century to strengthen the banks and to help prevent evaporation, since they grow rapidly and they furnish quick shade.'

'So they've been here around two hundred years? Why on earth would you cut them down now?'

'No choice.' He hunched his shoulders. 'Over the last decade or so it's become clear that many of them were diseased, possibly from a fungus brought to France in contaminated World War II ammunition boxes used by US troops. Plus boat users often lash ropes around the trees to moor their boats and as they moved up and down the canal it no doubt helped the disease to spread.'

'So they're taking out this whole section and replanting.' Alex pulled a face. 'So many trees.'

'More than you think, since it isn't just this section. So far over twenty thousand trees have been felled along the two-hundred-and-fifty-kilometre canal length but there's a real chance that all forty-two thousand of them will ultimately need to go.'

Her cry was typically heart-on-sleeve Alex. And he loved her for her passion.

'That's awful. All of them?'

'If something is diseased and corrupting, then doesn't it make sense to eradicate it completely? Before you can start again?'

He hadn't intended it, yet it seemed to spill off his tongue. She peered at him tentatively.

'Are we still talking about the trees here?'

'What else?' he stalled, trying to gain himself time to think.

She pursed her lips before plunging on.

'I don't know. You?'

She expected him to deny it, to scoff at her. He could see it in her expression. Instead, he met her intelligent gaze head on and they lapsed into silence, the ducks on the canal the only sound.

'So…' She broke the silence at last. 'If they all are felled then they would need to be replaced…but what would be the cost?'

He cocked his head to one side. To anyone listening, it would sound like a dry conversation. Only he could hear the quiver in her voice, and could feel the waves of desire coursing between them. The heat, the solitude, the setting, they were all conspiring to remind them both of the attraction that had been there from the start. The one that they'd spent the last few weeks quashing but which was now, inexplicably, back and seemingly stronger than ever.

'For the trees? Millions. It's a huge undertaking.'

'And for you?'

'I'm still working that out. But I already know the gain is peace of mind. And you.'

* * *

He looked so confident, so unruffled. While for her part she seared.

She wanted to move but she couldn't. Part of her expected him to reach for her, but he didn't.

The moment stretched out, circling around them, encompassing only the two of them. When he spoke, his breezy tone scratching over her, it was as though they had never touched on such a topic.

'Still, this isn't what we're here for. I just wanted to show you how we could offer canal cruises, either as a group or partnering some of the small boat-hire companies operating in the area.'

It amazed her the way he could switch so easily but she couldn't shake the moment with the same ease. Louis was a different man. No longer anything like the arrogant playboy of the media and, with each passing day, it was getting harder and harder for Alex to remember that they were still supposed to be playing a game. A charade.

And, if only for one afternoon, she desperately wanted to stop fighting the attraction.

'What if, right in this instant, I'm less interested in what the region has to offer and more interested in what you have to offer?' she hedged, nervous exhilaration flooding through her.

He eyed her slowly.

'And are you?'

'Am I what?' she mumbled, scorched by the heat of his stare.

His lips quirked upwards.

'Interested in what I have to offer? Because if you are, there's a bed in the cabin in there that I've never used before.'

Was it really that simple?

She just had to ask him? Abruptly her body felt too tight, too constricting for her bones. She wasn't sure how she persuaded her shaking legs to stand, but suddenly she was in Louis's arms.

The best place she'd been in a while.

'No one else has ever got to me the way you do,' he muttered. 'I must be crazy.'

'We both must be,' she breathed, her skin scorching everywhere he touched her, even through their clothing.

'If I'd realised taking you on a guided tour would make you want me, I'd have done it a week ago.'

'It isn't the guided tour,' she squeaked. He knew exactly what he was doing, moving his mouth so close to hers without actually kissing her. Like some exquisite form of torture. 'Talking isn't some kind of foreplay, you know.'

'I know exactly what foreplay is,' he rumbled. 'Allow me to demonstrate.'

And then he kissed her. Or more like possessed her, staking his claim and making her his. And she would be, she realised. In a heartbeat she would be with him. She was *in love* with him. Even if everything with Rainbow House fell through now, she would still marry him. If he asked. Which, of course, he wouldn't.

But she could fantasise. She could press herself against him and loop her arms around his neck, every inch of her body pressed against him.

His for the taking.

Louis claimed her mouth, investing every slide of his lips and every stroke of his tongue with all the promise he intended to fulfil for the rest of the night. The rest of their stay. The rest of the charade.

He thrust any other unwanted thoughts of it ever having to come to an end from his head, cupping her face in his hands, taking his time to explore every single element of it. From the soft, plump lips to the tiny dints in her cheeks that were only visible when she really laughed.

God, he loved to make her laugh so hard that those dimples showed.

Just for him.

He staunched the ferocity that consumed his insides, forcing himself to slow down. Reacquainting himself with her every curve and dip, revelling in the way her body quivered against him when he ran his hand up and down her spine, thrilling in the soft sounds that seemed to vibrate from her throat straight into his chest as he cupped her backside, knowing he was making her melt.

He took his time, plundering her mouth, exploring her face and her neck with his kisses, not even attempting to stifle his grin as she moved against him, her body clearly urging him to do more. His hand tangled into her soft, flowing hair, twisting a lock around his fist and tugging, only gently but enough to make her gasp and press against him harder.

He was too consumed with kissing her. He tested first one breast and then the other, before dropping feather-light kisses from her neck downwards until he was hooking a finger over the neckline of her sexy dress and taking the first straining rosy bud in his mouth. He hardened instantly at her gasps of pleasure. Need almost overtaking him for the first time in his life, he just about remembered they were still on the deck of the boat. Although the footpath was deserted for now, people could walk past at any time.

He'd never lost himself like that before. It felt good. Still, Louis made himself scoop her into his arms, carry her into the cabin to the compact bedroom, and lower her reverently on the bed. Slowly, deliberately, he stripped her, but then she pushed herself up with a litheness he couldn't help but admire and tugged him towards her so that she could hurry things along. Her shaking fingers fumbled with his buttons as she shed him of his clothing, too. And when she unzipped him, her hands moving greedily to his length, Louis lost all attempts at easy control.

'Even more beautiful than I remembered,' he muttered, his hands gliding over her soft skin when they were both finally naked, her body reacting to his touch.

He pressed her back onto the bed, only too happy to follow as her hands snagged his shoulders and she pulled him down to her.

Propping himself on one arm, his eyes skimmed over her, drinking her in, gorging themselves on her. Everything about Alex was so sweetly feminine, from her crooked, nervous smile—which only served to stoke him further—down to the perfect flare of her hips. His hands traced whorls on her body, his lips moving over hers before dropping hot kisses to her neck, her chest. Her smooth flesh was so delicate to the touch.

Louis revelled in the way her fingers explored his body, moving over his shoulders, his arms and his chest. But what he really remembered, what he ached for was to taste her again as he had that night. Her sweet honey taste that had ensured he had been hooked from the moment he'd first licked his way into her.

He grew harder at the memory. So hard it was almost painful. No one had ever driven him this wild before.

He shifted, preparing to slide back down between her legs when Alex decided she had other plans and shifted herself, trying to roll him over until his chest was over hers. He could have resisted, carried on with his plan. Instead he relented and gave her what she wanted, moving over until his chest covered hers, his body between her impossibly long legs.

And then she wriggled her hips, settling him at her apex and then wrapping her legs around his thighs as though anchoring him in place, and Louis lost the ability to think straight.

He'd intended a slow seduction. Tasting, toying, teasing. Instead desire consumed him, a slave to his most primal instincts, and to Alex's urgency.

The only time any woman had come close to being the master of him.

If he didn't slide inside her now, she was going to die from need.

She was certain of it.

The last few days since their encounter in his bedroom had been unbearable. Every fibre of her body still mourned what hadn't quite happened between them. And now he wanted her, that much was undeniable, yet still he insisted on setting a cruelly controlled pace. The tantalising moves of a rhumba when all her entire body ached for the driven, passionate pace of a tango.

She arched her hips and rocked against him, her already molten body searing as his sex flexed against her, his sharp intake of breath like a roar inside her head. Why was he holding back, tormenting them both this way? Louis was barely in control himself—at least she could take some small comfort from that.

'Please,' she whispered, curving her body into his, the stunning beauty of his physique with the planes and ridges almost too much to process. And when he nudged at her entrance again she was sure she was going to come apart.

His gaze snagged hers and she wasn't prepared for the fire that raged in their smoky depths. Savage, needy and wholly, utterly male.

'I can't take any more.' She bit out the desperate plea.

'I want us to take our time,' he rasped, reaching to re-trieve a condom and sheathing himself. But she didn't miss the slight shake to his voice. It gave her strength.

'We've got all night, all week to take our time. I've been imagining you since that morning, I just need you now.'

Her voice cracked before she could say any more but it didn't matter. It was as if she'd uttered the magic words. Told him what he'd been waiting to hear. With a groan Louis shifted, testing himself against her, his face tighten-ing at her slick, wet heat. It filled her with old Alex cour-age, a kind of mischievousness, an impulse, and she raised her legs to wrap them higher around his body, drawing him in faster than he'd intended.

She didn't know whether the guttural sound came from Louis or from her. In truth, it made little difference. He was thrusting into her, filling her, stretching her in every direction, but there was no discomfort. If anything, it felt as though they were made for each other.

The perfect fit.

He drew back and thrust in again. A deliberate, lazy rhythm that drove her half-mad with pleasure and frus-tration. Again and again he slid in and out of her, and just when she thought she couldn't take any more teas-ing, he picked up the pace, leaving her little choice but to grip his shoulders and let him take her with him, meet-ing him thrust for glorious thrust and trying to remem-ber to breathe.

Shudders were already beginning to burst through her when he slid his hand between their bodies and down to her core, expert fingers dancing over the very centre of her desire, heightening everything and propelling her towards the edge. Then she catapulted off, bursting apart under his skilful touch and crying out his name.

She hadn't even come back down when she realised he

hadn't followed her. He was still inside her, still in control of himself, if only by a thread.

'Louis…'

'Shh,' he growled, a dark, deeply satisfied smile lifting his mouth. 'Hold on tightly.'

Before she could answer, he was moving inside her again. Thrusting harder, faster, deeper, his fingers still playing with her, sending her hurtling back over the edge. And this time when her body shattered into a thousand fragments, her muscles rippling around him, he toppled with her.

It took her long, long moments to come back to herself again, and when she did, Louis was cradling her as though she was the most precious jewel in the world.

'You're so beautiful,' he murmured. 'So perfect.'

'So are you.' Still in a haze of bliss, Alex barely heard the words slipping so naturally from her lips. 'I love you.'

Beside her, Louis froze. And then her world came tumbling down.

'You do not love me.' Louis bundled her off him so fast that she almost fell and he nearly put a hand out to catch her, only just stopping himself in time. 'You cannot. That isn't what we agreed.'

If he'd thought she was going to crumble, to fall, then he'd thought wrong. But a part of him had known that she wouldn't. Not his Alex. He admired the way she tilted her chin, meeting his eyes even as she tugged the tangle of sheets over her chest to protect what little modesty she had left. It made his chest tighten with something that felt dangerously close to regret.

'No.' Her soft voice wrapped around him, hot and tight, just as she'd wrapped around his sex only minutes earlier. 'it wasn't what we agreed. And yet here we are.'

'I won't accept that.' He tugged his jeans on furiously.

That, surely, was the point. *Sex.* She was confusing sex with love. And so, to some degree, was he. Why else did he want to pull away all the barriers between them and crush her body until they were so close he didn't know where he ended and she began?

Alex merely shrugged lightly, her hurt evident, and yet she refused to apologise.

'It isn't your choice to make, it's mine. And it appears I've made it. But tell me, Louis, what are you so afraid of?'

He snorted. An ugly sound.

'I'm not afraid of anything. Or anyone.'

'I think you are,' she pressed. 'I think you're afraid of the one person who truly counts. Yourself. You're afraid to be that good surgeon version of yourself because, for some reason, you can't allow yourself to be happy. And so you keep throwing the two-dimensional playboy side out for the world. Why do you do that? Are you afraid you won't measure up to the man you ought to be? And so you won't even try in case you fail?'

It was too close to the mark. He couldn't bear it.

Every time she talked to him like this she made him feel more and more like he could be the man he should have been from the start. She made him *want* to be. If only for her. But now it was too late. He was too like his father. He destroyed things, he didn't create them.

'You think you know me, just because we slept together?' He shook his head. 'How many other women do you think have been exactly where you are now, Alex?'

It was cruel. He had to slide his eyes away so that he didn't see the pain clouding hers. But it was the only way. He couldn't give Alex what she wanted. He wouldn't.

She hoped he would take on the Lefebvre Group, guide it, nurture it. In her mind, he could build the Lefebvre Group into the force that the Delaroche Foundation could have been if not for his father's ego. How was it she couldn't see that his own ego was just as out of control? That, despite every choice he'd ever made—*because* of every choice he'd ever made—he had turned himself into the one thing he most loathed. He was his father's own son.

She couldn't be allowed to love him. He would end up destroying her. Just as his father had destroyed his mother. It was inevitable.

'This was sex, Alex. Just sex.' The lie practically lodged itself in his throat. 'This is exactly who I am and I *am* happy with that. But since you insist on reading more into it than that, it cannot happen again. We will marry, as agreed, I'll gain control of the Lefebvre Group and I'll appoint a new board to pass it on to, to ensure that Rainbow House, and any other assets, are protected.'

'So you want to protect your mother's legacy from your father, yet not get your hands dirty?' It was the sad, almost sympathetic edge to her tone that really twisted in his chest the most.

He gritted his teeth. Alex must never know how much it cost him to answer her.

He'd been foolish to let himself get caught up in their charade, allowing himself to think, even for a moment, that there was anything real to it. He'd been stupid to allow her to convince him to look into the stable block conversion that his mother had once planned. And he'd been reckless to even consider taking over the role of Chairman of the Lefebvre Group and appointing a board of his own.

He needed to get back to the original plan. Stop his father from destroying his mother's legacy and then walk away. Run, if he had to.

'That's exactly what I intend to do,' he growled, unsure whether he was more furious at her or himself. 'Now get dressed, we're leaving. You have a dress fitting and I have a life to get back to once this is over.'

CHAPTER THIRTEEN

THE NEXT FEW days bled into each other, a tense blur for Alex, until one week stretched into two, then three.

Gone was the Louis who had caused her to abandon herself to the wanton desire that had seemed to fuel them both equally. The Louis who had taught her to revel in his obsession with her body as he'd licked and kissed and tasted his way over every last square centimetre of her trembling flesh.

They had reached an uneasy truce following their argument. They'd had to. Not only for the paparazzi but also for the estate hands and chateau staff, none of whom could be allowed to suspect there was any animosity between the soon-to-be-wed couple.

Alex was almost grateful for the whirlwind of planning and decisions, from her wedding dress to the music, the flowers to the food. At least they kept her mind occupied and the pain at bay.

But it wasn't always so easy. When Louis showed her around the estate, ostensibly so that he could teach his future bride about its history, and how the estate had employed people from the local area for centuries, she could almost fool herself into thinking it was real all over again. Especially when he so proudly recounted to her how his great-grandfather had been unmasked and hunted down as one of the most effective, dogmatic leaders of the Resistance during the Second World War, and local farmers had been prepared—only too willing—to conceal and protect such a man as Albert Delaroche on their farms, even after several of them had been tortured or taken prisoner.

But when she called her father, after she had finally been granted permission to advise him of the highly guarded date of the wedding, she wasn't prepared for what he had to say.

By the time Louis returned, Alex still hadn't moved from the chair by the window, her mobile phone still clasped in her hand. He knew something was wrong the moment he walked in, the immediate concern etched onto his face only making her feel worse.

He strode across the room and for a moment she thought he was going to haul her out of the chair and into his arms.

Ridiculous notion.

Instead, Louis stopped dead in front of her.

'Did something happen? Did your father upset you?'

She shook her head.

'He didn't like the respite holiday idea? Rainbow Court?'

She'd turned the words over and over in her mind all afternoon, but they still didn't come any easier. There was no soft way to put it. She just had to tell him.

'I told my father we had set a date, I explained. He thanked me for letting him know.'

But he hadn't congratulated her, or celebrated with her, or anything really. He'd just listened politely, thanked her and then, to her surprise, he'd asked her if she was doing it to save Rainbow House. She couldn't tell Louis that she'd harboured some secret fantasy he might tell her that wasn't something she needed to do. At least, not for him.

Maybe tell her he did love her, and that she should only marry Louis if she wanted to.

No, she couldn't tell Louis. She could barely admit that to herself. Alex shook her head as if to dislodge the fanciful idea.

'He did tell me something about your mother.'

'My mother?'

The sense of foreboding swelled up inside her even though she tried to quell it. He waited in silence for her to continue.

'He asked why you had never taken up your role as chairman of the Lefebvre Group before now. I told you Jack was at Rainbow House around the time your mother used to visit regularly?'

'Yes, yes.' He shrugged irritably, but she got the sense there was more going on beneath the surface. If only he would let her in.

But he never would.

'Apparently your mother's desire for you to take over was widely known.'

'Indeed?'

'Well, my father knew her well, Jack was around seven and your mother was very involved with the residents.'

'I am aware of that.'

'Well, we were talking...' If one could call their conversation *talking* in that sense. She flicked a tongue out over parched lips. 'Conversation got around to your mother's death and...basically he said she didn't take her own life. That it was an accident.'

He raked his hand through his hair. In that moment it seemed floppier and more playboyish than ever. It also made him seem more vulnerable than ever and her heart twisted and knotted.

'Yes. Your father would think that. They told everyone it was an accident.'

'No.' She was explaining this badly. 'I mean, I know that. What I mean is, it really *was* an accident.'

He stared at her, first in disbelief, then in exasperation.

'They covered it up, I told you that. It was the only decent thing my father ever did for her.'

'You're wrong. He didn't cover anything up. That is… he did, but not your mother's suicide. It really was an accident. My father was there. He saw exactly what happened.'

Cold fingers inched over her body. She hated the way he looked at her, as though she was lying, deliberately trying to hurt him. How could he think that?

'I saw the photographs, Alex,' he bit out coldly. 'The evidence. Or the lack of it. I know there was a cover-up.'

'There was. But not how you think.'

She touched his arm but he pulled away, unable to bear the contact. Something inside her shrivelled up even smaller. But she couldn't stop now, she had to tell him what she knew.

'Louis, your mother died trying to save someone's life.'

He froze, waiting for her to go on.

'There was a single mother, twenty-three, and her six-year-old daughter. The daughter was severely disabled and the young mother had borderline learning difficulties herself. That particular day it all got too much for her. She went to the child's room and smothered her in her sleep. She was in the process of taking her own life when your mother went past the room and spotted them. Celine hit the alarm and then ran in to try to save the woman by hoisting her up, but her body was convulsing and your mother got knocked over.'

'My mother fell?' It didn't even sound like his voice.

'She hit her head on the metal corner of the bed as she

went down. By the time the ambulance crew got to her, she was already gone.'

'It was an accident?'

'Yes. My father was there. He'd heard her in the refectory barely a few hours before, talking about you as usual, he said.' She reached a tentative hand out to hold his arm again.

This time he didn't move away or throw her off, he simply stared at it. Seeing but not seeing. She doubted he could feel anything at all. She could only imagine he felt numb.

'She always talked about you, apparently,' Alex continued softly. 'She told people you were her whole world. Her *petit prince*.'

He actually staggered back. *Him*, Louis Delaroche. And in that moment Alex knew if she could have taken his pain on in his stead, she would have.

She loved him. And that would cause her far more pain than her father had ever caused her.

Anguish ripped through Louis, like something yanking him in a million different directions at once. He'd forgotten that, her affectionate nickname for him. She'd called him her prince and he'd told her she was more beautiful than even the Princess of England who she had always so loved.

How could he have forgotten?

'They covered it up,' he managed at last, his voice sounding so, so far away. Lost in his own head.

'Yes, to protect the young mother and her child. The press would run stories because of Celine's death, and therefore the circumstances would have been front-page news. The family of the mother and daughter would have been hounded for months. Maybe years. He said it was felt that Celine would have wanted to protect them.'

Louis jerked his head up and down in what passed for a nod.

'She would never have wanted those families to go through any more pain than they would already have been in. Neither would she have wanted people pointing the finger at Rainbow House. Back then there were people who already objected to having a place for people with learning difficulties on their doorstep. My mother wouldn't want to have given them any more ammunition.'

'No one could never have anticipated that your father would use the cover-up to tell you such a cruel lie. You can't blame yourself.'

Fury howled inside him, tearing and clawing. He wanted to rage. At the world. At his parents. At himself.

'I don't,' he ground out.

And he didn't, at least not for that part of it. But how could he have believed his father—a man who made his career on lying and being vindictive as much as his talent—over what he knew in his heart to be true about his mother? How could he have ever imagined she would have chosen to take her own life? What kind of a son did that make him?

What kind of a person did that make him?

No loyalty. No trust. No belief.

Suddenly he realised Alex was cupping his face in her hands as though she could anchor him while the terrible storm wailed around his head. As though she could save him.

But she couldn't.

No one could.

He had to protect her. She deserved better, so much better, than him. She deserved someone loyal and honourable, someone who would stand by her side no matter what. Clearly, he wasn't that person. He never had been. The press were right.

'Tonight you will pack to leave. The wedding is off.'

'No,' she cried. 'That doesn't make sense.'

He'd only felt helpless once before in his life. The night his father had told him that his mother had given up on existence, on herself, on *him*, and taken her own life. Louis was determined that tonight, the night he had discovered it was all a lie, wasn't going to be a second time.

'It makes perfect sense.' He finally found the strength to move. To take Alex's hands and tear them away from his face. To step away from her. To cross the room. Seeing her desperation only made him feel furious, powerless and mournful all at once. He couldn't understand the emotions raging through him. He only knew that, whatever they were, they had to be as far removed from *love* as it was possible to get.

Because that was the one thing he clearly wasn't capable of.

'The only person at fault here is your father—you can't let him win. You must learn to forgive yourself.'

A tear tracked its way down her cheek and his stomach churned at the realisation that he'd hurt her. Immeasurably. He'd been a fool to imagine it could have turned out any other way.

But equally quickly, anger washed over the guilt. For her part, had Alex been honest with him? She certainly hadn't been honest with herself.

'Alex, we've been through this before. You talk about me forgiving myself, but you still haven't forgiven yourself.'

Her eyes flashed, but he didn't miss the shadow of panic.

'Of course I have. That's why I volunteer at Rainbow

House. Because I've accepted my past and I've made peace with it. I don't push it away like you do.'

'But you still haven't accepted it, Alex. You don't volunteer at Rainbow House because you're at peace with yourself, you volunteer because you're still trying to earn your father's love. You might have stopped blaming yourself for your mother's death, and for not being the saviour sibling you had been intended to be, but deep down you don't think your father has stopped blaming you.'

'That's enough,' Alex gasped, her hand pressed to her chest as if he was ripping out her very heart.

He knew he might as well have been.

But he couldn't stop now. He had to tell her, lay it all out there. She deserved better and he couldn't bear the thought of being the one to tie her down, trap her and disappoint her.

'You've spent decades trying to prove to him that you were worthy of being born. It's what's driven you to be a doctor, to volunteer at Rainbow House, to make a difference. It's why you're so determined to save me. You're trying to turn me into the son my mother wanted me to be because you can't turn your father into the dad you've needed him to be.'

'Stop!'

The strangled cry constricted his chest, tightening until he could barely breathe. It was nothing compared to Alex's ashen appearance. But she had to hear this, she had to understand what she was doing. And why.

'He loved your mother, he loved your brother and now he loves Rainbow House,' Louis said quietly. 'All the volunteering you do forces him to keep the door open to you, and appreciate your hard work. But I can't imagine how much it must eat away at you that he's never loved just *you*.'

'How could you be so cruel?' She shook her head, the words so quiet he had to strain to hear them.

'It may be cruel, but it's also the truth. You and I aren't so different. We have each buried our demons yet convinced ourselves we've dealt with them. If you stop thinking I'm deliberately trying to hurt you just long enough to think clearly, you would see that all the pushing you've been doing to get me to take on the Lefebvre Group is motivated by your need to go back to your father and tell him that Rainbow House is safe.'

'No.' She shook her head but the way she bit her lip betrayed her uncertainty.

'In your eyes, marrying me would be the ultimate sacrifice. The one thing that would prove to your father that you would do anything for him. But it won't work, Alex. He'll have Rainbow House but it won't be the magic cure you think it will be. It won't change the way he either does or doesn't love you.'

'You don't know that,' she managed hoarsely. It was all the admission that he needed.

Until that moment he hadn't realised how badly a tiny part of him wanted her to tell him that none of that mattered any more, that she loved him. The fact that she hadn't cut him deeper than he could have imagined possible.

'And then you'll just be left married to me. As miserable as my mother was with my father.'

'That's not true.'

He couldn't allow her tears to get to him. This was the best thing. For him and for Alex.

'It is true. And I won't do that to someone. Alex, I won't do that to *you*.'

He would find another way to save Rainbow House, whether it meant gaining control of the Lefebvre Group or not. But Alex would be free and he wouldn't be in her life to darken it.

She deserved better than that. Better than him.

He stalked across the room, the heavy walnut door bearing the full brunt of his frustration. And there, her face white and pinched, stood Brigitte, her hand raised to knock.

Shock bounced around the trio and then the older lady spoke, her voice as dignified as ever.

'Monsieur Étienne Morel is in the drawing room with his father Monsieur Alain Morel. They ask me to tell you that they have found a loophole. Something about there is no need for you and Mademoiselle Vardy to marry?'

'This proves nothing,' Jean-Baptiste sneered as he raised his head from the papers Louis had set on his desk barely a day later. 'I'm not signing a thing.'

'As you wish.' Louis dipped his head as though it didn't matter to him one way or another. 'Then the contract will go to the board instead.'

For perhaps the first time he realised that it *didn't* matter. He'd wasted so much time fire-fighting all the little blazes his father had always set in his path that he hadn't realised they'd sapped all his energy and stopped him from battling the infernos that he really wanted to tackle.

There were more important things than wasting time on Jean-Baptiste.

Like Alex.

Ever since last night he'd been replaying the argument in his head, wondering if he'd done the right thing, if he could have done things differently.

'You can't send it to the board. I won't authorise it,' his father ground out, desperately trying to appear in control.

Louis turned as if to leave, pausing only at the door.

'It isn't a matter of authorisation. There's a legal obligation for your board to see all documents that pertain to the Lefebvre Group. It will be dealt with by both teams of lawyers. I have no control over that.'

'I am Chairman of the Delaroche Foundation and I won't allow it,' Jean-Baptiste growled. Rather like a child throwing a playground tantrum, Louis realised abruptly.

He shrugged and reached for the door handle.

'As I said, there is a legal obligation. Neither of us can interfere with that.'

'You're threatening me.'

'No.' Louis shook his head. 'I'm telling you the facts. I'm even offering you the opportunity to emerge with your reputation, not to mention your dignity, intact. Which, frankly, is more than you deserve.'

'You're blackmailing me into signing the Lefebvre Group over to you. You? Chairman? It's laughable.'

'No more laughable that letting you get away with snatching control of the group before my mother's body was even cold.' Louis didn't know how he restrained himself. 'And, for sake of clarity, I'll say again that I am not blackmailing you, I am presenting you with the facts.'

'If I sign the Lefebvre Group over to you then my reputation will be safe?' Jean-Baptiste's eyes glittered malevolently. 'You seem to forget that the Delaroche board is *my* board. I own them, every single one of them, and I'll destroy the Lefebvre Group before you even get there.'

'You can try, I suppose.' Louis felt unbreakable, totally in command, and he intended to hold onto that feeling for as long as he could. 'But I don't think you can. The Lefebvre Group is my mother's legacy, and you already tried to destroy it once before and failed. Now I owe it to her to keep it alive.'

'You think you owe anything to the woman who abandoned you?' Jean-Baptiste was almost incandescent. 'Do you forget that she took her own life rather than watch her only son, her only child, grow up? Is that what your little whore has taught you? To be weak and pathetic, and so desperate you'll pretend your mother didn't know what her choice would do to her kid?'

Not now. Not yet.

The madness that ravaged its way through him was destructive. Louis recognised that, and it was all he could not to let it cripple him at the knees. He bit back any response that might alert his father to the fact that he knew the truth. He needed those papers signed first.

'I'm claiming it, as she always wanted me to.'

'You're that desperate that you, of all people, are getting married. Do you think I didn't realise what it was all about, you making such a public spectacle of asking your nobody girlfriend to marry you?'

Something fired inside him. It was one thing for Jean-Baptiste to come after him, quite another to go after his sweet Alex. He wanted to lay his father out on the floor right now, but he couldn't afford to let his fury show.

'I asked Alex to marry me because I wanted to. Because I—' Shock hit him. He took a deep breath, the realisation washing over him. 'Because I love her.'

'You?' Jean-Baptise mocked. 'You don't know the first thing about love. You never had it, and, if your less than stellar history is anything to go by, you never gave it either.'

Because he hadn't thought he deserved it. Because he'd been ashamed that his mother hadn't loved him enough for it to stop her taking her own life. Because that's what his father had told him, and he'd stupidly believed everything Jean-Baptiste had said back then.

'Your mother never loved you enough. How could she?

Look at you. But if she did, then maybe it was your inability to love her back that made her commit suicide.'

Louis steeled himself. But the pain never hit.

Not the way it once had.

Something inside him stood strong, true. Like a beacon of light. Something that Alex had put there.

'I love Alex,' Louis reiterated, barely recognising his own raw voice or the admission that he had tried to pretend wasn't true for far too long.

It was there, and it was real. He loved her. He wasn't sure when it had happened. Perhaps it had started from that first meeting, but now there was no denying it. No hiding.

'There is no wedding tomorrow, we called it off. We won't marry for you, or for a contract, or for Rainbow House. But one day we will marry. And it will be for love.'

'Beautiful sentiment.' The acidulous words were matched only by the unpleasant sneer and slow handclap. 'Though I'm not sure the press will buy it. Not when I tell them exactly what kind of sham your engagement has been.'

Louis stood, his palms flat on the table, his body leaning over, and took in the vicious gleam in his father's eyes as the old man waited for him to lose his temper.

Well, not today.

He could almost hear Alex's soft voice in his head as he dredged up an icy smile, but a smile nonetheless. His voice was low and even.

'Fine. Go ahead and tell the media whatever you want. You're going to anyway. But don't pretend it's anything other than to destroy her reputation for your own revenge. And it won't change anything. You've still lost. I will take control of the Lefebvre Group and Rainbow House, which my mother and my grandfather worked so tirelessly to support. I don't need to marry Alex. I *want* to marry her.'

'I won't sign.'

'Then you'll end up losing the Delaroche Foundation, too,' Louis warned. Though, perhaps surprisingly, he took no pleasure from it. It was simply a fact that his stubborn father needed pointing out to him. 'If they see these papers—and they'll have to, there's no avoiding it—then you could lose everything.'

'No,' his father ground out, his composure beginning to crack. 'Take the Delaroche Foundation from me? I'd like to see you try.'

'I don't want your foundation,' Louis scorned. 'I never did. But I want to honour the legacy my mother created. The first seven years of my life were the happiest I've ever had, until now. She taught me how to laugh, how to be kind, and how to feel. I recognise now what I've always known, and that is that the only reason she would have chosen to leave me behind is if she hadn't been in her right mind. And that comes down to you. And you alone. We both know how cruelly you treated her.'

'You think you can blame her death on me? You dare to threaten me? *Pah,* the press will never believe a playboy bastard like you.'

He'd never seen his father's hand shake like that before.

Somehow it only helped Louis feel all the calmer.

'I wasn't threatening you at all.' He straightened up, making a show of taking a step back from the table. Away from his father. 'I have no intention of going to the media. I can't think of anything that's less their business. However, it will come out. The truth always does.'

'Then I'll destroy you,' Jean-Baptiste roared, his anger making him miss Louis's warning.

Wordlessly, Louis stood up straight and took a further step back from the desk. The moments ticked by as they remained motionless in their respective places. At an impasse. But Louis knew he held the key. He drew in a steadying breath, then another, and another. One image locked in his brain. Alex, in her wedding dress. And he knew with bone-deep certainty that he had to win her back. She was the one thing that made his life make sense. He could live without her if he had to, but he didn't want to have to.

'Sign the papers. It will return the group to me as my mother's will had always intended, and the fact that you manipulated the documents will never have to come out. Once the tie is severed between the Delaroche Foundation and the Lefebvre Group, all documents pertaining to the latter, including these, are no longer valid. As the new chairman of the Lefebvre Group, I can file them away wherever I see fit and neither your board, nor anyone else, need ever see them. It's your choice.'

'And yet it isn't really a choice at all, is it?' sneered the older man. Still, Louis found himself holding his breath as his father, with no other choice, lifted his pen and began to sign.

Personally, he would have liked nothing better than to let the whole world know what Jean-Baptiste had done, let him get his comeuppance. But that would destroy the Delaroche Foundation and there were too many good people, too many truly charitable projects that would be irreparably damaged by such an action. It would destroy far more than it would achieve.

And that wasn't something he could imagine Alex approving of. It was strange how much she factored into his thoughts. How, over their time together, he had begun to weigh things against what she might approve of or not.

He'd thought cutting her free was the right thing to do. The only thing to do. But now he wasn't so sure. She'd once told him she loved him. Had that been true? Could she love him again?

'There, you have your pound of flesh.' The resentful tone pulled Louis back to the moment.

He leaned over to take the papers but his father gripped them all the more tightly, one final insult at the ready.

'What would your mother think of you now?'

The insidiousness scratched at Louis, scraping away until a rage was rushing in to fill the vacuum. He twisted around and the sardonic smile on Jean-Baptiste's face revealed the old man thought he had won.

At any other time, he might have. But Louis had a weapon now, one he'd never had before—Alex's belief in him. He knew it was pointless but he couldn't stop the glimmer of possibility that maybe, just maybe he could one day win her love for real.

He had to be the kind of man she deserved.

'I don't think you have the right to talk to me about my mother. Not now. Not ever.' He sounded as close to the edge as he felt. But that couldn't be helped.

The cruel twist of his father's mouth was sharp enough to draw blood. Like a scalpel slicing him from within.

Now.

'No wonder you weren't enough to make her want to live.'

It was all Louis could do to swallow the bitter, acid taste in his mouth.

'Except that she did want to live, didn't she? She never committed suicide, she never even considered it. The day she died she was trying to save a life, not take one. But you told me otherwise simply to keep me in line. To exact some kind of revenge.'

He'd never seen that expression on his father's face before. So hateful, so ugly.

'So you finally know the truth. How does it feel, Louis, to know that you believed so badly of her so easily?'

'You're really trying to turn this onto me?'

'How much guilt do you feel, knowing that she believed in you so much that she bought a house a few streets away from Rainbow House, where she thought you and she could live, and yet you didn't believe in her enough to trust that she hadn't taken her own life?'

'She bought a house?' Louis echoed dully, as Jean-Baptiste's face contorted all the more.

'You must feel sick to the stomach to realise how pathetically easy it was to convince you that she had left you. You didn't have enough faith in her to question what I told you for even a moment.'

'You're sick.'

'I'm a winner. I do whatever it takes. And you're just like me. As this…' he waved his hand over the papers he'd just signed '…proves.'

He had a choice. He could let his father get to him, as he had always done. Or he could be the man Alex would want him to be, the man his mother would have wanted him to be, but, more importantly, the man *he* wanted to be.

And suddenly it was so clear. He was finally free. Free from guilt and responsibility for things over which he actually had no control. Alex had freed him. Maybe she'd started to from the moment they had first met on that balcony, and now it was time he did the same for her.

And he knew just what he needed to do to win her back. If she'd let him, as he knew he'd really hurt her. But he had to try. Starting with resurrecting the plans for the stable block. Taking the papers from his father's hands and striding across to the door, Louis felt lighter and less weighed down than he had in years. Possibly ever.

'No,' he cast over his shoulder with a genuine smile that wasn't aimed at his father in the least. He felt jubilant, untethered, victorious. 'I'm nothing like you. I never have been.'

CHAPTER FOURTEEN

THE NEWS THAT Louis was back at Silveroaks reached Alex's ears at the end of a long afternoon of surgeries, her legs wobbling perilously as she checked on her last patient in the recovery unit. It had been three weeks, two days, seven hours and a handful of minutes since that awful row back at the chateau.

She knew the timings by heart. How could she not? The moment he'd walked out of that door it had been as though her life had been stripped of every last drop of colour. And now he was back.

But was it for work? Or for her?

She knew what was most likely, and yet hope still gurgled inside her like a trickling brook. The past few weeks had been like nothing she could describe—a deep, hollow emptiness that tumbled around her chest.

And as much as her heart ached for herself, it also ached for Louis. For what the two of them had almost shared. For how far he'd almost come. For the way she'd hurt him without intending to. He'd hurt her too, she knew that, but it didn't stop her caring for him. She should have told him that he was becoming more important to her than Rainbow House, than her father. She knew what it was like, playing second best. Why had she made him feel as though he was?

It may not have changed anything, but at least she would

have been brave enough to have been honest. For once. Because nothing eased the dull pain that still ached inside her every time she read a news story about a possible sighting of the uncharacteristically low-profile Louis, who still appeared to be working from the relatively secure confines of the chateau. Nothing, that was, until the news had filtered down that he was back.

And despite all attempts by her brain to caution her, it was as though that very fact in itself caused the colour to flow back into her lonely black and white world. And the voice in her head, which she'd been trying to silence for almost a month, finally broke free of its cage.

If you want him, go and find him.

She had no recollection of moving through the hospital, its maze of corridors which she knew so well, but one minute she was leaving the recovery unit and the next she was outside Louis's door. She lifted her hand to knock, then decided against it and simply stepped right in. This time her legs really did give way.

The room seemed to shrink around him, as though he overpowered it without doing a thing. Sitting behind the desk as he was, his shirtsleeves rolled up to reveal his tanned forearms, his tie loose and a stack of paperwork in front of him, how could he have grown more powerful, more handsome, more... *Louis* in a matter of weeks?

Stumbling back, she felt the door swing with her, heard it slam shut with such force the room shook.

Not exactly the entrance she'd been intending but at least he wouldn't know just how weak at the knees he made her.

He narrowed his eyes.

'Alex? What are you doing here?'

Her mouth had never felt so parched. She still couldn't

find the strength to push off the door and so she stayed there, leaning against the cheap wood veneer, effectively trapping him.

'I came to see you.'

'Evidently.'

There was no trace of sarcasm in his tone and yet she could feel the heat rising from her toes.

'I came to apologise,' she said calmly. As if she wasn't shaking inside.

Even the frown that drew his features together was handsome. How had she forgotten quite how striking he was?

'I believe I should be the one apologising. I came here to tell you as much. I said things to you that were unforgivable.'

He'd been intending to see her? To talk to her? Something tiptoed through her but she didn't dare to examine it too closely. Not yet.

'You said things to me that were true.' Alex forced herself to maintain eye contact, but that familiar heat burned low in her. 'What's more, I needed to hear them. I know I've said this before, but you were right, I was just as tethered to my past as you. I was using you, our marriage, to try to convince my father that I would do anything for him. To try to make him love me the way he loved my brother.'

Was that sadness that skittered across his expression before he shut it down? She couldn't quite tell. He leaned back in his chair, his eyes raking over her even though his voice was gentle.

'Did it turn out the way you hoped?'

'No. But it turned out exactly the way you said it would.' And somehow, with Louis, it didn't hurt as much as it had. 'My father was pleased, perhaps grateful, but he didn't have some epiphany. He didn't suddenly tell me how much he loved me, or how proud of me he was. And I realised that he never would.'

'I'm sorry.'

She blinked back the tears that pricked her eyes.

'I realise that he never will. He loves me in his own way, but it will never be the limitless, unconditional way he loved Jack or my mother. I'll never know what he really feels about me, and whether deep down a part of him blames me or not, but I do know that I don't blame myself. I live my life as well as I can and if that's enough for him then great. If not, I refuse to twist myself inside out for him any longer. I'm me, and I'm happy with who I am.'

'That's good.' Louis smiled softly and it tugged at her chest, her stomach, lower.

'And I have you to thank for helping me to see that.'

Finally, finally, she found the strength to push off from the door, to make it halfway across the room before she stopped.

'You gave me the strength to trust in myself. You've allowed me to believe in myself,' she murmured. 'But you were wrong about one thing.'

He was watchful, immobile.

'And what was that?'

'I may not have recognised my underlying intentions, but I was genuine when I told you I wanted to help you stop punishing yourself. I thought I could help you move on.'

The silence stretched out between them. For a moment she thought he wasn't going to answer.

'You did help me,' he said abruptly. 'Because of you I realised I no longer felt the isolation I'd never realised I'd been experiencing. My brain was fired up with a renewed drive. I had this…this energy effervescing in my blood. Alex, you made me feel *alive*.'

The hot—even savage—need in his eyes was almost her undoing.

* * *

He didn't remember reaching into his drawer, or standing up to cross the room and stand in front of her, the pretty leather box offered to her with as much ceremony as if it were a ring.

Her arrival had been as unexpected as it had been incredible, filling him with feelings he hadn't dared to let himself experience these last few weeks. Pouring hope and light right through him. He fought the urge to scoop her into his arms and hold her close to him to try to make her feel safe, secure, cared for—to make *him* feel all those things—and simply waited for her to open the box.

'A key?'

Her surprise was evident and, despite himself, laughter spilled from his lips. *His* Alex. If she would let him.

'Not just any key. It's the key to Rainbow Court Respite Holidays in what was once the stable block of Chateau Rochepont.'

'Rainbow Court Respite Holidays?' She turned the words over and over on her tongue as though she couldn't quite believe it.

'It was what my mother had always intended to do with the place,' he said softly. 'It's what you kept pushing me to do. I told you I'd consider it.'

'I remember.' She flushed. 'But I was pushing for all the wrong reasons. I should never have done that to you. It doesn't matter any more. I don't need it. I just need you.'

'And I didn't do this for you.' He pulled a wry face. 'Well, not entirely. I did it for myself. Because seeing her legacy come to fruition was something I needed to do for me. I made it one of the first things I did as the chairman of the new board of the Lefebvre Group.'

She blinked at him, then back down to the key.

'I thought you would sell the group after all.'

'Someone convinced me to change my mind. Someone whose opinion I respect. Someone who…I love.'

'Love,' the word was echoed with such awe that it scraped and teased across every inch of his body. It felt more right than he could have ever imagined to take her hands and repeat his vow to her.

'I love you, Alexandra. You enrich my life and make me want to be a better man than I ever dreamed I could be. Marry me. Not for Rainbow House, or for the Lefebvre Group, but simply to be my wife. To spend the rest of our lives making each other happy.'

And when she kissed him, the certainty in her eyes shining out brighter than any jewel that could ever exist, any last shadows of the demons that had lurked inside both of them were finally banished for good.

'Say the words,' he commanded, finding himself wanting to hear them. Needing her to voice them.

'Which words?' she murmured against his mouth, hot and inviting and sensual. Teasing him as though they had all the time in the world. And maybe they did. 'Oh, you mean tell you I love you?'

'I warn you.' He bit gently at her lip as she squirmed in pleasure. 'Two can play that game.'

'I'm counting on it.' She rocked against him, deliberately slowly, provocatively. 'Which is exactly *why* I love you.'

'Again.'

'I love you, Louis.'

And he knew, with bone-deep conviction, that his redemption was complete. Alex was his just as he would always be hers. Not because there was a means to an end but because this *was* the end. And the beginning.

This time was for real.

* * * * *

MILLS & BOON

Coming next month

ONE NIGHT WITH DR NIKOLAIDES
Annie O'Neil

"Cailey *mou*. I've always felt we had a connection, you and I. Don't you know that?"

She shook her head against his finger, fighting the urge to open her lips and draw it into her mouth. Any connection they'd had had been more master and servant than anything. She'd grown up working in his house. Scrubbing, cooking and cleaning alongside her mother, who had spent her entire adult life serving as the Nikolaides housekeeper.

She'd thought that kiss they'd shared all those years ago had been a dare. A cruel one at that. For it had been only a day later when she'd overheard him telling his friends he'd never marry a housemaid.

She was surprised to see him looking hurt. Genuinely hurt.

"Not in the strictest sense," she whispered against his finger.

"We're peas in a pod. You must know that. And today, working together, wasn't that proof?"

"No. It only proves we work well together. Our lives... we're so different."

She wanted to hear him say it. Say he'd held himself apart from her because of her background.

"You *are* different from me," he said, lowering his head until his lips whispered against hers. "You're better."

Before she could craft a single lucid thought they were kissing. Softly at first. Not tentatively, as a pair of teenagers might have approached their first kiss, more as if each touch, each moment they were sharing, spoke to the fact that they had belonged together all along.

Simply kissing him was an erotic pleasure on its own. The short walk to Theo's house had given his lips a slight tang of the sea. Emboldened by his sure touch, Cailey swept her tongue along Theo's lower lip, a trill of excitement following in the wake of his moan of approbation.

The kisses grew in strength and depth. Theo pulled her closer to him, his lips parting to taste and explore her mouth. The hunger and fatigue they'd felt on leaving the clinic were swept into the dark shadows as light and energy grew within each of them like a living force of its own.

Undiluted sexual attraction flared hot and bright within her, the flames licking at her belly, her breasts, her inner thighs, as if it had been waiting for exactly this moment to present itself. Molten, age-old, pent-up, magically realized and released desire.

Continue reading
ONE NIGHT WITH DR NIKOLAIDES
Annie O'Neil

Available next month
www.millsandboon.co.uk

LET'S TALK
Romance

For exclusive extracts, competitions
and special offers, find us online:

 facebook.com/millsandboon

 @millsandboonuk

 @millsandboon

Or get in touch on 0844 844 1351*

For all the latest titles coming soon, visit
millsandboon.co.uk/nextmonth